Protect And Serve

Rebecca Shamhart

Rebecca Shamhart
2015

First Printing: 2015

ISBN – 10: 0692429743

ISBN - 13: 978-0-692-42974-7

Registration Number: TXu 1-890-204

Cover design copyright © 2015
By (http://digitaldonna.com)

This book is dedicated to my amazing husband, Kevin. Thank you for your love and support.

It is also dedicated to my friend, Gail. Thank you for being my biggest cheerleader.

Chapter 1

"Would you hurry up?" Morgan screamed at the car in front of her. "The light is green!"

Morgan honked the horn and slowly began to move through traffic. She couldn't believe how busy the streets were but it was always hectic this time of year. Christmas time made the streets wall to wall traffic and it seemed like everyone was out. Big cities always made it feel that way.

Morgan glanced at her watch. Ten after nine, it read. Great, she thought. I'm going to be at least twenty minutes late for work.

Morgan hurried through traffic and finally arrived at the parking garage where she always parked her car. After parking on the second floor, she ran down a flight of stairs and across the street. Upon reaching the firm of Parker, Barnes, and Newman, she went inside to the elevator. After a slow and bumpy ride, she stepped off the elevator at the sixth floor and hurried to her office.

"You're late!" Senior Partner, Charles Winston Parker, exclaimed.

"Yes," the petite blue eyed blonde agreed. "I know."

"This will be deducted from your pay," he informed her.

"I know that too," Morgan responded with a cocky tone.

"Don't let it happen again," he warned.

"But sir," she argued. "If you haven't noticed, the traffic is awful. I tried my best to be here on time."

"Always the lawyer, aren't we, Ms. Garrett?" he said, as she pleaded her case. "Next time leave home earlier. Good day."

Before Morgan could say anything else, Mr. Parker was gone. She turned to her secretary, who was watching in awe. "Are there any messages for me, Jaime?" she asked.

Jaime handed her a white piece of paper. "Oh no!" Morgan said, disappointed. "Not Mrs. Landing and her poodle again."

"I'm afraid so," Jaime replied. "Here's a file on a new client. Mr. Parker wants you to work on this case."

Morgan took the file from Jaime. "Is there anything else?" she asked.

"Yes," Jaime replied. "Some of us girls are going out tonight. Do you wanna come?"

"I don't think so," Morgan answered, shaking her head.

"Oh, come on," Jaime insisted. "You never do anything anymore. It will be fun."

"I don't know," Morgan replied, unsure of herself. "I'll get back to you."

Morgan entered her office and sat down in the chair behind her desk. She opened the file Jaime had given her but was too lost in thought to read it.

Jaime was right, Morgan thought. She hadn't been out since her husband died. She shook her head not wanting to think about the horrible night. She needed to work. "Jaime," Morgan called over the intercom. "When is my meeting with our new client?"

"You are meeting with Craig Masterson at ten o'clock tomorrow morning," Jaime answered.

Morgan thanked her and turned back to the file on her desk. She began to read it slowly. It stated that Mrs. Masterson was filing for a divorce on the grounds of neglect and abandonment. It also read that Mr. Masterson worked long hours and was called away from home at all hours to do his job.

Morgan began to read the file more carefully. She was concentrating so intensely that she didn't notice Jaime had entered the office. Jaime cleared her throat causing Morgan to look up. "I'm sorry to bother you," she said, "but I was wondering if you wanted to go eat."

"Yes," Morgan replied, looking at her watch. "I can't believe it's that late already."

Morgan got up with the file in her hand. She grabbed her coat and was ready to leave. "You're not taking your work with you, are you?" Jaime asked in a disappointed tone.

"Oh, I guess not," Morgan replied in surprise. "It's just another divorce case."

Plenty of questions filled Morgan's mind on her way to the elevator with Jaime. They hopped on the elevator and took a bumpy ride to the first floor. As they stepped off, Jaime said, "Someone needs to fix that elevator. I'm almost afraid to ride in it."

"I know what you mean," Morgan replied.

They hurried to a small restaurant down the block from the office and sat down at a table in front of the window. "It is really busy out there," Jaime said, as she watched the shoppers.

After a moment of silence, Morgan replied, "Did you say something?"

"Morgan," Jaime said, staring at her with a puzzled look on her face. "What's on your mind? You have been in your own little world since we left the office."

"I have just been thinking about the Masterson case," Morgan answered. "I have so many questions about it."

"You can get all the answers you need tomorrow," Jaime replied. "Just please don't be late. I don't want to be interrogated again."

"I'm really sorry about that," Morgan said. "I promise it won't happen again."

As the two conversed, the waiter interrupted them for a moment to take their orders. Jaime always ordered the club sandwich. She was predictable and didn't handle change very well.

"You can judge for yourself about your new case tomorrow," Jaime said, changing the subject back to the original topic. "I wonder if Mr. Masterson is cute!"

"Jaime!" Morgan exclaimed in shock. "Now you know that he is going to be our client. We can't have any opinion on that matter. Anyway, you have Bryan, remember?"

"Yes, how could I forget him," she replied, dreamily.

Morgan shook her head. "Where is that man anyway?" she asked. "Why didn't he join us?"

3

"Bryan has a date with a real estate broker," Jaime explained. "We are going to buy a new house."

"A new house!" Morgan repeated. "Why didn't you tell me?"

"We weren't sure until last night," Jaime answered. "And this is the first time I have been able to tell you."

"What is it like?" Morgan asked.

"It's big," she answered. "It has three bedrooms and two baths. Bryan thinks the best part about it is the huge kitchen."

"You knew that when you married my brother you were getting a man who likes to work in the kitchen," Morgan reminded her. "Most women would kill for a man like that."

"I know," Jaime replied, as she tucked a section of her short raven hair behind her ear.

The waiter arrived with their food. The two ladies hurried through their meals and back to the office.

Morgan began to prepare for her meeting with Mrs. Landing. She knew what the case was about. The woman always had the same complaint. Someone was trying to kill her poodle, Miss Clairy.

"You don't have a case unless you can prove it, Mrs. Landing," Morgan heard herself telling the older lady for the tenth time.

"But this time I do, Ms. Garrett," she stated.

"Oh, do you?" Morgan questioned. "Where is it?"

"My witness couldn't make it," she answered.

"I can't help you until I hear from your witness," Morgan explained.

"You are being extremely rude," the older woman stated. "Won't you at least hear me out?"

Morgan sat back in her chair and gave Mrs. Landing her undivided attention. "I was taking Miss Clairy for her daily walk when this child asked me who I was," she explained. "After I told him, he replied by saying things that I wouldn't dare repeat. He ended up threatening Miss Clairy's life. She is very sensitive. I had to take her to the veterinarian to calm her down."

"Now Mrs. Landing," Morgan said. "I'm sure it's not that bad. You know how children are. Anyway, by law, I can't do

4

anything until someone harms your pet. What do you want me to do? Get a restraining order against the whole city?"

Mrs. Landing stood up in protest. "If you aren't willing to help me, Ms. Garrett, I'll go elsewhere. I'm talking to your boss."

She stormed out of the office before Morgan could stop her. Frankly, Morgan was glad she was gone.

Jaime rushed into the office. "What is going on?" she asked.

"That is what I would like to know," Mr. Parker said, standing at the door.

Morgan stood there like she was on trial. "What do you have to say for yourself?" he asked.

"I'm getting tired of dealing with that paranoid old woman," Morgan replied. "She is in here every week with a different story. I can't take it anymore."

"Morgan, I'll talk to Mrs. Landing," Jaime offered.

"No," Mr. Parker said, rejecting the idea. "It's Morgan's case. But if she can't handle it."

"I can handle it," Morgan replied. "Jaime, would you send her back in here?"

"She left," Mr. Parker stated. "We may have just lost a client. Now go home, Morgan. I don't want you to mess anything else up."

Morgan gathered her things and headed for the door. "I'll call you later," Jaime told her.

"Don't forget about the Masterson case tomorrow," Mr. Parker reminded her. "Try not to mess it up too."

Morgan left the building angrier than she had ever been. She couldn't believe what she had just been through. She just wanted to go home and sleep the rest of the day away. She was just so tired of getting the cases no one else wanted. She would prove herself to everyone if it was the last thing she did.

Morgan arrived home. It felt so good to be there. She changed clothes, curled up on the couch, and drifted off to sleep.

The phone rang awakening Morgan from a restless sleep. "Hello," she whispered.

"Morgan, are you all right?" Jaime asked.

"I'm fine," she answered. "I was asleep."

"I'm sorry I woke you," she said. "I was wondering if you were going with us tonight."

Morgan knew she wouldn't take no for an answer. "When are you leaving?" she asked.

"Probably seven-thirty," Jaime answered.

"I guess I'll go," Morgan replied.

"I'll pick you up," she said. "See ya later."

Morgan struggled to get herself up and going. She didn't feel any better but she had to get out and do something. She went to her bedroom and grabbed something to wear. Nothing fancy, she decided.

Jaime rang the doorbell at exactly seven-thirty. She was always prompt. That was the difference between Morgan and Jaime. Morgan never rushed anything except when it came to work. Jaime always had to have things done on time. "Are you ready?" Jaime asked. "We need to meet Judy and Sara at eight o'clock."

"Yes," Morgan answered. "Would you relax? We'll be there in plenty of time."

"I want to get a good table near the dance floor," Jaime replied.

Morgan shook her head. She couldn't believe this. The last time the girls went out, Jaime sat and watched everyone else. Morgan couldn't resist the temptation. "Why do you do this?" she asked.

"Do what?" Jaime questioned, very confused.

"You have all this energy now," Morgan explained. "But when you get there, all you will do is sit there."

Jaime glared at Morgan. Morgan was sure she had made Jaime mad. "I will have fun, Morgan," she replied, sternly. "You are a real bitch."

"A bitch?" Morgan repeated.

"Yes, that's what I said," Jaime replied.

"I have had a really rough day," Morgan explained. "I'm entitled to be bitchy."

"Can we go now?" Jaime asked, getting frustrated.

Morgan smiled knowing this was going to be one heck of a night. "Let's go," she said.

The music was playing loudly when they arrived at the club. "Do you see Judy and Sara?" Jaime yelled, as she looked through the crowd.

Morgan shook her head. "No," she answered. "I can't see anything with this crowd."

They sat down at a nearby table. Jaime continued to look for Judy and Sara even as the waitress took their drink orders. "There's Sara!" Jaime exclaimed. "I'll be back."

Jaime got up and hurried over to a group of people. Morgan sat there alone but she didn't mind. She looked around to see if she knew anyone and noticed a fight going on near her. She hated the thought of eavesdropping but she couldn't resist.

"How could you bring my best friend here?" the girl asked.

"She needed a ride," the man replied, defending his actions.

"I'm sure she did," the girl stated, being snotty.

"What are you implying, Amy?" the man asked.

"Matt, I think you can figure that out for yourself," Amy said. "I'm glad I figured you out before we went any further."

"Baby, we never started," Matt replied.

"Good," Amy stated. "Consider us finished."

Amy walked away as Matt stood there making no effort to stop her. He turned, smiled at Morgan, and walked away.

Morgan was bored again. That was the only form of entertainment she could find. She lost track of Jaime in the crowd.

Someone sat down at Morgan's table and this alarmed her. "Hi!" the girl said.

"Hello!" Morgan replied.

"I need a rest," she said. "Do you mind?"

"No, I guess not," Morgan replied.

"I'm Leslie," she introduced herself, extending her hand.

She shook Leslie's hand and introduced herself. "Nice to meet you," Leslie said. "Are you here alone? You can sit with us."

"No, I'm not alone," Morgan informed her.

"Here with your husband?" Leslie asked.

"No, just some friends," Morgan said, feeling resentment.

"I'm here with family and friends," Leslie told her.

7

Leslie waved to a group of girls out on the floor. "Come dance with us," she invited.

Morgan followed Leslie out to the floor and was introduced to the group. She danced a couple of fast songs with them but returned to her seat when the slow songs played.

"Where were you?" Jaime asked her, when she sat down.

"I was dancing," she answered. "Where's Judy?"

"Her daughter is sick," Sara said. "She couldn't make it."

"That's too bad," Morgan commented.

It grew quiet at the table. Morgan examined her friends' faces. Sara stared aimlessly at her drink. She did that a lot. Sara, a really shy person, didn't like to make eye contact. Jaime was the opposite. She always said that she could learn something about people by their eyes.

"Come on, girls," Jaime said. "Lighten up. We came here to have fun. Let's go out and dance."

"You two go on ahead," Sara said, quietly.

"Suit yourself," Jaime replied. "But if you change your mind, you know where we'll be."

They walked out to the dance floor and joined Leslie and her friends. Morgan stared at Jaime the whole time. She couldn't believe Jaime was actually out on the dance floor. Morgan decided to keep her mouth shut.

It was so crowded that it was getting hard to move. A few people bumped into Morgan and immediately excused themselves. But the real surprise came when a man spilled his drink down the front of Morgan's pink sweater.

"I'm sorry," the man said. "But if you would have watched what you were doing, I wouldn't have spilled this drink on you."

"Me!" Morgan exclaimed. "If you weren't already plastered, I wouldn't have to watch out for you."

"For your information, I'm not drunk," he said. "Lady, I haven't had a good day. Let's just forget this happened."

"Forget this happened?" Morgan shouted angrily at him. "You ruined my sweater!"

"Let me pay to get it cleaned," he offered.

"Red wine won't come out," she told him. "Just forget it."

She turned and hurried back to the table to grab her coat. "That was quite interesting," Sara noted.

"I'm not really in the mood, Sara," Morgan replied.

"You don't have to bite my head off!" Sara snapped.

"I'm sorry," Morgan said. "I have had a very bad day and I just want to go home."

Morgan hurried to the exit. "Where are you going?" Jaime demanded.

Morgan turned and glared at Jaime. "I'm going home," she answered, as she turned and walked out the door.

Morgan wrapped her coat around herself and hurried to the corner to catch a cab. There weren't any around which she fully expected.

Jaime came up beside Morgan several minutes later. "Would you please come back inside?" she asked.

"No!" she answered. "How many times do I have to tell you? I'm going home."

"Oh!" Jaime replied. "Your evening just started off bad. It will get better."

"Get it through your thick skull!" Morgan yelled. "It's not getting any better! I am going home!"

Before Jaime could reply, a cab pulled up to the curb. Morgan jumped in and waved goodbye to Jaime. She directed the driver to her destination and sat back in the seat, trying to relax. She had a rotten day and just wanted to get it over with.

Morgan arrived home and dropped onto the couch. She wanted to cry. She hadn't felt this bad since the night the police came to the door to tell her that Edward was dead. Morgan picked up the picture of Edward she kept on the desk. As she wiped away her tears, she whispered, "Edward, why did you have to leave me? I need you so much."

Morgan stared at the picture a few minutes longer. She set it back down on the desk and went to the bedroom. She stopped in the doorway and glanced around the room. She stopped at the bed. It had been so long since she had slept in the bed. Six months, to be exact. She couldn't bear to be in that bed without Edward.

A knock at the door brought Morgan out of her thoughts. She moved to the door quickly and opened it. There stood her brother, Bryan.

As he entered the apartment, he said, "Next time check to see who it is before you answer the door."

"Hello to you too," Morgan said.

"Don't get smart with me," he replied. "I'm just concerned about you."

"Well, don't be," she told him. "I'm fine."

"I don't think you are," he stated. "Jaime told me what happened."

"It wasn't a good night," she explained. "Can't you tell by the red wine stain on my sweater?"

After pausing to look at her sweater, she decided she needed to change. "Make yourself at home, Bryan," she invited. "I'll be right back."

After changing into something more comfortable, she returned to the living room. "Are you going to tell me what's bothering you?" he asked.

"I just had a lousy day," she answered.

"I think it's more than that," the spiky haired blonde stated, knowingly.

"Do you know how it feels to have a lousy day and then come home and find no one to comfort you?" Morgan questioned. "I used to have someone to do just that but now he is gone."

Bryan put his arms around his sister. "We all miss Edward," he said. "But he is gone and we need to move on."

Morgan pulled herself away from her brother. "I need a little more time," she replied. "I'm not ready to move on."

"You will be someday," Bryan replied in a soothing voice. "Maybe you need to get some help to get past this."

"I don't need any help," she said. "I prefer to take it one day at a time."

Bryan got up and walked to the door. "Can I offer a suggestion?" he asked. "I think you need to get out more and find a man. That may be the only way to move forward."

10

With that, he was gone. Morgan sat in her favorite chair, stunned. How could he even suggest she find another man? She couldn't picture herself with anyone but Edward.

Morgan wandered aimlessly around her small apartment. Edward crossed her mind. They had such a wonderful life planned. They were in the process of buying a new house but after Edward's untimely death, Morgan decided that plan was dead too. She remained living in the one bedroom apartment that she was renting when she and Edward married. That was over a year ago and she was back where she started.

Morgan shook her head. She had to quit thinking about Edward. She picked up the Masterson file she'd left lying on the counter. It was time to worry about someone else's problems.

She studied the file. Craig Masterson is a policeman with five years on the force. Wait a minute, Morgan thought as she set the file on her lap. I know that name. "Officer Craig Masterson," she whispered. "Where do I know that name from?"

Morgan concentrated on his name but couldn't place him. She eventually shrugged it off and read on.

Valerie Masterson is an interior decorator. The only interesting thing about her is that she's five years older than Craig. Morgan wasn't too impressed with Valerie. She was a member of about every club or group that met in town. She even owns her own business, Val's Designs. She's accusing Craig of abandonment, Morgan reflected. This lady's life is hectic.

Morgan decided to move on to the profile she had on the youngest Masterson. Four-year-old Stephanie led a normal child's life. She spent most of the time at her grandparents' houses and is anxiously awaiting the start of school.

What a great family, Morgan thought sarcastically, as she rummaged through the rest of the file. She stopped quickly when she noticed the family picture. They were sitting on a porch swing smiling from ear to ear. The Mastersons looked very happy. Morgan turned the picture over. "This was taken over a year ago," Morgan said aloud. "What could have happened in a year's time?"

11

Morgan flipped the picture back over and studied the face of Craig Masterson. Where had she seen him before? After pondering the question for a few minutes, Morgan decided it was time to call it a night.

She wandered into the bedroom and put on her nightclothes. She stopped to stare at the bed. "Not tonight," she whispered. "Not tonight."

Chapter 2

Morgan awoke the same way she did every morning, restless and sore. The couch had never been comfortable and she should have realized that by now. But Morgan didn't feel ready to sleep in that bed just yet.

She went through her morning ritual, which included skipping breakfast, and then made her way to work through the Christmas traffic.

Morgan entered the law firm with three other lawyers and a paralegal on her tail. The lawyers bypassed her without even a hello. The paralegal, on the other hand, talked Morgan's ear off. "Hello!" she said. "I'm Abby Lewis."

Morgan glanced at the lanky brunette. "Hello," she replied, extending her hand.

Abby gladly shook it and asked, "You're Morgan Garrett, aren't you? I've admired your work for sometime now. I really liked the way you handled that child custody case a few months back. Oh, what was it?"

"Collins versus Murphy," Morgan helped, knowingly.

"Yes, that's it," Abby interrupted. "I was overwhelmed with the way you proved Miss Murphy to be an unfit mother. I could really tell that Mr. Collins loved his daughter and would take good care of her."

Morgan stopped walking and turned to Abby. "I don't want to be rude but I really have to get to work," she explained. "Thanks for the compliments but I really can't talk now."

Morgan hurried towards her office. She opened the door and was surprised to see Jaime standing there. "Good morning, Jaime," Morgan said.

"Don't good morning me, Morgan," she replied. "I'm very upset with you."

"If it's about last night, don't even start with me," Morgan warned. "I don't want to hear it."

"Well, you're going to hear it whether you like it or not," Jaime informed her. "Bryan and I always have your best interest at heart. We are just looking out for you. Anything we have said or done has been for your own good."

"Sometimes I don't appreciate some of the things you two say," Morgan said.

"Someone needs to say them to you so you'll snap out of this depression you are in," Jaime replied.

"I don't have to listen to this," Morgan stated, as she turned and walked into her office.

Morgan sat at her desk for some time evaluating her situation. Maybe Bryan and Jaime were right. Maybe she needed to move on. But how could she when she couldn't even sleep in the bed that she and Edward shared? Something would have to give but which would it be, her memory of Edward or her sanity?

Morgan opened the Masterson file hoping it would keep her mind occupied until Mr. Masterson arrived. She studied the picture again. It was then that she realized where she had seen him before. He was the officer who visited her the night Edward died. She was now starting to remember things from that night that she had been desperately trying to forget. She wanted to cry but she knew she had to pull herself together because Mr. Masterson would be arriving soon. As Morgan wiped her eyes, there was a knock on the door. "Come in," Morgan announced.

Jaime opened the door and told Morgan, "Mr. Masterson is here and you are not going to believe this."

Mr. Masterson entered the room. Morgan smiled and let out a little laugh.

He stopped dead in his tracks when he recognized the woman from the night before. "You're the one from the bar," he acknowledged.

"The one you spilled your drink on," she replied.

"I'm really sorry about that," he stated.

14

"I accept your apology," she returned.

"I did offer to pay for the sweater," he pointed out.

"You could buy me twenty sweaters to make up for it," she explained. "But you can't give me back the sentimental value. Just keep your money."

"I'd like to do something to make it up to you," he offered.

"It's ok," she said. "You don't have to. Just forget it."

"Ok," he said, smiling.

"Have a seat Mr. Masterson," Morgan instructed.

"Please call me Craig," he said, as he took his seat. "I haven't been called Mr. Masterson in a really long time and frankly, I hate it."

"Alright, Craig," Morgan replied. "Let's start by talking about your marriage."

"Ok. Val and I will be married six years in February," Craig explained uncomfortably. "But we aren't going to last that long."

Craig stopped talking and went into a deep train of thought. The whole last year was a blur. All the days seemed to run together. Val left at eight-thirty every morning to go to work at her latest business endeavor. She took their daughter, Stephanie, to the day care center and then spent an eight-hour day at her designer shop. Craig, on the other hand, came in at eight in the morning after a long night on patrol and went directly to bed. He would wake up every evening at five and wait for Stephanie to come home. This was his favorite time of day. He spent a few hours of quality time with his daughter before he went back to work at eight.

No wonder our marriage turned out this way, he thought. After what Val did, our family life has turned into a shambled routine. It was time to put a stop to the whole charade.

"Craig," Morgan called. "Are you still alive?"

"Oh, I'm sorry," Craig apologized. "Where were we?"

Morgan laid a comforting hand on Craig's arm. "I know you are uncomfortable with this," she said. "But I need to understand your situation if you want me to help you. I have all the facts. I just need to know what happened to bring about this divorce."

Craig took a deep breath. "I don't know where to begin," he said. "Val and I decided about six months ago to call it quits. There was nothing left in our marriage to hang on to except Stephanie. That's a hell of a reason to keep a marriage together. Don't get me wrong. I love my child with my whole heart but there is no use making Stephanie miserable because she knows Val and I are miserable."

"How long have you both felt this way?" Morgan asked.

"About a year," Craig answered. "Something happened about a year ago that almost destroyed our marriage. But it took a lot of strength and patience to give us another chance."

"What happened?" Morgan questioned. "As your lawyer, I really need to know."

Craig stood up and began to pace around the room. "I'm not really comfortable with this," he told her.

Morgan got up from her desk and approached Craig. She looked him straight in the eye and saw the hurt he was trying to hide in his dark, mysterious eyes. "I wish there was something I could do for you," she whispered, as she placed her hand on his. "I know this is difficult but if you want me to help you, you need to talk to me."

Craig looked into Morgan's intense blue eyes. A feeling of calm came over him. It was at that point he realized how comfortable he felt around her. He smiled at her and squeezed her hand.

"Please tell me what happened," she said.

"About a year ago, Val met a rich, married man who wanted her to redecorate his office," Craig explained. "Well, one thing led to another and she had an affair with him. To say the least, I was devastated but it was probably my fault. I'm sure she got tired of my long hours at the station and needed something that I couldn't give her."

"Craig," Morgan replied. "Don't tear yourself up over this. It's not your fault your wife had an affair. Did she give you any indication that she was feeling neglected and needed your attention?"

"No, I had no idea she was feeling that way," Craig said.

"Then don't blame yourself," she stated. "There was nothing you could do if she didn't tell you how she felt."

Craig thought about what Morgan had said. After a few moments of silence, he said, "Thank you."

"For what?" she asked. "Are you thanking me for doing my job?"

"You are very good at it," Craig said. "Thanks for making me feel better."

"It was my pleasure," she told him with a smile. "I remember how you helped me on the night my husband died."

Craig stared at her. "I didn't want to bring that up," he said, uncomfortably, knowing how emotional she was that night. "How are you doing?"

"I would like to say that it gets easier each day," Morgan replied. "But it doesn't. Most days it hurts like hell."

"I understand," Craig said. "I know our situations are different but the emotions are the same. It is hard to adjust when the one you planned to spend the rest of your life with is gone."

Tears filled Morgan's eyes. Craig quickly wrapped his arms around her. "Just let it all out," Craig whispered. "You know I am here for you just like I was before."

Morgan pulled away from him. "You have your own problems," she said, wiping her eyes. "You don't need this."

"That's what friends are for," he told her. "We are friends, right?"

Morgan smiled at him. "That's more like it," Craig said. "Why don't I get you out of here for awhile? Do you have lunch plans?"

"I would like to have lunch with you," she retorted. "But I can't. I have work to do. I have two meetings today and I'm not as prepared for them as I would like to be."

"What about dinner?" Craig asked.

"Craig," Morgan replied, fighting the urge to say yes. "I make it a point not to get involved with clients, especially married ones. I can't have dinner with you."

"I'm not talking about a romantic dinner," Craig explained. "I don't think either one of us is ready for anything like that. I was thinking more along the lines of a business dinner."

"A business dinner?" Morgan questioned. "Well, I guess that would be alright."

"Have you been to the new pizza place downtown?" Craig suggested.

"No, but I know where that is," she said. "I will see you at seven."

"See you then," Craig replied, as he opened the door. "Take care of yourself, ok? That means make time to eat lunch."

"I will," she said, with a laugh.

After Craig left, Morgan took a seat behind her desk. "One, two, three," she counted.

As if on cue, Jaime rushed into the office. "Yes, Jaime," Morgan said, not looking up from her desk.

"So how did it go?" she asked.

"Fine," Morgan answered.

"You know he is going to be available soon," Jaime pointed out. "And for an extra plus, he is extremely gorgeous."

"What's this have to do with me?" Morgan questioned, already knowing the answer.

"You two would look cute together," Jaime stated.

"Jaime, stop it!" Morgan demanded. "I can't believe you would say such a thing. He's my client, for heaven's sake. Plus he's a married man with a four-year-old daughter."

"So," she replied. "He's going to be divorced soon. That makes him open for business. Come on, Morgan. You can't tell me that you don't think he is gorgeous."

"I didn't notice," Morgan lied.

"Uh-huh, right," Jaime said.

Morgan stopped what she was doing and glared at Jaime. "Is Elizabeth here?" she asked. "If she is, would you please send her in?"

Jaime jumped up from her chair and hurried out the door. A few seconds later, Jaime entered the room pushing a wheelchair. Twenty-six-year-old Elizabeth Brinkman sat peacefully in the chair. Jaime situated Elizabeth near the desk. "Is there anything I can get you?" Jaime offered.

"No, thanks," she replied.

After Jaime left the room, Morgan asked, "How are you feeling today, Elizabeth?"

"I'm managing," she answered. "This chair's a bit of a burden."

"I'm sorry you have to go through this," Morgan replied.

"I'm not going through it alone," she pointed out. "My family and friends have been very supportive and helpful, especially Craig."

Morgan glared at Elizabeth. "Craig who?" she asked.

"Craig Masterson," Elizabeth answered. "You know. The police officer who helped me out the day of the accident."

Morgan shook her head in disbelief. "What's wrong?" Elizabeth questioned. "Do you know Craig?"

"I've known him for quite awhile now," she answered.

"How do you know him?" Elizabeth asked, very interested.

"Well, for starters, Jaime and I went out last night and he and I bumped into each other. The glass of red wine he was carrying is now all over my pink sweater," she explained.

"Oh, no," Elizabeth said, disappointedly. "Not the sweater Edward gave you."

"That's the one," Morgan replied. "It was the last present he gave me before he died. Now it's ruined."

Morgan cleared her throat and fought back the tears. With a little laugh, she continued. "The funny thing about it is I had no idea it was Craig I ran into last night until he walked into my office this morning."

"Why was he here?" Elizabeth asked. "Was he here about my case?"

"No," Morgan answered. "He was here with his own case."

"You're his divorce lawyer, huh?" Elizabeth announced with a smirk. "Good choice."

Morgan smiled at her. "Can we move on to something else?" she asked.

Morgan rummaged through the papers on her desk. She handed one to Elizabeth. "This is a copy of the statement you gave to the police," Morgan explained. "I need you to read it over and tell me if that's everything you can remember."

Morgan studied the auburn haired woman as she read the paper. She still couldn't believe that this had happened to her. Morgan remembered Elizabeth as the cheerleader and tennis player during their high school and college years. She was outgoing and fun in those days but now Elizabeth mostly kept to herself. That probably had to do with her job though. She

19

worked as an assistant to a United States Senator. Her father threw his weight around, and probably a little money too, to get her the job. Some job, Morgan thought. Because of her job, she now sits in a wheelchair.

Morgan thought back to the day of the accident. She was sitting at her desk reading the local newspaper when the phone rang. After she received the news, she slammed the phone down and rushed out the door. She hurried through traffic and arrived at the hospital where Elizabeth was being prepped for surgery. Morgan stood outside the waiting room in disbelief. She didn't understand what was happening and no one would tell her anything. She wandered into the waiting room and took a seat. A few minutes later, a police officer entered the room. Morgan knew he had bad news. She didn't feel comfortable about any of this when she realized that this was the second time in four months the police had visited her.

"Are you Morgan Garrett?" he asked.

"Yes," she answered, anxiously. "Please don't beat around the bush. Give it to me straight. How is Elizabeth?"

"You need to talk to my partner," the officer explained. "He was there when it happened. He'll fill you in."

Morgan's thoughts were interrupted by the sound of Elizabeth's voice. "I think everything on this statement is correct," she said. "What are you thinking about?"

"I was just thinking about the day of the accident," she told her.

"I don't like to think about it," Elizabeth stated. "It wasn't horrible or anything like that. It's just the fact that it happened to me."

"I'm sorry," Morgan replied.

"It's not your fault," she said. "It's that obnoxious senator's fault. I'm lucky I'm not dead."

"Why don't you tell me what happened again?" Morgan suggested.

Elizabeth took a deep breath. "It happened so fast," she said. "We were driving, just minutes away from the office, and I was unaware that the senator had one too many cocktails at lunch. I would have never gotten into the car with him if I had known that. Anyway, he started swerving all over the road and

I thought he was only kidding around. You know what kind of a character he is. I noticed the police car behind us and I begged him to quit messing around. Before I knew it, there was a truck coming right at us and WHAM! Thank God Craig was there. He saw everything that happened and helped me out a great deal. He held my hand, made sure I arrived at the hospital, and was by my side the whole time. I don't know what I would have done without him."

Morgan ignored Elizabeth's remarks about Craig. "What did the doctor tell you?" she asked.

"He said that the impact of the accident caused serious injury to my back and spinal cord," Elizabeth answered.

"Will you be able to walk again?" Morgan questioned.

"The doctor said that it's a possibility but it doesn't look promising," she replied. "We are trying different things but we haven't had any luck."

"Don't worry about any of this," Morgan told her. "We are going to make the senator pay for all of this."

"Morgan," Jaime announced over the intercom. "Elizabeth's father is here to pick her up."

Elizabeth wheeled herself to the door as Morgan opened it. "Thanks for everything," she said.

"Not a problem," Morgan replied. "I will be in touch."

Morgan glanced at her watch. She had an hour to kill before her next appointment. She decided to grab a quick bite to eat and head to her appointment. "Jaime," Morgan said, as she passed by her desk. "I'm going out for a couple of hours. I'll be back later."

Morgan exited the building and crossed the street. She entered a small café and took a seat. After the waitress took her order, Morgan glanced around the café and noticed a young couple sitting at the corner table. They looked so happy just like she and Edward were before he died. Everything was so perfect. Edward was a sweet and charming man who would have given the world to Morgan on a silver platter. She thought back to the night he gave her the sweater. It was a week before he died and they had a huge fight the night before about something that didn't seem to matter now. Edward came home from work with a dozen roses in one hand and a white box in the other. "I'm sorry about last night, Angel," he said, as he handed her the gifts. "Will you ever forgive me?"

"Yes, I forgive you," she whispered. "But I know it will happen again."

"I'll try not to let it happen again," Edward replied. "Can I have a kiss?"

Morgan moved closer to give him a quick kiss and before she knew it, she was locked in a tight embrace. "I love you so much, Angel," he told her. "I hate it when you're mad at me."

"I'm not mad," she said. "What's in the box?"

"Well, open it," he insisted.

When she did, she found the beautiful pink sweater she had been eyeing the day before. How he knew she wanted it, she will never know.

"Miss," the waitress said, intruding on Morgan's thoughts. "Here's your meal."

Morgan picked at her food. She caught herself watching the couple in the corner. They were laughing and having a great time enjoying each other's company. Morgan really missed that. She really missed Edward. But she knew she couldn't bring him back and that she needed to move on with her life. That is what Edward would have wanted. Now if she only knew how to do that, she would be happy.

She glanced at her watch and left her uneaten meal on the table. She paid the waitress and went to her next appointment.

After her appointment, which resulted in a huge settlement for her client, she returned to the office. When she noticed the look on Jaime's face, she knew something was definitely wrong. "What's wrong?" Morgan asked.

"Where have you been?" Jaime demanded.

"I had a meeting," Morgan answered, impatiently. "You knew that."

"The meeting wasn't until two," she replied.

"Who do you think you are?" Morgan questioned. "My mother? For your information, I can take care of myself."

"I'm not so sure about that," Jaime informed her. "I worry about you. You have been through too much in the last six months. With everything that has happened, you know, Edward's death, Elizabeth's accident, and the..."

"Don't say it," Morgan threatened, cutting Jaime off in mid sentence. "I don't want to be reminded of that."

"I'm sorry," Jaime replied. "You don't have to get so defensive."

"Well, if you would just stop attacking me, I wouldn't be so defensive," Morgan said, as she entered her office and slammed the door.

Morgan sat at her desk, trying to keep herself busy until it was time to go home. She rummaged through the papers on her desk, putting everything in order for the next day. She impatiently waited for five o'clock to approach so she could run some errands before meeting Craig for dinner. Oh, Lord, what had she done? She hadn't been out with a man in a long time and just the thought of that made her sick to her stomach. Morgan took a deep breath to try to calm her nerves. It was just a business meeting. It wasn't a date.

Morgan walked to the window and stared at the people on the street below. Everyone was Christmas shopping. Oh joy! She wasn't looking forward to that at all.

Jaime's voice came over the intercom. "Morgan, I'm leaving," she announced. "See you in the morning."

With that, Jaime was gone. Good riddance, Morgan thought. She didn't think she could handle any more grief. She decided to wait a few minutes longer and then head to the grocery store and home.

When she arrived home, she realized another problem. She didn't know what to wear. She wanted to be comfortable but not look like a slob. She rummaged through her closet and finally decided to wear a pair of jeans and a sweatshirt.

She went back into the living room and started to pace. Morgan was nervous but she didn't know why. Maybe it was because an extremely good-looking man invited her to dinner. No, that wasn't it, Morgan tried to convince herself. It had to be something else.

Morgan realized that she hadn't felt this way since Edward. She thought back to their first date. It was so romantic. He brought her a single red rose and they ate dinner at the Italian restaurant down the block. They danced after dinner and then came back to her place for a nightcap. As a matter of fact, the very couch she was sitting on was the same couch where they shared their first kiss. It was so magical and so passionate. She knew there would never be another night like that.

Morgan looked at her watch and realized she needed to go if she was going to make it on time. She grabbed her briefcase and her keys and headed out the door.

As she drove to the restaurant, Morgan tried to calm herself down. She reminded herself that it was only a business meeting. It wasn't a date.

Morgan arrived at the restaurant and found Craig waiting for her. "This is for you," he said, as he handed her a single red rose.

"What is this for?" she asked in a you-didn't-have-to manner.

"A peace offering," he announced. "I'm sorry about your sweater."

"It's ok," Morgan replied, faintly. "It was just my favorite sweater."

"You said it had sentimental value?" Craig questioned.

"Edward gave it to me," she answered with tears in her eyes.

Morgan turned away from Craig. She didn't want him to see her cry. "I know you miss him," he said.

Morgan wiped her eyes and turned back towards him. "I don't want to talk about it," she replied. "Let's just get a table. I am so hungry."

"Did you eat lunch like I told you to?" Craig asked.

"Not exactly," she answered.

"What does that mean?" he replied.

"Well, I ordered it," she said, "but I didn't feel like eating."

"You need to take care of yourself," Craig told her.

"Please don't lecture me," she retorted. "I get enough of that from my brother."

Before Craig could say anything, the waitress came over and led them to their table. After they decided on what to eat, the waitress returned to take their order. "Let's get started," Morgan said. "Tell me about your relationship with Elizabeth Brinkman."

"I forgot you are friends," Craig said.

"We've been friends since we were four," Morgan replied.

"You are lucky to have a friend like her," Craig said. "She is a great lady."

Morgan cleared her throat and decided it was time to work. "What kind of relationship do you and Elizabeth have?" she repeated.

"Elizabeth and I are only friends," Craig replied, as he glanced at Morgan's intense eyes. "What? Can't a guy and a girl be friends without someone thinking they are sleeping together?"

"Not when one of the people are married," Morgan answered, getting irritated.

"Why are you being so bitter?" Craig asked.

"I don't think I am being bitter," she answered. "I just don't want it to come out later that you and Elizabeth have more than just a friendship. I don't want any surprises."

"I am not involved with anyone," Craig stated. "I promise you that there won't be any surprises."

Morgan grabbed the picture from the file and handed it to Craig. "Tell me about this picture," she instructed.

"It was Stephanie's third birthday party," he explained. "We had a huge party for her. It turned out to be a good day. Stephanie was really happy and had a good time."

"It sounds like you didn't," she said.

"I did until Val and I started fighting about the puppy I bought Stephanie for her birthday," Craig replied. "Val got mad because I didn't consult her about my decision."

Morgan could already tell she wasn't going to like Val. "What happened?" she asked.

"Stephanie begged Val to let her keep the puppy," he answered. "After Stephanie got on Val's nerves, she agreed to let her keep it. A couple of days later, Stephanie and I were headed home after buying a doghouse and found him dead in the backyard."

Morgan was devastated. "Oh, no," she said.

"Needless to say, Stephanie was heartbroken and Val claimed she had nothing to do with it," Craig stated.

Morgan was speechless. "That's how I reacted," Craig said, staring at Morgan. "But now we have a cat which Val just adores but Stephanie and I are allergic to."

"Val doesn't sound like the right type of woman for you," Morgan stated.

"She was at first," Craig replied. "She was everything I thought I wanted at the time. But after we got married, she turned into some kind of monster. She always had to be perfect and keep up with everyone else. It wasn't a fun marriage. I had to put up with her failed business endeavors and when her best friend had a baby, Val was bound and determined to have one too. That caused another problem. Val decided she wanted this baby now. We tried and tried but nothing happened. She naturally blamed me and I began to get frustrated with the whole thing. She didn't talk to me for days after that. She finally told me that if I couldn't give her what she wanted, she would get it someplace else."

"She must be a real pain to live with," Morgan said.

"That's not the word I would use," Craig replied, with a grin. "I loved Val at one time but over the years, things changed. She changed. I see so much of Val in Stephanie and that scares me a little. Val can be manipulative and very demanding and I don't want those qualities picked up by Stephanie."

"I can understand that," Morgan stated. "Parents want their children to be well behaved."

"Parents want their children to be perfect," Craig informed her. "You don't have any children, do you?"

"No," Morgan mumbled.

"I didn't mean to make you sad," Craig replied, with great concern. "I know you and Edward were planning on having children."

"We planned to do a lot of things," she answered.

The waitress arrived with their large pepperoni and sausage pizza. Morgan was relieved to see her.

As they ate, Morgan began questioning Craig about his job, home life, and social life. "Do you feel your job is causing you to neglect your family?" she asked.

"No," he answered, quickly. "I need to support them somehow. I know my hours don't suit Val but they are going to be that way until I am promoted."

"When will that be?" she asked.

"I go in front of the review board in a couple of weeks," Craig answered.

Morgan sat in thought for a moment. "Do you want a divorce, Craig?" she asked after some hesitation.

Craig sat silent for a moment. "I think it is the best thing for everyone," he answered.

"I don't think that I need to tell you that the custody battle over Stephanie is going to be the most difficult part of this," she explained.

Craig sat in silence. "Morgan," he muttered.

"Yeah," she replied.

"I can't lose my baby," he pleaded.

Morgan returned her slice of pizza to her plate and stared at Craig. "I'll do everything in my power to make sure that doesn't happen," she said.

"I appreciate that," he told her.

Morgan smiled at him and continued eating. "I am going to need a list of people that I can talk to about your case," she stated.

"Ok," he said. "I will work on that and get it to you."

Morgan continued to question Craig as they ate their dinner. After a few minute, they agreed to stop talking about the case and just relax.

"I had a really good time," Craig said, as he walked Morgan to her car.

"Once we got past all the serious legal stuff, it was fun," she replied.

Morgan climbed into her vehicle. "I will see you in a few days," she said.

"Ok," Craig said. "I am just going to make sure that you get out of here alright. My mom would kill me if I didn't."

Morgan turned the key in the ignition only to find that her car wouldn't start. Craig instructed her to pop the hood so he could see what the problem was. "I don't see anything wrong," he said. "Maybe it just needs a jump start. Let me go get my truck."

Craig soon returned with the vehicle and charged the battery in Morgan's car until it finally started. "I am going to follow you home to make sure you get there ok," he told her.

When they arrived at her apartment building, Craig instructed Morgan to have the battery checked. "Thanks for your help!" she said. "Do you want to come up for a cup of coffee? I think there is some cheesecake in the refrigerator if you want some."

Craig took Morgan up on her offer. "I am glad you invited me in," he said, after they entered the apartment.

"Why?" Morgan asked.

"I think there are some things we need to talk about," he answered.

"Like what?" she questioned.

"I want to talk about these feelings I am having for you," he stated. "Don't tell me you don't feel them too."

"Craig," she said, angrily. "I can't do this."

Morgan glared at him. Craig, in turn, glared back and saw the fire in her eyes. She was beautiful, Craig decided, even with her hot temper. He felt very drawn to her, which seemed very strange to him. He had experienced these feelings before but he had to ignore them. Six months ago was the wrong time to even think about a possible relationship with Morgan. She was mourning her husband's death and he was trying to save his marriage. Even now, he wasn't sure a relationship with Morgan was the right thing to do. What he did know was the feelings he was having couldn't be ignored this time. "What are you thinking about?" Morgan asked, not wanting to know the answer.

"I have a very strange question for you," Craig replied, still looking into her eyes.

"Ok," she said, alarmed.

Craig cleared his throat and ran a hand through his dark brown hair. Morgan could tell that he was nervous about asking this question and that frightened her. "May I kiss you?" he finally asked.

Morgan's heart skipped a beat as she tried to hide her excitement. "Craig," she said.

"I know," he stated, interrupting her. "You just want this to be a professional relationship. I just have this overwhelming desire to kiss you. Forget I asked."

Craig began pacing around the room. Morgan walked over and stood in front of him. "Are you going to let me finish what I was saying before you interrupted me?" she asked.

"Sorry," Craig apologized.

Morgan decided not to say anything. She moved closer to him and looked into his eyes. She gave him a sexy smile, which caused Craig's temperature to rise. She placed her lips on his and they shared a passionate kiss. "Wow!" Craig said.

"Was that what you wanted?" she asked, with a smile.

"Yeah," he answered. "Actually that was more than I expected. I think that was better than the first time we kissed."

"Oh God!" Morgan exclaimed, covering her face with her hands.

"You don't remember that?" Craig questioned.

"I blocked out a lot of things that happened the night Edward died," she explained. "I wasn't at all myself."

"I think on some level I blocked out things too," Craig replied. "I didn't even remember the kiss until we shared that one just now."

"Despite my actions, I want to thank you for being there for me that night," Morgan said. "I appreciate it more than you will ever know."

"I know," he said.

"I need to get the coffee started," Morgan said, changing the subject. "I invited you up for coffee and I don't even have it going."

Craig followed Morgan into the kitchen. "Do you like cream and sugar?" she asked.

Craig let out a sigh and ran his fingers through his hair again. "Is something wrong?" Morgan questioned.

"I just wanted to talk about that kiss," he answered.

"We will," she replied.

"Good," he said. "I'll take just sugar."

Morgan grabbed the cheesecake out of the refrigerator. She grabbed a plate from the cabinet and scooped a piece onto it for Craig. After handing the plate to him, she grabbed another plate and stared at it. Edward's sister had given them to her and Edward as a wedding gift. Morgan thought back to the wonderful day as if it were yesterday. It was a perfect day. She had all her loved ones around her. Elizabeth and Jaime tried to keep her from being nervous. Her mother helped her pick out the most beautiful gown she had ever seen. Her brother, Bryan, walked her down the aisle. Everything went perfectly.

"Morgan," Craig called, placing a hand on her shoulder. "Are you alright?"

Morgan jumped at the sound of Craig's voice. She watched as the plate she was holding crashed to the floor. She immediately went down to her knees and began to clean up the mess. Craig followed her lead and began to help. Morgan held up one of the broken pieces. "Just like my life," she explained. "It's all shattered to pieces."

Craig grabbed hold of her hands. She was shaking. "What has gotten you so upset?" he asked, as he tried to stop her trembling.

Morgan sighed and willed herself not to cry. "Why does my well being concern you so much?" she asked.

"I care about you," he answered. "Also it goes with the job. Police officers are supposed to take care of people in need."

"I'm not in need," she informed him. "I can take care of myself."

"I am sure you can," he replied. "I just want to be here if you need someone to lean on."

"I don't depend on others for help," she explained. "I get hurt that way."

"Well, for what it's worth, I am here if you need me," Craig told her.

Morgan cleaned up the mess and sat down with Craig to eat. "Maybe we can work on your list of names while we eat," she suggested.

"I'll get started on it," he replied. "Do you have a pen?"

"In the top drawer of my desk," she answered, without looking up.

Craig got up and walked over to the desk. As he opened the drawer, he noticed a picture of a man staring at him from the corner of the desk. He picked up the picture and stared back. Craig could feel the jealousy building up inside him. "It might be easier to move on if you start letting go of Edward," he said.

Morgan's head shot up in an instant. Edward, she thought. She jumped up and hurried over to Craig. "What I do is none of your business," she snapped at him, as she grabbed the picture out of his hand.

"I was just surprised to see it on the desk," Craig replied.

"I'm not going to hide it," she responded. "I wish everyone would understand that it's been really hard for me to adjust to his death. It's been a really slow process."

"I'm really sorry about all the pain you've been through these past few months," Craig stated. "I tried really hard to help him but it was out of my hands."

"I know you did everything you could for him," she replied, softly. "Please don't feel guilty about it."

"I'm sorry but I don't know how else to feel," he said. "We don't have to talk about this if you don't want to."

Morgan stared at Craig with a painful look on her face. "No, it's alright," she replied. "I really need to talk about this, if you don't mind."

Craig thought back to that horrible night when he had to break the news to Morgan about her husband. "No, I don't mind," he replied. "You can always talk to me."

Morgan began to pace around the room. "Sometimes it seems like a lifetime ago," she told him. "Then again, when I start to miss him, it seems like it happened yesterday. Do you understand what I'm saying?"

"Yes, I do," Craig said.

"I'm indebted to you for being there for me that night," Morgan replied. "I want to thank you for your help."

"Don't mention it," Craig stated. "I made a promise to your husband. I was determined to follow it to the letter."

"I lost a lot that night," Morgan stated. "I don't ever want to feel that kind of pain again."

31

"I never told you this but I felt something that night," Craig explained. "I felt a connection with Edward and you. It's something I can't quite explain. I told you that night I stayed with him up until the time they wheeled him into the operating room. I also tried so desperately to find you. I'm sorry I didn't find you in time. I feel so guilty about the whole night."

"Craig, please don't feel guilty," Morgan pleaded. "You were here for me when I needed someone. It's not your fault you couldn't find me. Edward and I had a special evening planned. What a rotten thing for him to do to me."

Morgan burst into tears. On impulse, Craig grabbed her and pulled her into his arms. "I'm sorry, Angel," he whispered with a tear in his eye.

"Edward used to call me angel," Morgan cried.

"He called you 'his angel' that day," Craig replied. "He told me to take care of his angel."

"You did a good job taking care of me that night," she stated.

Morgan pulled away from Craig just enough to place a gentle kiss on his lips. "What was that for?" he asked, shocked.

"For helping and taking care of me," she answered.

"I think I'll do it more often," he said with a smile.

"Craig," Morgan replied. "I don't know what you are expecting from me. But all I can give you is friendship. I'm not ready for anything more than that. I'm not sure I'll ever be ready."

"You need to let go," Craig told her. "It's hard to lose something that you love but time passes and we learn to adjust."

"I'm not sure I know how to move on," she said.

Craig moved away from Morgan. She could tell that something was on his mind. "I need to know what was behind that kiss we shared earlier," he stated.

"I am not going to lie to you," Morgan responded. "I am very attracted to you."

"I am very attracted to you too," Craig replied. "I think I have been since the moment I first saw you."

"I can't allow myself to get involved with anyone right now," Morgan told him.

"Why did you kiss me then?" Craig asked.

"Why did you ask me if you could kiss me?" Morgan questioned.

"Because I wanted to," he answered.

"I think you have your answer then," she replied.

Craig looked away from Morgan. "If things were different, I would consider being with you in a heartbeat," Morgan explained. "I just need time to get over the last six months of my life."

Craig grabbed hold of Morgan's hand and directed her to sit next to him on the couch. "There is a part of me that just wants to be with you," Craig told her, as he caressed her hand. "I know that it's not the right time for either one of us. Maybe if we try though, we can get through all of this together."

"That is so sweet," Morgan said. "But I don't want you to settle for the first girl that comes along."

"I wasn't planning on doing that," Craig replied. "When I see something I like, I go after it."

"Aren't you going to take any time to get over your divorce?" she asked. "I'm not going to approve of any relationship you may have with any female until you are divorced and have custody of Stephanie."

"My little girl means the world to me," Craig said. "I'm not going to ruin any chance I have of getting custody of my daughter."

"I am going to do everything I can to make sure that you get custody of her," Morgan replied.

"I appreciate that," he said.

Morgan glanced at the wall clock and said, "Craig, it's getting late. Let's call it a night."

"You're right," he replied, as he returned to the table and finished his dessert and coffee. "I have to get up early and work the morning shift."

Craig headed for the door. "Please think about what I said about us. Will I see you tomorrow?" he asked.

"Probably not," she answered. "I have a busy day but I will call you about my meeting with Valerie's lawyer."

"I'll drop the list of names off at your office sometime tomorrow," he replied. "That way, I'll be able to see you."

Craig gave Morgan a quick kiss on the cheek. "Thanks for everything," he said, as he walked out the door.

Chapter 3

Craig awoke to the sound of pots and pans banging in the kitchen. He sat up on the couch and rubbed his tired eyes. It was seven o'clock and time to get up, he decided. He wandered to the kitchen and found a very angry Val standing there with a cup of coffee in one hand and a pan in the other. "Where the hell were you last night?" she demanded.

"Would you keep your voice down?" he asked. "You're going to wake Stephanie."

"Stephanie isn't here," the short haired brunette replied. "If you would have been home, you would have known that."

"Where is she?" Craig questioned.

"She's with my parents, Craig," she answered, with an attitude.

"My parents are supposed to have her this weekend," Craig reminded her.

"Don't worry," Val said, getting bored. "They will."

Craig sighed loudly. "You didn't answer my question," Val stated. "Where were you?"

"Oh Val. I'm so touched that you're so concerned about me," Craig replied, sarcastically.

"I couldn't care less about you," Val said. "Are you having an affair?"

"That's not a bad idea," Craig stated, deep in thought. "After all, you had one."

"Sure bring that up," Val said, like it was no big deal. "Just because I made a mistake doesn't mean you get to."

"Why does it matter to you what I do with my life?" Craig asked.

"Because I am still your wife!" Val screamed.

"Not for long," Craig said. "I'm through talking to you."

Craig hurried down the hall and slammed the bedroom door. The nerve of that woman, he thought. Every time he did something he had to answer to her. There would be no more of that.

Craig grabbed a towel and headed towards the shower. As he stood under the flowing water, thoughts of Morgan entered his mind. She was a remarkable woman. She listened to him and made him feel important. He would love to have someone like her to share his life with. He knew that would never be possible because of all the heartache she had been through recently. He wanted so badly to take Morgan in his arms and take her pain away. Something interrupted Craig's thoughts. He turned towards the new presence in his shower and let out a life-wrenching scream. "What the hell are you doing in my shower?" Craig yelled, grabbing his chest. "You almost gave me a heart attack."

"I don't think I look that bad," Val replied, sweetly. "I'm sorry I scared you."

"Don't do it again," Craig said. "Now get out of my shower."

"But Craig," Val pleaded. "We haven't spent any time alone together. Please let me stay."

Val moved closer to Craig and ran her hand through the hair on his chest. She stood on her tiptoes and began kissing his neck and behind his ear. "Do you like this?" she whispered.

Craig rolled his eyes. "No," he said, as he took a step back.

"You used to like it," she reminded him.

"That was before you cheated on me," Craig said, exiting the shower.

Craig grabbed his towel and headed for the bedroom, dripping water as he went. "Craig," Val yelled. "You're making a huge mess on the new carpet."

Val hurried into the bedroom. "Val," Craig said, mimicking her. "You're making a huge mess on the new carpet."

"Would you stop doing that?" Val asked. "It is so irritating."

Craig stopped dead in his tracks. "Only if you quit your damn bitching," he yelled. "I'm really sick of it."

36

Val flopped down on the bed and began to cry. Craig rolled his eyes again. "Don't," Craig demanded.

"What do you expect me to do?" she cried. "You obviously don't love me anymore and don't want to be with me."

"You're the one who wanted to get a divorce," Craig reminded her. "You're the one who cheated on me. That's why I feel the way I do about you. So don't even bother to ask me for sympathy because you're hurting. I'm hurting too."

Val got up and hurried over to Craig. "It's not too late to call our lawyers and cancel this divorce nonsense. Let's get back together," she said, hopefully. "We can even start on having another child. Stephanie is old enough and I can close the business. Oh please, Craig! What do you say?"

"No," he replied. "It's too late for a reconciliation. Now if you'll excuse me, I have to go to work."

Craig arrived at the precinct and shoved his way through a group of people. "Craig," someone called. "Chief wants to see you."

He hurried to the Chief's office and took a seat. "How's it going, Craig?" he asked.

"Just fine, Sir," Craig replied.

"Good," he said. "The reason I asked to see you was to tell you the review board wants to see you at nine o'clock tomorrow morning."

"I thought that wasn't going to be for a few weeks," Craig exclaimed.

"Things are being moved up," the chief replied. "Are you sure you are in the right frame of mind for this?"

"Yes," Craig said. "I'm not going to let my personal life interfere with my job."

"Good," the chief replied. "Be in full uniform and here at nine o'clock."

Craig left the office and hurried to the lounge to grab a quick bite to eat. When he entered, he immediately noticed his partner and best friend, John Martin, finishing a cup of coffee. "Hey Buddy," John said, as he threw his cup in the trash. "How did your date with that lady lawyer go?"

"Things went well," Craig informed him. "But it wasn't a date."

The older gentleman stared at Craig. "What's wrong?" John asked. "You seem distracted."

"I am," Craig answered. "But there's nothing you can do unless you want my wife."

"No Sir," John protested. "I swore off women a long time ago. Divorce will do that to you. What did Valerie do now?"

"She's just being herself," Craig answered. "Manipulative, demanding, and bitchy."

"That's Valerie alright," John agreed.

Craig laughed. "Let's go to work," he said.

The morning seemed to go by very slowly. The area they usually patrolled was quiet and deserted. This didn't help Craig's train of thought. It always went back to the same person, Morgan. She haunted his thoughts. He was absolutely certain he dreamed about her last night. He needed to stop doing that. She already made it clear they couldn't be together right now and he knew she was right. It wasn't the right time for them. He had to get this divorce taken care of and get custody of Stephanie. After that, he could concentrate on a relationship with Morgan. A voice over the police radio interrupted Craig's thought. The two officers were informed about a hostage situation at a nearby convenience store.

"10-4," John responded. "Unit 12 will be on scene."

John flipped on the siren and lights and raced to the location. John and Craig hurried over to the other officers to find out what was happening.

"From the information we have gathered from the other employees of the convenience store, a young man is holding a cashier hostage," Officer Mel Stone explained.

Craig let out a sigh. "Do we have any information on the two in the building?" he asked.

"Their names are Tom and Julie," Mel answered. "They used to date but she broke up with him."

"I hope this isn't one of those situations where if he can't have her, no one can," John replied, as he ran his hand through his salt and pepper colored hair.

"I am almost certain that it is," Craig said. "Has anyone tried talking to this guy?"

"I did," Mel answered. "He doesn't want to listen to reason. I'm going to try again. I figure while I distract him, someone can get inside and get that girl out of there."

"I'll do it," Craig volunteered.

Craig and John hurried around the back of the building. Before entering the building, they quickly formulated a plan to rescue Julie. Craig entered the building quietly and hunched behind a crate waiting for the right time to act. "Why did you leave me?" Tom asked Julie. "You know I love you. How could you just walk out on me?"

"You were suffocating me," she replied. "Would you please let me go? You're scaring me."

"No!" Tom yelled, in a threatening voice. "If I let you go, you'll find someone else. I won't allow that. I'll kill you first."

On impulse, Craig stepped into the room. "I don't think you want to do that, Tom," he said.

Tom turned to him. "Who the hell are you?" he yelled.

"I'm Officer Masterson," he answered. "I decided to come in here and talk to you since you wouldn't listen to the officer outside."

"You made a huge mistake coming in here, Cop," Tom threatened. "I'm going to have to kill you too."

"Why are you doing this?" Craig asked.

"Because I love her," Tom answered. "And I want her back."

"You have a hell of a way of showing her that," Craig replied, as he inched closer to the counter.

"There was no other way," he said. "She wouldn't return any of my calls and she refused to see me."

"Tom, sometimes life goes that way," Craig replied. "People change and decide that they don't want to be in their present situation. I don't know anything about your relationship with Julie but I can speak from my own experience. I'm going through a divorce right now and I can understand your pain."

"Yeah, right," Tom said, not believing Craig. "You're just making that up so I'll let Julie go."

"No, I'm not," Craig said. "Honest. I can't stand my wife so we are getting a divorce."

Tom chuckled. Craig reacted to it by waving for Julie to come closer to him. When she was close enough, Craig grabbed her arm and pulled her behind him. "Stay behind me," he ordered. "And you'll be okay."

"What are you doing?" Tom yelled.

"I don't believe you really want to hurt Julie," Craig explained calmly. "I want to get her out of here before you do something you'll regret."

Tom raised his gun. "Julie, either get out from behind him or I'll kill you both."

Julie caught her breath. "Don't worry, Julie," Craig whispered. "Everything is going to be alright."

Craig moved slowly towards the door. "One more step and you're both dead," Tom threatened.

Craig stopped just short of the door. He had to get Julie out of there. On impulse, he drew his gun. "Tom," he said. "I guarantee you I'm a lot better shot than you. You'll be dead before you pull the trigger."

Tom stared at his gun and thought about the situation. Craig edged Julie closer to the door. He turned his head to look at her. "Run," he mouthed.

Julie did as she was told. She was out the door in seconds with John waiting for her.

Craig stepped closer to Tom. "You shouldn't have done that," Tom said. "Now you'll pay."

"I don't think you want to kill me," Craig stated, stepping closer. "Or you'd have done it already."

Craig took another step forward watching the gun in Tom's trembling hands as he moved. "Don't come any closer, Cop!" Tom exclaimed. "Or I'll...I'll."

"Kill me," Craig finished, grabbing the gun out of Tom's hands. "I don't think so."

About that time, four cops rushed into the building. "It's about time," Craig called, as he dropped to the floor.

"Are you okay?" John asked.

"I am now," Craig answered.

"You're lucky you didn't get killed," John replied.

"Lucky's not the word for it," Craig said, as John extended his hand to pull him up.

"It took guts to do what you did," he stated. "Please don't do that again."

"I hope I don't have to," Craig told him. "But sometimes that's the job, isn't it?"

John patted Craig on the back as they hurried outside. Julie walked over to Craig and expressed her deep appreciation. "I wouldn't be alive if it wasn't for you," she said.

"I'm just glad nobody was hurt," Craig said. "You, me, or Tom."

Julie stood on her tiptoes and gave Craig a kiss on the cheek. "Thanks again," she said.

As John and Craig headed back to the station, Craig became lost in thought. He knew he had done a good job. Even with the praise he got from some of his co-workers, it didn't seem to be enough. He wondered if Morgan would have been proud of the way he handled the situation. Oh Morgan, I wish I could get you out of my mind, he thought. He decided he had to see her today. He had to think of some excuse. He did promise he would deliver the list of names to her.

When John and Craig arrived at the station, he felt a lot better. Just thinking about Morgan made him feel good. He wanted to keep her in his life.

When Craig entered the station, a room full of smiling faces greeted him. He thought they were congratulating him on a job well done. He soon found out it was for something totally different. "Legs was here looking for you," Mel told him.

"Legs? Who's Legs?" Craig asked, baffled.

"I don't know who she was," Mel replied.

"What did she look like?" Craig questioned.

"She had blonde hair, blue eyes, and great legs," he answered. "A knockout."

Morgan, Craig thought. "Oh, that was my lawyer," he replied, like it was no big deal.

"Is that what your lawyer looks like?" John said, interrupting the conversation. "Where was she when I was going through my divorce? I could have used her services."

41

Craig smiled as he walked away from Mel and John and their comments about Morgan. He would see her today and that made him feel like the happiest man in the world.

Craig entered the lounge and grabbed a soda from the machine. He leaned against the wall and let his mind wander. He had to quit thinking about Morgan, especially at work. Things on the job were bad enough without the added distraction. He had to keep focused. A knock at the door brought him back to reality. "Craig," Morgan called. "Do you have a minute?"

"Sure," he said, smiling. "Let's step into the next room and talk privately for a moment."

Craig opened the door to an interrogation room down the hall and directed her inside. "I wanted to let you know I talked to Valerie's lawyer today," Morgan told him. "Things didn't go well. Apparently, Valerie's demands have changed again. We can talk about that when we have more time."

"She can have whatever she wants," Craig replied. "All I want are the things I moved in with and Stephanie."

"Would you be willing to share custody with Valerie?" Morgan asked. "That is, if we can talk her into it."

"I'll have to think about that," Craig replied. "I don't want to keep Stephanie away from her mother but I don't want to lose custody of her either."

"I didn't want to tell you this while you're working," Morgan told him. "Valerie has been telling her lawyer that you and I are having an affair and because of that, she wants full custody of Stephanie."

"The nerve of that woman!" Craig exclaimed. "How dare she lie to manipulate the situation! But after all, it is Val and she's lied before to get what she wants. Why should this time be any different?"

"Try not to worry about it," Morgan stated. "I will get it all worked out. Do you have that list for me?"

"Yes," Craig answered, still shaking his head over Val's latest stunt.

Morgan glanced at her watch. "I don't have time to go over the list with you now."

"When will we be able to talk about all of this?" Craig asked.

"Just call my office and make an appointment," she answered. "That is the best I can do right now."

"How about dinner tonight?" Craig questioned.

"No, Craig," Morgan said. "After the accusations that your wife is making, I don't think we should see each other outside the office. The only time we should meet is to discuss your case."

"Ok," Craig agreed. "I will make an appointment and see you then."

Morgan got up and headed for the door. She couldn't believe Craig didn't try to persuade her to have dinner with him. She decided not to press the issue. "I have another appointment," she told him. "I'll see you later."

After she was gone, Craig whispered to himself, "You can count on it, Legs."

The day went by quickly for Craig. He called Jaime and made an appointment for 4:30 p.m. the following day. He made it perfectly clear to her he wanted to be Morgan's last appointment of the day and Jaime was more than happy to oblige.

Craig hurried home to Stephanie. When he entered the house, a smiling four-year-old greeted him. "Hi Daddy!" she exclaimed.

"Hi Sweetheart!" he said, as he picked her up and swung her around.

"Craig, how many times have I asked you not to do that?" Val questioned, angrily.

"Stephanie likes it," Craig told her.

Stephanie giggled as Craig swung her around once more. "Craig, please stop!" Val exclaimed.

Craig put Stephanie down. "Finish coloring, Honey," Craig instructed. "Your mother and I will be right back."

"What the hell is your problem?" Craig asked.

"I want you to move out," Val answered.

"This is my house!" Craig exclaimed. "Why should I leave?"

"My lawyer said that it would be for the best," Val said.

43

"I don't care what your lawyer said," Craig stated. "I'm not leaving."

"Then Stephanie and I will leave," Val replied.

"You are not taking my daughter anywhere," Craig threatened.

"How do you know that she's your daughter?" Val asked, in a nasty tone.

"Oh, please," Craig said, disgusted. "Don't start playing that game again."

"Then you stop playing your game," Val demanded.

"And what game would that be, Val?" Craig asked. "You're the one who cheated on me and now you're using my child against me."

"Mommy! Daddy! Stop!" A little voice yelled from across the room.

"Stephanie," Val said, softly. "Your father and I are just having a disagreement. Don't be scared."

Stephanie ran over to Val and gave her a hug. "Mommy, I love you so much!" she exclaimed.

Craig knelt down and looked at Stephanie. "What about me?" he asked.

"Oh, Daddy," she said, wrapping her arms around his neck. "I love you too!"

Craig kissed the tiny tip of her nose and asked, "What are you doing tonight, Miss Stephanie?"

"Grandma and I are going shopping for Christmas stuff," she answered. "Then I'm staying with her and Grandpa."

Craig glared at Val. Val caught Craig's stare and immediately directed her attention to Stephanie. "Sweetie," she said, in her motherly tone. "Why don't you get ready to go? Grandma will be here shortly."

Stephanie quickly ran from the room. "Craig," Val said, walking across the room. "I know exactly what you're going to say. Why must we go through this?"

"Because my parents have as much right to see Stephanie as your parents do," Craig replied.

"You know how my parents are," Val said. "They really enjoy their time with Stephanie. Please don't deprive them of it."

Craig went to the phone. He couldn't believe he was actually giving into Val's manipulation. After a lengthy talk with his crying mother, he hung up the phone. "I hope you're happy," Craig said, coldly. "My parents get her the next two weekends, Val. Don't forget that! Now if you'll excuse me."

Craig hurried down the hall with Val in hot pursuit. "Where are you going?" she demanded.

"For your information," he replied. "I'm first going to take a shower alone and then I am going out."

"Going out?" Val stated, shocked. "Where? I can't believe you can't spend at least one night at home with me."

"It's none of your business where I'm going," Craig told her. "And why would I want to stay here with you? You're the reason I'm leaving."

Val burst into tears. "I can't believe you would say such a thing," she cried. "You can be so cruel. Is this the way you treat your mistress?"

Craig stopped dead in his tracks. "I don't have a mistress, Valerie," he replied, calmly. "How many times do I have to tell you that?"

"What about Morgan?" Val questioned. "I bet she's more than just your lawyer."

Craig turned and glared at her. "You leave her out of this," he threatened.

"She is the reason for all this hostility towards me, isn't she?" Val questioned.

"She has nothing to do with us," Craig answered. "Now just shut up! I'm so sick of your constant yelling, mocking, and manipulation. I'm leaving."

"Tell Morgan I said hi," Val called after him.

After a quick shower and an even quicker exit, Craig left the house. He wasn't sure where he was going but it didn't matter as long as he was far away from Val. He needed to talk to someone but he wasn't sure whom. He drove by John's townhouse and saw that the lights were on. "I'm not interrupting anything, am I?" he asked, when John opened the door.

"No! Come on in!" John replied. "I was just sitting down with my beer getting ready to watch the game. Partner, you don't look so good."

"I have a lot of things on my mind," Craig replied.

"Do you want to talk about it?" John asked.

"If you have time," Craig answered.

John motioned Craig into the townhouse. "What's going on?" he asked.

Craig explained to John his situation with Val. "She absolutely drives me crazy," he said. "She has taken total control of Stephanie's life. I would hate to think of what our constant fighting is doing to Stephanie. I don't want her upset. Val suggested I move out. Maybe that will make things better for Stephanie. I don't know what to do anymore."

"What do you want to do, Craig?" John asked. "You know I've been through this so I can speak from experience. It's not easy especially when children are involved. Do you still love Valerie?"

"No," Craig answered, quickly. "I can't even stand being around her anymore."

Craig began to pace around the room. "Maybe it would be best if you move out," John suggested. "You two are only hurting each other not to mention Stephanie."

Craig ran a hand through his hair. "Yeah," he agreed. "Maybe I should."

"It's your call, Buddy," John replied. "If it were me, I wouldn't want to live with Valerie either."

Craig smiled. "Now that that is settled, I need to find a place to live," he stated.

"No problem there," John said. "There's plenty of room here. The kids are out of town for a few more weeks. Alec is spending the holidays with his mom and Kim is in Colorado skiing. You can stay here for awhile, if you need to."

"If you don't mind," Craig replied. "It would only be for a short time."

"I said that it wasn't a problem," John said. "Is there anything else you need to talk about?"

"Yeah, but I think it will keep," Craig answered.

"I have been wanting to ask you something," John told him. "Is that lady lawyer of yours single?"

"Yes," Craig answered. "Why?"

"I think she is absolutely gorgeous," John replied. "I would love to take her out sometime."

Craig felt a bit uncomfortable, not to mention jealous. He didn't want anyone taking Morgan out but him. "Well, while we're on the subject," Craig stated, carefully. "That's the other thing I wanted to talk about."

"Legs? What about her?" John asked.

"You're right," Craig replied. "She is very attractive. And that's a huge problem for me. I find myself thinking about her constantly. In the short time we have spent together, I have realized she's the one I want to be with."

John shifted in his chair. "Well, that causes a big problem, doesn't it?" John said.

"You got that right," Craig stated. "She has already made it perfectly clear she doesn't want a relationship with me right now. She wants to wait until the divorce is final. She doesn't want to jeopardize my custody of Stephanie. I think there might be more to it though."

"What makes you say that?" John asked.

"Do you remember about six months ago when that stock broker got killed in that hostage situation downtown?" Craig questioned.

"Yes," John answered. "You and Mel handled that. His name was Edward Garrett."

"Well, he was Morgan's husband," Craig explained. "She is still having a rough time getting past it. I know six months isn't enough time but she needs help moving on. I want to be the one to help her. I feel like I owe it to her."

"I reviewed the case afterwards," John stated. "You did everything you possibly could do. You were with him up until the point they wheeled him into the operating room. You tried so desperately to find Morgan with no luck. Hell, you even killed the man who killed Edward."

"That was only because he shot at Mel," Craig reminded him. "He came close to killing him too."

47

"What I'm saying is I think you have done enough for Morgan," John explained. "You even stayed with her that night to make sure she would be fine. Man, I consider you a hero."

"Some hero," Craig replied. "I couldn't even prevent what happened the next morning to her. I feel like I messed up everything."

"What happened to Morgan was unpreventable," John stated. "There was nothing you could do to stop that. And as for being a failure, you did the best possible job you could do under the circumstances."

"I don't feel like I did enough," Craig said. "Listen. I better go. You've got things to do and I have something I need to take care of."

"Well, anytime you need to talk," John replied. "I'll be here."

Craig left the townhouse and decided to drive by Morgan's apartment. He had a need to see her. He knew it was wrong and he should keep his distance but he wanted to make sure she was all right. After parking his car, he ran up two flights of stairs to get to her apartment. "Who is it?" Morgan called, knowing she wasn't expecting anyone.

"It's Craig," he replied. "May I come in?"

Morgan opened the door slowly. "What are you doing here?" she asked.

Before Craig could answer, he had to take in this vision. There she stood dressed in only a short white bathrobe and nothing else as far as he could tell. He wanted to carefully slide the robe off her and...

"Excuse me!" Morgan called. "I hate to bother your little fantasy but would you please tell me why you are here?"

"May I come in?" he asked again.

"Is this about business?" she questioned. "You have an appointment with me tomorrow. We can talk then."

"No, it's not about business," he answered. "I just need to talk."

Morgan held open the door and let Craig inside the apartment. After she shut the door, she asked, "What's the problem?"

48

Craig turned to look at Morgan. "You're very distracting in that robe," he commented. "I can't think straight."

"I'll go change," Morgan said, heading towards the bedroom.

Craig grabbed her arm and pulled her over in front of him. "There's no need to do that," he whispered.

Morgan shifted uncomfortably. "You said that you wanted to talk to me," she replied.

"Yeah," Craig answered, as he stared into her gorgeous blue eyes. "You are so beautiful."

Craig touched Morgan's face softly. "Don't," Morgan whispered, pulling away.

"Please don't pull away from me," Craig pleaded. "I want you."

Morgan closed her eyes and took a deep breath. She didn't want to fight with him. She hated to admit it but she wanted him too. But was she ready to take this big step especially with a married man? He was her client and they were supposed to have only a professional relationship. Was she ready to open the door to a whole new relationship?

She opened her eyes and immediately was drawn to Craig's dark, soulful eyes. She stood on her tiptoes and gently placed her lips on his. Craig gathered her into his arms and returned her kiss. "Are you sure you want to do this?" he asked.

"I want to," she said, hesitantly. "But we probably shouldn't."

Craig turned away from Morgan, not believing what he was hearing. Morgan put her hand on his shoulder. "Craig," she said. "I'm sorry. I didn't want to stop it but you have to understand. It's been a long time since I've been with a man. I'm really scared not only for me but for you too. If something were to happen between us, it may jeopardize your case. I don't want us to feel guilty about this in the morning. I want to be with you when we are both available to be with each other, not because we are lonely and need comfort."

Craig turned back to Morgan. "I understand what you're saying," he replied. "I don't want to do anything that will hurt any chance I have at getting custody of Stephanie. But I don't

49

know how long I can fight my feelings for you. I care a lot about you. I think I have ever since the first time I saw you."

"Craig, before you say anything else," Morgan interrupted. "I care about you too. I am very grateful for all your help on the night Edward died. You're a wonderful, giving, and caring person. I would love to have someone like you in my life but you have to understand. I lost my husband six months ago. I am not over that yet and I don't know if I will ever be."

"I know what happened to you," Craig replied. "I don't want to see you throw away what we have here. You can't tell me you don't see what is going on here. We have this connection."

"I feel it too," she told him. "I don't want to throw it away. I am not doing that. I just need time to get through this. For now, we need to keep this relationship on a professional level."

Craig pulled Morgan into his arms. "I'm not giving up on you," he assured her, getting lost in her eyes.

"Please don't push me," Morgan replied. "As soon as your divorce is final, we can talk about this again."

Craig pulled Morgan closer and kissed her passionately. Morgan's heart skipped a beat and her head started to spin. Boy, could he kiss. She could get used to this if she would let herself. No, she couldn't get involved in this. She had to stop it. "Craig," she said, as she pulled away. "I can't do this. Please leave."

Craig stared at her. He slowly walked to the door and then turned back towards her. "I'll slow down and lay off for now," he said. "But once I'm divorced, you better be ready."

After Craig walked out the door, Morgan dropped to her knees and began to cry.

Chapter 4

"You look terrible," Jaime said, as Morgan walked by her desk.

"Don't remind me," Morgan replied. "I didn't sleep very well."

After pouring herself a cup of coffee, she walked back over to Jaime's desk. "Who's my first client?" she asked.

"Her name is Louise Cramer," Jaime answered. "She'll be here in a few minutes."

"She must be a new client," Morgan said, trying to recall the name. "Let me see her file."

"I don't have it," Jaime stated.

"What do you mean you don't have it?" Morgan questioned.

"She called yesterday wanting some legal advice," Jaime answered. "She made it clear that she must speak with you."

"I guess I'll find out what she wants when she arrives," Morgan replied. "Send her in when she gets here."

Morgan settled in behind her desk. All she could do was wait.

The time moved by slowly but finally, there was a knock at the door. "Come in!" Morgan called.

The door opened and a woman at least ten years older than Morgan entered the room. "Ms. Garrett, I presume," the woman said in a confident voice.

Morgan stood up and extended her hand. "That's me," she replied. "You must be Ms. Cramer."

The woman glared at Morgan's hand and chose to ignore it. "No," she answered. "I used that name as a front. I'm actually Mrs. Craig Masterson."

Morgan fell back in her chair not waiting for Mrs. Masterson to sit. She couldn't believe her eyes. The woman standing in front of her looked so much older than the one she saw in the family picture. "What can I do for you?" Morgan asked, hesitantly.

Valerie glared at Morgan. "I took time out of my busy schedule to come by and speak to you," she replied. "Would you at least act curious?"

"Mrs. Masterson," she said. "I really shouldn't be speaking to you without the presence of your attorney."

"Oh, it's no problem," Val replied. "My attorney knows I'm here. I assured him that I didn't want to talk to you about the case."

"Then what else could you possibly want?" Morgan asked, impatiently.

"Ms. Garrett or should I call you Morgan like Craig does?" Val questioned, with an attitude.

Morgan rolled her eyes. "And while we're on the subject of my husband," Val continued. "That's why I'm here."

"Your husband is my client," Morgan stated. "I can't discuss anything with you about what we've talked about."

"I don't want to know any of that," Val snapped. "Let me get to the point. Are you having an affair with my husband?"

Morgan wanted to laugh. She knew she wanted to be with Craig but she couldn't admit that to his wife. "No," Morgan answered. "Your husband and I have a professional relationship. That's it."

"Why was he at your apartment last night then?" Val questioned.

Morgan felt like she was cornered. What was she supposed to say? She wasn't a very good liar and she didn't want to tell the truth, for obvious reasons. "I don't know what you're talking about," Morgan lied.

"I know he was at your apartment building!" Val yelled.

"Mrs. Masterson," Morgan replied, calmly. "I suggest you calm down. There is no need for you to yell at me."

"Don't you dare talk to me like that!" Val yelled, getting up in Morgan's face. "I know you're sleeping with my husband!

I won't stand for it! The next time I catch you with my husband, you'll regret it!"

Jaime rushed into the office with Mr. Parker on her heels. "What's going on in here?" she asked.

"Mrs. Masterson was just leaving," Morgan announced. "Jaime, will you please show her out?"

Jaime grabbed Valerie's arm and started out the door. "You better watch your back, Morgan," Val threatened.

After Valerie was out of the room, Morgan began to relax. "What happened?" Mr. Parker asked. "Who was she?"

"She and one of my clients are getting a divorce," Morgan explained. "Obviously, she isn't taking it very well. She accused me of having an affair with her husband and then she threatened me."

"She's not your client?" he questioned.

"No," Morgan answered. "This is the first time I have met her."

"I think you better call her attorney and let him know what happened," Mr. Parker suggested.

After he was gone, Morgan called Jeff Harris, Valerie's attorney. She explained what had happened and told him about the accusations and threats Valerie had delivered. He said that he would take care of it.

Meanwhile across town, Craig was having about as bad a morning as Morgan. He was sitting in front of the review board awaiting their verdict. "Officer Masterson," Captain Brown said. "We have reviewed your record and it looks quite impressive. I would like to make a comment about yesterday though. It was quite a risk you took with the girl in the hostage situation but we would like to commend you for a job well done. With that being said, we feel we should proceed with your promotion. I have to ask though. Do you feel like your pending divorce is affecting your job performance?"

"I don't feel I have a problem distinguishing between my personal and professional lives," Craig replied. "Neither one interferes with the other."

"We are not so sure," the captain said. "We just want you to be free of distractions when you are promoted. Because of this, your promotion might be delayed."

As the group left the room, Craig sat there in disbelief. He couldn't believe how much his life was in shambles. His marriage was falling apart, his job was making him miserable, and Morgan made it perfectly clear they couldn't be together right now. His heart broke for her last night as he stood outside the door and listened to her cry. He wanted desperately to rush back in and take all her pain away. He knew he couldn't though not until he was free.

Craig got up and walked out into the busy precinct. A few people said hello to him but he passed them in silence. He had to get out of there.

He left the precinct and decided to pick up Stephanie and spend time with her. "Daddy!" she called when he entered Val's parents' house.

"Good morning, Sunshine!" he said, as he gave her a huge hug.

"What are you doing here?" Val's mother, Emily, questioned.

"I have the day off so I decided to spend it with Stephanie," Craig informed her.

"Well, you can forget it," Emily replied. "We have plans already made."

"You'll just have to break them," Craig stated. "My daughter and I are leaving. Get your coat, Stephanie."

Stephanie ran from the room. "How dare you!" Emily shouted. "This is our weekend with her!"

"Correction. This was my parents' weekend with her," he replied. "That's where she'll be staying tonight. If you'll excuse me, I'll go get her things."

Craig gathered her things and the two went out the door. "I'm calling Valerie," Emily threatened.

"Go right on ahead," Craig insisted.

Craig and Stephanie returned to their house in silence. "Daddy," she said, when they entered the house. "Are you mad at me?"

Craig knelt down in front of her. "No, Sweetheart," he answered. "I could never be mad at you."

"Then why do you and Mommy always fight?" she asked.

Craig sighed. "Let's sit down. There are a few things I need to tell you," Craig replied.

After they were comfortable on the couch, Craig continued. "Your mom and I are very unhappy right now. We do fight a lot but it is not your fault. Do you understand?"

"Yes, Daddy," she replied.

Now for the hard part, Craig thought. "I'm not really sure how to explain this to you," he told her.

"Just give it to me straight, Dad," she replied, trying to sound grown up.

"Ok," Craig said. "Your mom and I are getting a divorce."

"What's a divorce?" Stephanie asked, interrupting him.

"A divorce is when two people decide they don't want to be married anymore," he explained, carefully. "Your mom wants me to move out of this house."

Tears welled up in Stephanie's big brown eyes. Her bottom lip quivered when she asked, "You won't be living with me anymore?"

"No, Honey," Craig answered, wrapping his arms around her.

"Why?" she asked. "Doesn't Mommy love you anymore?"

"That is something you will have to ask her," he replied.

"Don't you love me and Mommy anymore?" Stephanie asked. "Why do you have to leave?"

"I love you very much, Sweetheart," Craig said, his heart breaking. "I don't want to leave but I think it would be for the best."

Stephanie began to cry. "I don't want you to leave me," she cried. "Please let me go with you."

Craig held her tighter as she cried harder. "Stephanie, it will be all right," he said. "You can come see me anytime you want."

"No," she replied. "I want to live with you."

The phone rang. Craig answered it with Stephanie still in his arms. "Hello," he said.

"Craig," Val replied. "Why did you take Stephanie from my mom's house?"

"Because I have the day off and I want to spend it with my daughter," Craig answered, bitterly. "For your information, she's going to my parents' tonight whether you like it or not."

"No, she's not," Val protested.

"Yes, she is," he replied. "Goodbye."

Craig hung up the phone and said, "Stephanie, I'm going to change clothes and then we are going shopping."

As Craig drove to the mall, Stephanie asked, "Why are we going shopping?"

"Don't you want to?" he questioned.

"Yes," she answered.

"Good," he said. "I thought we could do some Christmas shopping."

Stephanie seemed pleased with that answer because she didn't say another word until they were inside the mall. "So what are we going to buy?" she asked.

"I want to pick up a nice gift for a friend of mine," Craig answered.

"Is this friend a girl?" Stephanie questioned.

"Yes," Craig answered with a smile.

"What about something like that?" she exclaimed, pointing at something in a display window.

Craig looked where she was pointing. There sat a display of beautiful, sparkling engagement rings. "Sweetheart," Craig said. "I don't think my friend is ready for that yet."

Craig and Stephanie continued to look as Stephanie suggested everything they saw. Finally, after saying no about twenty times, he found the perfect gift. "What about this?" she asked. "I think the blue one is pretty."

A sweater would be the perfect gift, Craig thought. It would replace the one he ruined. It would also bring out the blue in Morgan's beautiful eyes. "That's perfect," he said with a grin.

After they finished their shopping, they grabbed a bite to eat before his appointment with Morgan. "Would you like to meet my friend?" Craig asked, between bites of his cheeseburger.

"Yes!" she exclaimed. "I would like to!"

As soon as they finished their meals, they hurried across town. "Hello!" Jaime greeted them. "Who is this beautiful little girl?"

"My name is Stephanie," she answered, proudly.

"Nice to meet you," Jaime said. "If you'll have a seat, I'll tell Morgan you're here."

Jaime called Morgan while Craig situated Stephanie in her seat. "Will you be all right out here while I go in and talk to Morgan?" he asked.

"Yes, Daddy," she answered. "Don't worry about me. I'm a big girl."

Craig smiled. "Yes, you are," he agreed.

Morgan entered the reception area and immediately saw Stephanie. "Hi!" Morgan said.

Stephanie jumped out of her seat and extended her hand to Morgan. "Hello! I'm Stephanie and I am pleased to meet you," she said in one breath. "You are very pretty!"

Morgan smiled at her. "Thank you!" she replied.

Craig directed Stephanie back to her seat. "I'll be awhile. Will you be all right?" he asked again.

"She'll be fine," Jaime interjected. "I'll take good care of her."

Craig and Morgan entered her office. "I'm sorry about that," Craig apologized.

"Don't be sorry," Morgan insisted. "I think she is adorable. She looks so much like you."

"Thanks!" Craig replied.

"Have a seat," Morgan said. "Let's get down to business. Before we start though, there is something I need to tell you. Your wife was here this morning."

"What?" Craig interrupted. "What did she want?"

"She came in here under a false name and began throwing accusations at me," Morgan explained. "She accused me of sleeping with you and she also threatened me."

Craig was angry. He began to pace the room. "I can't believe her!" he exclaimed. "How dare she!"

"I agree," Morgan replied. "How dare she! I can't believe your wife is so insecure that she would waltz in here and accuse me of sleeping with you. I also can't believe that she is so unbalanced that she would threaten me!"

"I'm really sorry about this," he said. "I don't know what to do about her. She gets these crazy notions in her head and she doesn't care about anyone but herself."

"You know we could use this to our advantage," Morgan replied, deep in thought. "I could make it look like she's very unbalanced and she could do harm to you and Stephanie."

"Do whatever you need to do," Craig stated. "But I don't want Stephanie upset over it."

"I'm not going to do anything that will upset Stephanie," Morgan assured him.

Morgan rummaged through her desk looking for the list of names Craig had given her. "As far as Val goes, I wouldn't worry about her," Craig said. "She is all talk and no action."

"I'm not going to let her bother me," Morgan replied. "We have better things to do."

"I met with the review board today," Craig stated.

"What happened?" Morgan asked.

He explained to her what was said at the meeting. "Well, maybe it is for the best it was delayed," Morgan replied. "It will only be for a few weeks."

Craig sat there in deep thought. He didn't want to talk about his job anymore. "I have an idea," Craig replied. "What do you say we go out tonight and have some fun?"

"Craig," Morgan said in that we have been through this before tone.

"We need this, Morgan," he said.

"You're right," she agreed. "We do need this. But there is absolutely no way I can go out with you. I'm sorry but we can't jeopardize your case."

"I have no intention of doing that," he replied. "I told you that I'm going to give you time but once I'm divorced, you better be ready."

"And I told you," Morgan stated.

"Yes, I know what you told me," Craig interrupted. "But I believe in fate. You and I were brought together on that very tragic day six months ago and we have been thrown together on three separate occasions since then. Now you tell me we weren't meant to be together."

"I'm not ready for all of this," she replied. "Please don't push me."

"I'm not meaning to push you," he said. "I just want to be the one there when you're ready."

"If you really want to help me and be there for me, that's fine," she stated. "But remember, for now we can only be friends."

"I think we are more than friends," he said. "I have never seen people who are just friends kiss the way we do."

Morgan smiled at him. "I think we should talk about something else," she stated.

She grabbed the list of names and they carefully went through it. They eliminated a few names from it and narrowed it down to four people Morgan could gather information from about the Masterson family. "I will contact these people as soon as I can," Morgan told him.

"I will let them know," Craig replied.

"I think that is all I have for now," she stated. "Unless you have something else you want to talk about."

"Actually I do," he responded. "I have been thinking about our situation and I think I have come up with a way for us to spend time together without anyone knowing about it."

Morgan sat back in her chair, wondering what he was going to try to talk her into doing. "I thought if we met here, we could make it look like we were meeting about my case," he explained. "That way we could have some time alone and no one would know the difference."

"I don't know if that is such a good idea," she said.

"It was just a thought," Craig replied. "I just want to be able to spend time with you without causing any problems for the case."

"Why don't you schedule an appointment for Monday?" Morgan suggested. "We need to go over some things before meeting with Valerie and her lawyer on Tuesday."

"I will do that," he said.

Morgan got up from her chair and walked to the door. Before she could open it, Craig wrapped his arms around her waist. "Does this mean we are finished?" he asked.

She turned to face him. "Stephanie is waiting for you," she answered.

"She can wait a few more minutes," he replied.

Morgan wrapped her arms around his neck and they shared a few passionate kisses. "I just want to stay like this," Craig whispered.

"That would be nice," Morgan replied. "But you know we can't."

"I know," Craig said, feeling dejected. "I will talk to you soon."

After Craig and Stephanie had left, Jaime began to interrogate Morgan. "So, what's happening between you two?" she asked.

"Nothing," she answered. "We are just friends."

"Sure you are," Jaime replied. "Well, I think I am going home. I have a lot of packing to do."

"Are you moving this weekend?" Morgan asked.

"No," she answered. "I just have a lot of organizing and things like that to do."

"Let me know if you need any help," Morgan offered.

"Oh, we will," Jaime called, as she walked out the door.

Morgan gathered her things but before she could leave, the phone rang. "Hello! Morgan Garrett's office," she answered.

"So they have you answering your own phone now?" Leslie questioned, jokingly.

"Seems that way," Morgan replied. "What can I do for you?"

"Craig wanted me to call you about his case," she told her.

"That was quick," Morgan stated.

"When my brother wants something, he'll stop at nothing to get it done," she replied.

"Yeah, I know that all too well," Morgan said.

"Do you have a few minutes to meet with me?" Leslie asked. "I can meet you at the corner café in five minutes."

"I'll meet you there," Morgan agreed.

When she arrived, Leslie was already waiting. After taking a seat, Leslie jumped right into things. "What kind of questions do you need to ask me?" she inquired.

"I need to build a strong case against Valerie," Morgan answered. "Tell me about Craig's relationship with her."

"Valerie and Craig had a fairly good marriage in the beginning," Leslie explained. "But as time passed, Valerie became a vindictive and manipulative pain in the butt. I don't think very highly of her, if you haven't noticed."

"I noticed," Morgan replied. "How is her relationship with Stephanie? Has Valerie ever put her in danger or showed neglect?"

"Not as far as I know," Leslie answered. "Craig and Valerie leave Stephanie at her grandparents' houses a lot because they don't want her to be emotionally scarred because of all their arguing. I would never say they neglect Stephanie."

"Well, I'm not sure how this case is going to turn out," Morgan replied, hopefully. "Maybe I'll find something out when I talk to everyone else."

"So, you're trying to find some dirt on Valerie?" Leslie questioned.

"Exactly," Morgan replied.

"I'd be more than happy to help," Leslie said with a wicked smile.

Morgan laughed. She knew she was going to like Leslie. Morgan sat back and relaxed. She studied Leslie. She had some of the same features as Craig. The nose, eyes, and smile were the same. Her long brown hair cascaded over her shoulders. "You know my brother likes you, don't you?" Leslie asked.

"I have a pretty good idea," she answered.

"I think you like him too," Leslie replied.

"Don't be silly!" Morgan exclaimed.

"I don't think it's silly at all," she stated. "I can see it when you talk about him. Your whole face lights up."

"I wasn't trying to be obvious about it," Morgan told her.

Leslie smiled. "You know I have connections," she said. "I could pull some strings and get something started."

"A relationship between Craig and me wouldn't work right now," Morgan explained.

"Because of the case," Leslie said.

"Yes," she replied. "It wouldn't look good plus he's still married. I have no business getting involved with a married man."

"He won't be married for much longer," Leslie pointed out. "Let me tell you something about my brother. He doesn't care about the marriage anymore. He and Valerie have been estranged for quite some time. He feels nothing for her. Not a thing! She cheated on him, which I'm sure you know, and ever since then, he has tried to hold it all together. But since he was the only one doing this, he decided he should just give up. If Craig believes strongly in something, he will fight to hold on to it. But in a relationship, it takes two to make it work. My advice to you is if you want to be with Craig, you should just go for it. I know Craig has set his mind on being with you and he'll fight until he gets what he wants. But if he ever feels he's the only one fighting for the relationship, he'll eventually give up and move on."

"You have given me something to think about," Morgan replied.

"All I am asking you to do is think about it," she said. "I hate to cut this short but I told my husband I wouldn't be gone too long. We are going to the club tonight if you would like to join us later."

"I will think about that too," Morgan told her.

"It will probably be around 8 o'clock before we get there," Leslie explained. "I hope to see you."

Morgan arrived at home with a lot of things still weighing heavy on her mind. She wanted to be with Craig but she didn't like the idea of having to sneak around. She just wished this whole case was over and she could concentrate on her life again. "What am I going to do?" she asked herself, while she paced around the room. "Would I be betraying Edward if I started dating again?"

Morgan mulled things over as she sat down for a quick bite to eat. She knew she wanted to have another relationship. She didn't like being alone. What would be so wrong with having a relationship with Craig? He was an amazing man who would do anything for her. He was a little pushy though, which bugged Morgan but she understood his ambition. She knew she could be happy with Craig, if only she could convince herself of that. What was wrong with being happy? She was entitled to a little happiness.

After eating, she tried to decide what to do next. She had the invitation to go out with Leslie. She wasn't sure if she really wanted to go but what other options did she have? She didn't want to sit in her empty apartment all night staring at the walls. She decided she was going to go out. Maybe it would take her mind off things.

She wandered into the bedroom and selected something to wear, which took no time at all. After sliding her short, black skirt and button-up shirt on, she grabbed a brush and stroked her long, blonde hair. She then applied her makeup and took a long look in the mirror. It would have to do. No matter how hard she tried, she just couldn't disguise the anguish she found in her eyes even with her best smile. She slipped on her shoes, which made her five foot five frame two inches taller.

Morgan arrived at the club in a taxi. She entered the building and immediately found Leslie sitting at a table with a group of friends near the dance floor. "I am so glad you decided to come," she said, as she hugged Morgan.

Leslie quickly introduced Morgan to her friends and instructed her to have a seat. "Have you thought about what I said earlier?" she asked.

"You get right to the point, don't you?" Morgan questioned.

"That's the way I am," she replied. "So, have you?"

"Yes," Morgan answered.

"And?" Leslie asked.

"I don't know," Morgan stated. "I'm confused about the whole thing."

"Let me ask you something," she said. "Would it really be so bad to have a romantic relationship with Craig?"

Morgan was relieved when Leslie's husband, Mark, interrupted the conversation to ask Leslie if she wanted to dance. Morgan really didn't want to answer the question. "We will finish this conversation," Leslie warned, as Mark took her hand and led her to the dance floor.

Morgan sat back in her chair and watched the crowd of people dancing. She felt someone come up behind her. She was ready to reject any man with the usual come-on line. "You look incredible tonight," the familiar voice whispered.

Craig, she thought. She was surprised to hear his voice. "What are you doing here?" she asked.

"It's a public place," he replied.

"Did you know I was going to be here?" she questioned.

"I was hoping," Craig answered.

"You know we shouldn't be seen here together," she told him.

"We just happen to be in the same place at the same time," Craig replied. "I don't see anything wrong with that."

"Some people might not see it that way," Morgan responded.

"I don't care what people think," Craig stated. "I am really glad you are here."

Morgan couldn't help but smile. She was glad she decided to accept Leslie's invitation. "Can I get you a drink?" Craig asked.

"A diet soda would be great," she answered.

As Craig headed to the bar to get Morgan's request, Leslie sat back down at the table. "So, where were we?" she asked.

"I haven't decided what to do," Morgan informed her. "We need to be careful until the divorce is finalized."

"Just to let you know," Leslie told her. "This waiting is not going to be easy for Craig. He works hard to get what he wants and things always seem to come easy to him. I am just afraid someone might try to snatch him up before you have a chance to start anything with him."

Leslie drew her attention to the bar and motioned Morgan to do the same. The envy built up inside her when she realized who Craig was talking to. "Excuse me," she said.

Morgan hurried to the bar. "Hi Morgan!" Elizabeth said. "I'm surprised to see you out."

"I do get out occasionally," Morgan replied. "Do you mind if I borrow Craig for just a moment?"

"No," Elizabeth answered. "Go right on ahead."

Craig ushered Morgan to the dance floor. "Dance with me," he whispered, as he pulled her into his arms.

Morgan decided not to fight him. She melted into him. "What did you want to talk about?" he asked.

Morgan looked into Craig's deep brown eyes. "I saw you with Elizabeth," she answered. "I just don't want to lose you to someone else."

"You could never lose me," he replied. "Who gave you that idea?"

"Your sister," Morgan answered.

"She is just trying to be helpful," Craig said. "I promise you I am not going anywhere."

Morgan drew herself closer to Craig. She knew she was right where she needed to be. "I am sorry I have been so impatient about all this," Craig stated. "I don't mean to be. I just believe you and I belong together. I don't know why we have to waste any time starting a relationship."

"It is only going to be for a few more weeks," Morgan reminded him. "I think you can wait."

"I hope I can," Craig told her. "I just want to start my life with you."

Morgan was touched by Craig's statement. "I really have this overwhelming desire to kiss you," she whispered, smiling.

"I was just thinking the same thing," Craig replied. "So what are we going to do about it?"

"I don't think we should kiss here," Morgan stated.

"Do you mind if we go back to your place?" he asked.

"Let me get my coat," Morgan said. "We probably shouldn't leave together though."

"Probably not," Craig agreed. "Why don't you stay here for a few more minutes and I will just meet you at your apartment?"

"Ok," she replied.

They walked back over to the table where Leslie and Mark were sitting. "I have to go," Craig said. "I promised Stephanie I would tuck her in."

"Give her a kiss for me," Leslie told him.

As Craig grabbed his coat, he leaned over Morgan's shoulder. "I will call you when I am finished with Stephanie," he whispered.

As Morgan watched Craig leave, Leslie said, "I saw you two dancing. What are you two up to?"

"Nothing," Morgan answered. "We have to wait until the divorce is finalized then we will see what happens. I don't know who is more impatient about this, you or Craig."

"I just want him to be happy," Leslie replied.

Morgan appreciated Leslie's concern for Craig. She just couldn't understand why they couldn't wait a few more weeks.

Morgan preoccupied herself with the conversation at the table. It was hard to do though because she kept wishing the phone would ring. "Hello!" she said, when it finally did.

"Are you ready to meet me?" Craig asked.

"Yes," she answered. "I can be there in a few minutes."

"Ok," he replied. "I'll be waiting."

"I have to go," Morgan announced to the table.

"It is still early," Leslie said, disappointedly. "Can't you stay a little longer?"

"No," Morgan answered. "I have somewhere else I have to be."

After Morgan grabbed her coat, she exited the building and hailed a taxi. After a few minutes, she was on her way home to Craig. What a nice thought that was. She was so excited she couldn't stop smiling.

After the taxi dropped her off, she entered her building and made her way to her apartment. As she opened her door, she saw Craig out of the corner of her eye. She opened the door and the two hurried inside. Craig backed Morgan up against the closed door and immediately accepted the first of many long, passionate kisses. "This is all I could think about the whole drive here," he said.

"I didn't think you were ever going to call," Morgan replied.

"I can't believe you agreed to this," he told her.

Morgan moved away from the door. "What?" Craig asked.

"We shouldn't be doing this," she answered.

"Please don't ask me to leave," Craig replied. "We can think of something else to do."

"Are you hungry?" she asked.

"I could eat," he answered. "Do you want to order something?"

"No," Morgan replied. "We can eat something here."

"You're going to fix me dinner?" he questioned, surprised.

"I can cook," she said, a bit offended. "I'm a woman of many talents."

"Oh, really," he commented. "And what would some of those be?"

"I don't think we know each other well enough for me to tell you that," she informed him.

"Let me guess," he said. "I am going to have to wait."

Morgan smiled at him. "Why don't you look and see what we have in the refrigerator?" she suggested.

Craig opened the door. "Do you have a pet rabbit?" he asked.

Morgan squeezed between Craig and the refrigerator. "We have all we need in here to make a salad," she explained. "Here's a tomato, a head of lettuce, and carrots."

Craig piled everything on the counter as Morgan handed it to him. "So you're going to make a salad," Craig said. "Is that all you have to eat?"

"I eat salads all the time," she answered. "They are very nutritious and I need to watch my weight."

Craig pulled her into his arms. "I'll watch it for you," Craig said, smiling at her.

Morgan blushed. "Anyway, you have a beautiful body," he continued. "I can't even imagine you having anything less than a perfect one."

Morgan smiled at him. "You are so wonderful," she whispered.

When their eyes locked, Morgan knew she couldn't fight this any longer. She wanted to be happy again and she knew Craig would be the one to do that. She couldn't resist running her hands through his hair. "You are a very attractive man, Officer," she said.

"And you are the most beautiful woman I have ever seen," Craig replied, as he ran his hands up and down her sides.

Morgan couldn't take it anymore. She placed her lips on his. It started with a few small kisses, which turned into several long ones. "You're making me want you," Craig whispered between kisses. "I don't know how much more I can take."

Morgan backed away from him. "Now that, you will have to wait for," she told him.

"I would wait forever for you," he replied.

Morgan smiled again. "I'm hungry," she said. "Let's eat."

Morgan made two salads with all the trimmings. "What are we going to do about us?" Craig asked.

"I have made a decision," she announced. "I'm not going to fight my feelings for you anymore. It's no use. I can't fight the fact every time I'm with you, I want to touch you and kiss you. So since this is obviously what we both want, we might as well go for it."

"I knew you would see things my way," Craig replied with a smile.

"I just want to be happy," Morgan explained. "I think you can do that."

"I will do my best," he stated.

"You know we're going to have to keep this relationship under wraps until after your divorce papers are signed," Morgan warned him.

"And that won't be for a few weeks," Craig replied.

"We have a meeting with Valerie and her attorney on Tuesday," Morgan answered. "We'll get the papers together as soon as we can. If you can't wait, I do have a solution."

"What's that?" he asked.

"I can have another lawyer appointed to your case," Morgan told him.

"No," Craig objected. "I want you to be my lawyer."

Morgan took a bite of her salad. She didn't know how she was going to pull this off. "What are you thinking about?" Craig asked.

"I think you are right about what you said earlier at my office," she answered. "If we want to spend time together, we are going to have to schedule it as a meeting."

"I really wish this divorce was final," Craig replied, as he pushed his empty bowl away from him.

Morgan stood up and gathered the dirty dishes. "It will be over before you know it," she said. "Then we can be together whenever we want."

Morgan went to the sink and began to wash the dishes. "Can't those wait?" Craig whispered, as he wrapped his arms around her waist.

"I'll be done in a few minutes," she replied. "Why don't you go make yourself comfortable on the couch?"

"I would rather do this," he stated, as he placed kisses on her neck.

Morgan tried to control the feelings she was experiencing. "Craig," she said. "Just give me a minute to finish these dishes and then I will join you on the couch."

Craig stopped what he was doing and decided to do what he was told. When Morgan was finished, she sat down next to him. "Are you happy now?" she asked.

"Very," he answered, as his stomach rumbled.

Morgan laughed. "Oh my!" she said.

"Sorry. That was my stomach," he replied, a bit embarrassed. "I am used to eating more food than that at a meal."

"Do you want me to fix you something else?" she questioned.

"No," he answered. "I'll be ok. You aren't a vegetarian, are you?"

"No," she replied.

"I was just wondering," Craig asked.

"I'll tell you what," Morgan stated. "When the divorce is final, we will go out for a meal at a nice restaurant. You can decide where since I made you eat a salad tonight."

"If I take you to a steakhouse, you aren't just going to order a salad, are you?" he asked.

"No," she answered. "I do eat more than just salads. I enjoy a cheeseburger and fries sometimes but I want to look good too. That is why I watch what I eat."

"I think that you are beautiful just the way you are," Craig stated.

"You are sweet," Morgan replied.

Their eyes locked and Craig moved in for a kiss. Each kiss they shared became more intense. Before Morgan knew it, she was lying on her back with Craig on top of her. She tried to adjust her body into a more comfortable position but with no luck. Craig stopped kissing her neck. "Are you ok?" he asked.

"I am just in an awkward position," she answered.

Craig sat up and pulled Morgan into a sitting position. "I am sorry," he said. "I wish you would have told me to stop."

"But I don't want you to stop," she whispered.

"Are you sure?" he questioned.

Morgan nodded. "Well, ok," Craig said. "You just tell me how far you want to go and I will stop."

"I don't want to send you home to a cold shower," Morgan replied.

"I don't want to go home to one," he stated. "I am not going to lie to you, Morgan. I want to make love to you."

Morgan took a deep breath. "Ok," she whispered, as she stared into his eyes.

"Are you sure about this?" he asked.

"Yes," she answered. "I want to be with you."

The couple exchanged several passionate kisses. Morgan kissed Craig's neck, as she started to unbutton his shirt. She slid her hands inside and softly caressed his chest. She tried to position herself on his lap but didn't have any luck there either. She had forgotten she was wearing a tight, short skirt. "You are having a lot of problems, aren't you?" Craig asked.

"I can do this," she said, unable to stop laughing.

"Maybe if we go into the bedroom," he suggested.

Morgan hesitated. Now what was she going to do? "Is that a problem?" Craig questioned.

"No," she answered, as she stood up, took hold of his hand, and led him to the other room.

Craig pulled Morgan into his arms and they started to kiss again. Morgan pulled his shirttails from his pants and slid his shirt off him and onto the floor. She ran her hand through the patch of hair on his chest. Craig slowly unbuttoned Morgan's shirt and he kissed every inch of skin that was exposed. In one motion, he picked her up and laid her on the bed. He removed her skirt from her body and climbed in bed beside her. "Are you forgetting something?" she asked.

"Do you want me to take my pants off?" he questioned, smiling.

"No," she answered. "I will do it myself."

Morgan unbuttoned his jeans. As she unzipped them, she gently rubbed her hand against him. Craig moaned. After she had removed his jeans and tossed them on the floor, she cuddled up beside him in the bed. Morgan began kissing Craig, which made him moan more. Craig became alarmed when Morgan stopped abruptly. "What's wrong?" he asked.

"What's that noise?" she questioned.

Craig listened closely. "That is my phone," he answered. "They can just leave a message."

"Your phone plays the Mickey Mouse theme?" Morgan asked, trying not to laugh.

"That is Stephanie's ringtone," he replied. "That lets me know she needs me."

"If you need to get it, it's ok," Morgan stated. "Do what you need to do. We have time."

Craig got up and retrieved his phone from his pants pocket. "I got to take this," he said, as he exited the room.

Morgan sat up on the bed and waited to hear what was going on. A few minutes later, Craig returned. "I am sorry I have to do this," he told her. "It's Stephanie. Apparently, she had a bad dream and has been calling for me. My mom can't calm her down. I tried to talk to her on the phone but she wants to see me. I need to go."

"I understand," she replied.

Craig gathered his clothes and quickly put them on. Morgan grabbed her bathrobe and followed him into the other room. "I am really sorry," he apologized.

"It is ok," she said. "Your daughter needs you. Go take care of her."

"Thank you for understanding," he stated. "I will call you later."

After a few goodbye kisses, Craig was gone. Maybe this was for the best, Morgan thought. Maybe this was a sign they were not ready for their relationship to go to this level. She decided she would have to be more careful next time.

Chapter 5

Several days had passed since Morgan and Craig had seen one another. Morgan had spent the weekend helping Jaime organize and pack for moving day. Craig worked the entire weekend. They finally spent some time together as they prepared for their meeting with Valerie and her lawyer.

It was now the morning of their meeting and Morgan and Craig sat anxiously, awaiting the arrival of Valerie and her lawyer. "Where the hell are they?" Craig asked, as he glanced at his watch.

"I don't know," Morgan answered.

"This is just like Val," Craig stated. "She is doing this on purpose."

"I doubt that," she replied. "They are just running late."

Craig sighed. "I just want to get this over with," he said. "I am not looking forward to my wife and my girlfriend being in the same room. You know Val is going to make this a living hell for you."

"I can handle her," Morgan replied.

The door swung opened and in walked Valerie and her lawyer, Jeff Harris. "Sorry we're late," Jeff apologized.

"Can we just get this over with?" Val asked, impatiently. "I have other things to do."

"Well, let's get started," Jeff suggested.

"I can make this really easy for you," Val stated. "I want everything. I want the house, Stephanie, and alimony."

"You can't be serious!" Craig exclaimed.

"Oh, I am," she said. "This is what you get for abandoning me and cheating on me with her."

Morgan shook her head. "You have quite an imagination, Valerie," Morgan told her. "By the way, we are not agreeing to any of your demands."

"Let her have the house," Craig said. "I am moving out and I want to know Stephanie has somewhere to live."

"Ok," Jeff replied, as he took notes.

"As for alimony," Craig continued. "I don't know how she is going to take anything. I don't make much money."

"We can talk about that later," Jeff suggested. "Let's discuss Stephanie."

"I want her!" Val exclaimed. "I will not share her."

"Why are you acting like a child?" Craig questioned.

"I am not acting like a child," Val answered. "I just know what I want."

"No," Craig replied. "You are deliberately trying to hurt me."

"You deserve it," she told him. "You have done all you can to hurt me."

There was no use trying to reason with an irrational woman, Craig thought. "I would like to have custody of Stephanie," Craig stated.

"Have you two thought about joint custody?" Morgan asked. "I handled this case once where the couple decided they would alternate weeks so they both could have equal time with the child. You might want to consider that."

"I would consider that," Craig said.

Morgan glared at Valerie, daring her to say something. "It is something for you both to think about," she replied.

"We aren't getting anywhere with this," Jeff told them.

"Valerie isn't working with us," Morgan stated. "This would be easier if she would be reasonable."

"I am not going to let you take everything away from me," Valerie pleaded. "You have already taken my husband. What else do you want?"

"I haven't taken anything away from you," Morgan responded. "You did all this to yourself."

Valerie burst into tears. It was Craig's turn to shake his head. "See what I have to put up with," he said.

Valerie glared at Craig. "I have known you for a long time," he told her. "I know all your tricks. That doesn't work with me."

"Are we finished here?" Valerie asked, as she rose from her chair.

Valerie didn't wait for an answer. She hurried to the door and made a quick exit. "I will try to talk to her," Jeff said. "I will try to make this easier for all of us."

After Jeff left, Morgan began to relax. "She is going to make this impossible," she replied.

"I do have to say I am proud of you," Craig stated. "You did very well."

"There were a few times I wanted to reach across the table and slap her," Morgan told him. "If she continues to act like she did today, this could take longer than expected."

"I don't know what to do about her," Craig responded. "She is making this difficult on purpose. She likes to be melodramatic."

"So what do we do now?" Morgan asked. "How do you suggest we handle this?"

"I can try talking to her," Craig answered. "I don't know if that would help though."

"Maybe we can think about this a little longer," she suggested. "Maybe she will come to her senses and be reasonable."

"She isn't going to," he stated. "She feels like she has been wronged and she is going to carry this out for as long as she can."

"I don't know what to do," she replied. "She won't listen to me. Let's just stop talking about this. Maybe an idea will come to us if we just stop thinking about it."

Morgan and Craig sat in silence. They knew what they really needed to talk about but neither one was willing to bring up the subject. A few minutes passed and Craig decided to say something about the other night. "I think we need to talk about what happened between us the other night," he said.

"I know we do," Morgan replied.

"I would like to continue where we left off," he told her.

"I don't think that is such a good idea," she responded.

"How can you say that?" he asked. "You thought it was a good idea at the time."

"I have had time to think about it," she answered. "We shouldn't have gone as far as we did."

"I thought we had something special going on here," Craig said, feeling dejected.

Morgan reached across the table and put her hand on his hand. "We do," she replied. "I just think we should wait before we take that step."

"Maybe you are right," he agreed. "I would like to wait until I am divorced so I can give myself completely to you."

"I think that is the way it should be," Morgan stated.

"Well, I need to go," he told her, as he rose from his chair. "I have to work tonight and I need to get some sleep."

"I don't want you to be mad at me," Morgan said, worried that she had hurt his feelings.

"I am not mad," Craig replied. "I just need to control myself until the time is right for us. It is taking all I have right now to not make love to you on this table."

"Well, that will give me something to think about now," Morgan said, as she flashed a sexy smile at Craig.

"Don't do that," he said.

"Do what?" she asked, innocently.

Morgan got up and moved over to Craig. She placed her hands on his chest and looked into his eyes. "Don't do that either," he warned.

"Do what?" she asked again.

"You are making this extremely difficult," Craig told her. "Oh, what the hell."

Craig gathered her into his arms and the two shared a passionate kiss. "Why are you doing this?" he asked. "You are making it very hard for me to leave."

Morgan giggled. "I just want you to think about me when you're gone," she answered.

"I don't think you have to worry about that," he said. "I think about you a lot."

"What time do you have to be at work?" she questioned.

"Eight," he answered. "I am just filling in for a few hours."

"Do you want to come over for dinner before you go to work?" she asked.

"I could probably arrange that," Craig answered. "We aren't having salad again, are we?"

"No," she said. "Why don't you come by about six? I will have dinner ready."

"Ok," he agreed. "That sounds like a plan."

Craig walked Morgan back to her office. "I will see you later," he said.

Morgan entered the office and sat down in a chair facing Jaime. "There you are," Jaime said. "I have a few phone messages for you."

"That's nice," Morgan replied.

"What is wrong with you?" Jaime questioned.

"That was a very frustrating meeting I just had," she answered. "Valerie is not going to make this easy for us."

"That doesn't surprise me," Jaime stated.

"Oh, well," she said. "I will just have to think of some way to persuade her that she needs to be more reasonable."

Morgan got up and gathered the phone messages from Jaime's desk. "I guess I will call these people back," she said.

Morgan spent most of the morning on the phone. She stepped out for a quick bite to eat and then prepared for her meeting with Elizabeth and her father. "I called you both in for this meeting today because I have some good news," Morgan told them.

"What is the good news?" Elizabeth asked, excitedly.

"The senator has decided to give you a huge settlement," Morgan explained. "He has also agreed to pay for all your medical treatments, including your physical therapy. He also wanted me to let you know that your job is still yours and you can come back whenever you're ready. I have the paperwork here for you to look over and sign."

"Wow!" Elizabeth exclaimed. "That is so much more than I expected. What do you think, Dad?"

"Let me look at that paperwork," Richard Brinkman instructed. "I need to make a phone call. I will be right back."

After he had left the office, Elizabeth said, "I was hoping he would leave for a few minutes. There is something I want to ask you."

"Ok," Morgan replied.

"I got the impression the other night at the club that you are mad at me," Elizabeth explained. "Are you mad?"

"No," she answered. "Why would I be mad at you? I was a little surprised to see you there."

"My friend, Dave, works there," Elizabeth replied. "I was there talking to him and then I saw Craig approach the bar. I was just saying hello. I saw you two dancing. Is there something going on I should know about?"

"No, nothing is going on," Morgan stated. "We are just friends."

"It would be nice if you two would get together," Elizabeth told her. "It would be great if something wonderful could come out of these last few months."

Before Morgan could say anything, Richard entered the office. "I think everything is acceptable," he said. "Elizabeth, you need to sign this."

Elizabeth did as she was told. "I would like a copy of this," he stated.

Morgan handed him the copy. "And when can we expect the money?" he asked.

"As soon as I get this signed agreement to him, he will give me the check," she answered.

"Just let us know when you have it," he replied, as he opened the door and pushed Elizabeth's chair over to it.

"Thank you, Morgan," she said. "I will talk to you soon."

Morgan worked diligently the rest of the afternoon. She wanted to leave early so she could stop by the store and buy a few things for her dinner with Craig. She couldn't wait to see him. She knew it would only be for a few hours but just the idea of spending time with him excited her. She found herself wishing they could be together all the time but she knew that was impossible. Valerie was going to make the divorce proceedings difficult for everyone involved. Morgan knew she was just going to have to be patient and wait.

Morgan left the office as planned, picked up a few groceries, and headed home. Once there, she immediately started dinner and prepared for Craig's arrival. "Hello Beautiful!" he said, as she opened to door to let him in.

After he gave her a big hug, he continued by saying, "I wasn't sure what to bring. So I just brought you these."

"Thank you!" she told him, as she took the flowers. "They are beautiful."

Morgan put them in a vase and set them in the middle of the table. "So what is for dinner?" Craig asked.

"I bought you steak and potatoes," she answered. "And cheesecake for dessert."

"Sounds good," he replied. "I have been looking forward to this all day."

"Well, I hope it is good," she said. "I don't cook very often. I would hate to disappoint you."

They sat down and began to eat. "So how did things go at work today?" he asked.

"It was a pretty good day," Morgan answered. "I have good news for you. They settled Elizabeth's case out of court today. You don't have to testify in court now."

"That is good news for her," Craig replied. "I know she was worried about that."

"I think she is very happy with the way things worked out," she told him.

After a moment of silence, Craig said, "This meal is really good. Thank you for inviting me over."

"I just was trying to come up with some way we could spend some time together," she replied.

"I am glad you thought of this," Craig told her. "I have missed you."

"It was a long weekend, wasn't it?" she questioned.

"Too long," he agreed.

After the couple finished eating, Morgan began to clear the table. Craig stood up and grabbed Morgan's arm. "Don't worry about those now," he said, referring to the dishes. "Come over to the couch and sit with me. I want to spend some time with you before I have to leave."

Morgan took Craig's hand and he escorted her to the couch. "It feels so good to sit," Morgan told him.

"Long day?" he asked.

"Yeah," she answered, as she rubbed the back of her neck. "I need a massage."

"Move over here in front of me," he instructed. "I'll rub your shoulders and neck."

She did as she was told. Craig placed his hands on her shoulders and gently squeezed. "Oh," Morgan moaned.

"You are tense," he stated. "Relax."

"It is hard for me to relax," she explained. "Your wife is going to make the divorce difficult for both of us. It is extremely frustrating."

"I know it is frustrating," he replied. "Once Val is finished throwing her temper tantrum, she will grant me the divorce. Like you keep saying, we need to be patient."

Morgan closed her eyes and tried to relax. She sighed. "I know how to get you to relax," Craig said, as he leaned forward and whispered in her ear.

"How's that?" she asked.

"By doing this," he answered, as he began kissing the back of her neck.

"That feels really good," she told him. "I hope you're not trying to start something. You have to go to work."

"I know," he said, as he wrapped his arms around her and rested her back against his chest. "I wish I could stay."

After a few minutes of cuddling, Craig decided it was time to get up. "I would like to have two things before I leave," he told her.

"And what would that be?" she asked.

"I think I have time for some cheesecake," he replied. "And I also need this."

Craig pulled Morgan into his arms for a passionate embrace. "Is that all you need?" Morgan asked, smiling.

"That should do it," he answered.

Morgan headed into the kitchen and dished up two plates of cheesecake. "Are you expecting anything from the office?" Craig asked, as he entered the kitchen.

"No," she answered. "Why?"

Craig waved the envelope he retrieved from the living room floor in her direction. "What is it?" she asked, setting the plates on the table.

"I don't know," he answered. "Do you want to open it or should I?"

"Go on ahead and open it," she told him.

Craig carefully opened the long white envelope. As he unfolded the letter, Morgan could tell by the magazine cut out letters that it was far from a friendly letter. "What's it say?" she asked hesitantly.

Craig took a deep breath. "I know what you're doing," he read. "I won't stand for it. You better watch your step, Morgan."

"What the," Morgan said, taking the note from Craig. "You know who this is from, don't you?"

"Val," Craig answered.

"It has to be," Morgan replied. "She knows where I live. She threatened me in the exact same manner. Who else could it be?"

"She seems to be the likely suspect," Craig stated. "I'm going to go talk to her before I go to work."

Craig grabbed his coat and headed for the door. "Do you think this is wise?" she questioned.

Craig pulled Morgan into his arms. "Don't worry, Angel," he said. "I'll be ok."

After a passionate kiss, Craig instructed Morgan to keep her door locked. "I'll call you later," he told her.

Craig hurried across town to have it out with Val. He never thought she would stoop this low. "Val!" he called, as he entered the dark house.

"Valerie!" he called again.

"What are you screaming about?" she said, as she entered the living room.

"What is the meaning of this?" Craig asked, throwing the letter at her.

"Of what?" she replied, as she flipped on the light. "I didn't do this. Why would I?"

"You threatened Morgan," he reminded her. "Don't deny it."

81

"Craig, I have been here all evening," Valerie told him.

"Valerie," a voice from the hallway called. "Is everything ok?"

A man came into the room wearing Craig's robe. "Is there a problem?" he asked.

"No, Nick," Valerie assured him. "There's no problem."

Craig couldn't believe this. She was sleeping with someone under their own roof. He was even wearing his robe! "Craig, I don't know anything about this," Val said. "Yes, I did threaten Morgan but I was just messing with her. I would never carry it out. I didn't do this."

"For some reason, Val," he said. "I believe you. But you and I will have a talk about him later. Right now, I have to get to work."

As soon as Craig jumped into his car, he called Morgan. "Hey! It's me," he said.

"What did you find out?" she questioned.

"I don't think she had anything to do with this," he answered. "She has done a lot of horrible things but I don't think she did this."

"You know her better than I do," Morgan replied.

"I wish I had better news," he said. "I can tell you though that she had company when I got there. Apparently, she is having an affair with someone named Nick."

"You're kidding," Morgan commented.

"No," Craig stated. "I wish I was. He came out of the bedroom wearing my bathrobe."

Morgan wasn't sure how to respond to that. "I don't know why we are waiting to be together," Craig told Morgan. "Val is obviously moving on. What is stopping us from being together?"

"Let's not talk about this while you're angry," Morgan replied. "We can talk about it when you have cooled off."

"You're right," he said. "I have to get to the station before they think I'm not coming to work. Save a piece of cheesecake for me, ok?"

"Ok," Morgan said. "I will see you later."

Morgan cleaned the kitchen and washed the dishes from dinner. She kept thinking about the letter. She was so sure

Valerie was the one who sent it. Who else could it have been? Morgan didn't have any enemies that she knew of. She always tried to get along with everyone. Who would want to threaten her and for what reason? She just couldn't figure it out.

After the dishes were finished, Morgan curled up on the couch and watched television. She must have fallen asleep because she was awakened by the sound of her phone ringing. "Hello," she said.

"Hello," she repeated, after getting no answer on the other end. "Who is this?"

After receiving no answer, she hung up the phone. As soon as she did, the power went out. "This is not happening," she said, feeling more paranoid with each passing moment.

Morgan moved towards the door. She wanted to check and see if she was the only one without power. Before she could look, the door flew open, knocking her to the floor. She looked up and saw a dark figure standing over her, shining a light in her eyes. She began to scoot backwards, keeping her eyes on the figure. Before she could stop him, he grabbed her arm and dragged her across the floor. He kneeled down next to her. "You are going to pay for what you have done," he said.

Morgan began to shake. "What do you want?" she asked.

"You sure are pretty," he replied, ignoring her question.

He ran his hand across her cheek and down her neck, which made Morgan cringe. "Please don't," she pleaded.

"I will do whatever I want to," he said, as he grabbed the front of her shirt and ripped it open.

As he slid his hand inside her shirt, Morgan began to fight back. She struggled but to no avail. The man was much stronger than she was and he had pinned her to the floor. "Kiss me," he said, as his face inched closer to hers.

"NO!" she screamed.

Morgan felt the sting of his hand slap her face. "Do it!" he threatened.

"I will not," she screamed.

"You will do as you are told," he replied, as he slapped her again.

Morgan could hear the police sirens in the distance. Another person had entered the room. "We have to get out of here," he said. "The cops are on their way."

"Consider this a warning," the man whispered in Morgan's ear. "If you don't stay away from Craig, I will be back to teach you a lesson."

With that, both of the men were gone. Morgan began to cry. "Are you ok, Morgan?" her neighbor, Otis Jackson, asked as he and his wife entered the apartment.

Morgan couldn't move or speak. She couldn't do anything but tremble and cry. "She is over here," Helen Jackson called, as the police entered the room.

Craig was immediately by her side. "Morgan, are you ok?" he asked.

Craig examined her. She had a bruise that covered most of the right side of her face and her shirt was ripped. Craig took off his coat and covered her with it. "Don't touch me!" she snapped at him. "You are the reason this happened to me. I want you to leave me alone!"

"What?" Craig asked, confused. "I didn't do this to you."

"You are the reason this happened," she cried. "You should have just left me alone."

"I don't understand," he replied.

"I want you to leave me alone," Morgan yelled. "I don't want you here."

Morgan slowly got up and walked to the other officers who were in the apartment. "Can you tell me what happened?" Craig asked the Jacksons.

"We didn't see anything," Otis Jackson answered.

"We heard all the noise and we called the police," Helen Jackson said.

"Thank you," Craig told them. "If you think of anything else, please let me know."

Craig walked over to Morgan and Officer Bill Adams. "I think she needs to go to the hospital and get checked out," Bill said.

"I'll take her to the hospital," Craig volunteered.

"I am not going anywhere with you," Morgan replied.

"I am going to take you to the hospital," Craig told her, as he picked her up.

"Put me down!" she immediately protested. "I can't believe you! You are the most impossible man! Why can't you just leave me alone?"

Craig carried her out the door. "What is your problem?" he asked. "Before I left, we couldn't keep our hands off each other. Now you want nothing to do with me. I didn't do anything wrong."

Morgan wanted to cry. "Craig, please!" she said. "You have to leave me alone."

"Why?" Craig asked, losing his temper. "Why? Give me one good reason!"

"Because I'm no good for you!" Morgan screamed. "Because you'll never be happy with me! Why do you have to be so damn stubborn?"

Craig put Morgan in the car and climbed in beside her. "What happened to you?" he questioned. "Who got to you?"

"What do you mean?" Morgan asked. "No one got to me."

"Please don't blame this incident on me," he pleaded. "I can't understand why you're pushing me away."

"It's for your own good," she replied. "Just forget you ever met me! I'll find you a different lawyer."

"No!" he said, angrily.

"Craig, just face it," she replied, calmly. "It's over! I don't want to see you ever again."

Officer Adams arrived at the car. "A couple officers are still in the apartment looking for clues," he said. "The landlord will be fixing the door when they are finished. Are you going to the hospital with us?"

"No," Craig answered, getting out of the car. "I don't care anymore."

Morgan watched as Craig walked back to the building. "Ms. Garrett," Bill said. "With all due respect, I think you have made a huge mistake."

"You're not the only one," she whispered between sobs.

Once Bill and Morgan had left, Craig decided to return to the apartment. He had to find a clue as to why Morgan was behaving this way. Somehow, he had to piece this whole thing together. He figured somehow the note and the break-in were connected. He wasn't sure though. All he knew was Morgan's life was in danger and he would do anything to protect her.

Craig wandered across the hall to speak with the Jacksons again. "I don't know if there is anything else we can tell you," Otis said. "All we heard was a loud noise and I looked out the peephole of the door while my wife called the police."

Craig studied the older couple. He figured they were in their middle to late sixties. "We didn't know what else to do," Otis continued, as if he was reading Craig's mind. "We aren't spring chickens anymore. We couldn't have fought them off."

"Them?" Craig questioned. "There was more than one?"

"I was watching," Otis replied. "I saw one man go into the apartment and two men leave."

"Can you both come down to the station and give us a statement?" Craig asked.

"Can we do that tomorrow?" Otis questioned. "It is really late and we don't drive at night."

"Just as soon as you can would be great," Craig answered. "Here is my card. Just ask for me or Officer Adams."

Craig said goodnight and left their apartment, wishing the couple had more to tell him. He entered the crime scene one last time before he decided to call it a night. He had to find something, anything that would tell him what happened. He had no luck. The only person who could tell him what happened was Morgan and she hated him. He had no choice though but to go to the hospital and question her again.

"Did she give you a statement?" Craig asked Officer Adams, as he entered the waiting room.

"No," Bill answered. "I am waiting for the doctor to finish with her."

"Why don't you go get a cup of coffee and I will question her?" Craig asked.

"I don't know if that's a good idea," he replied. "She really doesn't want to talk to you. I don't think you will get anything out of her."

"Just give me a few minutes," Craig said. "If she doesn't tell me anything, I will let you take the statement."

The doctor walked into the room. "How is she?" Craig asked.

"She is still shaken up from the whole ordeal but I think she will be fine," he answered. "Does she have any family here?"

"Not yet," Bill stated. "Her sister-in-law is on her way."

"Does she have anyone that can stay with her tonight?" the doctor asked. "I don't want her to be left alone and there is no need for her to stay here."

"I'll take care of her," Craig volunteered. "Do you mind if I go in and talk to her?"

"No, go right in," the doctor said.

Craig walked down the hallway and knocked on the first door to his left. "Come in," Morgan said.

Craig entered the room and saw Morgan sitting at the foot of the bed. "What are you doing here?" she asked, once she noticed it was him.

"I brought you some different clothes," he said, tossing them on the bed. "I am also here to take your statement."

"I thought Officer Adams would be doing that," she replied.

"There has been a change in plans," Craig stated.

Morgan wanted to cry. She couldn't handle acting this way with him. All she wanted was to have his arms wrapped around her. She wanted to hear him say that everything was going to be just fine. "Are you ready to give me a statement?" he asked.

Morgan described the incident. She started to cry when she explained to Craig the way the man had touched her. "He didn't rape you, did he?" Craig questioned.

"No," Morgan answered. "I don't know what he would have done if that other man hadn't come into the room."

Morgan broke down. Her tears fell like rain. Craig swallowed his pride and walked over to her. "Come here," he said, holding out his hand.

"No!" Morgan yelled, as she jumped off the bed and put some distance between her and Craig.

"I understand you are scared," he said. "I am sorry for what you are going through. I just wanted to comfort you."

"I just need you to stay away from me," Morgan replied.

Craig glared at her. He knew she probably wouldn't want him touching her because she was attacked. What he didn't understand was why she was so cold towards him even before he arrived in the examining room to question her. "I am going to need your clothes," he told her. "I will be outside. Just let me know when you are finished."

Craig exited the room. "How is she doing?" Bill asked.

"She is a bit uncomfortable around men right now, which is understandable," Craig answered. "Here is her statement. Do you want to work on this?"

"I can do it," Bill answered.

"If you need anything else, just let me know," Craig said. "I am going to make sure Morgan gets home ok. Has the crime scene been cleared?"

"Yes," Bill stated. "We didn't find any evidence."

The door opened and Morgan peeked out to see where the officers were. Craig walked over to her and grabbed the bag of clothes. "Thank you," he said, as she turned and went back into the room.

Craig handed the clothes to Bill. "I am going back to the station," he said. "I will take care of this paperwork."

"While you are at it, take the envelope and letter that are in a Ziploc on my desk and have them checked for fingerprints," Craig replied. "There may be a connection between the two."

As Bill left, Jaime entered the hallway. "How is she?" she asked.

"She is a little shaky but I think she will be fine," Craig answered.

"Have you talked to the doctor?" she questioned.

"Yeah," Craig told her. "He wants someone to stay with her tonight."

"I don't know who that is going to be," Jaime said. "We are in between houses right now."

"I'll take care of her," Craig offered.

"Are you sure?" Jaime asked.

"Yeah," Craig replied. "She doesn't like me much right now. She keeps blaming me for what happened. I just need to find out why she is acting the way she is."

A nurse wheeled Morgan into the lobby. "What are you still doing here?" Morgan asked, angrily. "I thought I told you to stay away from me!"

"Well, that's going to be hard to do, Angel," Craig replied, relieving the nurse of her duty. "I'll be staying with you."

"Excuse me!" Morgan protested. "I'm a big girl. I can take care of myself."

"The doctor said that someone needs to stay with you," Jaime said.

"So you stuck me with him?" Morgan questioned. "You must really hate me!"

"Morgan, I don't hate you," Jaime replied, with a laugh. "We are in the middle of moving. Craig is your only choice."

"I don't need him," Morgan stated. "I'll be alright on my own."

Morgan jumped out of the wheelchair and immediately got lightheaded. Craig caught her before she hit the floor. "I don't need your help!" she yelled, pushing him away.

"You're going to get it regardless," Craig replied, lifting Morgan into his arms. "You're stuck with me."

Morgan rolled her eyes and glared at Jaime. "I'll get you for this," she warned.

Craig set Morgan back into the wheelchair. "It's regulation, Sweetheart," he said. "You have to ride in it out to the car."

"Don't call me sweetheart!" she replied. "I'm not your sweetheart."

Morgan took control of the wheelchair and wheeled herself out of the building. "Thanks for allowing me to volunteer," he told Jaime, as they followed her out. "This is going to be so much fun."

Craig chased Morgan to the parking lot. After helping her into the car and taking the chair back, he climbed into the car. "You might as well start liking this because you're stuck with me for awhile," he informed her, as he pulled out of the parking lot.

"Over my dead body," Morgan replied.

Craig slammed on the brakes and came to a standstill in the street. "That can be arranged," he yelled, losing his temper. "I'll just take you home and let you fend for yourself. When they call me in the morning reporting a dead body, I'll try not to say I told you so. Don't you realize I want to help you and I care so deeply for you? It's breaking my heart having you push me away like this without even an explanation. Tell me what I'm supposed to do. I haven't a clue."

Morgan willed herself not to cry. What was happening to her? She didn't know how much longer she could keep up this act.

They rode in silence to Morgan's apartment. When they arrived, Morgan waited patiently in the car until Craig came around to help her. When they got to the apartment door, he asked, "Is there anything else you need?"

"No, I'm fine," she answered.

"I guess I'll leave," he replied. "You'll be ok on your own."

"Yes," she said. "Just leave."

Craig stopped at the door. "I have no reason to stay," he stated. "Unless you want to hurt me some more."

"No," she replied. "Just get out!"

"Better yet," Craig said. "I'll just keep watch outside the door."

"Fine," she responded, as she watched him take her keys and one of her kitchen chairs.

Craig kept guard outside her door for most of the night. He must have fallen asleep because when he checked his watch, it was two o'clock. He listened at the door and could have sworn he heard the television set on. "Is she still up?" he asked himself.

He quietly let himself into the apartment and noticed her asleep on the couch. After going to her, he gently picked her up and carried her to bed. After locking the door, he decided to camp out on the couch for the remainder of the night.

About 4 a.m., Craig was awakened by a loud scream. He ran to the bedroom thinking the worst and saw Morgan tossing and turning. She must have had a bad dream because she kept saying "why?" over and over again.

Craig went to her side. "Morgan," he called. "Wake up! It's just a dream."

Morgan sat up instantly and realized where she was. She turned to Craig and glared at him. "Why?" she asked. "Why did you put me in this bed?"

"Isn't this where you always sleep?" he asked, dumbfounded.

"No," she answered, angrily. "I haven't slept in this bed for more than six months. I can't believe you put me here."

"I had no idea," Craig said, angrily. "Would you like to go back to the couch?"

"No," Morgan said. "You take the couch. I'll sleep on the floor."

"I'm not going to let you sleep on the floor!" Craig stated, outraged. "What is your problem with this bed?"

"I can't sleep in it alone," she cried.

With that, she melted against Craig and cried on his shoulder. Despite how angry he was at her, he wrapped his arms around her to comfort her. "Would you like me to stay in here with you?" he asked.

Morgan lifted her head and looked into his eyes. "Yes, please," she whispered. "I would like that."

Craig held Morgan through the night as she slept. It was like a dream come true for him but it wouldn't last long. Things would be completely different in the morning.

Chapter 6

Craig awoke from a well deserved sleep with Morgan nestled by his side. He studied her as she slept. She was so beautiful especially in the morning light. It seemed to encircle her. She looked like an angel.

Craig carefully moved onto his side, making sure not to wake her. He still couldn't believe where he was. It seemed like a dream and he didn't want to wake up.

Morgan began to stir. She moved closer to him as if she was checking to see if he was still there. Craig ran his hand up and down her cheek, moving her hair out of her face. "Good morning," she whispered.

"Good morning, Angel," Craig returned.

Without opening her eyes, Morgan moved her head so she could kiss Craig. When she placed her lips on his, Craig was taken back. He wasn't sure what to think. The only thing he knew for certain was that he liked this surprising action of hers.

Before Craig could figure any of this out, Morgan was lying on top of him. She was consuming him, making him her own. "I knew you would be here," she whispered. "I've missed you so much."

This brought Craig back to reality. Morgan thought she was with Edward. Craig's suspicion were confirmed when Morgan called Edward's name.

"Morgan," Craig called.

"What is it, my darling?" she asked, between kisses.

"Morgan," Craig repeated. "It's Craig, not Edward."

Morgan's eyes shot open. She stared at Craig, realizing what she was doing. She quickly rolled over to the other side of the bed. "I'm sorry," she mumbled. "I thought…"

"I know exactly what you thought," he interrupted, angrily. "You're just lucky I'm not the type of guy who would have taken advantage of the situation."

"Yes, I guess I am," Morgan replied. "I'm going to take a shower."

After Morgan left, Craig laid in bed for the longest time. He couldn't figure out what was behind this change in her. He had come too far to just let her ruin this relationship for the both of them. He decided he wasn't going to give up on them. He had an idea he hoped would win her back.

Craig wandered into the kitchen to get a much needed cup of coffee. He searched everywhere for some but came up with only a jar of tea and two diet sodas. What the heck was going on here, Craig thought. How did Morgan survive?

There was a knock at the door which brought Craig into his policeman mode. "Who is it?" he asked, cautiously.

"Leslie," she answered.

Craig opened the door. "I brought you a cup of coffee," Leslie said as she entered the room. "After your phone call last night, I thought you might need it this morning."

"You read my mind," he said, as he took it from her.

"Where's Morgan?" Leslie asked.

"She's in the shower," he answered. "Can you stay with her for awhile? I have something I need to do. It shouldn't take long."

"Yeah," she replied. "That's not a problem."

Craig went back into the bedroom to grab his shoes. "Oh good! You're leaving," Morgan said, when she entered the room.

"Don't worry," he replied. "I'll be back."

Craig walked to the door but instead of exiting the room, he shut the door. "I don't understand what is going on here," he said, as he walked over to her.

"What are you talking about?" she questioned.

"I just don't understand," he explained. "We almost made love in your bed last week. And now, you hate me. When I left here last night, we were in a great place. And now, you hate me. I don't understand what happened between great and hating me."

"I explained this to you last night," she said.

"Your explanation didn't make any sense," he replied. "You said that I wasn't here for you. I was at work and as soon as we got the call, I was here. I got here as soon as I could."

"You need to stay away from me," she told him.

"Like the way you stayed away from me this morning?" he asked. "What was that about?"

"That was a mistake," she answered. "I was thinking about someone else."

"I got that," he replied, hurt. "I just wanted to hear you say it."

Morgan turned away from Craig. She wanted to cry. This was the most difficult thing she ever had to do. "I want you to leave me alone. I want you to get your things and get out. Please don't come back."

Craig turned Morgan around until they were face to face. "I don't think that is what you want," he said, as he pulled her close.

Craig kissed Morgan passionately and to his surprise, she didn't resist. After the kiss, Craig turned and walked to the door. "I knew you didn't mean it when you told me to leave you alone," he said, as he walked out the door.

Morgan laid down on the bed. She couldn't help but think about what happened between her and Craig earlier. She was having the wildest dream about him. They were on a beach lying under the stars. It was very erotic and turned her on. When she realized what she was doing to Craig, she had to cover. That's when she called Edward's name. She knew it was wrong and that she had hurt Craig deeply but she had to push him away.

She got up and made the bed. While fluffing the pillows, she could smell Craig's faint scent. She would love to have him in her bed every night with her but it was impossible. She had to keep him out of danger.

She grabbed a pair of jeans and a sweater from the dresser drawer and slipped them on. After fixing her hair, Morgan examined the bruise across her cheek. It was purple in color and sore to the touch. Flashes of the attack flooded her mind and she closed her eyes, praying she could forget the whole night.   After frantically applying some makeup to try and conceal the bruise to no avail, she gave up and ventured out to the kitchen.

Leslie was sitting on the couch watching television. Morgan opened the refrigerator and grabbed an apple from the crisper drawer. "I guess you are my babysitter, huh?" she said to Leslie.

"That's what it looks like," Leslie replied.

"I really don't need one," Morgan told her. "I can take care of myself."

"We are just trying to protect you," Leslie stated.

"I don't need protection," Morgan retorted. "I don't know why your brother can't leave me alone like I asked him to."

"He just wants to take care of you," Leslie said.

Morgan could see she wasn't getting anywhere by having this conversation. "So where did Craig go?" Morgan asked.

"He said that he had an errand to run," Leslie answered.

"Well, I will be fine until he gets back," Morgan stated. "You can leave if you want."

"I am not going anywhere," Leslie told her. "Are you trying to get rid of me?"

"Yes," Morgan answered. "I feel like a prisoner in my own home."

Before Leslie could say anything, the door opened and in walked Craig with Stephanie in tow. "Hi everyone!" she said in her cute little voice.

Leslie went to her and gathered her up. "You're so lucky, Craig," she said. "You have such a sweet little girl."

"And you have two holy terrors," Craig stated, laughing.

Stephanie approached Morgan very slowly. "Are you ok?" Stephanie asked, as she pointed at Morgan's bruised cheek.

"I'm fine," Morgan answered.

"Is there anything I can do for you?" Stephanie asked.

Morgan was so touched by this sweet girl. "No, I'm fine," she repeated. "Thanks!"

Stephanie hurried to Craig, who was watching the whole thing in disbelief. He couldn't get over how Morgan lit up at the sight of Stephanie. "Can I have my chocolate milk now?" Stephanie asked. "Please?"

"Yes," Craig answered.

As Leslie helped Stephanie, Craig went to Morgan. "I hope you don't mind that I brought Stephanie here," he said.

"I don't mind at all," Morgan replied.

"Daddy! Daddy!" Stephanie called. "Can we go get Morgan's present now?"

"It was supposed to be a surprise," Craig reminded her.

"What present?" Morgan asked. "I'm not going to accept any presents from you."

"It's not from me then," he replied. "It's from Stephanie."

Craig walked away from Morgan before she had a chance to say another word. "I think Morgan should pick it out," he told Stephanie. "Let's persuade her to go."

"I'm not going," Morgan said.

"Why not?" Craig asked, irritated.

"Because I don't want to be seen with you," she answered. "You know how I feel about you being here."

"Can't you even put your feelings aside for one day?" Craig questioned. "Do this for Stephanie. I hope you don't hate her as much as you hate me."

"I don't hate you!" Morgan exclaimed.

"You could've fooled me," Craig replied.

Stephanie dropped to the floor and began to cry. "All you ever do is fight with everyone, Daddy," she mumbled. "First with Mommy and now Morgan. Please don't fight anymore. I beg you!"

"It will be all right," Morgan said, motioning Craig and Leslie back.

Morgan hurried to Stephanie. "It's all my fault your dad and I aren't getting along," she explained, wrapping her arms around the little girl.

"Why do you fight?" Stephanie questioned.

"Your daddy and I are having a disagreement," Morgan answered. "It's not about you."

"Mommy and Daddy fight all the time," she said. "I want it to stop. My daddy cares about you. Why can't you get along with him?"

Morgan looked at Craig not sure how to answer the girl's question. "Stephanie, you have to understand," Craig told her, as he knelt next to her. "Not everyone is going to get along. I do like Morgan but right now, she doesn't like me. The only thing we can try to do is change her mind."

"I can do that," Stephanie said. "I already know you're a great guy."

Craig pulled her into his arms and gave her a big hug. He glanced at Morgan not sure what to think. Morgan was so understanding with Stephanie. Why was she being so good with her? Would she ever be that way with him?

"Daddy," Stephanie said. "Can we go get the surprise now?"

"Ask Morgan," Craig replied, daring Morgan to say no to Stephanie.

"Please?" she asked in her little voice.

How could Morgan say no to this little girl especially with Craig refusing to take no for an answer? "I really shouldn't," Morgan replied, glaring at Craig.

"But you will," Craig insisted.

"Is that an order, Officer?" Morgan asked, sarcastically.

"I'll drag you there kicking and screaming if I have to," Craig warned.

"I guess I have no choice then," Morgan said, angrily.

"Damn right you don't," Craig whispered close to her ear. "Get your coat, Stephanie. Are you going with us, Leslie?"

"Well, as much as I'd like to go and referee you two," she replied. "I really need to get home."

"Suit yourself," Craig said. "Are we ready?"

On the way to the parking lot, Morgan stopped Craig, letting Stephanie get out of ear range. "I want you to know," she told him. "I'm doing this in protest."

"Why can't you just relax and have a good time?" he asked. "Do I have to show you what that is?"

"No," Morgan answered, rolling her eyes. "I want to remind you that I told you to stay away from me. Why do you insist on hanging around where you're not wanted?"

"Because I care about you," Craig replied. "I don't want to see you get hurt again. I want to take care of you."

"I can take care of myself," Morgan reminded him for the hundredth time.

Before Craig could reply, he heard Stephanie's voice. "Come on, Daddy!" she said, tugging on his coat.

Stephanie grabbed his hand and began to pull him along. He held his other hand out to Morgan, who reluctantly grabbed it. "I knew you'd see things my way," Craig said.

Morgan sighed and rolled her eyes. This would be the last time she would let Craig manipulate her. She had to start keeping her distance. She was scared of what might happen to her if she didn't stay away from Craig.

They climbed into the truck and headed for their destination. "This surprise was Stephanie's idea," Craig told Morgan, hoping to end the silence that filled the truck.

"I hope you like it!" Stephanie exclaimed. "It's not much but Daddy said that you didn't have one."

Morgan glared at Craig, who was glaring back at her. Craig turned his attention back to the road. He was starting to wish he had never agreed to help Morgan. He couldn't understand why every woman he ever got involved with ended up treating him so badly. He decided as soon as his divorce was final, he would concentrate solely on Stephanie and his job. He didn't need a woman in his life. It didn't seem to matter anymore what he wanted.

When they arrived at the place, Stephanie announced, as she got out of the truck, "Here's your surprise! Take your pick!"

Morgan looked at all the Christmas trees in the lot. After turning her attention back to Stephanie, she questioned, "You want to buy me a Christmas tree?"

"Everyone needs a Christmas tree," the little girl replied. "You don't have one."

"I don't think I need one," Morgan responded. "Thanks for thinking about me though."

"Why don't you need one?" Stephanie asked.

Morgan knelt down in front of Stephanie. "Because people who are going to be alone on Christmas don't want to be reminded of it," she answered.

"I'll spend Christmas with you," Stephanie replied. "Daddy will too."

Morgan wanted to cry. It was a nice thought having Craig with her on Christmas but it was impossible.

"Please let us do this for you," Stephanie begged. "We really want to."

"Ok," Morgan agreed. "Let's go pick one out."

Stephanie ran ahead of Craig and Morgan. "I'm surprised you agreed to this," he said. "You know you don't have to spend Christmas alone."

"Don't fight with me about this," Morgan pleaded.

"I'm sure Jaime and Bryan will let you celebrate with them," Craig stated.

"I'm not going to impose on them," Morgan replied. "Besides, they usually spend the holiday with Jaime's parents."

"What about your parents?" Craig asked.

"My mom lives in Florida now," Morgan answered. "My father died when I was four."

"I'm sorry," Craig apologized.

"Daddy," Stephanie called. "I found the perfect tree."

Craig hurried to Stephanie and swung her around. "Morgan should pick out her own tree," he said, over Stephanie's giggles.

"Is there anything I can help you find?" the owner asked Morgan.

"No," she answered. "We're just looking. Thanks!"

"You have such a beautiful family," the lady said. "Your little girl is so adorable."

Before Morgan could correct the lady, Craig thanked her. "I wish you hadn't done that," she snapped at Craig.

"What?" Craig questioned.

"I'm not part of your family," she answered.

"I didn't say you were," Craig replied, blowing her off. "Let's get a tree."

Craig walked ahead of Morgan with Stephanie in his arms. "Well, isn't this a nice surprise?" Morgan heard someone ask her.

Abby Lewis, she thought. What did she do to deserve this? "Hello Abby," Morgan forced herself to say.

"Oh my God!" Abby exclaimed. "What happened to you?"

"I had an accident," Morgan explained, as she touched her cheek. "It's fine."

"What a relief," Abby replied.

99

Morgan glanced over her shoulder, looking for a savior. Craig was nowhere in sight. "Who's that hunky guy you're with?" Abby asked. "He looks so familiar."

"Craig Masterson," Morgan answered, wondering where he could be.

"Oh yeah," Abby replied. "He's a cop, I think. Are you two an item?"

"No," Morgan stated, a little too harsh. "It's a long story."

"You two look really great together," Abby stated. "Did you know I worked with him on a case once? It was really exciting."

"Let me go see if I can find him," Morgan offered, trying to get away. "You two can get reacquainted."

Morgan hurried as fast as she could with Abby on her heels. "He probably doesn't remember me," she said. "It was a short case. I was just gathering information for my boss."

"Craig," Morgan called. "Come here!"

Craig hurried over to them, thinking something was wrong. "What's wrong?" he asked.

"Nothing's wrong," Morgan replied. "Craig, this is Abby Lewis. She said that you worked together once."

"I remember," Craig responded. "How are you, Abby?"

Craig extended his hand which made Abby swoon. "I'm fine," she answered. "Are you looking for a tree? Oh, of course you are or you wouldn't be here, right? That was a really stupid question. I'm sorry."

Craig and Morgan glanced at each other. This woman was a nervous wreck. They both knew they had to get out of this. "Where's Stephanie?" Morgan asked.

"I'm not sure," he replied. "I'd better find her."

Craig made a quick exit, leaving Morgan alone with Abby again. "I need to go too, Abby," she said. "I need to get home."

Morgan hurried to find Craig. "Thanks for making me meet her again," Craig told her. "If working with her wasn't bad enough."

"I'm sorry," Morgan apologized. "If it's any comfort to you, I think she has a crush on you."

"That's reassuring," Craig replied, laughing. "Let's not make any wedding plans just yet."

They walked through the lot looking for Stephanie. They found her standing in front of her apparent tree of choice. "Can we get this one?" she asked.

Craig looked at Morgan, who was totally mesmerized by the sight. "You did a wonderful job picking out a tree," Morgan told Stephanie. "I would be really happy to have this one in my house."

Stephanie gleamed from ear to ear. She was so proud of herself. "Can we help you decorate it?" she asked.

"You sure can," Morgan answered.

"Let's go!" the little girl replied, unable to control her enthusiasm.

After Craig paid the bill and they loaded the tree into the truck, they headed back to Morgan's place. "How are you feeling?" he asked.

"I'm a little tired," she answered.

"I'm really sorry about last night," Craig stated. "I should have been there for you."

"I really don't want to get into this right now," Morgan warned.

"What are you smiling about?" Craig asked, turning his attention to his daughter.

"Nothing, Daddy," she answered, innocently.

After arriving at the apartment, Craig set up the tree while the girls went to get the decorations. "Can I ask you a question, Stephanie?" Morgan asked. "How do you feel about all of this with your mom and dad?"

Stephanie remained silent. "I don't want to upset you," Morgan explained. "I just want to know if you can help your dad's case."

"I really want to help my daddy," she whispered. "It makes me sad they are getting a divorce."

"It's not an easy thing," Morgan said. "I've seen a lot of kids go through this. If you want to talk to me, you can."

Stephanie began to cry. "I want my daddy to be happy," she said. "Can you help him?"

"I'll do the best job I can with his case," Morgan answered.

"What is going to happen to me?" the little girl asked.

"Well, after it's all over," Morgan explained. "You'll either live with your mom or dad or they'll share you."

"I want to live with my daddy," Stephanie whispered. "Please. I don't want to live with Mommy and Nick."

"Who's Nick?" Morgan asked, knowing the answer but wanting Stephanie to confirm it.

"Mommy's new boyfriend," Stephanie answered.

"You don't like Nick?" Morgan questioned.

The little girl shook her head. "He's always so mean to me," she said.

"How is he mean to you?" Morgan asked, expecting the worst.

"He is always yelling at me," she explained. "He doesn't want me around when he is with Mommy. He is always telling her to get rid of me."

Morgan pulled Stephanie into her arms as she cried. "Does your dad know about this?" Morgan asked.

"No," Stephanie cried.

Morgan held her for several minutes. She had to calm Stephanie down and figure out a way to tell Craig without showing she cared too much. This couldn't be kept from him. "Let's go decorate the tree," Morgan suggested, wiping away Stephanie's tears.

Morgan grabbed the heavier of the two boxes and Stephanie dragged the other one into the living room. "There you are!" Craig exclaimed. "How does it look?"

"Great!" Morgan replied.

As Stephanie rummaged through the boxes, Morgan directed Craig to the other side of the room. "Stephanie just mentioned Nick to me," she asked.

"I still can't believe the nerve of that man," Craig stated, thinking back to what he saw during his visit with Valerie. "I hope Val didn't have him spending the night with Stephanie there. I wouldn't put it past her though. What did Stephanie tell you?"

As Morgan explained to Craig what Stephanie had told her, she could see the fury glowing in his eyes. It really hurt her to see Craig so upset. "I'm really sorry," she replied. "I thought you should know."

Craig hurried over to Stephanie, who was hugging a huge teddy bear she had found in one of the boxes. "Are you ok?" he asked, picking her up.

"I don't want to get yelled at anymore," she replied. "Please don't make me live with Mommy and Nick."

"I'm going to do everything I can to make sure that doesn't happen," he told her. "I love you so much. I will protect you."

"I love you too, Daddy," Stephanie said, as Craig placed a kiss on the tip of her little nose.

Morgan watched in awe. She wished for a little baby that she could love and protect but her chance was gone. She would give anything for another chance. "Let's decorate the tree," Craig announced. "Come on, Morgan."

Morgan watched as Craig helped his daughter empty one of the boxes. He was so good with Stephanie. She wished she could be as happy as that little girl was right now. Before she could stop herself, she wished that Craig and Stephanie were her family. If only wishes came true, she thought. She knew this one never would.

"Do you have any lights?" Craig asked. "No tree is a Christmas tree without lights."

Morgan grabbed the other box of stuff. "These should be long enough," she said, as she handed him the lights.

As Craig put the lights on the tree, Morgan switched on the radio and found some Christmas music. Stephanie began to dance around the room with the bear in her arms. After putting the lights down, Craig asked Morgan if she wanted to dance. "Well, ok," she answered, knowing he wouldn't take no for an answer.

Craig pulled her into his arms. He twirled her around while she laughed. "It's nice to hear you laugh," he said. "I missed it."

Morgan stopped laughing. "I've never danced to Christmas music before," she stated.

"There's a first time for everything," Craig replied.

Craig caught Morgan's intense eyes and held them for a brief moment. He could still see the desire burning in them that he saw last night. He knew it was still there even with her strange behavior. He wanted to kiss her just like he did before. Craig was just about to make his move when the phone rang. "I'd better get that," Morgan said.

After Craig released her, Morgan hurried to the phone. "Hello!" she said.

"One big happy family," the male voice said. "I could have sworn I warned you to stay away from Craig. You don't take hints very well, do you?"

"Craig, I need to take this call," she said, trying not to panic. "I'll be right back."

Morgan headed to her bedroom and shut the door. "What do you want?" Morgan whispered harshly into the phone.

"I want you to stay away from Craig," he said. "Do you want me to pay you another visit?"

"No," Morgan answered, shaking. "I want you to leave me alone."

"I can't do that, Sweetheart," he said.

"What do you want me to do?" she asked. "Because of what you did last night, Craig will not leave my side. He feels like he has to protect me."

"You need to come up with something to keep him away from you permanently," he replied. "You're a smart woman. You'll think of something. But if you don't, I will be seeing you very soon."

"I will think of something," Morgan told him. "Just leave me alone."

Morgan hung up the phone and start to pace around the room. She had to get out of the apartment quickly and make sure Craig didn't follow her. She exited the room and passed Craig and Stephanie to get to the door. "Where are you going?" Craig asked.

"I have somewhere I need to be," Morgan answered. "Please lock up when you leave."

Morgan ran to her car and quickly got in. She had to figure out a way to get rid of this stalker. She wasn't sure what to do or who she could even turn to for help. She knew it was wrong to keep this information from the police but she had to protect herself. She didn't want that man visiting her again.

Morgan decided to stop for a bite to eat and to do some Christmas shopping. She tried to think of a solution to this whole mess but couldn't. The only thing she could do was stay away from Craig but just the thought of doing that broke her heart.

Morgan stayed away from the apartment for several hours. When she returned, Craig and Stephanie were gone. They did leave behind a Christmas present under the tree, which Morgan left laying there. She didn't have the heart to open it.

Morgan retired for the evening but she couldn't sleep. She had to think of every way possible to eliminate Craig from her life. She began to cry. She didn't understand why this was happening. She had finally found someone she really cared about and now she had to let him go. Why would someone do this to her? She needed to figure that out before she lost Craig forever. "I hope it is not too late," she said, as she drifted off to sleep.

Chapter 7

"Mister Masterson is no longer our client, Jaime," Morgan announced, as she entered the office. "I need you to take his file to Tom Warner's office and direct his calls there too."

"Why is he no longer our client?" Jaime asked.

"Because that is the decision that has been made," Morgan answered. "Now please do what I have asked you to do."

Jaime turned to the filing cabinet and grabbed Craig's file. "Anything else?" she questioned, not liking any of this.

"Yes," Morgan answered. "I am only working half a day today. Please reschedule my appointments for this afternoon."

Morgan knew Jaime was angry with her as she left the office. Morgan didn't care though. Dropping Craig as her client was the best thing for everyone.

Morgan walked into her office and decided to tackle the pile of paperwork that she had accumulated all week. In between the paperwork and the few clients she was meeting with, she figured it would keep her mind focused on work. But she soon found that wouldn't be the case. Her mind kept finding its way to Craig. She felt so bad about the way things had to be handled when it came to their relationship. She didn't know what else she could do. She knew he would probably hate her for not confiding in him. She needed to take care of herself and she prayed he would understand that.

Morgan's morning flew by. As soon as her last client had left, there was a knock at her door. "Are you too busy for some company?" a familiar voice said.

Morgan looked up from her paperwork and saw her high school sweetheart, Daniel Milano, standing there. "I am never too busy for you," she replied.

Daniel entered the room and sat down. "So what are you doing in town?" Morgan asked.

"My company is thinking of opening a new division here and I am in town checking out locations," he answered.

"Does that mean you might be moving here?" Morgan questioned.

"Not sure yet," he told her. "We will have to see how things go."

"So how are your parents?" Morgan asked. "Are they still living in Florida?"

"They are fine," Daniel answered. "They also say that moving to Florida was the best thing they ever did. They love it. My mother is constantly reminding me about the one that got away."

Morgan smiled. "She has never understood why we broke up," Daniel added.

"Our lives were just going in different directions," Morgan said. "It wasn't anyone's fault."

"She understands that but I think secretly she wants us back together," Daniel replied, with a laugh.

Morgan smiled. She was pretty sure that wasn't going to happen but she didn't have the heart to say anything. "What are you doing for lunch?" Daniel asked.

"I haven't thought too much about it," she answered.

"I want to take you to lunch if you would like to go," he offered.

"That sounds like fun," Morgan stated, as she gathered her things.

After Morgan and Daniel left the office, Jaime got a visit from Craig. "Is Morgan here?" he asked. "I need to talk to her."

"No, she isn't here," Jaime answered.

"Maybe you can tell me why she doesn't want to be my lawyer anymore," Craig said, voicing his frustration.

"I don't know," Jaime answered. "I wish I could tell you what was going through her head when she made that decision. The only thing I know is that was the decision that was made and you now have a different attorney."

"How could she do that without even consulting me?" he asked.

"I don't know that either," Jaime answered. "She has changed some since the attack and she doesn't confide in me like she used to."

"I would really like to talk to her," Craig told her. "Will she be back later?"

"No," Jaime said. "She has the afternoon off."

"Will you leave her a message that I stopped by?" he asked. "Maybe she will call me and let me know what is going on."

****

"Thank you for a very nice lunch," Morgan said. "I don't think I have eaten that much in a long time."

"It was my pleasure," Daniel replied. "It isn't everyday that I get to take a beautiful woman to lunch."

"So what does your afternoon look like?" she asked.

"It is wide open," he answered.

"Good," she said. "If you want to, you can come with me and look at this townhouse I am buying."

"Are you moving?" he asked.

"There are too many memories at the apartment," she explained. "I need a fresh start."

"I heard about Edward," he replied. "I am really sorry."

"It has been really hard to deal with but I am managing," Morgan told him.

"If you need to talk," Daniel said. "I am here for you."

"I think I am fine," she stated. "Thanks anyway."

Morgan and Daniel met the realtor at the townhouse. Morgan immediately fell in love with the place when she first saw it the week before. At that moment, she knew this was the right place to start her life over. "I really hope everything is ready for me to sign," she told the realtor. "I am so excited about this move."

After Morgan signed the papers to officially become a home owner, Morgan lead Daniel to the next destination. "Hi Morgan!" Mrs. Peters said, as Morgan entered the furniture store. "We haven't seen you in awhile."

"It has been awhile," Morgan replied. "How are you?"

"Fine," the older lady answered. "What can we help you with today?"

"I need some new furniture," Morgan told her. "A couch, a couple of chairs, and a bedroom set."

"We have a huge selection of furniture," Mrs. Peters said. "Just look around and let me know if you need any help."

Daniel followed Morgan around the store, as she tested out the mattresses. "Hello Miss Garrett," a voice called from behind her.

Morgan turned around and found Abby standing there. "Hello Abby," she said.

"Who's your friend?" Abby asked.

"This is Daniel," Morgan answered.

"Is he a client of yours?" Abby questioned.

"No," Morgan said, wondering why Abby would ask that.

"Let me ask you a question," Abby continued. "Do you really think it is ethical to become personally involved with a client?"

"What are you talking about?" Morgan questioned.

"How does it feel to break up a marriage?" Abby asked. "It is apparent though that you have had your fill of Craig and now have found someone else. I do have to say that you have great taste in men."

"Why don't you just mind your own business?" Morgan asked, a little too defensively.

"What's the matter, Morgan?" Abby questioned. "Did I hit a nerve?"

Morgan glared at Abby. Had this woman finally lost her mind? "So will you be sleeping alone in your new bed or will a certain police officer or maybe your new lover be joining you?" Abby asked, as she stepped closer to Morgan.

"What is your problem?" Morgan inquired. "I don't understand this attitude you have towards me."

"Well, let's just say," Abby replied. "You need to learn a thing or two about keeping your hands off things that don't belong to you. Do you always steal other women's husbands or is this a first for you?"

"You don't know what you're talking about," Morgan said, hatefully.

"I think I do," Abby said. "I have seen you with Craig on several different occasions outside of the office. Are you that desperate that you have to throw yourself at a man?"

"I don't have to listen to this," Morgan said, as she turned to walk away.

Abby grabbed her arm, which caught Daniel's attention. "One day, you'll get what's coming to you," Abby threatened. "I just hope I'm there to see it. You'll learn that you can't treat people the way you treat them and get away with it."

Morgan stood in disbelief as Abby walked out the door. She couldn't believe all of that came from Abby. "What was that all about?" Daniel asked.

"I don't know," Morgan answered.

"Is what she said to you true?" Daniel questioned. "Did you break up a marriage? Are you dating a married man?"

"Are you ok, Dear?" Mrs. Peters asked, as she hurried over to Morgan and Daniel.

"Yes, I'm fine," Morgan answered.

"What was her problem?" the older lady asked.

"Tell me something," Morgan stated, suspiciously. "Did she buy anything while she was here?"

"No," Mrs. Peters answered. "She came in right after you did and immediately approached you."

Morgan stood there in deep thought. Could "plain Jane" Abby be capable of masterminding the attack on her? It wasn't possible.

Morgan quickly dismissed the thought, thinking it was preposterous, and continued shopping for the right furniture for her new townhouse. "Did you find everything you wanted?" Mrs. Peters asked, as Morgan and Daniel approached the sales counter.

"Oh, yes!" Morgan answered.

"When do you want it delivered?" the older lady asked.

"As soon as possible," Morgan answered, handing the woman a piece of paper. "Here is the address you can deliver it to."

After Morgan was finished with her excursion, she and Daniel headed to her apartment. "I have a company party to go

110

to this evening," Morgan said. "Would you like to go with me?"

"Before I agree to go anywhere, I would like to know what that woman at the furniture store was talking about," Daniel told her.

"It is a long story," Morgan said. "I had this client and the professional relationship became personal. It didn't last very long. Apparently, Abby was a little upset about it."

"How personal was it?" Daniel asked, feeling a little jealous.

"We didn't sleep together if that is what you are getting at," Morgan stated. "I really need to get ready for this party. If you still want to go, the invitation stands. Just make yourself comfortable and I'll be with you shortly."

Morgan curled her hair and put on her make-up. She then slipped into her red dress and proceeded to present herself to Daniel. "Wow!" he said. "You look incredible."

"Thank you!" Morgan replied, as she ran her hand along his jacket lapel. "I am really glad that you are coming with me. You should fit in with a suit and tie."

Morgan arrived at the party on Daniel's arm, which made Jaime and Bryan's heads turn. "What are you doing here with him?" Jaime demanded. "Where's Craig?"

"Craig isn't my boyfriend," Morgan answered, harshly. "I'm not going to spend every waking hour with him just because you want me to."

"But I thought you two were getting closer," Jaime said.

"What would give you that idea?" Morgan questioned.

"I just hoped," Jaime replied, obviously hurt by the tone of voice Morgan was using.

"You can quit hoping," Morgan told her. "It's not going to happen."

Morgan found Daniel talking to Bryan and interrupted them to ask Daniel to dance. "Do I sense some animosity between you and Jaime?" he asked.

"Very much so," she answered. "She was hoping I would show up with someone else."

"Oh, really," Daniel said, surprised. "You said that you weren't dating anyone."

"No," Morgan stated, sharply. "I am not seeing anyone."

"We could change that," Daniel replied. "If I do move to this area, would you consider dating me again?"

"I don't know," Morgan answered. "So much has happened in the last several months. I am still recuperating."

"It was just an idea," Daniel replied, feeling rejected.

"If you do move here, we'll see what is going on then," Morgan told him. "Just don't move here because of me. I can't promise you anything."

"I understand," he said. "I just appreciate you being honest with me."

Morgan and Daniel danced the night away. Morgan could feel Jaime and Bryan's eyes burning a hole through her. They were watching her every move.

After Morgan rejected Jaime's endless persuasion to take her home, Daniel drove Morgan to the apartment. "Do you want to come in?" she asked.

"No, it's getting late," Daniel answered. "I better get back to the hotel."

"Ok," Morgan said. "Don't be a stranger."

Daniel turned away from Morgan. Just as quickly, he turned back to her. "Let me kiss you goodbye," he said.

"What?" Morgan questioned, shocked.

"Oh, come on," Daniel said, as he pulled her into his arms. "Just one little kiss. What could it hurt?"

Daniel moved in and pressed his lips to Morgan's, who wasn't sure what to think. Little did she know Craig was standing at the end of the hall watching as they kissed.

Chapter 8

"Tell us again what happened the day Edward Garrett was killed, Officer Masterson," Morgan demanded.

"I have told you several times," Craig explained. "Why do we have to go through it again?"

"I want to make sure the court is clear on the events of the day," Morgan told him.

The events from that dreadful day flashed through Craig's mind. "It was around four o'clock and we got a call at the station," Craig explained. "My partner and I hurried across town to the reported hostage situation. When we got there, the man was in Edward's office harassing him about a stock deal that had fallen through. We planted ourselves outside the office door and waited for the right moment to take action."

"You waited?" Morgan questioned. "You did nothing while my husband was being held at gun point."

"In situations like this," he said. "You have to consider all involved. Anyway, a shot was fired from inside the room. We then rushed in and the man started shooting at my partner. I shot and killed the man."

"Where was my husband during all of this?" Morgan asked.

"He was lying on the floor," Craig answered. "He had been shot in the chest."

"So while you were waiting outside the door," Morgan clarified. "My husband was dying. Tell me Officer Masterson. Did you do everything you could do?"

Craig awoke with Morgan's words echoing in his head. He struggled to catch his breath. "Why do I keep having that dream?" Craig asked.

He glanced at the clock. It read 5:15 a.m. Craig got up and went to the kitchen. He knew he wouldn't be able to sleep after having that dream again.

He started a pot of coffee and waited for it to finish. His mind began to wander. He had other things on it besides the dream. He couldn't get over the show he viewed as he entered the hallway to Morgan's apartment. He also couldn't believe she lied to him. It was now apparent that he meant absolutely nothing to her.

"You're up a little early, aren't you?" John questioned, as he entered the kitchen. "Your shift doesn't start until eight."

"Yeah," Craig said. "I couldn't sleep. I had that dream again."

"The one where you're on trial," John stated. "Craig, you did everything you could do. You need to quit feeling guilty about this."

"Did I do everything I could do?" Craig questioned. "I knew the man had a gun. That's why I didn't work on impulse. Because of that, Edward was killed."

"You can't reason your way out of this," John said. "In our line of work, bad things happen. We can't control that."

"I wish I could have saved him though," Craig replied.

"I have to get to the precinct," John said. "Try not to think about this too much. You'll go crazy. I'll see you later."

Craig decided he needed to get out for awhile. He got dressed and went for a morning jog. Craig couldn't believe everything that was happening or that it was happening to him all at one time. He couldn't be with the woman that he loved because so many things were keeping them apart. Not to mention, the kiss she shared with another man. Morgan was playing him for a fool and he didn't like that one bit. He thought they had something special. He was dead wrong.

Craig finished his jog and decided it was time to get ready for work. He got into the shower in hopes that the water would wash away his problems. It just made things worse. "Let me wash your back," Morgan said, as she came alive through his daydream.

Morgan took the soap from Craig and began to lather her hands. "That's not my back," Craig told her.

114

"Yeah, but that's one of my favorite parts," Morgan teased. "I thought I'd start there."

Craig turned to face her. "I'm so glad you are in my life," he said. "I love you so much."

Morgan flashed him her sexy smile. "I love you too, Craig," she returned.

As they kissed, Craig returned to reality. "It's just a dream," he said. "It will never happen."

Craig arrived at work and began doing necessary paperwork that had been cluttering his desk. "Craig, I need the paperwork for the Clarkson case," Officer Adams told him.

Craig searched the desk for the paperwork but couldn't find it anywhere. "I can't find a damn thing on this desk," he yelled, as he cleared his desk with one motion of his hand and watched everything fall to the floor.

Craig turned to the window and ran a hand through his hair. He had to gain control. "That's usually the way I clean my desk too," John said, as he entered the office and shut the door.

Craig let out a huge sigh and turned to face John. "I don't know how much more of this I can take," Craig said. "I am so frustrated. I can't keep my mind on this."

"You have to," John stated. "We can't have a cop acting this way. You're like a time bomb and I'm not really sure I want to be around when you go off."

"This whole situation with Morgan is driving me crazy," Craig explained. "She is constantly on my mind and I am dreaming about her. I love her, John."

"Have you tried talking to her?" John asked.

"I have talked to her until I'm blue in the face," Craig replied. "I thought things were going well between us and now she won't speak to me."

"So you haven't talked to her since she dropped you as her client?" John asked.

"I went over to her apartment last night," Craig explained. "When I turned the corner to go down the hallway to her apartment, I saw her kissing another guy."

"No wonder you can't sleep," John replied. "I hope things start working out for you."

John left the room as Craig began cleaning up his mess. He had never let anyone affect him the way Morgan had. He knew they had no future. He would have to get over her.

Craig worked non-stop on the paperwork he had to finish. He didn't even look up to see who had entered the room. "Hi!" Elizabeth said. "Do you have time for lunch?"

"Hey Elizabeth," he replied, as he looked at his watch. "Yeah, I could probably leave for awhile."

Craig helped Elizabeth out of the building and maneuvered her chair down the block to a corner café. "How are things going for you?" Craig asked, after they were directed to their table.

"Things are going fine," she answered. "My physical therapy is going slowly. I have made a little progress."

"Sometimes it takes time," Craig replied. "It's only been a few months."

"Enough about me," she said. "How are you?"

"Alright," Craig replied.

"That was really enthusiastic," she returned. "What's wrong? You seem distracted."

"It's nothing," he answered. "I'm just bogged down with work and this divorce mess."

After ordering, Elizabeth asked Craig, "Are you sure nothing else is wrong?"

Craig was a million miles away wondering what Morgan was doing. "Now I know there is something wrong," Elizabeth stated. "Craig."

"Yeah," he said.

"Where were you just now?" she asked.

"I'm so sorry," Craig apologized. "I have a lot of things on my mind."

"You said that," Elizabeth stated. "Is this about Morgan? I saw you two dancing at the club the other night but she told me that you two weren't involved."

"Well, that's just one side of the story," Craig responded.

"You're in love with her, aren't you?" Elizabeth questioned, smiling.

"Is it that obvious?" he asked.

"This is so great!" she exclaimed. "What's the problem then?"

"Morgan told me that she never wanted to see me again," Craig told her.

"Why would she say that?" Elizabeth questioned.

"I don't know if she told you," he explained. "But the other night, Morgan was attacked."

"Oh, my," she said. "Is she ok?"

"She is fine," Craig answered. "But I think the attack had something to do with her not wanting to see me anymore. She has been acting differently towards everyone since that night."

"Craig, I don't know what to tell you," she replied. "I love Morgan like a sister and I want her to be happy. Do you want me to talk to her?"

"Would you?" Craig asked. "After what I saw last night, I don't think I should."

"What did you see?" she questioned.

"I went to her apartment," he answered. "I saw her kissing another man."

"Ok. Time out!" Elizabeth said. "What other guy?"

"He was about six feet tall with brown wavy hair and a dark complexion," Craig explained.

"That sounds like Daniel," she stated. "Why would he be in town?"

"Who's Daniel?" Craig asked, eagerly.

"Morgan's high school sweetheart," Elizabeth answered.

"That would explain a lot," Craig replied.

"She shouldn't have been kissing him though," Elizabeth stated.

Craig replayed the scene of Morgan and the guy kissing over and over again in his mind, as he picked at his food. Elizabeth noticed he wasn't eating but didn't say a word.

After several more minutes, Elizabeth told Craig that her ride was there. "I have to go," she said.

"I'll take care of this," Craig said, as he picked up the check.

"Thanks!" Elizabeth returned. "I'll talk to Morgan and we'll get this all worked out."

Craig watched as Elizabeth left. He paid the waitress and returned to work.

Craig sat down behind his desk and returned to his paperwork, which seemed to have multiplied in his absence. He took a deep breath and closed his eyes. "You're not doing so well, are you?" Morgan asked.

Craig opened his eyes. "No," he answered. "I'm going crazy without you. I can't concentrate. All I think about is you."

"I can't stop thinking about you either," she said, as she approached him. "I'm sorry about what has happened between us."

"Me too," Craig replied.

"Do I get another chance?" Morgan asked.

Craig pulled her onto his lap. "You can count on it," he said.

"Craig," John called, awaking him from yet another daydream.

Craig opened his eyes and said, "Yes."

"There's a call for you on line one," John told him. "It's Valerie."

"Hello!" he said.

"Hi Craig! It's me," Valerie said. "I was wondering if you could come by today after work. We need to talk."

"I'll be over around five," Craig told her.

What does she want now? Craig thought. I guess I'll find out when I get there.

Craig decided to take a break and go to the lounge to get a soda. "Hey Craig!" John called. "How are things going?"

"Alright," he said. "I wish I knew how long I am going to be doing paperwork. I am really tired of sitting behind a desk."

"You didn't miss much today," John said. "We arrested a couple of women for solicitation and a man for indecent exposure. You know, same old thing."

"Sounds like fun," Craig said.

"What did Valerie want?" John asked.

"She wants me to come by the house when I get off work," Craig explained.

"Is this another attempt to get you back?" John asked.

"I hope not," Craig said. "I am not in the mood for that."

"Hey John!" Officer Adams called. "We need you in here."

"Got to go," John said. "Duty calls."

Craig grabbed a soda from the machine and hurried back to his office to finish the paperwork. Around five, he decided to call it a day. He headed to Valerie's to see what she wanted.

"Valerie!" Craig called, as he entered the house.

"Hi!" she said, as she entered from the kitchen. "I'm glad you could make it by today."

"What do you want to talk about?" Craig asked.

"I wanted to give you this," she answered, handing him an envelope full of papers.

"These are our divorce papers," Craig said, surprised.

"Yeah," she confirmed. "My lawyer said that everything was in order. As you can see, I already signed them. You can have Morgan look at them if you want."

"She isn't my lawyer anymore," Craig replied. "I'm going to have to read these before I sign them."

"What happened with you and Morgan?" she asked.

"I am not sure," Craig answered. "I thought you were against this divorce. What changed your mind?"

"I wasn't exactly against it," she stated. "I decided not to fight with you about this anymore. We are both unhappy and want to be with other people. This is the best thing."

Craig glanced at the papers and stuffed them back into the envelope. "Are you sure you want to be with Nick?" he asked.

"Yes, I am," she answered. "He is really good to me. Don't you want to be with Morgan?"

"Morgan and I are not together," Craig said. "I don't think there's a future for us."

"Let me fix you some dinner," Valerie offered. "You look like you could use a friend."

"That would be great," Craig replied. "If you don't mind, I'm going to pack up some stuff."

Craig wandered down to the other end of the house and started putting things in boxes. As he packed, he came across some pictures and a small box with his wedding ring in it. "It's not easy, is it?" Valerie asked from the doorway.

"Not as easy as I thought it would be," Craig answered.

119

"Nothing ever is," Valerie replied, as she sat down next to him on the bed. "I'm really sorry about everything."

"I know," Craig said. "Me too."

"I'm even sorry for all the things I said to Morgan," Valerie added.

"I know you were trying to make her mad," Craig stated.

"She's pretty tough," she said. "She didn't even crack."

"She's a very tough lady," Craig replied.

"Is that why you like her so much?" Valerie asked.

"That's one of the many reasons," Craig answered.

"Things will get better," Valerie said, touching his shoulder.

"What happened to us?" Craig questioned. "Did I miss something along the way?"

"I think we just grew apart," Valerie answered, taking the pictures Craig had in his hand. "Do you remember when these were taken?"

"Honeymoon," Craig answered.

"Yeah," she replied, thinking back. "We had a wonderful time."

"We sure did," Craig agreed.

"Dinner's ready," Valerie said. "We can talk more while we eat."

Craig sat down at the table while Valerie served up pot roast, potatoes, and carrots. "Wow!" Craig said. "You can fix something other than hamburgers and frozen pizzas."

"Don't make fun of me!" she protested. "I have come a long way."

"Yes, you have," Craig said, taking a bite. "This is really good."

"Thanks!" Valerie said with a smile.

Valerie sat down at the table and fixed herself a plate. "Now that the divorce is final," she said, "we need to discuss Stephanie. I think a custody battle would be really traumatic for her."

"What do you suggest?" Craig asked.

"Well, I think you should know," Valerie said. "Nick has asked me to move to Virginia with him."

"I don't think I can handle Stephanie being that far away," Craig explained.

"That's why I think you should keep her," Valerie said. "It's going to be really hard for me but at least here, she'll have her grandparents and your family to help out."

"I hate to see you give up your child for Nick," Craig replied.

"Well, Nick's not really a kid person," Valerie told him. "And I'll be back probably a couple of times a month to see Stephanie."

"I think the best place for Stephanie is here," Craig said. "She said that Nick yells at her a lot."

"Nick works a lot of hours at his job," Valerie explained. "We don't see each other much. A perfect example is tonight. I actually fixed this dinner for him. But he called and said that he had to work late. The time we do spend together he wants it to be just us, alone. I guess you can say he's a little possessive of me."

"Why do you want someone like that?" Craig questioned. "You could do so much better."

"That coming from my ex-husband," Valerie stated, dipping up some more carrots.

"I'm really sorry, Valerie," Craig whispered.

"I'm sorry too," she replied.

"I need to pack a few more things," Craig stated. "If I forget anything."

"I'll make sure you get it," Valerie finished.

Craig finished packing his things and loaded them into his truck. "Well, I think I'm going to go," Craig said. "Thanks for dinner."

"You're welcome," she replied. "There's one more thing. I'm going to sell the house, unless you want it."

"No," he said. "I think we need a new start."

"I know someone who wants to buy it," she told him. "I figure we can just split the amount of money we get for it. It should be enough for both of us to make a new start."

"Sounds good," Craig said.

Craig approached her and gave her a hug. "In spite of everything that has happened, I am going to miss you," she whispered in his ear.

"Me too," Craig replied. "Let me know if you need anything."

With that, Craig left and headed back to John's townhouse. "Hey!" John said, as Craig walked in. "How did things go with Valerie?"

"I think I am still in shock," Craig answered. "She was very nice and accommodating. She finally agreed to the divorce."

"That's great!" John said, as he watched Craig set his copy of the divorce papers on the table.

"Yeah," Craig replied. "This is just what I wanted but now I don't have Morgan. This is just too bittersweet."

"You have got to work things out with Morgan," John told him.

"I don't see how," Craig stated. "She won't take any of my calls and she definitely won't see me."

"If this is what you want, then you have to fight for it," John replied. "Why are you giving up? This is not like you."

"I don't know what else to do," Craig said. "Maybe I should just forget about her and move on."

"Stop kidding yourself," John stated. "We both know you can't do that."

"I need to figure out what happened," Craig replied. "Everything took a bad turn right after she was attacked."

"I'll review her file tomorrow and let you know what I think," John told him.

"I would appreciate that," Craig said. "I have been over it a hundred times and a different perspective might help."

"I will do what I can," John replied. "I think I am going to get me a beer and relax in front of the TV. The game will be on shortly. Do you want to join me?"

"No, thanks," Craig answered. "I need to call Stephanie and then I think I am going to try to get some sleep. I haven't gotten a lot of that lately."

Craig retired to his room and called Stephanie. The little girl told him about her exciting day. She went to a friend's birthday party and they had a new puppy. He promised her that as soon as they were settled, they would talk about getting a puppy.

As soon as he hung up the phone, it rang. "Hey Craig!" Valerie said. "Did I catch you at a bad time?"

"No," he answered. "I just got off the phone with Stephanie. What's up?"

"I called to talk to you about Stephanie," Valerie explained. "I think that we should talk to her together about what is going on."

"I think that would be for the best," he replied. "When do you want to do it?"

"I am not sure," Valerie said. "Let me call you later."

Craig hung up the phone. He laid down in bed but knew he wouldn't get much sleep. He couldn't stop thinking about Morgan and what went wrong. Something had to have happened the night she was attacked. Things were going really well for them until that night. He had to find out what changed her mind and then change it back. He had to win her back if it was the last thing he ever did.

Chapter 9

"We have a new neighbor," John announced, as he entered the townhouse.

"Really?" Craig questioned.

"I saw her while I was jogging," John said. "She lives in the blue one across the street."

"What are you getting at?" Craig asked, setting the newspaper he was reading on the table.

"If she is single, this could be your new start," John stated.

"Last night you wanted me and Morgan together," Craig said. "Why are you pushing this?"

"I just thought you might want to go introduce yourself and get to know our neighbors," John explained. "She is a very attractive woman."

After John left for work, Craig thought about what he had said. What would it hurt to go see the new neighbor? He would just stop by for a few minutes and introduce himself. It was time for him to get out and do that anyway. This would be a good place to start.

Craig walked across the street and down a few houses to the blue townhouse. He took a deep breath and rang the doorbell. He couldn't believe who opened the door. "What are you doing here?" Morgan questioned. "How did you find me?"

"I live across the street," Craig answered. "John told me that someone new moved into the neighborhood and I thought I would introduce myself."

"Well, I already know you so you can leave now," Morgan said, as she started to close the door.

Craig put his hand up and slammed it against the door. "I am not going to let you shut me out again," he replied, frustrated. "We need to talk now. You at least owe me that much."

Morgan was so tired of this. "Fine," she said, as she held open the door and let him in. "Just make it quick."

"I don't think it is going to be that simple," Craig replied. "This will take awhile, Sweetheart."

Morgan rolled her eyes. "Just to let you know this isn't going to change anything," she warned.

Craig glared at her. "I am going to talk and you are going to listen and answer my questions," he said, sternly. "First of all, I want to know why the hell you decided to drop me as your client without even consulting me."

"It was a decision that was made," Morgan answered. "It, or should I say you, were interfering with my work. I wasn't being objective. It was getting too personal."

"But you didn't even ask me," he said. "You just did it. I wouldn't be so upset about it if I were the only person your decision affected. But this also involved Stephanie and if your decision would have messed up any chance I had to get custody of her, you would have had more trouble than you could ever imagine."

"I couldn't continue being your lawyer," she explained. "I had to get your case reassigned. I tried to talk to you about it a few times and you were dead set against it. I had to do what I thought was best."

"Don't you think that decision should have been mine to make?" Craig questioned.

"I did what I had to do," Morgan told him.

"So why did you run out on me and Stephanie the other night?" Craig asked. "Was that something you had to do too?"

"I had to leave," Morgan answered. "It was important."

"I don't understand why you couldn't wait for us to come with you," Craig said. "Stephanie was upset because she thought she had done something wrong and I didn't have any idea what to say to her. I couldn't even console my own child. How do you think that made me feel?"

"I had things to do," Morgan replied. "I had to leave."

"No, I think you had to get away from me," Craig replied. "I don't know why I expect anything different from you. You have been trying to push me away ever since you were attacked. I am not the only one who has noticed a change in you."

"You have been talking to people about me?" Morgan asked, angrily. "What gives you the right?"

"I went to your office and Jaime told me that you had left for the day," Craig explained. "I had to get some answers somewhere but Jaime didn't know anything either. She said that you don't confide in her like you had been and that you have changed since the attack."

"Well, you and everyone else can think what you want," Morgan replied. "I don't have to answer to anyone and I don't have to tell anyone anything that I don't think is their business."

"I think you changing lawyers on me was my business and you should have told me what was going on," Craig stated.

"We are not getting anywhere here so let's just drop it," Morgan said. "Is there anything else you want to interrogate me about?"

Craig ran a hand through his hair. "I want to know what happened to us," he replied, frustrated. "I don't understand how things could be so good one minute and then bad the next."

"Things changed," Morgan stated. "It was never going to happen for us. It just wasn't right."

"You never gave it a chance," Craig replied, harshly. "You didn't want it to work from the beginning."

"That's not true," Morgan yelled at him. "I tried. I really tried."

"You didn't try hard enough," Craig yelled back, interrupting her.

Morgan wanted to cry. She wanted this whole thing to be over with. She wanted Craig to hold her and tell her things were going to be all right. She didn't know how long she could continue to keep the truth from him and play this game that she was forced to play. "So who's the new guy?" Craig asked, not wanting to hear the answer.

"What new guy?" Morgan questioned. "What are you talking about now?"

"Don't play stupid with me," Craig said. "I saw you, Morgan. I saw you kissing him in the hallway of your apartment building the other night."

"Are you spying on me?" she asked.

"I stopped by to talk to you about the change in my case," Craig informed her. "I didn't know what else to do. You didn't answer my calls and you were not at the office when I stopped by. What did you want me to do?"

"I want you to leave me alone," Morgan replied, angrily. "That is all I have asked of you lately but for some reason, you just don't listen."

"I don't think that is what you want," Craig said. "I have never believed that is what you want."

"Well, believe it," Morgan stated, her heart breaking. "I don't want anything to do with you."

Craig stood there silently. He didn't know what to say. Her statement had cut him deep and he wasn't sure he would recover from it. "I can't believe you just said that to me," he finally said. "We were getting close. We almost made love a few weeks ago. You can't tell me that means nothing to you. How can you dismiss all of that? You need to tell me because I need to move past this. I need to get over you."

Those were the words Morgan was afraid she was going to hear. She hoped she would get through this whole mess without ruining her relationship with Craig but it had gone too far. What was she going to do? How could she fix this? "I never said those things didn't mean anything to me," she told him, trying not to cry. "I never said I was over you."

"Then why are you pushing me away?" Craig asked.

"I am scared," she answered. "I have been through so much and I couldn't bear to lose someone else I care about."

Morgan felt bad about what she had just told Craig. She couldn't tell him the whole truth about why she was pushing him away. She was so afraid the man who attacked her would return and she had to prevent that. "You'll never lose me," Craig said, trying to reassure her.

"How can you promise me that?" she questioned. "Edward promised me that and now he's dead."

Craig didn't know what to say. "I couldn't bear to go through that again. For your own sake, you have to leave me alone," she pleaded.

"I can't leave you alone," Craig replied. "I want to be with you."

"But I can't be with you," Morgan told him.

"How can I change your mind about this?" he asked. "I can't stay away from you."

"You have to!" Morgan argued.

"I can't," Craig repeated.

"Why are you being so stubborn about this?" Morgan questioned, angrily.

"Because I love you!" Craig blurted out.

Morgan was taken back. "You can't," she exclaimed.

"Yes, Morgan, I do," Craig said, looking directly into her eyes. "I love you."

"No!" Morgan screamed, putting her hands over her ears and shaking her head.

Craig grabbed her arms. "Look at me," he ordered. "I love you. I can't live without you. I don't want to spend another minute without you beside me. Plus, you're great with Stephanie. I know she adores you just like I do. Please, Morgan. Give me a chance."

Morgan saw the tears in Craig's eyes, which made her cry. "I can't do this, Craig," she whispered. "It wouldn't be fair to you. I can't give you everything you need."

"Let me decide what I need," Craig said. "If I have you, that's all I need."

"I can't make you completely happy," Morgan cried. "I can't give you any children. I know you want more."

"I know," he replied, thinking back to the morning after Edward died.

"That miscarriage did a number on me," Morgan whispered, shaking. "Edward didn't even know."

Craig held Morgan as she cried. "I so much want a baby, Craig," she said. "I'd give anything to have one."

"I love you and with that, we can do anything," Craig whispered, so desperate to give her the chance. "Let me love you."

Morgan pulled away from Craig. He honestly cared about her, which made her want him even more. She would probably regret what she was about to do but she needed this. They both did. "My bedroom is upstairs," she told him. "First door on the right."

Craig picked Morgan up and carried her up the stairs to her room. Morgan gently placed her lips on his and initiated the first kiss. Craig began kissing her lips, cheeks, and neck. Morgan surrendered herself to him mind, body, and soul. She didn't want to think about this big step they were taking. She just wanted it to happen with Craig. "I want you, Morgan," Craig whispered. "Let me make love to you."

Morgan's heart skipped a beat. She really wanted this to happen but for some reason, she hesitated. "What's wrong?" Craig asked.

"I am just a little scared," she answered. Not caring anymore about anything but being with Craig, Morgan placed her lips on his for another kiss. The kisses grew more intense with each one. "Are you sure about this?" Craig questioned.

"As sure as I've ever been about anything before in my life," Morgan answered. "Make love to me, Craig."

"With pleasure," he responded, with a smile. "I promise I won't hurt you. Do you trust me?"

"Completely," she whispered.

Morgan pulled Craig on top of her and held him close. He kissed her neck and face. He nibbled on her ear lobe, which made her moan softly. "You like that, huh?" Craig questioned, intrigued. "What else do you like?"

"Do whatever you want," Morgan answered. "I'll let you know if I don't like something."

Craig began to slowly undress Morgan and caress every part of her exposed body. Craig gently touched her breast, which caused her to quiver. She caught her breath when he began to nibble on one of her nipples. Craig stopped to look up at Morgan. She wanted to plead with him to continue. "Let me get undressed," he said, teasing her.

He stood up but before he could do anything, Morgan began unbuttoning his shirt. She entwined her fingers into the hair on his chest. "I like what I see so far," Morgan said, playfully. "What else do you have to show me?"

"You first," Craig replied.

Craig grabbed hold of the front of Morgan's jeans and unbuttoned them. As her jeans fell to the floor, he stared at her in awe. She took his breath away. "You are absolutely beautiful," he said, as he relished this sight.

Morgan stood on her tiptoes and kissed Craig slowly. "Your turn," she said, already unzipping his jeans.

"Be my guest," Craig replied.

As the jeans fell to the floor, Morgan caught her breath. "Oh my!" she laughed. "You are ready, aren't you?"

"I hope you're not making fun of me," Craig joked. "I'll just have to get dressed and leave."

"You better not," Morgan replied.

Craig laughed as he pushed Morgan to the bed. He explored every part of her body, making it his own. Morgan moaned softly every time he touched her. "I can't take it anymore!" she exclaimed.

"Would you like me to stop?" Craig asked.

"No!" Morgan answered.

Craig laughed. He couldn't remember ever having this much fun. Morgan took advantage of Craig's pause. She began to caress him, which sent sensations through his whole body. The moment seemed to turn serious when Craig looked into Morgan's eyes. "I love you," he said. "I needed to tell you that."

The tears welled up in Morgan's eyes as Craig began to kiss her passionately. The moment of tenderness turned into pure need. The passion overtook them. Craig entered her slowly, making sure not to hurt her. She shuddered at the pure pleasure of it. "I'm not hurting you, am I?" Craig asked, wiping the tears from her eyes.

"No," she whispered, as she squeezed him.

Craig moaned, never feeling this much pleasure before. They rolled over until Morgan was on top of him. She leaned over him and pinned his arms down. "Now, Officer Masterson," she teased. "What can I do to please you?"

Craig found this side of Morgan erotic. "Anything you want," he replied.

She began kissing Craig's lips, face, and neck. She sat up on top of him and rocked back and forth across him. As she squeezed him once more, he grabbed hold of her hips to help her move. Craig was on the edge of pure fulfillment with Morgan very close behind him. He began to say her name over and over again, which pushed them both over the edge. Morgan collapsed on top of him.

Craig held her tightly. She felt so safe and secure in his arms. She moved off him and cuddled up beside him. Craig ran a finger up and down her cheek. "You are wonderful," he told her. "You make me feel like a new man. I think you've taken me somewhere I've never been before."

Morgan studied Craig's face. "You mean to tell me you never felt this way with Valerie?" she questioned.

"Who?" Craig asked with a smile.

Morgan gave him a shove. "Your wife?" Morgan reminded him. "Remember her?"

"I really don't want to think about her at this particular moment," Craig laughed. "Actually, just to let you know, the papers were filed a few days ago and now she is my ex-wife. Valerie and I had decent sex. She was very demanding and manipulative. She was never aggressive like you are."

It was Morgan's turn to laugh. "Does that bother you?" she asked.

"Absolutely not," he answered. "It really turned me on."

"I'm glad you enjoyed yourself," she replied.

"What about you and Edward?" Craig asked.

"Edward and I had really good sex," she answered. "But sometimes it was very rough. Don't get me wrong. It was never rape. He just found it a good way to relieve stress. That was one thing I didn't like about him. He always was in control and I had no problem with that. I never got to be aggressive though. It was kind of fun."

"I'm glad you had fun," he said.

"Well, now that we are lovers," Morgan stated. "I want to know about all the women you have been with."

"Oh, there have been so many. Where do I start?" he teased her.

"You jerk!" she exclaimed, adding another shove.

Craig laughed at her. "I'm teasing you," he said. "Actually, contrary to what you might believe, I haven't been with very many women."

Morgan thought he was teasing her again but he seemed to be serious. "I dated a friend of my sister's," he explained. "There was another girl in college and then Val. Other than that, there's you."

Morgan gave him an unbelievable look. "It's true," Craig said. "I know a lot of guys who take sex casually. I'm not that type of guy. I think when you make love with someone; it should be with someone you care about, someone you love. I care very deeply for you."

Morgan remained silent. She laid there soaking it all in. "So what about you, Lady Lawyer?" he asked. "How many men have you been with?"

"Three now," she answered. "I was engaged to my high school sweetheart. We decided to go our separate ways though when we entered college. Then there was Edward. Then I was with this guy named Craig Masterson. Do you know him?"

Morgan began to laugh as Craig pulled her close and whispered, "How would you like to be with Craig Masterson again?"

"Oh, Officer," she said. "I surrender."

They made love again. This time, they found something new that aroused them even more than before and sent them to new heights.

Morgan laid in the bed next to Craig and watched him sleep. She was so happy even though she knew her problems were going to haunt her after Craig left. She wasn't going to let them bother her now though. She was right where she wanted to be. Everything felt so right, except for the psychopath that was stalking her. She couldn't for the life of her figure out what she had done to make this guy come after her. She didn't want to stay away from Craig and she didn't want to sacrifice a relationship with him. She had to find a way to stop this madman before he ruined any chance she had with Craig.

Morgan snuggled up next to Craig. She memorized everything about him from the way he slept to his scent. She still couldn't believe what had happened between them. She couldn't believe it happened even after the way she had treated him. She just hoped that when the truth about the attack came out, he would forgive her for lying to him.

Morgan decided to let Craig sleep while she took a quick shower. After a few minutes, she exited the shower and heard a knock on the door. "I woke up and you were gone," he said. "I thought I might have dreamed the whole thing."

Craig looked Morgan over from head to toe. He couldn't help but notice the small scar on her lower abdomen. "That's my little reminder of the worst day of my life," she told him.

Craig pulled her into his arms to comfort her. "I'm sorry," he whispered. "I'd do anything I could to take away that night. I don't want to see you unhappy."

Morgan began kissing Craig. She was touched by the way he genuinely cared for her. Craig lifted Morgan into his arms and took her back to bed.

Morgan and Craig laid there in each other's arms. "I don't want this to end," Craig said. "I wish I could stay here forever."

"Me too," Morgan replied, as she ran her hand through the hair on his chest.

"I think I better go," Craig said. "I need to call Stephanie before she goes to sleep. I can't believe what time it is."

"Well, time flies when you're having fun," she told him.

"Yes, it does," he agreed, as he rolled onto his side. "I meant what I said earlier about loving you. I didn't just say it to get you in bed. I do love you, Morgan. I understand if you can't say it in return. I will wait and one day, you will say it."

As they got dressed, Morgan thought about what he said. She wanted so badly to tell him she loved him too but she couldn't get the words to come out of her mouth. She knew she was just scared of getting hurt again. She had to get past that so she could tell Craig how she really felt.

The couple walked to the front door. Craig leaned in to kiss Morgan and she stopped him. "I don't want you to leave here without me telling you something," she said. "I do love you, Craig."

He smiled at her. "I know you do," he told her. "It is nice to hear though."

Craig kissed Morgan. "I will talk to you soon," he said, as he exited the townhouse.

Craig entered John's townhouse and found the place a mess. "John!" he yelled, as he set his keys on the table. "John?"

Craig entered the kitchen and flipped on the light. There was John lying on the floor. Craig reached for the phone and directed the dispatcher to his location. "I need an ambulance here as soon as possible," he ordered.

"John," Craig said, as he felt for a pulse. "John, come on, Buddy! Wake up!"

He examined John and saw bruises on his face and hands. He also noticed that he was having trouble breathing. "I think you have a few broken ribs," Craig told him, when he noticed John's eyes had opened. "I think you may have a punctured lung."

"Note," John said, breathlessly.

"Don't talk," Craig instructed, as John repeated himself.

Craig looked down and noticed an envelope next to John's body. Craig grabbed a plastic bag and slipped the envelope into it. "Read it," John whispered.

About that time, the paramedics rushed in with a stretcher. "What happened, Craig?" Officer Adams asked.

"I don't know," Craig answered. "This is the way I found him when I got home."

The paramedics examined John and carefully set him on the stretcher. "Why don't you go to the hospital and keep us updated?" the officer suggested. "We'll look around here and question the neighbors to see if they saw anything."

Craig followed the ambulance to the hospital and waited for the doctor to tell him John's condition. "He has a punctured lung and two broken ribs," the doctor told him. "He should be fine though. I need to get back in there."

After the doctor left, Craig took the plastic bag containing the note out of his pocket. After putting on his glove, he carefully took it out of the plastic bag and opened the envelope.

"Craig and Morgan, you have gone too far," he read. "There is no turning back now. What's done is done."

"Thank God!" Morgan exclaimed, as she entered the room. "When the officer told me that a police officer had been hurt, I was praying it wasn't you."

Craig stood up and glared at her. "You lied to me," he said.

"What are you talking about?" she questioned.

"This is what I am talking about," he answered, showing her the note. "I found this next to John's body."

Morgan read the note and began to shake. "Tell me what happened to you when you were attacked," Craig ordered.

"I told you the other night," Morgan replied.

"But you didn't tell me everything," Craig stated. "Now tell me what you left out."

Morgan took a deep breath. "The man threatened to come back and hurt me again if I didn't leave you alone," she told him.

"Why did you leave that part out?" Craig questioned.

"Because I was trying to protect myself," she answered. "I knew if I told you, you would want to protect me. I didn't want anything to happen to you."

"Is that why you have been treating me so badly?" he asked.

"Yes," she answered. "I had to get you to leave me alone. I was afraid of what he might do."

"Now you know what he is doing," Craig explained. "He is watching you. He knows that I was at your place today and how long I was there. My guess is he put two and two together and now he is out to get us."

"What does he want from us?" Morgan asked. "I didn't do anything."

"Someone wants us apart," Craig replied. "Apparently, we don't have to do anything anymore."

"We have to stay away from each other," Morgan said, raising her voice. "I don't want anyone else getting hurt."

"I don't know how we can stay apart after what happened today," Craig replied. "Don't tell me that didn't mean anything to you. Don't tell me you don't love me."

"I have to protect myself and the people I care about," Morgan told him. "I can't see you anymore."

"So we are over?" he questioned. "How can you throw what we have away?"

"I don't have a choice," Morgan answered. "What if this guy comes after Stephanie next? I would never forgive myself."

"The only thing to do is find this guy and put a stop to all this," Craig said. "As soon as I do that, everyone will be safe."

"This is what I was afraid of," she replied. "Don't you realize that you are in more danger than the rest of us? You are an easy target because you are a cop."

"I can take care of myself," he stated.

"The only solution right now is for us not to see each other," Morgan told him.

"Don't I get a say in this?" Craig questioned.

"No," she answered. "I can't take the chance of someone else getting hurt or worse. We have to stay away from each other. We have no choice."

"If you decide to throw this away now," Craig replied. "I can't guarantee that we can work this out later. It may be too late."

Morgan wanted to cry. She couldn't believe Craig had said that to her. She didn't have a choice. "Well, I guess this is goodbye then," she said, as she walked out the door.

Chapter 10

"Hey!" Craig said, as he entered John's hospital room. "How are you feeling?"

"I'm doing better," John answered.

"You really scared me last night," Craig replied. "What happened?"

"It happened so fast," John told him. "I was blindsided. I came into the house and these two men jumped me. I fought back but it was just too much. Before I knew it, I was on the floor and one of them starting kicking me."

"Did you get a good look at them?" Craig asked.

"No," John answered. "It was too dark."

"I am sure the guy who attacked you was the same one who attacked Morgan," Craig told him. "Morgan gave me some more information about her attack when I questioned her last night."

"Did you go by her townhouse?" John asked, smiling.

"You sent me over there knowing fully well she lived there," Craig replied.

"I was just trying to get you two back together," John stated. "So what happened?"

"Well, when I got there, we fought," he explained. "Then we ended up in bed."

"So you kissed and made up?" John asked, smiling.

"Not exactly," Craig answered. "After what happened to you, we got into another fight and she ended it."

"It was just a fight," John said. "Couples have them all the time. You can make this right."

"No, I'm afraid it is over for good," Craig replied. "There is no fixing this."

A nurse entered the room and began checking John's vital signs. "I better let you rest," Craig said. "I just wanted to see how you were."

"Before you go, I want to thank you for letting my kids know what happened," John stated. "They called earlier. They can't get home right now because of the weather but they said that they would be home as soon as they could."

"Not a problem," Craig replied. "I'll see you later."

As soon as Craig exited the building, his cell phone rang. "Hello!" he said.

"Hey Craig! It's Valerie," she replied. "I was wondering if today would be a good day for us to talk to Stephanie."

"Sure," he told her. "What time do you want to do this?"

"Right now, if that is okay with you," she answered.

"I'm on my way," he said.

When Craig arrived at Valerie's house, a smiling four-year-old greeted him at the door. "Hi Daddy!" she said, as Craig gathered her into his arms.

"Hello Miss Stephanie!" he replied.

"Come over here and sit down," Valerie said to them. "Stephanie, your dad and I want to talk to you."

Craig and Stephanie situated themselves on the couch. "Stephanie, I am going to try to explain this to you so you will understand," Valerie explained. "If you have any questions, just ask."

"Ok, Mommy," she replied.

Valerie looked at Craig. "Remember when I told you that your mommy and I were not going to be living together anymore?" Craig asked Stephanie. "I also explained to you what divorce was."

"Yes," Stephanie replied.

"Well, your mom and I are not married anymore," Craig told her.

"Does that mean you are going to be with Morgan?" Stephanie asked. "Is Mommy going to be with Nick?"

"I am not going to be with Morgan," Craig answered. "Things just didn't work out."

"I'm not going to be with Nick either," Valerie replied.

Craig looked at Valerie, not sure he had heard her correctly.

"What is going to happen to me?" Stephanie asked.

"Well, we are going to share you," Valerie answered. "We still need to work that out."

"Do you understand everything that we have told you?" Craig asked the little girl.

"Yes," Stephanie answered.

"Stephanie, why don't you get your things ready to go to Grandma and Grandpa's house?" Valerie suggested. "I need to talk to your dad."

After Stephanie left the room, Valerie said, "I am sure you have some questions."

"You aren't going to be with Nick?" he questioned.

"I have been thinking about some of the things you said to me the other day," she answered. "I realized that Stephanie is the most important thing in my life and I can't be with a man who doesn't love her as much as I do. If I move, I won't be able to see her as much and I don't know if I can live with that. I feel like I have missed a lot already. With that said, there is something I need to ask you."

"Ok," Craig replied.

"I don't think Stephanie should be spending so much time with our parents," Valerie stated. "She is our daughter and we should be raising her. Can you talk to your parents and explain this to them?"

"I agree with you," Craig said. "My parents will understand."

"I will talk to my parents too," she replied. "I also decided that I am going back to school. I need to decide what I am going to do and stick to it. I have a daughter to support and I just want to be happy."

"So I guess our parents can watch Stephanie while you are in class and I'm working," Craig stated.

"That is what I am hoping for," Valerie said. "I haven't told Nick yet I'm not going with him. I don't know how he will react."

"I hope things go well," Craig replied. "If he gives you any problems, let me know."

"I will," she said. "I am getting ready to fix Stephanie some lunch before she leaves. Would you like to join us?"

139

Craig accepted Valerie's invitation and accompanied her to the kitchen. "I think I might have a buyer for the house," she told him.

"You mentioned that the other day," Craig replied.

"They came by this morning to look at it," Valerie stated. "They love it. If things go well, everything could be finalized in a few weeks."

Stephanie entered the room. "I have all my things ready to take to Grandma and Grandpa's house," she announced.

"You are just in time," Valerie said. "Your lunch is ready and your daddy is going to stay and eat with us."

The three sat down at the table and had a meal together like a real family. Craig couldn't believe the change in Valerie. It felt like she had finally grown up and stopped playing games with him. She was almost the same person Craig had fallen in love with.

After lunch, Craig's mother came by to pick up Stephanie. After a lengthy talk about the new arrangements for Stephanie, the young girl and her grandmother left. "That went well," Craig announced as he entered the kitchen.

"What did your mom say?" Valerie questioned.

"She agreed with us," he answered. "We do need to raise our own child. She said that they would baby-sit whenever we need them to."

"I hope my conversation with my parents goes just as well," Valerie replied.

"Are you going to talk to Nick too?" Craig asked.

"Yeah," she answered. "He is coming over later. I hope that goes well too."

"Remember, any problems with Nick, let me know," Craig stated. "I better get going. I need to stop by the station."

"Thank you!" Valerie said, as she gave Craig a hug.

As Craig drove to the station, he thought about the events of the last few days. He couldn't believe the change in Valerie. It was like she was a totally different person and that scared him. It seemed that as soon as the divorce was final, she returned to the person she was when their relationship started. Was he the reason for her attitude over the last few years? Was being married to him a horrible experience for her? He hoped that wasn't true. He would hate to be the reason for her unhappiness. That was the last thing he wanted.

His thoughts soon turned to Morgan. He was so mad at her for not telling him the truth about the night she was attacked. But for some reason, it just didn't seem to matter. He still loved her and he missed not seeing her. He should have never told her that there might not be a chance for them after the case was solved. He wished he could take it back but it was too late. He couldn't believe that things were this bad between them. He understood her concern for her family and friends. He understood that she didn't want anyone else to get hurt. He just couldn't let go of her though. Images of their lovemaking took over his thoughts. He knew he would never be with her like that again. He also knew that Morgan was the woman for him and he had to find a way to fix this.

Craig arrived at the police station and immediately located Officer Adams. "I need to talk to you," Craig requested.

"Sure," Bill replied, motioning Craig into his office.

"Do you have any new information about John's attack?" Craig asked, as he sat down.

"I don't have much to go on," Bill explained, as he handed a file to Craig. "The note is the only piece of evidence I have."

"Let me see it again," Craig said, pulling the note from the file. "This could have come from any magazine."

"Yeah," Bill agreed. "And there are a million magazines out there with a million subscribers. That is a lot of suspects."

"Anything else?" Craig asked.

"No," Bill answered. "Just plain white paper and glue. Two common everyday things people have in their homes."

"That's a dead end," Craig replied. "Neither Morgan or John saw the men who attacked them. Did any of John's neighbors see anything?"

"No," Bill answered. "That was a dead end too."

Craig ran a hand through his hair. "How are we going to solve this if we have no hard evidence and no witnesses or suspects?" he asked.

"We are just going to have to see if they make a mistake next time," Bill said.

"I hope there is no next time," Craig replied.

Bill picked up the note. "Do you want to tell me about this?" he questioned. "Your name is mentioned here as well as Morgan's."

"Morgan and I were involved for a short time," Craig answered. "Apparently, someone wasn't happy about that and decided to threaten us."

"Who would want to do that?" Bill asked. "Do you know of anyone who would want you and Morgan apart?"

"I can't think of anyone," Craig answered. "We need to ask Morgan that question."

"Bill," another officer said, interrupting their conversation. "There is a situation downtown at a law firm. There have been shots fired."

Bill jumped out of his chair. "Craig, you need to come with me. We are a bit shorthanded with John gone."

A few moments before, Morgan was coming out of her office and heading home. She didn't like working on a Sunday but with the Christmas holiday just around the corner, she wanted to get some work caught up. As she locked her office and headed down the hallway, she had a strange feeling she was being watched. She dismissed it as paranoia and continued on her way to the elevator. All of the sudden, the power went out. She leaned against the wall and closed her eyes. She felt like she could hyperventilate. As the emergency lights came on, she felt a hand wrap around her neck. "I warned you I would be back," he threatened.

"Please don't hurt me," she pleaded, as his grip became tighter.

"You are not going to talk," he ordered. "You just need to listen. I know what you and Craig did yesterday. I was quite disappointed that I didn't get to see you naked because that would have been amazing."

Morgan began to tremble as the man caressed her face and neck. "You and Craig have gone too far," he said, as he came back to reality. "I ordered you to stay away from him and you couldn't do that one little thing. It is too late now. Everyone you love is in danger and there is no way you can stop it. So go on ahead and see Craig but I promise you that I won't stop

142

until you feel the same pain I feel. I also promise that each incident will be worse than the one before."

Tears ran down Morgan's face. "What did I ever do to you?" she whispered.

"I told you not to talk," the man threatened again, as he looked her up and down. "Let's just say that I am jealous because another man was with my girl."

"Hold it right there," a voice said from behind them.

Morgan recognized the man as James Nixon, the security guard from downstairs. "I am going to hate to have to do this," the man told Morgan.

In one quick motion, the man let go of Morgan, grabbed his gun from its holster, and shot the guard. "I will see you again soon, my love," he whispered in Morgan's ear.

As soon as the stalker was gone, Morgan hurried over to James. "I am so sorry," she said. "Where are you shot at?"

"My shoulder," he answered.

Morgan pulled her scarf away from her coat and used it to apply pressure to James's wound. "I have a security guard down," she announced as loud as she could in his police radio. "We are on the sixth floor."

"Help is on the way," a voice said over the radio.

"Hang in there, James," Morgan whispered. "They will be here soon."

After a couple more minutes had passed, Bill and Craig entered the floor. The paramedics hurried past them to tend to James. As the lights came back on, Craig noticed Morgan standing down the hall. He hurried over to her and wrapped his arms around her. "Thank God you are here," she whispered, as she began to cry.

"What did he do to you?" Craig asked, as he pulled away to examine her.

Craig noticed the faint bruises on her neck. "He wrapped his hand around my neck and squeezed," she explained.

"What did he say to you?" Craig questioned.

"He told me that he knows what we did yesterday," Morgan answered. "You were right. He has been watching me. I am so scared that he is not going to stop until he rapes me. He keeps making innuendoes about it."

143

Craig pulled Morgan closer as she cried. "I am not going to let anything happen to you," Craig said.

"He threatened to hurt the people I love," she explained. "Can you protect them too?"

"I will do what I can," Craig stated.

"We are going to have to get a statement from her," Bill told Craig.

"I'll take care of it," Craig replied.

Craig led Morgan over to a couple of chairs near the elevator. "Tell me what happened," he instructed.

Morgan told him everything from what happened to what the man said. "I did get a good look at his face," she said.

"You will have to come down to the station and talk to our sketch artist," Craig stated.

"I can do that," she replied.

"First, I want to take you to the hospital and make sure that you are alright," he told her.

The couple walked to the lobby and out to the parking lot to Morgan's car. As Craig drove, Morgan stared out the window. She couldn't understand what was going on. She didn't even know this man and he was threatening everyone she loved. She didn't know what she was going to do. "What are you thinking about?" Craig asked.

"I am just confused about all of this," she answered. "I don't even know this guy. Why is he doing this to me?"

They arrived at the hospital and a nurse escorted them to an examining room. "The doctor will be with you shortly," she said.

Morgan sat on the bed in silence. Craig walked over and stood in front of her. "Is there anything I can do for you?" he asked.

"Hold me," she whispered.

Craig wrapped his arms around her. "I am so sorry this is happening," she whispered, as she cried. "It is all my fault that John was attacked."

"It is not your fault," he replied. "There is a psycho running around out there."

"And he is obsessed with me," she replied. "What am I going to do?"

144

The doctor entered the room. He instructed Craig to leave while he examined Morgan.

After the examination, Craig and Morgan headed to the police station so she could talk to the sketch artist. Morgan told the woman every detail about the man's face. It was like it was seared into her memory. She couldn't close her eyes without seeing his face. When the artist was finished, Morgan stared at the drawing. She started to cry.

"Are you going to be ok?" Craig asked, as he approached her.

"I can't take this anymore," Morgan answered. "This is so frustrating."

"Now that we know what he looks like, we will catch him," Craig reassured her.

"Can you just take me home?" she asked. "I just want to go home."

"I don't think you should be alone tonight," Craig said, as he drove Morgan home.

"I just want to be alone," she replied, staring out the window.

"I don't think that is a good idea," he told her, as he parked her car in front of her townhouse. "I would feel a lot better if I stayed here with you."

"He told me that he would hurt everyone I love," she stated. "Each time would be worse than the last. I have to protect them. I think you should go home."

"I can't do that," he said. "I want to protect you."

"Nothing has changed," she informed him. "I still don't want to see you. Please leave me alone."

Craig exited the car, feeling rejected once again by the woman he loved. Morgan hurried up the stairs of the townhouse and disappeared inside.

As Craig walked across the street, he still couldn't believe that Morgan didn't want anything to do with him. She acted like she did earlier but he guessed it was just because it was convenient for her. She needed someone to comfort her and a shoulder to cry on and apparently, he was the man for the job. All he could hope for was to find this crazy man and win Morgan back before it was too late. But he didn't know if he could recover from this recent rejection. It was getting harder and harder for him to keep being there for her only when she needed him.

Craig entered the townhouse and sat down in the recliner. He didn't sit there very long. He was feeling restless and couldn't get his mind to stop racing. He went into the kitchen to make a bite to eat. As he ate a ham sandwich, he thought about Morgan and their situation. He knew that Morgan felt like she was between a rock and a hard place. He knew she just wanted to protect everyone but who was going to protect her? In her mind, she figured that if she stayed away from Craig, the damage would be minimal. She was sacrificing herself for the people she loved. It was a noble thought but not a safe one.

Craig's thoughts were interrupted by a knock at the door. "Maybe Morgan changed her mind," Craig said, as he opened the door.

"You told me that if I needed anything, I should let you know," Valerie told him, as tears ran down her face.

"What happened?" Craig asked, as he motioned her inside.

"I told Nick," she answered. "He wasn't happy about it. He started screaming at me and he really scared me, Craig."

"Where is he now?" he questioned.

"I don't know," she answered. "I am sorry to drag you into this. I didn't know where else to go."

"Tell me what happened," Craig said, as he directed Valerie to sit down.

"He just started yelling at me," she explained. "He wanted to know what changed my mind about going with him and why I didn't want to go. I am so glad Stephanie wasn't there because he starting blaming the whole thing on her. He said that she was the reason I didn't want to leave after I told him that I would go."

Craig went to the phone and called his parents. "I know it is late but I wanted to check on Stephanie," he told his mother. "We have a situation here and I need to make sure that she is safe and stays that way."

Craig explained to his mother the details about what was going on. She promised that she would let him know if anything out of the ordinary happened and that she would keep her eye on Stephanie.

"I hate to ask this, Craig," Valerie said, when Craig hung up the phone. "Can I stay here tonight? I am really scared. I don't want to go back to the house. If he shows up again, I don't know what I will do."

"Yes, you can stay here," Craig replied, as Valerie cried.

"Thank you," she said, wiping her eyes. "I think you thought I was someone else when you opened the door. Were you expecting someone?"

"No," he answered. "Just hoping, I guess."

"Were you expecting Morgan?" she asked. "I thought you two broke up."

"We aren't together anymore," he replied. "She had a scare this evening too. I offered to stay with her but she didn't want me to."

"What happened with her?" Valerie questioned.

"She was attacked at her office building this evening," Craig explained. "The guy shot a security guard."

"Are they alright?" Valerie asked.

"Yes," he answered. "The guard was shot in the shoulder. Morgan has a few bruises but she should be fine."

"That had to be scary for you," she stated. "It sounds similar to the incident when Morgan's husband was killed."

Craig stared at Valerie. "It was in all the papers," she said. "Don't think I didn't know about the night you spent with her."

"Nothing happened, Val," Craig told her.

"I know," she replied. "I did notice a change in you after that night though. I think that was about the time your feelings for me changed."

"How did we get on this subject?" Craig asked.

"I guess I was just trying to think about something else so I wouldn't be so scared," Valerie answered. "I guess we both have problems, don't we?"

Craig thought about Morgan and how rejected she made him feel. "Let me show you where you will be staying," Craig said.

Valerie followed Craig down the hall as he showed her the bedroom and the bathroom. "Can I borrow one of your shirts to sleep in?" she asked.

Craig went into his room and grabbed a t-shirt for her. "Thank you," she said, as she took the shirt. "I do appreciate you letting me stay here."

"I think it is sort of funny that you and I are getting along," Valerie continued, as she walked to the door. "It is almost like Morgan and I have switched places. Good night!"

As Craig climbed into bed, he thought about what Valerie had said. It was really weird that they were getting along so well and Morgan didn't want anything to do with him. Everything seemed so backwards. Ever since Edward died, all he wanted was to be with Morgan and now that chance was gone. He tried so hard to keep that from Valerie while they were married but somehow she knew what was going on. Now even after everything that happened, Valerie had turned into an ally. What kind of strange world had he entered and when were things going to be normal again?

Craig awoke to the sound of banging on his front door. Craig climbed out of bed and staggered half asleep to the door. "Valerie, I know you're in there," Nick yelled angrily. "I want to talk to you."

"If you don't quit yelling," Craig said, as he opened the door, "someone is going to call the police and have you arrested for disturbing the peace."

"I want to talk to Valerie," Nick demanded. "Where is she?"

"Nick, you need to calm down," Valerie said, as she walked up behind Craig. "You're scaring me."

"Is he the reason you're not going with me?" Nick asked. "Are you shacking up with him again?"

"No," Valerie answered. "I told you why I can't go with you."

"Because of the little brat," Nick replied. "You should just get rid of her."

Craig grabbed Nick and pulled him into the townhouse. "What did you say?" Craig asked, as he slammed Nick against the wall.

"Craig, please don't," Valerie pleaded. "He is drunk and doesn't know what he is saying."

"This isn't the first time he has threatened Stephanie," Craig reminded her. "I will not put up with that."

Craig heard the police sirens off in the distance. He opened the door and dragged Nick outside. "I suggest you go spend the night in jail and sober up," Craig told him, as the police cars stopped in front of the townhouse.

"We got a call about a domestic disturbance," the officer said. "Is everything ok, Craig?"

"I need you to take him in and let him spend the night in jail," Craig instructed. "It is for his own good. I'll call you in the morning and we'll see how he is doing."

After the police left, Craig returned to the townhouse and found a very terrified Valerie. "I'm so sorry about that," she said. "I should have never come here. I shouldn't have gotten you involved in this."

"I told you if you needed anything, you should let me know," he replied, as he pulled her into his arms.

Craig held Valerie as she cried. "I am so sorry," she repeated.

He had never seen Valerie this shaken up before. Usually she was a rock and didn't let anything bother her. Sure she could be a little melodramatic at times but it usually took a lot to get her that upset. "It will be ok," he told her. "He's gone now."

"I know," she replied. "I just don't know what he is going to do next."

"You are safe now," he said.

"Craig, can I stay in your room with you tonight?" Valerie asked. "I know I shouldn't ask and if you don't want me to, I'll understand."

"You can stay with me," Craig answered.

"I am really sorry about this," Valerie repeated, as she laid down next to Craig.

"It's ok," Craig replied.

"No, it's not," Valerie stated. "I should have never gotten involved with Nick. How could I be so stupid?"

"You didn't know this was going to happen," Craig told her.

"Well, I wish I did," she replied. "Then I wouldn't have to worry about Stephanie's safety. I am scared enough for me but if something happened to her, I don't know what I would do."

"I will keep you both as safe as I can," Craig stated. "I will not let anything happen to either of you."

"You shouldn't have to take care of me anymore," she said. "We are not married and you don't owe me anything."

"But I do care about you," he told her. "Even after everything that has happened, I still care."

Valerie moved closer to Craig. "Thank you for letting me stay in here with you," she said. "I know that you wish I was someone else though."

Craig thought about Morgan and the feelings of rejection flooded over him. It was true that he wished Valerie was Morgan but Morgan had rejected him earlier and he was finding it hard to get past that. "If this is uncomfortable for you, I can go to the other room," Valerie told him.

"No," Craig said. "I want you to stay."

Valerie smiled at him. At that point, Craig wasn't really sure what he was feeling. He knew he should have sent Valerie to the other room but something stopped him from doing that. He wasn't sure if the feelings of rejection played a part in him wanting her to stay. All he knew was he didn't want to be alone. "Don't worry, Craig," Valerie told him. "You are safe with me. I'm not going to try anything."

"It's not you I'm worried about," he replied, as he pulled her closer to him and kissed her.

Chapter 11

Morgan stepped out of her townhouse to retrieve the morning paper. She leaned against the door and took a drink of her coffee. She looked over at John's townhouse and feelings of regret came over her. She wished she hadn't turned Craig away last night. More than anything, she didn't want to hurt him anymore. They had both been through enough.

The door to the townhouse opened, which immediately caught Morgan's attention. She was extremely disappointed when she noticed Craig wasn't alone. "Is that Valerie?" she whispered to herself. "What is she doing there?"

Morgan soon got her answer as she witnessed what looked like a passionate kiss. She couldn't believe her eyes. It was obvious that he was hurt by her rejection and that he turned to Valerie for comfort. But how could he do that to her? He told her that he loved her. Was that all a lie to get her into bed?

Morgan returned to the townhouse and burst into tears. She felt so used. She couldn't believe that Craig had turned out to be someone she couldn't trust. She knew that it was officially over for them. He had reconciled with Valerie.

Morgan had to pull herself together. She had a busy day ahead of her and she couldn't let this interfere with that. She knew that was going to be hard to do but she had to try to forget what she saw.

After getting ready for her busy day, she jumped into her car and headed to work. She couldn't stop thinking about how betrayed and stupid she felt. She thought she had finally found someone who she could love and trust again. Boy, was she wrong. She knew that she would never make that mistake again. She had to get past this and move on with her life.

After arriving at her office, she decided to finish up the paperwork that she didn't get to the night before. She was interrupted by a knock at the door. "Come in!" she called.

"Morgan, I need to talk to you if you have a minute," Mr. Parker said, as he entered the office.

"What can I do for you?" she asked.

"I wanted to make sure that you were all right," he replied. "I heard about what happened last night."

"I am as well as can be expected," she told him.

"I have been wondering what's going on with you," he stated. "I have noticed the bruises."

"I have a stalker," Morgan told him, knowing she couldn't keep it from him. "I have been attacked twice and that is how I got the bruises. The first time he slapped me twice and the second time he wrapped his hand around my throat."

"What are the police doing to catch this man?" Mr. Parker asked.

"They don't have a lot to go on," she answered. "But I did get a good look at him last night and they now have a sketch of him."

"I hope they find him soon," he replied. "I don't want to see anything more happen to you."

Morgan smiled. Even when Mr. Parker was being rough on her, she knew that he had a soft side too. "I hope so too, Sir," she said. "I don't want anything more to happen."

After Mr. Parker had left, Morgan returned to her paperwork. She had to watch her time though because she was meeting Elizabeth for lunch. Elizabeth had called her last night and told her that she needed to speak with her. She didn't give details on what it was about but it sounded urgent. Morgan hoped nothing was wrong. She couldn't bear it if something else had happened to her friend.

After finishing her paperwork, Morgan left the office and made a trip out to the country to the huge mansion where Elizabeth lived. She reflected on all the time she spent there when she was a kid. She remembered all the walks she took through the woods and all the trees she climbed. She used to sit for hours in the trees and daydream about how her life would be. She missed those days. Everything seemed so much easier then.

She arrived at Elizabeth's house and was escorted inside by the butler. "Elizabeth is still in with her physical therapist," he told Morgan. "She will be with you shortly."

Morgan made herself comfortable in the living room. A few minutes later, Elizabeth arrived. "Hello!" she said to Morgan. "I am so glad that you could meet me for lunch."

"I am glad you invited me," Morgan replied, as she followed Elizabeth to the dining room.

After the two women were situated around the table, Morgan asked, "So what did you want to talk to me about? It sounded pretty urgent."

"I had lunch with Craig the other day," she answered. "After talking to him, I decided I should talk to you."

Morgan didn't like where this conversation was headed. "Why were you two talking about me?" she questioned.

"Because we are concerned about you," Elizabeth answered. "He is such a great guy, Morgan. I just don't understand why you won't give him a chance."

"There are too many things going on right now that are keeping us apart," Morgan explained.

"Like what?" Elizabeth asked. "If you two love each other, nothing should stand in the way of that."

"I have a stalker," Morgan told her. "He follows me wherever I go. He is probably watching me now. He has attacked me twice and he also sent Craig's friend, John, to the hospital. He told me to stay away from Craig or he would come back. I am really scared. That is why Craig and I can't be together. I am afraid of what will happen next."

"I don't know what to say," Elizabeth said. "I thought maybe there was a simple fix to this but I don't know what can be done about it. Do the cops have any leads?"

"No," Morgan answered. "They do have a sketch of the man who attacked me."

"Well, that should help," Elizabeth replied. "Maybe you and Craig can be together after this is all over."

"I doubt it," she said. "I think he is back together with his ex-wife."

"What makes you think that?" Elizabeth asked.

"I saw them kissing this morning as she was leaving the townhouse," Morgan explained.

"Let me give you some advice," Elizabeth stated. "You and Craig need to get your stuff together. He saw you kissing Daniel and you saw him kissing Valerie. You need to be together so stop messing around with these other people. Don't you want to be with Craig? I am pretty sure he wants to be with you."

"I do want to be with him," she confirmed. "But I can't risk my life and the lives of the people I love and care about to be with him."

The women sat in silence and ate lunch. "I am sorry to worry you with all my problems," Morgan finally said. "The whole situation is just so frustrating."

"I can understand that," Elizabeth replied. "I just wish there was a solution."

"There isn't," Morgan responded. "I just have to stay away from Craig. I couldn't bear it if something happened to you, Bryan, Jaime or anyone else I care about. I am afraid that this person may go after Craig or Stephanie."

"You don't think he would go after a little girl, do you?" Elizabeth asked.

"Crazy people do crazy things," Morgan answered. "At this point, I don't know what he is going to do. I couldn't even guess what his next move is going to be."

Elizabeth stared at Morgan, not sure what to say. "Let's talk about something else," Morgan continued. "I am so angry and frustrated with the whole mess and it would be nice to talk about something else. How are you doing with therapy?"

"It is going really slow," Elizabeth answered. "I don't think I will ever be out of this chair. My doctor said that there is a chance but it isn't a guarantee. This is so frustrating. I wish I could walk."

Morgan noticed a tear running down Elizabeth's cheek. "Is there anything I can do?" Morgan said, getting up from her chair and going over to her friend.

"No," Elizabeth answered. "I will just have to keep trying and pray for a miracle."

Morgan sat back down, as Elizabeth wiped her tears away. As they finished eating, the woman began to reminisce about their childhood. It felt good to get their minds off their problems and actually laugh. "Before you go," Elizabeth told her. "I want to give you your Christmas gift. It isn't much but I think you will like it. See the present with the big white bow. Could you get it for me?"

Morgan walked over to the tree and delivered the present to Elizabeth. "I brought you something too," Morgan replied.

As Morgan opened her gift, tears welled up in her eyes. "It's our tree house," she said.

"It is a replica of the one my father had built for us," Elizabeth explained. "I know how much it meant to you as a child and since I can't give you the actual tree house, I thought maybe this would do."

"This is the perfect gift!" Morgan exclaimed, as she gave Elizabeth a hug. "Thank you!"

It was Elizabeth's turn to open her present. When she did, she had the same reaction Morgan had when she opened hers. "I know how you love pictures," Morgan stated. "A friend of mine sketched the old photo of us I have. I thought it would make a great gift."

"This is perfect," Elizabeth said. "This means a lot to me."

After the two women hugged and exchanged goodbyes, Morgan drove back to the office. As she did, she thought about what Elizabeth had said. She should be with Craig but she wasn't sure that was an option anymore. She still didn't know what to think about the kiss she witnessed between Craig and Valerie. She also couldn't figure out why Valerie was there that early in the morning. She realized that Valerie and Craig must have spent the night together and just the thought of that made Morgan want to cry. She couldn't understand why Craig would profess his love for her and then end up in bed with his ex-wife. She hated to assume that but what else was she going to believe.

Morgan returned to her office and got back to work. She wanted to get everything done early and leave for the Christmas break. She had decided that she was going to Florida to visit her mom and her mom's friend, Jack. She hadn't seen her mom in quite awhile and she was due for a visit. Plus the break would be an added bonus. She needed to forget everything that was happening and concentrate on having a good holiday.

After her work was complete, Morgan decided to call it a day. She entered the elevator and pushed the button to the lobby. "Wait!" a voice called. "Hold the door!"

Morgan pushed the open door button and she soon wished she hadn't when Abby walked onto the elevator. "Well, isn't this just great?" Abby said. "If I had known it was you, I would have taken the stairs."

Morgan hit the stop button. "What is your problem?" Morgan yelled. "I am so sick and tired of all your comments."

"I am sick and tired of the way you have been treating me," Abby replied, harshly. "You dismiss me like you are so much better than I am. You and Craig made fun of me at the Christmas tree farm the other day. How do you think that makes me feel? I admired you. I looked up to you."

"You know what?" Morgan said, getting in Abby's face. "I don't want you to look up to me or admire me. I am ordering you to quit interfering in my life and to stop following me. I never asked for your opinion on how to live my life so stop acting like my mother."

"You don't have to worry about me anymore, Morgan," Abby replied, hatefully. "I will never bother you again. It was a mistake for me to even try to be nice to you. I am sorry I ever thought that you could be my mentor. I don't need someone like you in my life anyway."

Abby pushed the button to start the elevator. "One day, you will get what you deserve," she said. "I hope I am there to watch it."

The elevator doors opened and Abby was gone. Morgan walked slowly to her car. It was becoming more and more obvious to Morgan that Abby had something to do with the attacks on her and John. She didn't think Abby was the mastermind behind it but she had her hand in it somewhere. Morgan decided to call Officer Adams and tell him to add Abby to the list of suspects.

As Morgan walked to her car, she had the feeling that she was being followed. She picked up the pace but she wasn't fast enough. She felt a hand on her shoulder. "You scared the hell out of me!" she yelled, as she realized who it was. "Why are you sneaking up on me like that after everything that has happened?"

"I'm sorry," Craig said. "I called to you but you didn't hear me. I just wanted to check on you. I was very concerned about you all night."

Morgan found that hard to believe. "I doubt that," she said.

"What is that supposed to mean?" he asked.

"Nothing," she answered, just praying he would leave. "I am fine."

"I wish you would have let me stay last night," he said.

"What do you want from me, Craig?" Morgan asked, as she unlocked her car.

"You know what I want," he answered. "I want us to be together. Why am I explaining this to you again?"

"Because I can't believe a single word you say," Morgan replied, harshly.

"I have never lied to you about anything," he said. "Why are you questioning me now?"

"Because I have come to the realization that people will say and do anything to get what they want," she explained.

"Are you trying to start another fight?" he asked.

"No," Morgan said. "I just want you to leave me alone so no one else gets hurt. Why do I have to keep explaining that to you?"

"Because I don't believe that is what you really want," he replied.

Morgan opened the door. "I need to go," she said. "Please just leave me alone."

As she climbed into the car, Craig grabbed the door so she couldn't close it. "We are going to find a way to be together," he told her. "I can't stand being away from you."

"It isn't going to work," Morgan replied. "Just accept it."

"I will never accept it," Craig responded.

"I am starting to think that maybe you are the one causing all these problems between us," she explained.

"What are you talking about?" he questioned.

"You always seem to be right there when something happens," she answered. "And you are acting so obsessive when it comes to me. Are you trying to scare me so I'll run back to you and let you protect me?"

Craig was taken back. "How could you even suggest that I am the one behind all of this?" he asked. "I love you. I would never hurt you and John."

Morgan couldn't believe she just said that to Craig. She wasn't trying to hurt his feelings but she knew she had. "If that is the way you feel about me," Craig continued, "then maybe we shouldn't see each other. I don't think I can be with someone who doesn't trust me and questions my motives."

Morgan knew she should apologize but before she could get the words out, Craig said, "Just save it, Morgan. I am so sorry for bothering you."

Craig slammed the car door and left. Morgan put her head down on the steering wheel. She couldn't believe what she had said to Craig but she was so tired of this. She hated fighting with him and she was sick of him talking to everyone about her. She didn't want to have to explain to everyone why she wasn't with Craig and she didn't want to hear about how perfect they were together. She wished everyone would just shut up and leave her alone.

As Morgan drove home, she couldn't think of one thing that was going right for her. There was only one thing she could think of that would serve as a temporary solution to her problem. She needed to get away for awhile and there was only one place she could think of to go. She needed to go home for the holidays.

Morgan arrived at the airport and was greeted by her mom's friend, Jack Franks. "Where's Mom?" she asked, as she gave Jack a hug.

"She is getting things ready for you at home," he answered.

"I hope she isn't going to a lot of trouble," Morgan replied.

"You know how she is," he said, as he opened the car door for Morgan.

"So how are things going?" Morgan questioned, as Jack drove towards the beach house.

"Your brother called and told your mom what has been going on with you," Jack answered. "I just wanted you to be prepared."

"I just want to forget about all that for the next few days," Morgan told him. "She doesn't need to worry about me."

"She does and you can't stop it," he said. "She worries a lot about you. She wonders why you aren't married and don't have someone to take care of you."

"That's not in the cards for me," Morgan replied.

"So what exactly is going on?" Jack questioned.

"Will this stay between you and me?" Morgan asked. "I will tell Mom if she asks. I want her to hear it from me."

"I will let you tell her," he answered.

"I met this man," Morgan said.

"There is always a man involved," Jack replied, smiling. "Don't you know that we are nothing but trouble?"

Morgan smiled and continued to tell Jack the story of the last few months of her life. She told him about meeting Craig and starting a relationship with him. She explained the threats and attacks on her life and how she had been ordered to leave Craig alone. "Sounds like you got yourself in one hell of a situation," Jack said. "What do you want to do?"

"I want my family and friends to be safe," Morgan answered.

"So you have elected yourself to be everyone's protector?" he questioned. "You can't keep everyone safe. Bad things are bound to happen."

Morgan sat in silence, feeling hopeless. She was going out of her mind and she didn't know what to do anymore. "Do you want to be with this guy?" Jack asked.

"Yes," she answered. "But I think it is too late for us. We had a fight before I left and I said some things I shouldn't have."

Jack pulled up to the beach house and helped Morgan out of the car. As he took her suitcase, he said, "If it is meant to be, it will work out."

"I appreciate that," Morgan stated, as she gave him another hug.

159

"You're here," Morgan's mother, Linda, exclaimed from the front door of the house.

"Time to face the music," Jack told Morgan, as they walked to the door.

"Jack, take Morgan's suitcase to the back bedroom," Linda instructed. "I am putting you in the bedroom with the adjacent bathroom. It will give you more privacy. I am just so happy to see you. You don't visit nearly enough."

Linda wrapped her arms around her daughter and gave her a hug. "You are nothing but skin and bones," Linda said. "I am glad I made dinner. When was the last time you ate?"

"Mom, I'm fine," Morgan replied, following her mother into the kitchen.

"I wouldn't say that," Linda stated. "I talked to your brother and I am very concerned about you. Who is this Craig person and how did he get you in so much trouble?"

"What exactly did Bryan tell you?" Morgan questioned.

"That you have been threatened and attacked and that it is all Craig's fault," Linda answered.

"None of this is Craig's fault," Morgan replied, angrily.

"Isn't he a cop? Shouldn't he be protecting you from all this?" Linda asked.

"He has been trying to but I have been pushing him away," Morgan explained.

"Maybe he isn't the problem then," Linda responded. "The problem is you."

"Yes, it is me," Morgan agreed. "I am the one who this person hates so much that he would do anything to keep me away from Craig. This psycho has threatened my family and friends just because I can't do the one thing he has asked me to do."

"And what would that be?" Linda asked.

"What? Bryan didn't tell you?" Morgan questioned, sarcastically. "He told you everything else."

"Don't take that tone with me, Morgan," Linda warned. "I am talking to you about this because I am concerned."

"You may be concerned," Morgan agreed. "But that is not your only motive for asking these questions. Why are you interrogating me? I am so sick and tired of talking about this.

There is nothing anyone can do except sit back and see what happens next."

"Why don't we just sit down and eat?" Jack suggested, as he entered the room. "We can talk about something else."

"How was your flight?" Linda asked, as they sat down at the table.

Morgan knew that her mother was only exchanging pleasantries. It wouldn't be long before she started asking the questions that were on her mind. "The flight was fine," Morgan answered.

"Why didn't you bring Craig with you?" Linda asked.

"Well, that didn't take long," Morgan exclaimed. "How long have you been waiting to ask that?"

"I would like to meet the man my daughter is in love with," Linda answered.

"No one said anything about love," Morgan replied. "Anyway, we are not together anymore so there is no need for you to meet him."

"Now maybe you will be safe," Linda said.

"I am finished talking about this," Morgan stated. "Why are you always so critical of me?"

"I am not critical of you," Linda replied, hurt. "I am only concerned. I wish Edward were still here. He was the only one who could make you understand and I knew you were in good hands with him. I didn't have to worry but since he is gone now, that is all I do."

Morgan stood up. "I can't believe you," she yelled. "Are you trying to hurt me? Why did I even come here? I'm going to bed."

Morgan stormed off to her room and slammed the door. The nerve of that woman was unbelievable. All she ever did was ride Morgan about the choices she made. She couldn't seem to do anything right. Morgan began to cry. She couldn't understand what she had done that was so wrong. Nothing in her life was going right and she just wanted to run and hide. She felt like she had nowhere to turn and no one to talk to. The only person she wanted to talk to was off limits to her and that left her without any options. She had to suffer though this alone.

Morgan awoke and stared at the clock. It was 3 a.m. and she was wide awake. She climbed out of bed and went to the bathroom to splash some water on her face. She quietly made her way to the kitchen to find a snack and then curled up in her dad's old chair. "I thought I heard you moving around," Linda said, as she entered the room. "You know you're a night early, if you came out here to wait for Santa."

Morgan smiled. "You know I am too old for Santa," she replied.

"Yeah but it is always nice to believe in something," Linda stated.

"It would be nice to believe in something right now," Morgan whispered.

"Oh Sweetie!" Linda said, hugging her daughter.

"I'm sorry, Mom," Morgan said, trying not to cry. "I'm so sorry about stomping out of here earlier like a two-year-old."

"Well, I'm really sorry for pushing you," Linda replied. "I'm just concerned about you."

"You should be!" Morgan told her. "I have finally found the strength to move on after Edward died. I would have never found that without Craig. I really love him, Mom, and I can't understand why someone wants me to stay away from him. Why are they doing this to me?"

"Have you ever stopped to think that maybe they are after Craig and not you?" Linda asked.

"It's possible, I guess," Morgan answered. "I don't know anymore."

"Promise me that you will try to relax while you are here," Linda replied. "Jack and I are not going to let anything happen to you."

Chapter 12

Morgan stared out across the water. She always enjoyed sitting on the beach. It relaxed her. Today though, she was too tense to relax. She couldn't understand how things got so bad. Actually, the more she thought about it, the more she realized she was acting childish. She never thought of herself as an irrational person but ever since she fell for Craig, she hadn't been thinking clearly. Maybe a part of her was trying to sabotage the relationship before it even began. She had to admit she was hesitant about starting the relationship to begin with. That feeling soon turned into just being scared. She didn't want to get hurt again so her defense mechanism kicked in. She knew she had sent Craig on a never-ending roller coaster ride, which he didn't deserve. She never intended to hurt him but she had to face the fact that is exactly what she did. When she finally made up her mind she wanted to be with Craig, someone decided to put a stop to it. This person had made a complete mess out of everything. She hadn't helped the situation either. She should have never accused Craig of instigating everything that was going on. She wished she could take it back but she knew it had hurt Craig deeply. It would take a lot to make it up to him and she had to figure out how to do that.

First thing Morgan needed to do was figure out what she really wanted. She knew she wanted to be with Craig. The only thing she didn't know was what was going on with Craig and Valerie. Why was Valerie there that morning? Most importantly though, why was Craig kissing her? If Craig was back with Valerie, then there was no chance for Morgan and him. She couldn't live with that. She had to figure out how to win Craig back.

The biggest problem with all of this though was the fact that someone wanted to keep them apart. They couldn't be together until the psycho was caught. The only way that would happen was if Morgan used herself as bait. She had to devise a plan to make that happen.

After sitting there a few more minutes, Morgan decided to head back to the house. She didn't want anyone to worry about her. "There you are," her mother said, as Morgan entered the house. "You're just in time to help me make Christmas cookies."

"As long as we don't eat all the dough," Morgan replied.

As the ladies baked, they laughed and reminisced about Christmases past. "Your father always hated that we would bake all day and end up with six cookies," Linda said.

"If I remember correctly, he would eat all six cookies," Morgan replied.

They burst into laughter. "What is going on in here?" Jack asked, as he entered the kitchen with a bag of groceries.

"Oh good! You're back," Linda said. "Morgan and I are just having fun making cookies and reminiscing about old times."

"I'm glad you are on good terms now," Jack replied. "What kind of stories were you telling?"

"Just talking about my dad and how he hated the way we made cookies," Morgan told him.

"I remember Ben mentioning that a time or two," Jack stated. "He talked about you all the time."

"He loved her more than anything," Linda explained. "She was his little girl."

Morgan took a deep breath, trying really hard not to get emotional. Thinking about her dad always made her miss him but she knew he was watching over her. "Morgan," Linda said, as she unloaded the bag of groceries. "I had Jack pick up some of your favorite things. I thought I might make your favorite dinner."

Morgan loved her mother's turkey, mashed potatoes, and stuffing. She sometimes wished everyday were Thanksgiving.

She missed Thanksgiving with her family this year because of work but she knew her mother was making up for it now. "I decided to make turkey breasts instead of a whole turkey," her mother explained. "Less leftovers for Jack and me to eat."

Before Morgan could reply, there was a knock at the door that made all three of them turn to look. Standing outside the glass door was Daniel. After being invited in, he said, "I didn't mean to interrupt. I just wanted to invite all of you to my parents' house this evening for a Christmas party."

"I don't think we have anything planned for this evening," Linda responded. "If everyone wants to go, we could make an appearance."

Morgan and Jack agreed, "That's fine."

"Great! I'll see you around eight," Daniel said.

****

"Stephanie, you need to get your stuff together," Craig said. "Your mom will be here soon."

"Ok, Daddy," she replied.

"She is so cute," John's daughter, Kim, told Craig.

Craig smiled at her. "So what are you and your dad going to do today?" he asked.

"I think I'm going to the station for a little bit," John answered, as he entered the room. "We need to go over Morgan's case again and see if we can get this figured out."

"I think you and Bill can handle that," Craig replied. "I have lost interest and perspective."

"We need you," John stated. "You know more about it than we do."

"I don't know any more than you do," Craig corrected him, as he answered the door.

"Hey Craig!" Valerie said. "How are you doing?"

"Good," he answered. "Stephanie is still getting her stuff together. She'll be out shortly."

"I'll go check on her," Valerie replied, as she headed down the hallway.

A few minutes later, Valerie and Stephanie entered the room. "I think we are going to go," Valerie announced. "Tell your dad goodbye."

165

Stephanie gave her dad a big hug and a kiss on the cheek. "I will see you tomorrow afternoon," he told her. "I love you."

"I love you too, Daddy," she replied.

Craig walked Valerie and Stephanie to the door. "Merry Christmas, Craig," Valerie said.

The two shared a kiss. "Merry Christmas, Valerie," he said.

"What is going on between you and Valerie?" John asked, when Craig entered the room.

"Nothing," Craig answered.

"Don't feed me that line of bull," John replied. "You two have been acting a little too civil to each other ever since the divorce. You two aren't back together, are you?"

Craig remained silent. "I thought you were with someone named Morgan," Kim stated. "Isn't that what you said her name is, Dad?"

John and Kim stared at Craig, waiting for an answer. "Morgan and I are not together and there is no chance of reconciliation," Craig stated.

"That's too bad," John said.

"I'm going to work," Craig told them, as he grabbed his coat and headed for the door.

Craig entered the precinct and found Bill Adams. "Do you still want to go over the Garrett case?" he asked.

"I don't know if there is anything new to go over," Bill answered. "I think we have hit a dead end."

"Is there anything new from the other night?" Craig questioned. "I know we have the sketch."

"We don't have anything else," Bill told him.

"Well, let's hope we get a break soon," Craig stated. "I want this case solved as soon as possible."

Craig's cell phone rang. "Hello," he said. "Calm down, Valerie. We'll be right there."

"What's going on?" John asked, as he walked over to the men.

"I'll explain on the way," Craig said.

The men hurried over to Valerie's parents' house. Craig picked Stephanie up. "What happened?" he asked Valerie.

"We were out here building a snowman and my mom called me to the phone," Valerie explained. "I left Stephanie sitting on the porch swing while I went to answer it. I turned to check on Stephanie and there was a man standing on the steps talking to her."

"What did he say to you?" Craig asked Stephanie.

"He told me that he was a friend of yours," she answered. "He asked me about you and Morgan."

"Did the man look like this?" Craig asked, as he showed them the sketch of the man who attacked Morgan.

"Yes, Daddy," Stephanie answered. "That's him."

"I'll go question the neighbors and find out if they saw anything," John said.

"I want to go with you," Craig told him. "I'll be back as soon as I can."

Craig and John walked door to door asking the neighbors if they saw anything. Finally, they got the break they had been looking for. "I saw a black BMW sitting right over there," William Miller stated, pointing in the direction he saw the car. "It was parked there for about thirty minutes. I kept an eye on the driver. When he exited the car, I had the opportunity to write down the license plate number."

"Wow!" John said, stunned. "Not very many people can give us that much detail."

"I watch a lot of cop shows on TV," William replied. "We look out for each other around here. If we see something suspicious, we take notice."

"We appreciate all your help," Craig stated. "If we need anything else, we'll let you know."

The officers hurried back to Valerie and Stephanie. "Did you find out anything?" Valerie asked.

"A car description and a license plate number," John answered.

"Why was he here?" Valerie questioned. "Was he going to hurt me and Stephanie?"

"No," Craig answered. "He was here to send me a message. He wanted to show me that he could get close to you two and there is nothing I can do about it."

"Are we in danger?" Valerie asked, concerned.

"No, I don't think so," Craig told her, putting his hand on her shoulder. "Be careful though. If anything else happens, you call me immediately."

****

Morgan entered Neil and Susan Milano's house with Linda and Jack. "I'm so glad you made it," Daniel said, as he gave Morgan a kiss on the cheek. "Let me introduce you to some people."

Morgan wrapped her arm around Daniel's arm and the two made their rounds through the crowd. Morgan realized that most of the people there were Daniel's relatives. "Why did you invite us to your family function?" she asked.

"I invited you because I wanted you here," he answered. "Plus my mom insisted."

Morgan smiled. "I need to make sure I say hi to her," she said.

"She wouldn't let me live it down if you didn't," he replied.

It didn't take long for Morgan to find Susan. She was the loudest person in the room. "Oh my God!" Susan exclaimed. "Morgan! You're here!"

The woman sprinted over to Morgan and gave her a big hug. "Daniel told me that you were in town and I am so glad I got to see you. We have got to catch up before you head back home."

"We will do that," Morgan replied.

"It was so good to see you," Susan said. "I need to mingle but help yourself to the food."

As Morgan put some food on a plate, Daniel's aunt, Betsy, approached her. "Hi Morgan! How are you?" she asked.

"I'm doing well," Morgan answered. "You?"

"Things are great," she said. "I'm glad you are here. It is so good to see you and Daniel together again. I always knew you two would get back together eventually."

"Daniel and I are not together," Morgan informed her. "How did you get that idea?"

"Daniel told me that you two were back together," she replied. "He made a huge announcement earlier. He told all of us before you got here that he was dating you again."

168

Morgan set her plate down. "Would you excuse me?" Morgan answered. "I need to talk to Daniel."

Morgan searched frantically for Daniel. "I need to talk to you," she told him, when she found him. "Now!"

Morgan led Daniel to a quiet corner of the room. "What's wrong?" he asked.

"I just found out that you announced to the entire room that we are dating again," she informed him. "Why did you do that?"

"I didn't say that," Daniel answered. "Someone must have misunderstood what I said earlier. I told them that you were coming to the party."

"You're lying," she replied. "I'm leaving."

Morgan grabbed her jacket and headed out the door. "Morgan, wait!" Daniel called, as he went after her.

"What do you want from me?" she asked, turning to face him.

"I want us to get back together," Daniel answered.

"I can't do that," she replied. "Things have changed so much since we broke up. We can't go back there."

"Why not?" he questioned. "We can just start over."

"I can't do that," she repeated. "I don't want to hurt you but I am in love with someone else."

"And where is he, Morgan?" Daniel asked. "Why are you not spending the holiday together?"

"I don't have to explain that to you," she told him.

"Things aren't going so well, are they?" he questioned.

Morgan turned and walked away. She didn't want to listen to anymore of this. Daniel grabbed her arm. "You are not just going to walk away," he stated. "I'm not letting you go until I convince you that we are meant to be together."

Daniel pulled Morgan into his arm and passionately kissed her. "Stop it!" she yelled, as she tried to pull away.

Daniel pushed her down into the sand and before Morgan realized what was happening, he was on top of her. "I'm going to make you forget all about Craig," he whispered.

"Get off me!" she yelled.

As soon as the words came out of her mouth, she felt the weight of Daniel being lifted off her. "You heard her," Jack said, as he pulled Daniel up.

Linda helped Morgan up. "What the hell were you doing?" Jack yelled.

Daniel remained quiet. "I suggest you go home," Jack continued. "I don't ever want to see you near Morgan again. Don't think about her! Don't come near her! Don't think about coming near her! If you so much as look in her direction, it will be the last thing you do!"

The trio walked back to their house in silence. Morgan couldn't believe what had just happened. She thought she could trust Daniel and then he decided to do something stupid. She didn't understand why he would do something like that. Was he the one behind all the horrible things that had happened lately? It was obvious he had a motive. He wanted Morgan for himself and he would do anything to keep her and Craig apart. She would have to mention this incident to Craig.

After they returned home, Linda asked Morgan if she needed anything. "No," she answered. "I think I am just going to take a long bath."

Morgan entered her room and sat down on the bed. She started to cry. She couldn't stop thinking about Daniel. She couldn't understand why he would want to scare her like that? It became more obvious with each passing moment that he was the one responsible for all the attacks on her and the one on John.

After changing into her bathrobe, Morgan went into the bathroom and turned the water on for her bath. She found some candles and decided to light them with some nearby matches. She wanted to make the environment as relaxing as possible. She was so tense and decided every little bit would help her at this point. After she set the candles around the room, she slid off her robe and slipped into the tub. Morgan rested her head against the tub and closed her eyes. "Is there room in there for me?" Craig asked.

Morgan smiled at him. Craig stepped into the tub and took a seat behind her. "Better?" he asked.

"Much," she answered, as she leaned against him.

After a few minutes, Morgan continued by saying, "I'm so sorry about the way things have been between us. I wish we could just start over and forget what happened."

"Don't worry about it," Craig stated. "I think we should just kiss and make up."

Morgan turned and faced Craig. "You know. Sometimes you do come up with some great ideas," she replied.

As Morgan started to kiss Craig, there was a knock at the door that brought her back to reality. "Morgan, are you alright?" her mother called. "I don't want to disturb you but I did want to check on you."

"Yes, I am fine," she answered.

After her mother left, Morgan decided to call Craig. It was probably a mistake but she just wanted to talk to him. She wanted to tell him about what happened tonight anyway. "Hello!" he said, when he answered the phone.

"Hi Craig!" she replied. "Is this a bad time?"

"What do you want, Morgan?" he asked.

"I wanted to tell you we have another suspect to add to our list," she answered.

"Did something happen?" Craig questioned.

Morgan explained to Craig her incident with Daniel. "Are you ok?" he asked. "Did he hurt you?"

"I'm fine," she answered. "He just scared me."

"You need to stay away from him," Craig replied. "We will investigate him and see what we come up with."

"Thanks!" she said. "I appreciate it."

"That's my job," he stated. "We had some drama here today. The man who attacked you approached Stephanie today. Before you ask, she is fine. He didn't hurt her. A neighbor gave us a description of the car and license plate number but we ran into a dead end. We ran the plate number and found out the car had been stolen a few days ago. It was also wiped clean but we have a team going over it for any other clues."

"I hope they find something," Morgan told him.

"We'll keep you informed," Craig responded. "If there isn't anything else, I'm going to go."

"Craig, wait!" Morgan called.

"What do you want, Morgan?" he asked again.

"I was hoping we could talk about us," she answered.

"I don't have anything to say," Craig replied. "As far as I'm concerned, there is no us."

Morgan wanted to cry. "I'm sorry you feel that way," she responded. "I guess I will never bother you again."

Morgan closed her cell phone and disconnected the call. She started to cry. She hated herself for messing up everything. She wished she could go back in time and make things right but knew that was impossible. She had caused so many problems between her and Craig and now she was going to pay for it. Craig hated her and there was nothing she could do to change it.

After Morgan was finished, she returned to her room and put on her pajamas and robe. She needed to get a drink of water before she retired for the evening. "How are you feeling?" Linda asked, as Morgan entered the room.

"I'm fine," she answered.

"We were wondering if you wanted to open a present before you went to sleep," Jack questioned. "It has always been a tradition around here."

Morgan sat down in her dad's old chair and waited for her mother to hand her a gift. "I noticed you brought a gift with you from Craig and Stephanie," Linda told her. "Would you like to open it?"

Morgan wanted to start crying again. She wished she had just returned the gift to Craig but instead she accidentally packed it with the other gifts. "I don't care what you do with it," she replied. "Throw it in the trash if you want."

"You don't want to do that," Linda stated. "I think you should open it."

"I just talked to him on the phone," Morgan said, trying not to cry. "He doesn't want anything to do with me. Maybe I'll open it later. Actually, let's just treat it like a band-aid. The quicker I open it, the quicker I can forget I have it."

Linda handed the gift to Morgan. She opened it quickly and found a beautiful blue sweater with a note saying that it was to replace the one that was ruined. "How beautiful!" Linda said, admiring the gift.

Morgan told the two the story about her pink sweater. "That was nice of him to replace it," Jack replied.

"I wish he hadn't done it though," Morgan told them. "I will probably never wear it. He should have saved his money."

Morgan sat in silence as Linda and Jack opened their gifts. As soon as they were finished, Morgan excused herself and went to her room. She climbed in bed and cried herself to sleep.

Chapter 13

Several weeks had passed since Morgan returned home from her Florida vacation. She was surprised she hadn't heard from or seen her stalker. She wasn't about to put her guard down for one second though. She knew he would return eventually. She hadn't heard from or seen Craig either though but that really didn't surprise her. He made his feelings crystal clear to her the last time they spoke. She had time to think since then and decided she had to just let him go. He was too angry at her and she didn't know what to do to fix it. Maybe one day he would forgive her but right now, she wanted to give him time and space.

Morgan opened the front door and leaned over to pick up the morning paper. Before she turned to go back in, she noticed John jogging down the sidewalk. "Isn't it a little cold to be jogging?" she asked.

"No," he answered. "I love this weather."

"Well, you look cold," Morgan replied. "Wanna come in for a cup of coffee?"

"Sure," John said, as he climbed the stairs and followed Morgan inside.

"So how were your holidays?" Morgan asked, as she grabbed a coffee mug and filled it up with coffee.

"Not bad," John answered. "My daughter was home and I got to spend some time with her before she headed back to school. How was yours?"

"Good," she told him. "I went to visit my mom for a few days. She lives in Florida."

"I bet that was a nice vacation," John said.

"It was nice to get away from everything," she replied.

"Have you had any problems lately with your stalker?" John asked.

"Haven't seen or heard from him since before I left for Christmas," she responded.

"I hope we have seen and heard the end of him," John said. "But I am sure that isn't the case. They rarely give up on something once they start it."

"I am still very much on the lookout for him," Morgan reassured him. "I am not letting my guard down again."

"Probably for the best," John replied.

Morgan stood there contemplating what to ask John next. She wanted to know how Craig was but she didn't want to ask. "Anything new with you?" she questioned.

"Actually, I am up for a promotion," John answered. "I am pretty sure I will be a detective before too long."

"That is good news," Morgan replied. "I didn't know you were up for that."

"Well, the department didn't want to split up me and Craig," he told her. "He became a detective last week and we are just waiting on some paper work to go through for me."

"I see," Morgan said. "I am happy for both of you. I know Craig had been waiting for that promotion for awhile."

Morgan stared at her coffee cup. "We don't have to talk about him," John told her.

"I was wondering how he was doing," she explained. "I haven't seen or heard from him in weeks and just wondered if he was doing all right. You don't have to tell me anything. I wouldn't want you to betray your friendship."

"I haven't seen much of him either so I don't really have anything to tell you," John replied. "He works a lot and spends time with Stephanie. He isn't around the house much. So if you don't mind me asking, what happened between you two?"

"I messed it up," Morgan answered. "I was just trying to protect him and I ended up pushing him away. He doesn't want anything to do with me. He told me that we were over."

"I'm sorry," John said.

"Thanks!" Morgan replied.

"This may not be the right time for this," John stated, hesitantly. "But I want to tell you something."

"Ok," Morgan said.

"Before Craig told me that he was interested in you, I told him that I was going to ask you out," John informed her.

"You were?" Morgan questioned.

"Yeah, I was," he said. "But I didn't so you and Craig could have a chance."

"Why are you telling me this now?" she asked.

"Well, I thought I might ask you now," John answered. "I know it probably isn't the right time but would you go to dinner with me sometime?"

Morgan was speechless. "Won't that cause problems with you and Craig?" she finally asked.

"The way I see it is he already had his chance," John explained. "I think it would be a good idea to mention it to him, if you say yes. I think you are a very attractive woman and I would just like to take you to dinner."

Morgan blushed. "If you don't mind, I would like to think about it," she said. "I just want you to be sure this isn't going to cause a problem with you and Craig. I don't want anyone to get hurt."

"I'll give you some time to think about it," John told her. "Here is my cell phone number. It might be better for you to call it instead of calling the townhouse."

"Sounds good to me," she replied.

"I better go," John said. "Thanks for the coffee! I'll talk to you soon."

After John left, Morgan sat down at the table with a fresh cup of coffee and the morning paper. She couldn't believe what had just happened. She was flattered John had asked her out but she didn't want it to cause problems with him and Craig. Plus she felt a little weird going out with Craig's best friend. It suddenly occurred to her that this might be John's way of trying to get Craig jealous so he will come back to her. She prayed that wasn't the case. She really didn't want anyone to get hurt. There had been so much of that lately.

Morgan glanced at the clock and decided it was time to get ready to go. She was going to see Jaime and Bryan's new house. The last few weeks of her life had been so busy and she hadn't found the time to visit with them. In addition, they invited her out for lunch and she couldn't say no to her brother's cooking. She was so happy her brother loved to cook. She could live on it for the rest of her life.

After she got ready to go, she drove to the new house. She was looking forward to seeing it. She was hoping Jaime and Bryan would take her mind off her life for awhile. She hated the fact she was alone but decided maybe she needed this time to regroup and figure out what she really wanted. John's dinner invitation came to mind. Did she really care about what Craig would think? John was a nice guy and one dinner with him wasn't going to lead to marriage. She could just look at it as two friends hanging out for the evening and see where things go. If it didn't go anywhere, at least she would have another friend. She could always use more of them.

"Hello!" Jaime said, as she opened the door. "How are you?"

"I'm fine," Morgan replied. "I'm so sorry I haven't made it out here before now. You know how crazy things have been."

Morgan followed Jaime into the kitchen where Bryan was sitting at the table. "Hey Sis!" he said, looking up from the paper. "I'll start lunch in a little bit."

"No hurry," Morgan said. "I am just so glad to not be sitting at home today. Thanks for inviting me over."

"Don't mention it," Jaime replied. "Did you have a good time in Florida?"

"Yeah," Morgan answered. "Christmas was nice and it was good to get away from everything for awhile. Mom and I had our share of disagreements but I think I left on a good note. How was your holiday?"

"It was uneventful," Jaime replied.

"Maybe you should go see Mom," Morgan suggested. "I think she would like to see both of you."

"We might have to plan a trip to Florida this year and see them," Bryan said. "We'll see what we can work out."

After a moment of silence, Jaime decided to ask the burning question. "So what is going on with you and Craig?" she asked.

"Nothing," Morgan answered. "He told me he never wanted to see me again."

"What happened?" Jaime questioned.

"I messed up," Morgan told her. "I wasn't honest about the whole stalker thing and I constantly pushed Craig away. I guess he had enough."

"Do you blame him?" Bryan asked.

"No, I don't" Morgan replied. "I messed up and there is nothing I can do to fix it."

"That is too bad," Jaime stated. "I was hoping you two would be fine."

"Well, I appreciate that," Morgan said. "But things are not going to work between me and Craig so don't hold your breath that we will get back together."

"Would you like something to drink?" Bryan asked, wanting to change the subject.

"Sure," Morgan answered.

"I'll bring you both a glass of iced tea," Bryan said, as he got up and headed to the refrigerator.

"I'm so sorry about you and Craig," Jaime told Morgan.

"It's fine, Jaime," Morgan replied. "I wish I could change what happened but I can't. I just have to live with that."

"Here you go, ladies," Bryan said, as he set the two glasses on the table. "I'm going to start lunch now."

"Let me ask you two your opinion on something," Morgan stated. "Craig's best friend, John, asked me out. Do you think I should go?"

"I don't see why not," Bryan answered. "You're not with Craig anymore. Go for it!"

"She can't do that!" Jaime exclaimed. "He is Craig's best friend."

"So, they aren't together anymore!" Bryan replied, sarcastically.

"Isn't there a man code about dating your best friend's ex?" Jaime asked.

"Well, technically, John should talk to Craig first," Bryan answered. "But since he has already asked you, go for it."

Jaime let out a sigh. "I just wanted to know if you two thought I should go," Morgan said.

"What do you want to do?" Bryan questioned.

"I don't see any harm in going," Morgan answered. "We are friends."

"I think you should go," Bryan said.

"I am not so sure," Jaime replied. "I wonder if this is John's way of getting you and Craig back together."

"I thought about that but I don't think that is the case," Morgan told her. "I think his intentions are genuine."

"I think you should go and have a good time," Bryan stated. "I don't think there is any pressure to do anything else."

"I just hope going isn't a mistake," Jaime said. "It is your decision though."

"I think I will probably go," Morgan told them.

"You know Jaime is going to want all the details," Bryan stated.

"I'll tell her what I think she needs to know," Morgan said with a laugh.

After a moment of silence, Bryan suggested that Jaime take Morgan on a tour of the house. As Jaime lead Morgan through the house she said, "There is probably too much room in this house for two people but we fell in love with it the moment we saw it. I think it is beautiful."

"It is a very nice house," Morgan replied.

"Thanks!" Jaime said. "We thought we would get something big just in case we decide to start a family."

"You should be sure that is something you want to do before you do it," Morgan stated.

"We talked about it but nothing has been decided," Jaime explained.

"You have time," Morgan stated. "There is no rush."

Jaime continued the tour and when they finished, the ladies went back to the kitchen. "Just in time," Bryan said. "Lunch is ready."

The three of them sat down and enjoyed the turkey and bacon grilled panini sandwiches Bryan had made. "This is delicious," Morgan said. "You wouldn't mind if I sold my townhouse and move in here? I would let you cook for me all the time."

"Well, as tempting as that is," Bryan replied, "I think I will have to pass. Do you really think we could live together and not want to kill each other?"

"You're right. It wouldn't work," Morgan agreed.

She then cocked her head to one side and continued with a smarmy tone, "By the way, I want to thank you for calling Mom and telling her about all the problems I am having lately. It wasn't a very pleasant first day. All we did was fight."

"I didn't tell her so you two would fight about it," he stated. "I thought she needed to know and I knew you wouldn't tell her."

"I had no intention of telling her because I didn't want her to worry," Morgan replied.

"You should know by now that you can't hide anything from Mom," he told her. "She has a way of finding out things."

"This is true," Morgan said. "Do you think she has spies watching us?"

"That wouldn't surprise me," Bryan answered.

Morgan smiled at her brother. She couldn't have a conversation with him without having some sort of disagreement. It had always been that way and she wasn't sure why. It could have been because he felt the need to be her father and brother or maybe he was just too much like their mom.

"Have the police found out anything more about your stalker?" Jaime asked.

"The last time I talk to Craig, he told me that all the leads they had turned into dead ends," she explained. "They have the sketch of him and that is about it. I haven't heard anything else."

"Has anything else happened?" Jaime asked.

"Not since before Christmas," Morgan answered. "I wish I could be confident that this is all over with but it would be stupid to assume that."

"I wish they would catch this guy," Jaime said.

"Me too," Morgan replied. "I am tired of worrying about everyone and tired of watching my back."

"That would be frustrating," Bryan chimed in.

"I need to find a way to catch him," Morgan stated.

"You don't need to do anything," Bryan replied. "You need to let the police take care of this."

"I think I am the only one who can do this," Morgan told him. "The cops have nothing but a picture."

"I'm not going to talk you out of this, am I?" Bryan questioned. "Whatever you do, please be careful."

"You really do care about me," Morgan teased, smiling.

"Of course, I do," he replied. "You're like a sister to me."

Morgan smiled again. "You are goofy," she said.

"All kidding aside," he told her. "I do want you to be careful."

"I will," she reassured him.

Morgan glanced at her watch and was surprised to see how late it was getting to be. "I need to get going," she said.

The couple walked her to the door. "Thank you so much for lunch!" she told Bryan, as she hugged him.

"Don't mention it," he replied.

Morgan gave Jaime a hug. "I want to apologize to you," Morgan said. "I am so sorry about the way I have treated you lately. I have just been messed up. Can you forgive me?"

"There is nothing to forgive," Jaime told her. "I know you have had a rough time lately. Just know that we are here for you, if you ever need anything."

"I appreciate that," Morgan replied.

Morgan got into her car and started back home. She had so much fun at Jaime and Bryan's house but it was now time to get down to business. She had to figure out how to catch her stalker. She knew that she was the only one who could do it and was set to use herself as bait.

As Morgan drove along, she noticed someone following her. They could have just been going the same way she was but with everything that had happened lately, she was extremely paranoid.

Morgan watched as the car following her parked several houses down from her townhouse. She exited her car and calmly walked to the door of her house. She didn't want to alarm the stalker by appearing anxious. She wanted to act like everything was just fine.

Morgan changed into her workout clothes and decided to go for a walk. She thought if she appeared to be gone for a long time, the stalker would think he missed her return. She hoped he would then break into her townhouse and wait for her. He would be surprised to find her waiting for him instead. At least that was the way she pictured it in her head. She just prayed it went that way.

Morgan exited through the front door, making absolutely certain the stalker saw her. She walked as fast as she could and rounded the corner before he had an opportunity to chase after her. She sneaked back behind the townhouses and entered hers through the back door. She grabbed her gun and waited in the dark for her stalker to hopefully take the bait.

Morgan waited for what seemed like an eternity. About half an hour in, she decided to turn on a light to try to entice him but he didn't bite. This might take awhile, she thought. She would have to be patient.

After an hour had passed, Morgan was ready to give up. It was becoming obvious he was just sent to watch her, not approach her. She started to get up from her chair but the jiggling of the door knob stopped her. She sat back in her chair and tightly held the gun.

Morgan hadn't been around guns growing up. She was first introduced to them when her mother started dating Jack. He was a police officer at the time and in his spare time, he would take her to the shooting range. It was there she learned the finer points of aiming and shooting a gun. He always told her "to shoot, to kill." His words echoed in her head. She didn't plan to kill her intruder but she would do what she had to do to survive.

The man entered the house and walked passed her to the living room. Morgan followed him into the room and flipped on another light. The man turned to face her. "Put the gun down, Love," he said, looking at the weapon. "I just stopped by for a friendly chat."

"I doubt that," she replied. "I'm going to put an end to this once and for all."

"What are you going to do?" he asked. "I am only here to help you."

Morgan carefully walked around behind him. "Put your hands behind your back," she ordered. "If you even think about doing anything stupid, I will kill you."

Morgan put handcuffs around his wrists. "On your knees," she directed, harshly.

The man stood there with a smirk on his face. Morgan pointed the gun at him. "I do know how to use this," she stated. "Now, on your knees."

She didn't know if it was pure adrenaline or the anger she was feeling but she managed with one shove to knock the man onto his knees. "Now, tell me why you are terrorizing me or I'll call the cops and they'll get it out of you," she told him.

"I told you that I was here to help you," he replied. "This whole thing has gotten out of hand and it needs to stop."

"Damn right it needs to stop," Morgan agreed. "So tell me now."

"And what do I get in return?" he asked. "Are you going to let me go?"

"After everything you have done, hell no," Morgan answered. "You get nothing but time in jail."

Morgan grabbed the phone and called 911. "The cops are on their way so you better start talking," she demanded.

"You can't let the cops arrest me," he pleaded. "I'm as good as dead in jail."

"That's not my problem," Morgan replied. "Why are you terrorizing me?"

"Because that is my job," he answered.

Morgan raised her gun a little higher and aimed it at his head. "Tell me who you are working for?" she asked, demanding an answer.

"You need to let me go," he told her, as the police sirens were getting closer.

"No!" Morgan yelled. "After everything you have done and the people you have hurt, there is no way in hell you are getting away."

"Morgan!" John called, as he entered the townhouse.

"Tell me!" she exclaimed, harshly.

"The cops are here," he replied. "I'm not telling you now."

"Morgan, put the gun down," John ordered.

"Not until I know you have him," Morgan stated. "He is not getting away."

"This isn't over, Morgan," the man told her, as two cops took him into custody. "There is more in store for you and Craig."

"Are you okay?" John asked Morgan, as she put the gun down.

"Yeah," she answered. "He is working for someone. He wouldn't tell me who though."

"Well, because of you, we are one step closer than we were an hour ago," John said. "How did you overpower him?"

"Determination and adrenaline, I guess," Morgan answered.

Morgan gave John her statement for his report. "I'll let you know if we need anything else," he told her.

"Do you have a minute?" Morgan asked.

"Yeah, but just a minute," John answered.

"I just wanted to tell you that I have decided if you want to go to dinner sometime, we can," Morgan said.

"That's great!" John replied. "Does tomorrow night work for you?"

"Sounds good," she confirmed.

Another cop entered the room. "We have a report of a house fire just outside of town near the old water tower," he stated.

"Bryan and Jaime live in that area," Morgan said, in a panic.

The two men hurried out the door with Morgan in hot pursuit. When they arrived at the scene, the fire was under control but Morgan knew the house was destroyed. As she stood there in disbelief, she noticed Craig standing a few feet from her. She hurried over to him. "Do you know where Jaime and Bryan are?" she asked.

Craig turned towards her. "Bryan had to be taken to the hospital," he answered. "Jaime went with him."

"Are they ok?" Morgan questioned.

"Jaime is fine but I am not sure about your brother," Craig answered. "I need to go. I really don't have time for you right now."

Morgan stood there in disbelief. She didn't know why she expected anything different from Craig. There was one thing that she couldn't understand though. How could he dismiss everything that they had shared? How could the feelings he had for her just disappear? Was his hatred for her stronger than the love he once felt? She wished she could get over him as quickly as he had gotten over her.

Morgan turned to leave and ran right into John. "I'm sorry," she said. "I should have been watching where I was going."

"Are you ok?" John asked.

Morgan shook her head. "I ran into Craig," she explained. "He treated me like I meant nothing to him. He just dismissed me without blinking an eye."

John put his hands on Morgan's shoulders. "I just asked him about my brother," she told him. "I didn't go looking for him."

"I know," he said. "I wish I could tell you to just forget about him and move on. I wish it were that easy."

Morgan wiped the tears from her eyes. "This isn't your problem," she replied. "I'm sorry to burden you with this."

"Don't be sorry," John told her. "You can talk to me anytime about anything."

Morgan smiled at him. "I'm glad I ran into you," John continued. "The man we arrested earlier is Reginald Montgomery. He wants to talk to you."

"Ok, I'll stop by the station after I check on my brother," Morgan stated.

"Promise me you will not go in there alone," John instructed. "Make sure you have an officer with you."

"I promise," Morgan said.

"I have to go," John told her. "Call me if you need anything."

Morgan hurried to her car and decided to get to the hospital. She had to make sure her brother was fine and Jaime had some emotional support.

Morgan began to feel guilty with each passing mile. This fire was her fault. If she would have just followed her instincts from the beginning and stayed away from Craig, this could have been avoided. What made her even think she was ready for a relationship? Well, it didn't matter anyway. She still lost everything. Maybe she was just destined to be alone. That was probably the best thing for her anyway.

Morgan felt horrible. This was probably the lowest she had ever felt. She thought she could learn to cope with everything that had happened to her but it just seemed like it wasn't getting any better. She had tried to move on. She thought she was doing a good job at it too but once again, she was wrong. She had to quit feeling sorry for herself. What was done was done. She couldn't fix it even if she tried. Right now, she had to pull herself together and be strong for Jaime and Bryan.

Morgan arrived at the hospital and found Jaime sitting in the waiting room. "Morgan," she said. "Thank God you are here."

Jaime hurried to Morgan and gave her a hug. "How is Bryan?" Morgan asked.

"I don't know," Jaime answered. "I haven't heard anything since they brought him in. This is really scary."

Morgan instructed Jaime to sit down. "I am so sorry about this," Morgan said. "It is all my fault."

Morgan took a deep breath and willed herself not to cry. "This is not your fault," Jaime replied. "I am not blaming you for any of this."

"If I would have stayed away from Craig from the beginning, this wouldn't have happened," Morgan explained.

"You don't know that," Jaime said.

"I'm sorry," Morgan told her. "Here I am feeling sorry for myself when I should be supporting you."

"I could use the distraction," Jaime stated. "I want to know what is taking so long. Why won't they tell me anything?"

The door to the room opened and Jaime stood up, hoping it was the doctor. She was sadly disappointed when she realized it was Craig. "I was hoping you were the doctor," she told him, as she sat back down.

"Jaime, I need to ask you about what happened tonight," he stated, without acknowledging Morgan.

"I don't know what I can tell you," she said. "I left around 6:30 to go grocery shopping and when I returned, my house was on fire."

"You didn't see anything suspicious?" he asked.

"No," she answered. "You may want to talk to the neighbors. They may have seen something."

"I already did," he said. "I didn't get much from them but I'll keep looking."

"Could this have anything to do with what is going on with Morgan?" Jaime questioned.

"Not sure yet," Craig answered. "I'll know more after I talk to the fire chief."

Craig turned to leave. "Let me ask you something," Jaime said, as she got up and walked in Craig's direction.

Before Craig could say anything, Jaime continued, "Why are you being so cold towards Morgan?"

"Jaime, don't," Morgan said.

"I want to know what the problem is here," Jaime told her, as she turned back to Craig. "You didn't even acknowledge Morgan. There was no hello or anything from you. Why are you treating her like this?"

"This is between Morgan and me," Craig replied. "I suggest you keep your nose out of it. It's none of your business."

"It is my business," Jaime stated. "She is my family and she is very unhappy. I thought you loved her."

"I don't have time for this," Craig told her, as he headed to the door.

Jaime stepped in between Craig and the door. "You better make time," Jaime demanded. "Fix this now. I am going to check on my husband but I will be back."

"If you are thinking I put her up to that, you are mistaken" Morgan said.

Craig sighed and ran a hand through his hair. "What the hell do you want from me?" he asked. "You know what. Just forget it. I don't have time for this. I need to get back to work."

"Leave then," she told him. "Before you do though, I wish you would help me understand why you hate me so much."

"I don't hate you," Craig said. "I just don't like you very much right now. You hurt me. You broke my heart. Do you expect me to just forget about that and make believe that things are good between us?"

187

"I don't expect anything from you," she replied. "After the way you have treated me lately, I'm surprised you're even talking to me now."

Craig stood there, staring at the floor. "I don't know what to say to you right now," he told her. "I don't know how to fix it or even if I want to."

Morgan wanted to cry. "I need to get out of here," Craig continued. "I can't do this."

After Craig left, Morgan cried uncontrollably. It didn't matter what she did, she wasn't going to get Craig back. That ship had sailed. She had to get over him and move on. It was apparent he would never forgive her for what she had done. She couldn't forgive herself. Why should she expect him to?

****

Craig slammed the car door. That was the hardest thing he ever had to do. He still loved Morgan, even though he would deny it to anyone who asked. He wanted to take her into his arms but his pride stopped him. He couldn't forget the hurtful words she had said to him and that made it difficult for him to forgive her.

Craig arrived at the police station. "Detective," Officer Adams called. "Here's the report from the fire chief about the house fire."

"That was quick," John said, as he walked over to Craig.

"Damnit!" Craig exclaimed. "The fire chief said that it was arson. There was an accelerant found in the garage. It looks like just gasoline and a match."

"This guy isn't leaving us any real evidence," John replied. "The fire left nothing traceable."

"Yeah," Craig agreed.

"Do you think this has anything to do with Morgan's case?" John asked, even though he knew the answer.

"I would like to know the answer to that," Morgan stated, as she walked up behind the two men.

"Adams, go back out to the crime scene and see if forensics has found anything," Craig instructed, without acknowledging Morgan's existence. "I want everyone to go over everything one more time."

Morgan walked over to the desk sergeant. She knew not to ask Craig for help. "I'm here to see Reginald Montgomery," she explained. "Is he in holding?"

"What the hell are you doing?" Craig asked her as he grabbed her arm and led her away from the officer.

"I was told that the man I helped capture this evening wanted to see me," she answered. "I want to see him."

"No way that is happening," Craig told her. "You aren't getting anywhere near him."

"Have you gotten anywhere with him?" she questioned. "Judging by the look on your face, I would say no."

"I haven't had time to talk to him yet," he answered. "I had a fire to deal with."

"Are you going to talk to him now?" Morgan asked.

"Yes," Craig said. "No, you are not going."

"Why not?" she questioned. "He did ask to talk to me. He might tell me something that he would never tell you."

"If I let you go in there, you will keep your mouth shut," Craig ordered. "I will ask all the questions. One word out of your mouth and I will show you the door. I do not have time for games."

"Yes Sir," Morgan barked, like she was a new recruit in the army.

"John," Craig said. "Would you bring Montgomery up from holding and put him in interrogation room 2?"

After John left the room, Morgan followed Craig to the viewing room next to the interrogation room. "I'm going in alone and see what I can get out of him," Craig told her. "You can watch from here. I will signal you to come in if I need you. Don't argue with me."

Morgan and Craig stood in silence as they watched John bring Montgomery into the room. Craig waited a minute or two longer and then headed into the other room. "Hello Detective," Montgomery said, as Craig entered the room. "How are you on this beautiful evening?"

"This is the way this is going to work," Craig explained. "I will ask the questions and you will answer them."

"As I recall, I didn't ask to speak to you," Montgomery replied. "Where is that beautiful Morgan? No offense, Detective, but she is easier on the eyes than you are."

Craig chose to ignore Montgomery's comment. "Tell me who you are working for," Craig instructed, as he sat down across from Montgomery.

"What makes you think I am working for someone?" he questioned.

"Because the mastermind usually doesn't do his own work," Craig answered.

"Well, look at me!" Montgomery exclaimed. "I have chosen to play this game differently."

"If that is the case, then tell me what you have against Morgan?" Craig asked. "Why have you been terrorizing her?"

"Morgan is an incredibly beautiful woman," Montgomery stated. "What man wouldn't want to get her attention?"

"A normal man would have bought her flowers or taken her to dinner," Craig replied. "He would have never used force or terrorized her like you have."

"Is that what you did, Craig?" the prisoner asked. "Did you wine and dine Ms. Garrett just to get her into bed?"

Craig felt his hands ball up into fists. It was taking everything he had to not punch this guy in the nose. "Am I reading this all wrong?" Montgomery questioned. "Seems to me, you two aren't together anymore. Wasn't she good enough in the sack for ya, Detective? Maybe you need a second opinion."

"What I need are answers," Craig replied.

"Well, you aren't getting any here," Montgomery told him. "I want to see Morgan."

"He isn't making it easy for Craig, is he?" Morgan said to John, as they stood in the adjacent room watching the scene.

"I wonder if he would talk to you if you went in there," John replied.

"He would probably play more games," Morgan stated. "He isn't going to tell us anything. Has he asked for a lawyer?"

"No, not yet," John answered.

"He's not going to say anything then," she replied. "He'll want a deal eventually and he won't give any information until he gets one."

"We need to figure out who he is working for," John stated.

"He told me that he was working for someone," she said. "I don't know who though."

"Maybe you should go in there and see if he tells you anything," John suggested.

"Craig won't like that," Morgan told him.

"Well, Craig will just have to deal with it," he replied.

"So you haven't told him that we are going out tomorrow night?" she questioned.

"No," John answered. "I need to tell Craig."

"Tell me what?" Craig asked, as he entered the room.

Morgan and John looked at each other. "I'm not sure this is a good time," Morgan told him.

"I'll tell you later," John replied. "It's not important."

Craig stared at them. "You two look guilty about something," he stated. "Tell me what is going on. What are you hiding from me?"

"I asked Morgan to have dinner with me tomorrow evening and she accepted," John told him.

"It didn't take you long to move on, did it?" Craig asked Morgan.

Before Morgan could reply, Craig directed his attention to John. "Well, congratulations, Buddy!" he exclaimed. "I hope you two will be very happy together. Just some friendly advice though. You may want to be careful with this one. One minute, she'll act like she loves you and the next, she'll treat you like crap. Good luck with this one."

"You bastard!" Morgan said, angrily, as she pushed past both men and exited the room. She decided to do the only thing she knew of that would make Craig as angry with her as she was with him.

Morgan entered the adjacent room, not caring what Craig thought or how he even felt about it. "Hello Mr. Montgomery," she said.

"Why are you being so formal, Morgan?" he asked. "Please call me Reggie."

191

"Ok, Reggie," she replied, as she sat down across from him and flashed him a smile.

"That's more like it," Reggie stated.

"I am very upset with you, Reggie," she told him. "You hurt me and I would like to know why."

"It's nothing personal, Sweetheart," he explained.

"Does that mean it's business?" she questioned. "Did someone hire you to hurt me?"

"Morgan, you can flash that sexy smile and talk sweet to me but I'm not telling you anything," Reggie responded.

"I don't know what you are talking about," she whispered. "I just want to know how a man like you got mixed up in something like this."

"I'm not mixed up in anything, Sweetheart," he replied.

"Why did you come after me?" Morgan questioned. "I have never met you and I don't recall doing anything to you. Is this some kind of revenge? Did I break your heart in high school or something?"

"I had a lot more fun talking to your lover when he was in here," Reggie answered. "I was able to get under his skin. You ask too many questions."

"And you can stop asking them too, Ms. Garrett," George Peterson said, as he entered the room. "Stop talking to my client."

"Hello George," Morgan replied, rolling her eyes.

She had encountered George before and she wasn't a big fan of his. He was as ruthless as a lawyer could be. "Morgan, if you would excuse us," George ordered, as he sat down. "And tell your cop friends to exit the adjoining room."

Morgan headed to the door, knowing now that she wouldn't be getting any of the answers she wanted. "Bye Beautiful!" Reggie said. "I'll see you soon."

Morgan entered the hallway and immediately began getting the third degree from Craig. "What the hell were you thinking?" he questioned.

"Are you mad?" Morgan asked, in a sickly sweet tone. "That was my plan. I wanted to piss you off."

"That was dangerous," he replied. "You should have never gone in there alone."

"Why do you care?" she asked. "Anyway, John had my back. He would have taken care of me if Montgomery had done anything."

Craig stared at Morgan, not sure how to respond to her statement. "Don't give me that look," she said. "You are the one who gave up on me."

Craig grabbed Morgan by the arm and ushered her into the nearest room. "You gave me no choice," he told her. "I was sick and tired of your games."

"I wasn't playing any games," she explained. "I was trying to protect you."

"Well, it doesn't matter now what you were trying to do," Craig stated. "It is over between us. You have moved on. I can't believe you are going out with my best friend. After everything you have done, I think that hurts the most."

"You are such a hypocrite!" Morgan replied. "You moved on a long time ago. I saw Valerie leaving your townhouse early one morning a few weeks back. That happened long before John asked me to dinner."

"Well, it looks like you have drawn your own conclusions based on what you think you saw," Craig told her, calmly. "We have nothing left to say."

Craig walked slowly to the door, trying to decide if he should say something else to Morgan. He wasn't aware that she had seen Valerie leave that morning and he didn't know how to explain the situation to her without hurting her more. The last thing he wanted to do was hurt her because despite all that had happened, he still loved her. He decided to just leave the room without saying a word. That might have been the wrong thing to do but he didn't know what else to do.

Morgan stood there in disbelief. Craig didn't bother to defend or deny what she saw. He left without saying a word. Morgan wanted to cry but she knew she had to compose herself before she walked out into a room full of cops. She didn't want to embarrass Craig or cause a scene but she felt like he had ripped her heart out of her chest and stomped all over it. She may not have been completely honest with him about all the things that were going on but she would have never cheated on him. She would have never hurt him like that. She decided at that point that she needed to move on. Despite how much she still loved Craig, moving on was the only thing left for her to do.

Morgan left the police station and headed home. As she drove, she couldn't shake the feeling of dread. She knew that she had treated Craig horribly but she did what she thought was best at the time. She just couldn't believe that she would push him into the arms of another woman. Everything was such a huge mess and if she could fix it, she would. It was too late for that though and she just needed to let go and move on.

When Morgan arrived at home, she decided to just head to bed. She knew she wouldn't sleep well. Her mind was racing. As she entered the room and stared at the bed, the intimate moments she and Craig spent in it flashed through her mind. She caught her breath. She missed him and the realization of that made her cry.

She sat on the bed and reached for the phone. She wanted to call him and beg him to take her back. She knew it was a desperate move but she didn't want to feel this pain anymore. All she wanted to do was go to him and fall into his arms. She knew it was too late for that though. It was over and she had to live with that.

She laid down on the bed and continued crying. She hadn't cried this hard since Edward died. His death was nearly the end of her existence but somehow after several months, she was able to recover at least enough to function. Now she was feeling the same despair she experienced before. The heartbreak, like before, was unbearable. Why did she have to mess things up when everything was going so well for Craig and her? Maybe she just wasn't meant to be happy.

****

Before Craig entered the townhouse, he turned and looked in the direction of Morgan's place. He felt bad about leaving things the way he did with her but he didn't know how to respond to her comment. He knew saying nothing was worse than explaining things to her but he realized that part of him didn't want to explain. He didn't feel he owed her an explanation.

He turned and entered the townhouse. John was sitting on the couch waiting for Craig to come home. "Hey!" Craig said.

"Hey!" John returned. "I don't want there to be any problems between us. Are you ok with me taking Morgan to dinner?"

Craig walked to the refrigerator and grabbed a beer for him and John. After handing one to him and sitting down, Craig answered, "I'm fine with it. If you want to date her, I'm not going to stop you."

"I don't believe you," John replied. "You are my friend and maybe I should have talked to you about it first. In my defense though, I told you that I was interested in her before you started seeing her."

"I know you did," Craig said. "If you want to date her, it's fine with me. I don't think we'll be getting back together. Date her if you want to. I just hope you don't get hurt."

"I still don't think it is fine with you," John stated. "I'll take her to dinner tomorrow evening and we'll see how it goes."

"Good luck," Craig told him. "I'm going to sleep. I'll talk to you in the morning."

Craig went to his room. He didn't want John to date Morgan but what could he do about it? He wasn't seeing her anymore and he didn't think there was a chance for them again. He did some things that he wished he didn't do but he couldn't change them now. What was done was done and there was no going back.

He laid down and closed his eyes. Thoughts of Morgan flooded his mind. He wished that he could go to her and try to make up for the mistakes he made. He wished that he could go back in time and change the outcome. That wasn't possible though. He just wanted to see her smile again. He knew it was too late for them and he had to accept that.

It was going to be a long night. Craig prayed for sleep and for a better day tomorrow.

Craig was awakened by his overactive imagination, which came in the form of a nightmare. Craig's heart was pounding as he tried to recall what the dream was about. After a minute of trying to remember, he gave up and decided to get up for a drink of water. As he entered the living room, he heard John's voice. It sounded like he was on the phone. "I just wanted to check on you," he said. "I wanted to make sure you were ok."

Craig didn't want to eavesdrop. He decided to return to his room. He came to an abrupt stop when he heard John say Morgan's name. "I'm glad you're ok," John told her. "Morgan, you really need to get some rest though."

"I know I do," Morgan replied. "I just have a lot of things on my mind."

"I understand that," he stated. "Are you having second thoughts about going out tomorrow night?"

"No," Morgan answered. "I still want to go."

"That is good to know," he said with a smile. "I will let you rest then and I will see you tomorrow night."

Craig felt deflated as he returned to his room. Morgan was definitely planning to move on with John. The only thing he could do now was to move on too.

Chapter 14

It was the beginning of spring. This also meant it was a time for a new start and Morgan was prepared to take full advantage of it. As she sat on her back patio sipping her morning coffee, she reflected on the last few weeks of her life. A smile appeared on her face as she realized that finally the good was outweighing the bad. With the arrest of Reginald Montgomery, the threats to her family and friends had stopped. She wasn't ready to breathe a sigh of relief though. Over the last week, she had received more phone calls resulting in hang ups. She wasn't sure what to make of it but she did tell John about them.

Speaking of John, they had a wonderful first date. He took her to a restaurant that served the best French American cuisine she had ever tasted. After dinner, they went for a walk around the city. They talked about everything they could think of and she even felt like they had made a connection. It seemed perfect except for one thing. Craig was still in the back of Morgan's mind and no matter how she tried, she couldn't shake him. She had talked to John about it. She felt it was only fair since they had started spending a lot of time together. She also didn't want to feel like she was leading him on. John understood that and appreciated it but Morgan still felt some guilt. With as much time as the two had spent together, she still wasn't having any romantic feelings for John. She wasn't sure if that would change with time. She just prayed that John would continue to understand that and wouldn't push her into something she wasn't ready for.

"Hey!" Jaime said, as she walked onto the wooden deck. "What's going on?"

"Not much," Morgan replied with a smile. "I'm just enjoying this beautiful day. Are you and Bryan ready for your trip?"

"Yes," Jaime answered. "We are leaving late this afternoon after the cookout."

"So you are going to John's house?" Morgan questioned.

"We're planning on it," Jaime said. "It will be fun. I'm guessing Craig will be there. How are you going to handle that?"

"I guess I'll just avoid him," Morgan told her.

"Bryan and I will run interference if we need to," Jaime stated.

"I appreciate that," Morgan replied. "I don't want John to see me get into an embarrassing spat with Craig."

"This is going to be very awkward," Jaime said. "I'm going to go to the store and get a few things. Do you need anything?"

Morgan shook her head. "I think Bryan is going to stay here with you. He said that he was going to rest a little bit before the cookout."

"How is Bryan feeling?" Morgan asked.

"He is feeling better," Jaime answered. "I don't know if I could have said that a few weeks ago. But he is a fighter and I am so relieved that he has recovered. It was scary for awhile."

"I'm sorry about what happened to you two and your house," Morgan stated. "If it wasn't for me, none of that would have happened."

"Don't blame yourself," Jaime said. "Everything is fine. Thanks for letting us stay with you for the last few weeks. We really appreciate it."

After Jaime left, Morgan received a phone call. "Hello!" she said.

"Morgan, it's Daniel," the voice replied.

"What do you want?" she asked.

"I called to apologize," he told her.

"It's been three months and you're just now calling to apologize," she stated. "It's a little too late for that. I have nothing to say to you."

"If you would just let me explain," he pleaded.

"I don't want to hear it," she said. "You hurt me and I don't know how you can make up for what you did."

Morgan disconnected the call. How dare he have the nerve to call her and want to make amends? He attacked her and as far as she was concerned, there was no excuse for it. She didn't want to talk to him ever again.

Morgan wandered into the house and found Bryan relaxing in the recliner in the living room. Before Morgan could say anything to him, the doorbell rang. She opened the door and saw Daniel standing there. "I told you that I had nothing to say to you," she told him.

"I have a lot to say to you," he replied. "Can I come in so we can talk?"

"No!" she answered, as Daniel pushed his way in.

"Don't even think about taking another step!" Bryan threatened, as he stepped in between Daniel and Morgan, pushing Daniel back out the door.

"What is going on?" John asked, approaching the two men.

"John, please go check on Morgan," Bryan instructed. "I don't know if this jerk did anything to her."

John entered the house and found Morgan leaning against the wall. As soon as she saw him, she wrapped her arms around him. "Are you ok?" he asked. "Did he hurt you?"

"No," she answered. "He just scared me. He called here a few minutes ago. I hung up on him. Next thing I know he is here. I don't know what I would have done if Bryan wasn't here."

"You're safe now," John whispered. "Everything is fine."

"What do you want me to do with this scumbag?" Bryan asked.

"Do you want to press charges?" John questioned.

"No," she answered. "He forced his way in here but it would be his word against mine. He didn't hurt me so just let him go."

"Get the hell out of here!" Bryan told Daniel. "Stay away from my sister!"

Morgan finally let go of John as Bryan entered the house. "Are you ok?" Bryan asked.

"Yes," Morgan answered. "Thank you!"

"Maybe Jaime and I should postpone our trip," Bryan suggested.

"No," Morgan said. "Don't do that. I'll be fine."

"She can come over to the house, if she needs to," John offered. "I'll make sure she's safe."

Morgan hugged John again. "Thank you so much!" she said.

"Not a problem," John told her. "Glad I could help. Don't forget. Cookout is at four. If you need anything before then, let me know."

After John left, Morgan gave Bryan a hug. "I am so glad you were here," she told him. "I don't know what would have happened if you weren't here."

"What has gotten into Daniel?" Bryan asked.

"I don't know," Morgan answered. "After what happened in Florida, I thought I would never see him again. Now after three months, he is calling and showing up here to talk to me."

"Do you think he has something to do with the attacks on you and John and our house fire?" Bryan questioned.

"I wouldn't put it past him with the way he's been behaving," Morgan answered. "He is definitely a person of interest."

"You should have had John arrest him," he told her.

"It wouldn't have done any good," Morgan replied. "He would have been out on bail in no time or the charges would have been dismissed."

"Hey you two!" Jaime said, as she entered the house. "Could you help me with these bags? There are a few more in the car."

"I'll get the ones in the car," Morgan offered. "I need some fresh air anyway."

Morgan wandered outside and gathered the bags. As she turned towards the house, she saw Daniel. "I thought you were told to leave," Morgan said.

"Not until I talk to you," Daniel replied, taking a step towards her.

"If you want to talk, you can talk from right there," Morgan told him. "If you move one step closer, I will scream."

Morgan and Daniel stood at opposite ends of the car staring at each other. "You have two minutes," Morgan stated. "If you have something to say, say it."

"I just want to apologize to you for what happened at Christmas," he explained. "I don't know what I was thinking. I just thought maybe we could try again, start over."

"And you thought we could do that by attacking me?" Morgan questioned. "What were you planning on doing to me once you had me pinned to the ground?"

"I don't know," Daniel answered. "I wasn't thinking."

"That's right, Daniel," Morgan said, angrily. "You weren't thinking. Why would you do that to me?"

"I guess my emotions got the better of me," he answered. "I just wanted to have another chance with you and I had a lapse in judgment."

Morgan stared at Daniel. "You have had three months to apologize to me," she stated. "Why did you wait until now to do it?"

"I didn't think you would talk to me," he explained.

"Why should I talk to you?" Morgan replied, raising her voice. "I thought I could trust you and you hurt me. I will never trust you again."

"I thought I told you to get out of here!" Bryan shouted, as he approached Daniel.

"I just wanted to talk to Morgan," Daniel stated.

"I think you are done now," Bryan said. "You can leave and this time, don't come back!"

Bryan started towards Daniel. Morgan grabbed his arm. "Don't," she told Bryan. "He's not worth it."

"Is everything ok?" John asked, as he approached the group. "Is he bothering you again?"

John walked over to Daniel and told him, "I have an investigation going on that I think you have information about. Want to take a trip down to the station with me for a little talk?"

"What are you talking about?" Daniel asked. "I don't have any information about any investigation."

"I think you do," John replied. "I'll tell you more about it at the police station."

"Am I under arrest?" Daniel questioned. "I didn't do anything wrong."

"No, you're not under arrest," John told him. "You are a person of interest in an ongoing case. Because of your actions today, I just want to sit down and talk to you and see if you can help me with my case."

Daniel reluctantly agreed to go to the station with John. "I'll be back in plenty of time for this afternoon," John told Morgan and Bryan. "I just want to see what I can get out of Daniel before he disappears. I'll see you later."

A couple of hours passed and Morgan was getting anxious, waiting for John to return to tell her what Daniel said. "Looking out the window every two seconds isn't going to make John come home faster," Jaime said.

"I know," Morgan replied. "I'm just anxious. I want to know if John found out anything more about my case. I wonder if Daniel had any information that could help."

"You need to be patient," Jaime told her.

Morgan got up and walked to the kitchen. The waiting was driving her crazy. She had to find something to do to occupy the time. She had so many questions running through her mind and she was hoping Daniel could answer them. She wanted this nightmare behind her so she could feel safe again. She didn't want her family and friends to be in danger. It was time to solve this case and move past it. "Hey!" John said, as he entered the kitchen.

"Hey!" Morgan replied. "Did Daniel cooperate with you?"

"He was very cooperative," John answered. "Too bad he couldn't answer any of my questions."

"What happened?" Morgan questioned.

"He claimed he didn't know anything about your case," he told her. "I have a feeling though he is hiding something."

"Have you talked to Reginald Montgomery?" Morgan asked.

"Not since his lawyer showed up," John answered. "I wish I had more to tell you."

"I wish you did too," she stated. "I appreciate all you have done though."

John studied the look on Morgan's face. "I know you are scared," he told her. "I will do whatever I can to protect you."

Morgan smiled at him. "I need to get going," John said. "I have several things to do before people start showing up. Do you want to go with me?"

Morgan was designated as hostess for the cookout. Basically, she was in charge of answering the door. She was having a good time until she caught a glimpse of Craig as he went into the kitchen. She felt her heart sink and she wanted to disappear. "I don't think he saw you," Jaime said, as she approached Morgan.

"Probably a good thing," Morgan replied, as she answered the door.

"Morgan," Valerie said, as she entered the townhouse.

"Valerie," Morgan replied.

"I'm here to pick up Stephanie," Valerie told her.

"Craig is in the kitchen," Morgan informed her, as Valerie walked past her.

"That was pleasant," Jaime replied.

"Just another person to avoid," Morgan stated.

"Have you ever thought that maybe Valerie is the one behind all the attacks?" Jaime asked.

"At this point, I'm not sure who to suspect," Morgan answered. "I thought I could trust Daniel and look what he did. It wouldn't surprise me but why would Valerie put Stephanie in danger?"

"The guy didn't do anything to harm Stephanie though," Jaime pointed out. "He just wanted to talk to her. Maybe that was the plan all along."

"Craig would never believe me if I told him that I have suspicions about Valerie," Morgan explained.

"Probably not," Jaime agreed. "Probably wouldn't even talk to you."

After Jaime excused herself to go find Bryan, Morgan played door greeter a few more times. As everyone was directed to the backyard, Morgan took inventory of the guests. There were a few people she didn't know but she did recognize a few. Craig's sister, Leslie, and her family were in attendance, along with Elizabeth. Craig must have invited them, which meant he would be staying. Morgan never did see Valerie and Stephanie leave, which more than likely meant Craig invited them to stay too.

"There you are!" John said. "What's wrong?"

"Nothing," Morgan answered. "I just got a little distracted."

"I hope you don't mind that I had you answer the door for me," John replied. "Craig probably should have done it but you're better looking than he is. So you were the better choice."

Morgan smiled. "Should we join everyone else outside?" she asked.

"Probably should," he answered. "Promise me that you will try to have a good time today. I know this can't be easy for you but I am glad you are here."

"I'm fine," Morgan told him. "I would be better if Valerie wasn't here but I will just avoid her."

"Just please have a good time and don't worry about her," John replied. "Will you do that for me?"

"Yes," Morgan said. "I will do that for you."

Morgan made small talk with everyone as she asked them if they needed anything. She took several minutes to talk to Elizabeth and Leslie. Elizabeth told her that she was making progress with her physical therapy, which was good news. She was still confined to her wheelchair but she felt that it wouldn't be long before she was out of it and able to walk with a cane. Leslie, on the other hand, hounded Morgan about Craig. She wanted to know the real story as to why they weren't together. Morgan tried to tell her as politely as she could that it wasn't really any of her business. She didn't want to have that conversation with Leslie, especially with a backyard full of people. She didn't want to publicize it to everyone. Morgan finally told her that she didn't want to get into it and that Leslie needed to ask Craig.

John announced to the guests that dinner was ready and everyone lined up to get their food. Morgan helped Elizabeth with her plate and then returned to ask John if he needed anything else. After the crowd was taken care of, John and Morgan grabbed some food and sat down next to Jaime and Bryan.

As Morgan ate, she reflected on the evening. She was surprised that Craig hadn't approached her or even tried to talk to her. She looked up from her plate and immediately locked eyes with Craig. The moment didn't last but a few seconds but Morgan knew that she had exposed too much. She wanted him back but she knew there was no hope of that happening.

The crowd started to dissipate after dinner. A few guests left while a few others decided to start a game of football. John decided that he wanted to play so Morgan offered to clean up the mess and put everything away. After Morgan walked Jaime and Bryan to the door and wished them a safe trip, she returned to the backyard to gather things that needed to be refrigerated. Morgan made her first trip to the kitchen with an armful of miscellaneous condiments. "Hey!" Craig said, as Morgan closed the refrigerator door and turned towards him. "I just wanted to make sure that you were all right. John told me what happened to you today."

"I'm fine," Morgan answered, as she headed to the doorway.

"Morgan, wait," Craig said.

"What do you want?" she asked.

"I want you," he answered.

"Why?" Morgan questioned.

"Why? What kind of question is that?" Craig inquired. "Why would you even ask that?"

"Why do you want to be with me?" Morgan asked. "All we ever did when we were together was fight. All we did was hurt each other. Why would you want to put us through all that again? Plus the last time I talked to you, you acted like you wanted nothing to do with me. So what's changed? Are you jealous because I am with someone else and you can't have me now?"

"Yeah, about that," Craig replied. "I don't see this thing with you and John working. It just doesn't make sense to me."

"I'm not going to listen to anymore of this," Morgan said, as she turned to leave.

Craig grabbed hold of Morgan's hand and pulled her close to him. "I still love you," he told her.

"Sometimes that isn't enough," she stated.

Craig pulled her closer and whispered in her ear, "Tell me you love me too."

"I can't do this," Morgan said. "I'm with John."

The two locked eyes again. Morgan didn't know how much longer she could resist him. She didn't have to wonder for too long because before she knew it, Craig had pulled her into his arms and passionately kissed her. "What are you doing?" she asked, as she pulled away from him. "One minute you hate me and want nothing to do with me. Now you want me again knowing full well that I am dating your best friend. What has gotten into you? Is this a game to you?"

"Now you know how I felt when you were doing it to me," Craig replied.

"So this didn't mean anything to you?" she questioned.

"That's not what I meant," he stated.

"But that is what you said," Morgan replied. "I had very good reasons for what I did. I was trying to protect you. What you just did was dirty."

"That didn't come out the way I wanted it to," Craig told her. "I never meant to hurt you."

"And I never meant to hurt you," Morgan replied. "But that is what we keep on doing."

"This probably won't make any difference but there is something I need to tell you," Craig stated. "I still love you. I never stopped. I miss you like crazy. Maybe I am jealous of you and John but I want to be with you. I want to spend time with you. It hurts when I see you two together. I can't continue avoiding you. I can't continue pretending that I don't care about you."

"I don't know what to do," Morgan replied. "There are so many problems, so many misunderstandings that I don't know if we can get past all of them. Plus I'm dating John. I can't just dismiss that. I have someone else to consider."

"I'll wait then," Craig stated. "Not that I want something bad to happen to you and John but I don't see you two together very long. So like I said, I'll wait."

Morgan still wasn't sure what to think. She thought back to the morning that she saw Valerie leaving Craig's townhouse.

She wanted to ask Craig about it but wasn't sure she wanted to hear the answer.

Craig pulled Morgan back into his arm and kissed her again. "Am I interrupting something?" John asked, as he entered the room.

"No," Morgan answered, turning towards John.

"Craig, would you excuse us?" John asked. "I think Morgan and I need to talk."

"I'm sorry you walked in on that," Morgan told him. "I never meant for this to happen."

"Morgan, it's ok," John said. "I'm kind of glad it happened. I have something to tell you."

Morgan was confused. She wasn't sure what was going on but apparently she was about to find out. "I realized something earlier," John explained. "I think I started to feel this way a few weeks ago but chose to ignore it. I had hoped I would feel differently with time but apparently that isn't going to happen. I feel like you are more of a little sister to me than a woman that I am dating. I feel like all I am doing is protecting you. Don't get me wrong. I have had a great time with you but there is nothing romantic going on here. You know it as well as I do."

"I tried to be honest with you from the beginning about how I feel about Craig," Morgan replied. "I never wanted to hurt or mislead you."

"I appreciate that," he said. "There are no hard feelings. Don't feel bad about this. If I have to lose you to anyone, I would want it to be Craig. But I do reserve the right to take you to lunch or a movie on occasion."

She smiled at John. "I don't know if Craig and I can work things out," she told him. "There are a lot of things that have happened in the last few months."

"I just want you to be happy," John said.

"Thanks!" Morgan replied, as she gave him a hug.

"Now go find Craig," he ordered. "Sit down with him and start talking."

"I'm not sure I want to do that right now," Morgan explained. "A lot has happened today and I just need to soak it all in and decide what to do next. I think I'll head home."

John insisted on walking her home and inspecting the townhouse before he left. "Call me if you need anything," he instructed.

Morgan sat in her big comfy chair and sipped on a cup of coffee. She was still confused about what had happened earlier. Part of her was relieved that John had let her off the hook but she couldn't help but be suspicious. Why did he let her go so easily? Was there a conspiracy going on with John and Craig or was she just being paranoid? With everything that had happened, she couldn't help but be.

She set her coffee mug down on a coaster on the nearby coffee table. She was getting so tired of being paranoid. It was starting to get to the point where she didn't trust anyone and she knew that wasn't the way to live her life. She felt like she was jumping out of her skin every time someone she didn't know would approach her. She was trying so hard to be strong but the whole fiasco was starting to take its toll.

Morgan picked up her cup and wandered to the kitchen. As she set the cup in the sink, she started to cry. This was another low moment for her and she realized that she was alone. Everything that had meant anything to her was gone. She lost her husband and a chance to be a mother in the blink of an eye several months ago. She would admit to anyone who asked that it had gotten easier over the past couple of months but the emptiness was still there. That feeling would probably never go away and she had to learn to live with it.

When Morgan met Craig, she thought that maybe she was ready for a relationship and that she would begin to heal or at least maybe some of the void would be filled. When she finally decided to let Craig in, someone else decided they had other plans for her. She couldn't understand why someone would want to take away her happiness. Was it jealousy or revenge? How could someone hate her that much? Morgan had always tried to treat people with kindness. Lately though, she felt like she had allowed this situation to make her jaded. She didn't want to be a cynical person but life took a wicked turn and changed her into someone she sometimes didn't recognize.

Morgan went to the bathroom and washed her face. As she dried her face, she caught her reflection in the mirror. She looked sad, which was exactly how she felt. She never intended for anyone to get hurt but that is what happened. She thought about John and hoped that he wasn't feeding her a line of bull earlier when he ended their relationship. She had to agree with him though. It did feel more like a brother/sister or buddy/buddy relationship than it did anything romantic. They had never even shared a kiss. She didn't think it was because they didn't want to. It just never felt like the right moment. It may have also had to do with the fact that John didn't want to rush her. He knew how she felt about Craig and he wanted to give her the time she needed.

If John would have given her until the end of time to get over Craig, she was sure that wouldn't have been enough. What she felt for Craig was so much more intense than anything she had ever felt. She had loved Daniel and she still loved Edward but not with the kind of passion she felt for Craig. She wasn't going to get over Craig any time soon and she wasn't sure she wanted to. She realized that dating someone else or even being alone wasn't going to change the fact that she knew right where she needed and wanted to be.

Things weren't going to be that simple though. Morgan still had so many questions that had to be answered before she would tell Craig how she felt and that she wanted him back. Was he messing with her or did he genuinely want her back? What made him change his mind after he had told her months ago that he wanted nothing to do with her? What exactly was going on between him and Valerie? Would they be able to work through their problems and put everything behind them? These were questions she needed answers to before she would commit herself to him again. If there was no chance at happiness, she needed to know so she could either stay and work things out with Craig or go and start a new life without him.

The phone rang and Morgan rushed across the house to answer it. "Hello!" she said, a little out of breath.

"Hey Morgan!" Jaime replied. "I just wanted to let you know that we made it safely."

"I'm glad you called," Morgan stated.

"Are you ok?" Jaime asked. "You sound like you are a little down."

"I'm fine," Morgan answered. "I'm just thinking about things. There was a little drama at the cookout after you left."

"Did you have a run in with Valerie?" Jaime questioned.

"No," Morgan replied. "It was with Craig."

Morgan shared the story with Jaime. "What are you going to do?" she asked.

"Talk to Craig," Morgan answered. "Then I'll go from there."

"You'll have to keep me updated," Jaime told her. "We'll be home in a couple days."

As Morgan hung up the phone, there was a knock at the door. When she opened it, she saw Craig standing there. "We need to talk," he said.

Morgan motioned him to enter the townhouse. "John told me what happened earlier between you and him," Craig continued.

"I can't help but think that you had something to do with it," Morgan replied.

"I didn't have anything to do with it," he told her. "I didn't plan to kiss you when I walked into the kitchen. I just wanted to make sure you were ok. It was just bad timing on John's part."

"I don't understand why you decided at that moment to tell me how you felt," Morgan stated. "It just seemed to me that the timing was too perfect for you."

"You act like we had some sort of conspiracy against you," Craig said.

"What am I supposed to think?" she questioned. "You told me that you wanted nothing to do with me. Then out of the blue, John asks me out. Then at the cookout while his back is turned, you make a move on me and he walks in at just the right moment to catch us. It just seems a little too convenient to me."

"Morgan, there is no conspiracy," Craig explained. "John told me that he was interested in you right before I asked you out. He stepped aside to give me a chance with you. After I found out that you two were going out on a date, he told me that he saw you as available and he wanted to see what would happen. Today's incident was simply a coincidence."

"Why did you pick today to tell me how you felt about me?" she asked. "I know how I have treated you in the past but the last few months you have been very angry with me. What changed your mind?"

"I can't stand the thought of you with another man," he answered. "I want to be the only man who kisses you and makes love to you."

"That sounds a little possessive," Morgan replied.

"No, not possessive," Craig said. "I'm just a man in love."

"We have a lot of things to work out," Morgan told him. "Let's go into the living room and sit down."

"I never meant to hurt you," Morgan explained. "I was only trying to protect you. I wanted to be with you but after the first attack, I didn't know what to do. I didn't want to see anything happen to you so I had to let you go. I didn't have a choice."

"Why didn't you just tell me what was going on?" Craig asked. "We could have figured it out together."

"Because I was scared," Morgan answered. "I didn't want to see you get hurt. As I keep saying, I was just trying to protect you and it cost us our relationship. That is exactly what this person wanted. They wanted to keep us apart."

"We need to find this person and put a stop to this," Craig said. "Montgomery's not talking. John told me earlier that all of Daniel's alibis have checked out. It just makes me think that this is much bigger than we thought. There is someone else in charge and these people are just pawns in the game."

"I don't know much about Montgomery," she replied. "He had something to tell me the night he was arrested but decided not to say anything after the police showed up. As for Daniel, I am not sure what happened. He was always so good to me. He told me that he wanted to get back together but I told him that I wasn't interested. I told you about what happened when I went to Florida for Christmas. He had never been aggressive with me before. The only reasons I can think of as to why he attacked me are either because he was getting tired of hearing "no" or he was jealous."

"Do you know why he approached you today?" Craig questioned.

"He said that he wanted to apologize to me for what happened," Morgan answered.

"That seems odd," he replied. "He waited this long to apologize."

"That's what I thought too," she stated. "Maybe he is just feeling guilty."

"Or maybe he is trying to cover his tracks," Craig responded.

"Maybe," Morgan agreed.

"Don't worry," Craig told her. "I will figure this out. Is there anyone else I should look into?"

"Abby Lewis," Morgan answered. "I don't think it was a coincidence that she was at the tree farm the same time we were there. It's the same thing with the furniture store. It's like she seeks me out and when she finds me, she yells at me about stealing you away from your family. She usually throws a threat or two in there too."

"It is hard for me to believe that she would be the mastermind in all this," Craig replied. "But I will check into her background and see what I can find. Is there anyone else?"

"You are probably going to hate me for saying this but yes, I do suspect someone else," Morgan stated. "I think Valerie may have something to do with all of this."

"No, that is not possible," Craig told her. "She would never put Stephanie in danger."

"Yes, but she has motive," Morgan replied.

"She didn't do it," Craig said.

"How can you be so sure?" Morgan questioned.

"Val has done a lot of things," Craig answered. "But she would never do anything like this. To put it bluntly, she is too lazy to put this much work into what is happening."

"Well, if that is the case," Morgan replied. "Why would she do it herself if she could get someone else to do it for her?"

"It just doesn't feel right," he answered. "I don't think we are going to agree on this but I will keep an eye on her and if I see anything suspicious, I will look into it."

Morgan seemed to be satisfied with that response. "Is there anyone else?" Craig asked.

"No, I don't think so," Morgan answered.

"But there is something else," Craig said.

"I've mentioned this to you before and if it is none of my business, tell me," Morgan stated. "Is there something going on between you and Valerie? Are you back together?"

"You are referring to the time you saw her leaving the townhouse?" Craig questioned, wanting clarification.

"Yes," Morgan confirmed.

Craig told Morgan about the problems Valerie was having with Nick that night. "I had never seen Val that scared before," he said. "She asked me if she could stay with me and I told her that she could. In my defense, I was feeling rejected, vulnerable, and probably a little needy. I did instigate the first kiss and I probably shouldn't have taken it as far as it went. You would be surprised to learn though that Val was the one who stopped it before it went too far. She told me that she knew my heart and mind were somewhere else and she wasn't going to play second fiddle to you. So no, Val and I are not back together and we did not have sex."

Morgan breathed a sigh of relief. "When I saw you two that morning," she explained. "I was confused. I couldn't understand why you were with her after you had been with me. You had told me that you loved me and I was so upset because I thought you had lied to me. I wasn't sure if I could even trust you after that."

"We have had a lot of misunderstandings," Craig replied. "I understand that all you wanted to do was protect me but I felt it was my job to protect you. When you started pushing me away, I got frustrated. At that point, I started to think that I wasn't going to stay somewhere I wasn't wanted."

"I'm sorry for everything that happened," Morgan stated. "I know I didn't handle it very well but I was scared."

"I'm sorry too," Craig responded. "Hopefully, we can work things out."

Morgan smiled at him. "I have a couple questions for you," Craig stated.

"Ok," she said.

213

"Did you sleep with John?" he asked.

"No," Morgan answered. "You don't have anything to worry about. John and I never even kissed. We are just friends."

"But you were dating?" he questioned.

"Yes," she confirmed. "It wasn't going to turn into anything romantic."

"What about Daniel?" Craig asked. "You did kiss him."

"No, he kissed me," Morgan said. "I will admit that night I was flirting with him more than I should have been so I guess I encouraged his behavior. The kiss was all his idea."

"So where do we go from here?" Craig questioned.

"Honestly, Craig, I don't know," Morgan answered. "A lot has happened today and I really need some time to process all of it."

"I understand that," Craig replied. "I would like to tell you that I will give you all the time you need but we both know from past experience that I'm not very good at that. All I want to do is find the guy who did this to us."

"No one did anything to us," Morgan stated. "We allowed this to happen. We should have handled it better."

"You are right," he agreed. "But I promise you that I will find this guy and I will fix things with you. That is if you want to be with me."

"I don't know what I want right now," Morgan told him. "I just need some time to think."

"I can give you that," he said. "If you need anything, don't hesitate to call me or John."

"Are things good between you and John?" Morgan asked.

"We talked before I came over here," Craig answered. "We're good. I think he was disappointed that I didn't talk to him before I decided to approach you. But I think we're good."

Craig got up from his chair. "I better go," he said. "It's getting late. Are you here by yourself? I thought Jaime and Bryan were staying with you."

"They needed some time away," Morgan answered. "After everything that's happened, I think they earned it."

"I don't want to be presumptuous but do you need me to stay?" he questioned. "I could sleep on the couch. I just want you to feel safe."

"I'll be fine," Morgan told him. "John checked everything when he was here. Feel free to check everything again, if you want."

Craig checked all the windows and doors. "You haven't received any more threats, have you?" he asked.

"Not since Montgomery was arrested," Morgan answered. "I think this is the calm before the storm. I'm not sure why it has stopped but it is far from over."

"If you need anything, call," Craig instructed again.

Morgan walked him to the front door. "I'll check on you in the morning," he told her.

After she shut the door, Craig fought the urge to turn around and knock. He forced himself to continue walking and respect her wishes. Plus he decided he needed this time to think about everything too. He wasn't quite sure why things happened the way they did. He hadn't planned on kissing Morgan but he did and he wasn't sure why.

Craig entered the empty house and headed to the kitchen for a beer. He needed something to help him unwind. After the day he had, he wasn't sure one beer would be enough though. His mind was racing and standing in the kitchen where the kiss with Morgan occurred wasn't slowing it down.

He leaned against the counter and took a swig from the bottle in his hand. During that time, he allowed the memory of kissing Morgan flood his mind. He knew that granting this indulgence wasn't the best thing for him right now. It made him realize just how much he missed her and how much he wanted her back in his life.

This created another problem for him though. It intensified the battle between his heart and his brain. His heart was persistent on reminding him that he loved Morgan and no matter how hard he tried, he couldn't dismiss that. Next to Stephanie, Morgan was the best thing that had happened to him and he couldn't just let that go. He had felt their connection the first time they met and even now, that connection was still there.

His brain was singing a different tune though. He couldn't stop thinking about how she had treated him when the trouble began. At the first sign of problems, how could he be sure she wouldn't push him away again? Was he sure he could trust her to not do that? Did he really want to take that chance knowing that he might end up in the same place he was in now?

Craig set the empty bottle on the counter and grabbed another beer from the refrigerator. He wasn't sure what he was going to do about Morgan. He had told her earlier that he wanted her back but that may have been a little premature. He decided that he should take a step back and take some time to soak in the day. He acted impulsive earlier, which was his nature. This was a big decision to make and it shouldn't be taken lightly.

The first thing Craig needed to focus on was finding the person responsible for causing this whole mess. Morgan mentioned a few people that Craig needed to check into, which he would do first thing in the morning. The only person he felt uncomfortable investigating was Val. He had known her for several years and just couldn't get himself to believe that she could do something like this. He knew that she was capable of being hateful and vindictive at times but violence wasn't her style. Plus she seemed to finally be turning her life around. Why would she jeopardize that?

Craig thought back to the night that he and Val almost had sex. He was relieved that it didn't go any farther than it did. Not only would that have complicated things more, it would have been meaningless and he wouldn't have been able to forgive himself for that. He would have felt like he used Val and he didn't want to be that kind of man.

Every emotion Craig felt that night suddenly washed over him. He hated how he allowed Morgan to make him feel so cheapened. He couldn't believe that he had sunk so low as to try to seduce another woman in order to feel better or to even forget about her. The more he thought about it, the madder he got. He had never let a woman control him in that way and he wasn't about to start now. He was going to have to take his control back or this whole situation was going to destroy him.

Craig entered his bedroom and sat down on the bed. After setting his beer bottle on the nightstand, he rubbed his eyes and let out a sigh. He wasn't sure how he was going to do it but he had to save himself. He figured the best way to do that was to just walk away. That should be easy to do since Morgan didn't commit to anything during their earlier conversation. Maybe he would just let her off the hook. That would probably be the best thing for both of them.

Craig polished off his beer and collapsed onto the bed. Deciding to dump Morgan was a bit drastic. Maybe a good night's sleep would clear his mind and he would reconsider. He didn't think that was a possibility though. She was so indecisive about their relationship. If she wanted to be with him, she wouldn't have hesitated. She would have run into his arms and not thought twice about it. He finally came to the realization that you couldn't lose something you never had. His relationship with Morgan ended before it even began.

He closed his eyes and flashes of his time with Morgan appeared. He loved kissing her and feeling her body close to his. He caught his breath when he thought about her touch and her scent. They had an incredible passion but that wasn't enough to save their relationship. His trust in her had been shattered, at least to the point where he questioned her actions. He knew their relationship couldn't be based on their one sexual encounter. He also knew that love might not be enough to repair it. He needed to let her go which was going to be harder than he thought. It was time to quit pining for her and walk away.

Chapter 15

Craig poured his second cup of coffee and sat down at the kitchen table. It had been a long night and he didn't get much sleep, which he fully expected. Every dream he had involved Morgan and they seemed to go from one extreme to the other. He felt like he was on an emotional roller coaster this morning and he couldn't seem to shake it.

Leslie entered the room and announced to Craig her arrival. "I'm sorry I'm late," she said. "I had to settle an argument between the boys."

"That's fine," Craig replied, as he got up from the table. "Do you want some coffee?"

"Sure," she answered, as she sat down. "Then you can sit back down and tell me what is going on with you."

"Nothing," he said, as he set her cup of coffee down in front of her. "Everything is fine."

"No, everything is not fine," she responded. "It's Morgan, isn't it? What did she do now?"

"I kissed her yesterday," Craig told her.

"You did what?" Leslie questioned.

"You heard me," he replied.

"Why would you do that?" Leslie asked. "I thought she was dating John."

"She was until he caught us kissing," he explained.

"Craig," she responded, disappointingly. "Do you really want to get involved in all of this again?"

Craig left his chair to pour himself another cup of coffee. "I don't know," he answered, leaning against the counter. "I spent most of last night thinking about this. At one point, I even had myself talked into just walking away. I'm just not sure what I'm going to do."

"Walk away," Leslie suggested. "I'm just trying to look out for you, little brother."

"I know you are," he replied. "It is just easier said than done. If I didn't love her, I would just leave. This is a very difficult decision because once I'm gone, I'm gone. I'm not coming back."

"I'm sorry I pushed so hard to get you two together," she said. "I really thought that you two were good together."

"We were good together," Craig agreed. "I understand that she was apprehensive about entering a relationship after everything she had been through. Everything was going fine until she was attacked. I wish she had told me what was going on instead of pushing me away. She is the one who made that decision. She is the one who destroyed us."

"Morgan was just trying to protect you the best way she knew how," Leslie replied. "I'm not trying to defend her but can you blame her for what she did? She had just lost her husband. She was probably terrified she was going to lose you too. You are a cop and anyone can get to you."

"For someone who is trying not to defend her, you are sure doing a great job," Craig pointed out, jokingly.

Leslie smiled. "It is really hard for me not to like her," she told him. "I don't like the decisions she made. I think she could have handled all of this differently. I am just trying to see it from her point of view. She just didn't want the same thing that happened to Edward to happen to you. I understand that because I worry about you every time you go to work."

"You have given me something to think about," he replied. "I don't know if it will change anything. It is hard for me to forget all the rotten things that have been said and done. I'm not sure this can be repaired."

"I will support you in whatever you decide to do," Leslie stated. "If you need to talk, I am here to listen."

"I appreciate that," Craig told her.

"Well, I appreciate you letting me take Stephanie today," she stated. "I know that you are giving up your day with her. I am surprised you talked Valerie into it."

"Val didn't have much of a say in it but I thought I would be nice and ask her," Craig replied. "She and I have been getting along a lot better since the divorce. She has been very easy to work with."

As if on cue, the doorbell rang. Craig headed to the living room to answer it. "Daddy!" Stephanie exclaimed.

Craig gathered the child into his arms. "Is it ok with you if Aunt Leslie takes you for the day?" Craig asked Stephanie.

"Yeah," Stephanie answered. "But I will miss you, Daddy."

Craig smiled at her. "I will miss you too," he replied. "I promise you the next day I have off work, we will spend the whole day together."

Stephanie gave him a big hug and kiss. "It's a date!" she exclaimed.

After Leslie left with Stephanie, Craig asked Valerie if she had a few minutes to talk.

"What do you want to talk to me about?" Valerie questioned, as the two took a seat.

"It has been suggested to me that you might be a person of interest in a case I am working on," he explained.

"I'll do what I can to help but I don't know what you're talking about," she replied. "What case?"

"Do you remember the letter I questioned you about a few months ago?" Craig asked.

"Yes," she answered.

"Do you remember when that man approached Stephanie?" Craig questioned.

"Yes," Valerie repeated. "Didn't those things have to do with you and Morgan? You don't think I had something to do with that, do you?"

"I am just exploring every possibility," he answered. "This case has gone on long enough and I would like to have a break in it. I know you have had problems with Morgan in the past."

"The only problem I had with Morgan was she stole my husband," Valerie stated. "But I realize now you and I were having problems well before Morgan entered the picture. I hope you know all the things I said to you and her were said because I was hurt. I would never hurt anyone."

"I know that," he said.

"Plus I would never put Stephanie in danger," she replied.

"I know that too," Craig said.

"If I had any information about this, I would tell you," Valerie told him. "I don't know anything about this. I know I have been a horrible person in the past but I believe I have changed. I wouldn't want to do something like this."

"I hope you understand I'm not accusing you of anything," Craig explained. "I am just trying to find some answers."

"I understand," she replied. "We're good."

Valerie got up and headed to the door. "You and Leslie have made arrangements for you to pick Stephanie up, right?" he asked.

"Actually she is bringing Stephanie by the house," she answered.

"I hate losing a day with her," Craig stated. "Leslie asked if she could take her to the zoo with the boys. That works out for me though since I have some work I need to do today."

"Good luck with your case," Valerie replied. "I hope you find out who is doing this."

"Thanks!" he said. "I hope so too."

After Valerie left, Craig made a call to the police station asking Officer Adams to track down Abby Lewis and bring her in for questioning. He hoped Abby would give him the answers he needed to crack this case and give Morgan some peace of mind.

When Craig arrived at the station, there was no sign of Abby. While Craig waited, he decided to do some investigating of his own. He called in a few favors and got subpoenas for both Abby's and Daniel's bank and phone records. It was more difficult to get Daniel's records because he did all his business out of state but Craig accomplished it.

As he waited for the information he requested to arrive, he decided to find out what the problem was with locating Abby Lewis. Adams told him that he was unable to locate her. "I have checked her home," he said. "I am on my way to her work right now."

"I'll meet you there," Craig told him.

Craig headed over to the law offices of Parker, Barnes, and Newman to search for the paralegal. Craig found Adams waiting for him in the lobby. "I called here earlier but they told me that she hadn't arrived for work yet," Adams informed him. "The woman I spoke with earlier told me that she would be working on the seventh floor today in Alan Jameson's office."

They walked into the office and Craig immediately saw Abby in the corner by a filing cabinet. "Abby Lewis," he called to her.

Abby looked up. "Craig," she said. "Is there something I can do for you?"

She walked over to him. "I want to be discreet about this," he replied. "I need you to come down to the station. I have a few questions to ask you."

"Pertaining to what?" she questioned.

"You are a person of interest in an ongoing investigation," he answered.

"Me?" she asked, in disbelief. "You're kidding, right?"

"No," he said. "I need for you to come with me now."

"I'm at work," she replied. "Can't this wait until later?"

"No," Craig answered. "Do you have something to hide?"

"Helen," Abby called to another woman in the office. "I need to leave for a little bit. I'll be back as soon as I can."

When they arrived back at the station, Officer Adams escorted Abby into an interrogation room. Craig joined her a few minutes later with her records in hand and some surprising information. "How do you know Daniel Milano?" Craig asked, as he sat down.

"I have no idea who that is," she answered.

"You know what surprises me about you, Abby," Craig stated. "The last few times I have talked to you, you have been scatter brained and have acted very nervous. Today, you are very calm and self-assured. Why is that?"

"I've been visiting the self-help section at the local bookstore," she replied.

"Uh huh," Craig responded. "I'm going to ask you again. How do you know Daniel Milano?"

"And I'm going to tell you again," she answered. "I don't know him."

222

"Then why have you been in contact with him at least 3 times a week for the last month?" Craig questioned, showing her the highlighted phone records.

Abby sat in silence. "I also would like to know about this large deposit that was put into your account about a month ago," Craig inquired.

"My favorite aunt died and left me some money," Abby told him.

"Quit messing with me, Abby!" Craig threatened. "I know you have harassed Morgan Garrett on more than one occasion. I want to know how you are involved in the attacks on her, among other things."

"So this is about your girlfriend?" Abby questioned. "She's a home wrecking slut! I want to talk to my lawyer. I'm finished talking to you."

Craig grabbed the papers off the table and walked out. "She lawyered up," he told Adams. "Track down Daniel Milano and bring him back in. Is John here? I need to talk to him."

Craig found John in a nearby office. "I need to talk to you about your interrogation of Daniel Milano yesterday," Craig told John, as he took a seat.

"What do you need to know?" John asked.

Craig filled him in about the information he had received pertaining to Abby's and Daniel's phone and bank records. "Sounds like Milano was having some financial problems," John replied. "Enough for him to have to shuffle money from one account to another until he was in the black."

"And then about 3 months ago, large deposits were made into each account," Craig stated. "Looks like someone bailed him out."

"We need to get our hands on his business financial records and find out where these deposits came from," John told Craig.

"I got a buddy looking into that," Craig said. "Did Milano tell you anything yesterday?"

"Milano was very cooperative," John explained. "He claimed he didn't know anything about it. I told him not to leave town but I will bet you we won't be able to find him. Do you think he is the mastermind in all of this?"

223

"It wouldn't surprise me," Craig answered. "It's possible jealousy drove him to terrorize Morgan and when he couldn't have her, he went after the people she cared about."

"We know he's not acting alone," John replied. "We have Montgomery to prove that. I checked and Milano has an alibi for everything that happened. That doesn't mean he isn't involved though. Have you talked to Abby Lewis?"

"Yes and she is a smartass," Craig answered. "She asked for her lawyer."

"We need to find Milano then," John stated.

"I think I better go check on Morgan," Craig replied. "With him still out there somewhere, she might be in danger."

****

"I am so glad you could join me for lunch today," Morgan said. "Sorry we have to do it at the office though."

"That's ok," Elizabeth replied. "I am so happy to be out of the house. I don't seem to go anywhere but physical therapy."

"How is that going?" Morgan asked.

"Actually, I have made some progress," she answered, with a smile. "I walked with a cane the other day. The therapist told me though that I need to work up to using the cane and not to overexert myself. That is why I am in the chair today."

"You will get there," Morgan responded. "I have faith in you."

"That's what my dad keeps saying," Elizabeth replied.

"How is he doing?" Morgan asked.

"He is keeping busy," she answered. "Sometimes I feel like a burden to him. He really needs to get on with his life and stop worrying about me. I am hoping, as I get stronger and can start taking care of myself, that I can take the settlement I got and get my own place. I appreciate him and everything he has done but I think it is time."

"I understand," Morgan replied. "It wasn't easy for him to raise a teenage girl by himself but I think he did pretty well. I think he will understand if you want to get out on your own."

"I don't know," Elizabeth explained. "I tried to talk to him about it but he hasn't said anything. I think he just worries too much."

"He's a parent," Morgan responded. "That is what they do. I'm in my twenties and my mom still worries about me."

"I am glad that you got to see her and Jack over the holidays," Elizabeth stated. "She was probably happy to see you."

"Yes, she was," Morgan agreed. "We had a fight when I got there but by the end of the trip, we were probably as close as we ever have been."

Elizabeth smiled. "So what is going on with you?" she questioned. "Is there anything new to report about you and Craig?"

Morgan told her what happened after the cookout. "We had a long talk about things," she explained. "But I told him that I needed to think about things. So much has happened and I am still soaking it in."

"He is probably doing that too," Elizabeth said. "With everything that's happened, it's a lot to take in."

Morgan took a bite of her sweet and sour chicken that Elizabeth had brought her for lunch. "I am so glad you picked up Chinese," Morgan told her. "This is so good."

"I forgot to tell you," Elizabeth replied. "You will never guess who I saw when we stopped to pick up the order."

"I have no idea," Morgan said.

"Jake Waters," Elizabeth stated. "Remember him from school?"

"Yeah, he's the guy that all the girls had a crush on," Morgan answered. "I know you liked him."

Elizabeth smiled. "As I recall, you also liked him," she replied.

Morgan laughed. "Yeah, what were we thinking?" Morgan questioned. "So how is he doing?"

"He's doing well," Elizabeth answered. "He owns a few restaurants here in town and invited us to come for dinner one evening. He's married with a couple of kids."

"Another one bites the dust," Morgan replied.

The two ladies burst into uncontrollable laughter. "What were we thinking?" Elizabeth asked, as she tried to catch her breath.

"We were teenage girls," Morgan answered. "Who knows what we were thinking."

"I miss this," Elizabeth replied. "I miss hanging out with you."

Morgan smiled at her and said, "I'll tell you what. One evening soon, we will go to one of Jake's restaurants and have a girls' night out."

"Sounds good to me," Elizabeth responded.

Morgan's attention was drawn to the door as it opened. "Hello Ladies!" Craig said, as he entered the room.

"Hey Craig!" Elizabeth replied. "How are you?"

"I'm good," he told her. "Morgan, I need to talk to you when you get a free minute."

"We're in the middle of lunch," she stated, trying not to sound rude.

"It's ok, Morgan," Elizabeth replied, checking her cell phone. "I need to get going anyway. I have appointments this afternoon and my driver is here to pick me up."

Morgan got up from her chair and gave Elizabeth a hug. "I am so glad that we had lunch today," she said. "Do you need any help?"

"No," Elizabeth answered. "You just work things out with Craig."

After Morgan closed the door, she turned her attention to Craig. "Hello!" she said with a smile. "I wasn't trying to be rude."

"I know," he told her. "I should have called."

Morgan sat down in her chair and motioned for Craig to also take a seat. "So what can I do you for?" she asked.

"I have some information about your case," he answered. "We brought Abby Lewis in for questioning today. It didn't take her long to ask for a lawyer so she knows something. There was a large amount of money deposited into her personal account. Also according to her phone records, she has been in contact with Daniel Milano."

"Daniel and Abby has been talking on the phone?" she questioned.

"At least 3 times a week over the last month," he explained. "We are trying to find Daniel now. His bank records also indicated that he has deposited large amounts of money into his accounts. Funny thing about this though is that he had been shuffling money to cover withdrawals in several accounts but then this money was deposited. We think someone bailed him out."

"So there is someone else involved," Morgan replied. "We just need to figure out who it is."

"Another reason I came by was to check on you," Craig told her. "I was concerned about you."

"I appreciate it," Morgan said. "I would like to think that Daniel wouldn't hurt me but with everything he has done, I'm not so sure anymore."

"I don't like the idea of you being alone," Craig told her. "Now that it looks like we are closing in on this person, I am afraid this is going to accelerate. If this person feels cornered, they might slip up and hopefully, we can catch them."

"I don't want you to worry about me," Morgan responded. "Ever since the attack here at work, my boss has been keeping an eye on me. I am supposed to call downstairs when I am ready to leave and a security guard will escort me to my car."

"It sounds like you are taken care of here," he replied. "What about when you get home?"

"I don't know," she answered.

"I could assign an officer to you," Craig said.

Morgan closed her eyes and let out a sigh. "I don't like the thought of having a babysitter," she told him.

"I know," he replied. "I just want you to be safe."

"I know you do," Morgan said.

"I just wish I could do it myself," Craig stated. "But I feel I am too emotionally involved in this. I am afraid that will cloud my judgment. I just don't want anything to happen to you."

Morgan felt like she could cry. "I appreciate your concern," she said.

"I still care about you," he replied.

Morgan smiled at him. "I still care about you too," she confirmed, trying not to cry.

Craig cleared his throat. He didn't want Morgan to see how emotional her words had made him. "I'll check with John and see if he is available to watch you tonight," he explained. "If he is, you two can work out whether you want to stay at your townhouse or his. I trust John to watch over you for me. I just wish I could do it but I think it would be better for me to be at the station. I need to stay objective. I hope you understand that."

"I do," she said.

"It's not that I don't want to be with you," Craig told her. "You know that's not true. With as close as we are to solving this case, I just don't need the added distraction. Please don't take this the wrong way but you are definitely a distraction."

Morgan smiled. "I understand," she replied. "I'm not going to lie to you. I am still very attracted to you. I don't think us spending the night together would be a good thing right now especially with all of this going on."

"I agree," Craig responded. "As much as spending the night with you would excite me, I need to stay focused. We also have a lot of things we need to work out before that can happen. I'm going to check with John and I'll let you know what is going on. Do you trust me?"

"Yes," she answered.

"I'll take care of you," he said. "No one is going to hurt you."

Craig got up out of his chair and walked to the door. Morgan followed him. "Thank you for everything," she said.

Craig smiled as he grabbed hold of her hands. "All I want to do right now is hold you," he told her, as he looked into her eyes. "Even if it is just for a minute."

Morgan moved closer to him and wrapped her arms around him. Craig returned her hug. He thought about how good it was to hold her, wishing it would last forever. He hoped they could work things out because right now, there was nowhere else he wanted to be. He was sure Morgan felt the same way.

Craig returned to the station and immediately found John. "We still haven't found Daniel," John told him. "I don't think he has left the area though. He hasn't booked any flights and there has been no activity on any of his credit cards."

"He's in hiding," Craig stated. "After yesterday's interrogation, I am sure he knows we suspect him. Is Abby cooperating yet?"

"Her lawyer showed up and encouraged her to talk," John answered. "She said that her cell phone had been misplaced and she didn't know anything about the calls. She also told me that the money she received was given to her when her aunt passed away."

"Has her stories checked out?" Craig asked.

"Her lawyer confirmed that she had received money from her aunt's estate," John answered. "As for the phone, she claims that she didn't realize it was missing until a few days ago. According to the carrier, the account was closed when the phone was reported missing."

"So let me guess," Craig replied. "We had to let her go."

"Yeah," John said.

Craig let out a frustrating sigh and ran a hand through his hair. "What the hell is going on here?" he asked. "Why is it that every time we get a break we end up hitting a wall?"

John shook his head, not sure how to answer Craig's question. "How's Morgan doing?" John asked.

"She's fine," Craig answered. "She has people checking on her at work. Her boss ordered her to have a security guard walk her to her car. Do you have any plans for this evening? I discussed it with Morgan and we think it would be a good idea for someone to stay with her. I was wondering if you would be willing to do that. I figured if it was ok with you, she could either stay at the townhouse or you could go over to her house."

"I can watch her," John replied. "What are you going to do?"

"I am going to stay here and try to figure all this out," Craig answered. "I don't think it would be a good idea for me to stay with her. I need to be focused."

"I'll call her and we'll work out the details," John told him.

****

Morgan stood by the front door as John searched the townhouse. "It's all clear," he said, as he returned to the living room.

"Thanks," Morgan said.

"What are you thanking me for?" he asked. "I am just doing my job."

"This is so frustrating," Morgan told him. "I don't like to rely on others but this person has forced me to do just that. I really do appreciate all your help. I just wish I didn't need it."

"I understand," John replied, as he took her bag. "Let me show you where you'll be staying."

"Is this Craig's room?" Morgan asked, stopping in the doorway.

"Yeah," John answered.

"Do you think he would mind if I stayed in there?" she questioned. "Does that sound creepy?"

"A little bit," John said, laughing.

"Maybe I'll stay somewhere else then," Morgan replied, feeling a little embarrassed. "It's just that I thought it might make me feel safer. I know that you are here and I hope you know I really appreciate that. I just thought it might bring me a little more comfort and peace of mind to feel close to him. Now I do sound creepy."

"No, you don't sound creepy," he responded. "I understand what you are trying to say. I don't think he would mind if you stayed in his room tonight."

John set her overnight bag on the bed and walked back out of the room. "Are you ok?" Morgan asked, as she followed him into the living room.

"Yeah, I'm fine," he answered. "Why wouldn't I be?"

"I guess I just wanted to know if you are ok with what happened yesterday," she explained. "I know I'm not. I feel really guilty about it."

"You shouldn't feel that way," John stated. "I told you that I think of you more like a sister. We had some fun when we were hanging out but I didn't have any romantic feelings for you. Trust me when I tell you that everything is fine."

"I just want you to understand that I didn't plan on kissing Craig yesterday," she told him. "I was trying to avoid him."

"I know," he replied. "Morgan, you need to take a step back and see what the rest of us see. You and Craig have this bond, this connection that no one can break. I know it might seem grim right now but if you two want to be together, you will be. After we find this guy, you need to sit down and talk things out with Craig. I can promise you that you two will be back together, if that is what you want."

"I'm not so sure about that," she stated. "I said and did so many unforgivable things."

"He did too," he said. "I don't think it is anything unforgivable though. You want to be with him right?"

"I do," Morgan answered.

"I know he wants to be with you," John told her. "You love him right?"

"I do," she repeated.

"He loves you too," John confirmed. "You know that. Everything is fine between you and me. Everything is fine between me and Craig. You just need to have a little faith and forgive each other. We all do stupid things but neither one of you did anything that can't be forgiven."

"Thanks!" she said. "That is exactly what I needed to hear right now."

The two settled on the couch with dinner and a basketball game. As soon as the game ended, Morgan told John that she was going to go to bed. "Do you still want to go for that jog in the morning?" John asked.

Morgan turned around and smiled at him. "Yeah I do," she answered.

"It's a date then," John replied.

Morgan went into Craig's room and slipped into her night clothes. She crawled into his bed and immediately smelled his scent on the pillow. She snuggled up with his pillow and felt herself start to relax. "Hello!" Morgan said, as she answered her cell phone.

"Hi!" Craig replied. "How are you doing?"

"I'm doing well," she answered. "How are you?"

"I'm better now," he told her. "I got some rest earlier because I knew I would probably be here all night. What are you doing?"

Morgan smiled. "This is probably going to sound weird," she answered. "I am lying in your bed."

Craig caught his breath. "I wish I was lying there with you," he said. "After we catch this guy, we are getting back together."

231

Morgan smiled. "You sound pretty sure about that," she replied.

"I am," he stated. "I am going to do everything in my power to convince you that we belong together."

"I don't need any convincing," she responded. "I love you and I want to be with you."

"You don't know how long I have been waiting to hear you say that," Craig replied, with tears in his eyes. "I love you too, and more than anything, I want to be with you."

Morgan's tears of joy fell onto Craig's pillow. "I need you to catch this guy then," she told him.

"I'm doing everything I can," he said.

"I know you are," she told him.

"I better get back to work," Craig replied. "I'll see you tomorrow."

After Craig hung up the phone, he turned his attention back to the evidence he had collected. He had looked at it a million times and still couldn't connect the dots. He knew that Abby was lying but now he had to prove it. That was going to be hard to do without Daniel. "Craig," Officer Adams said, as he entered the office. "This package was just delivered for you."

Craig opened the manila envelope and found a note that read that the information included would help with Morgan Garrett's case. After setting the note aside, he pulled a book out of the package. He was shocked to find that the journal belonged to Elizabeth Brinkman. This confused Craig. He didn't understand what Elizabeth had to do with Morgan's case. He hoped that reading the journal would clear things up.

The first journal entry was dated two days after her accident. It didn't take long for Craig to find the first entry about him. Elizabeth praised him for being her savior. She expressed an interest in him, proclaiming that he might be "the one." That declaration didn't sit well with Craig. He knew he didn't feel that way about her and just reading what she had written made him think that maybe he led her to believe something more.

As he read more, he got the feeling that Elizabeth was jealous of Morgan. That would be a good motive for everything that had happened. That feeling was confirmed when he read the entry from the night he had seen her at the club. Elizabeth was excited that she had seen Craig that night but was upset with Morgan for interrupting their conversation. She was even more upset to see Craig and Morgan dancing. Elizabeth knew then that she had no chance with Craig. It wasn't anything unusual though. Morgan always had things come easily for her. She didn't even have to try. Things just fell into her lap. Morgan was well liked in school and always popular. She also had a lot of luck with men. She had a boyfriend all through high school and then Edward all through college. It was really hard for Elizabeth to not be jealous of Morgan.

Craig couldn't believe what he was reading. He felt like he had been the one to start this whole situation. He had no idea though that Elizabeth had romantic feelings for him. It was probably because he was concentrating on his marriage and then on a relationship with Morgan. He was oblivious to her crush on him. If he had known, maybe he could have let her down easy and avoided all of this. Instead, she was now the suspect in the investigation.

As he continued to read, he noticed that Elizabeth never once mentioned getting back at Morgan. She never talked about devising a plan to hurt her or to break up the couple. As the entries progressed, Elizabeth seemed to be fine with the relationship between Craig and Morgan and seemed genuinely happy for them.

Craig closed the book and let out a sigh. He was finding it difficult to wrap his head around all this. He couldn't believe that Elizabeth would pretend to be Morgan's friend one minute and plan her demise the next. The only way he was going to get to the bottom of this was to talk to Elizabeth.

Craig got up from his desk and exited the room. After he found Officer Adams, Craig directed him and Officer Stone to find Elizabeth and bring her in for questioning.

He returned to his office and emptied the rest of the contents of the envelope onto his desk. The first thing that caught his attention was pictures of him and Morgan. There were several of them together at the tree farm and outside of her townhouse.

They looked like surveillance photos. Was Elizabeth having them followed?

The last bit of evidence was a bank statement. The statement showed that large amounts of money had been withdrawn from Elizabeth's account over the last several months. He knew that she had received a settlement recently for her accident. Was she using this money to pay Daniel and Abby?

Craig grabbed the evidence off his desk and headed out the door. He wanted to find out why Elizabeth wasn't there yet. Craig was on his way to ask the desk sergeant when Officer Adams approached him. "Miss Brinkman is in interrogation," he told Craig.

Craig wasn't looking forward to this. He wasn't sure what Elizabeth's role was in all of this but he was going to find out. He prayed this was all just a misunderstanding.

"Hey Craig!" she said, as he entered the room. "I'm not sure why I am here. I hope everything is ok?"

"I'm sorry to get you out so late," he told her. "I need to ask you a few questions about a case I'm working on."

"Sure," she replied. "I'll do whatever I can to help."

Craig took a seat across from her. "I need to talk to you about Morgan's case," he told her.

"I don't know what kind of help I will be," Elizabeth said. "But I'll try."

"You and Morgan have been friends for a long time," Craig stated. "Have you ever been jealous of her?"

"Sure," she answered. "Morgan seemed to have it easy in high school. She had a boyfriend and I didn't. People liked her. Sometimes it was hard not to be jealous."

"What about recently?" he asked.

"I don't understand what this is all about," she replied.

Craig showed the journal to her. "Is this your journal?" he questioned.

"Yes," she answered. "Where did you get that?"

"Some new evidence has come to my attention regarding Morgan's case," Craig told her. "If you want a lawyer, now is the time to get one."

"Am I a suspect?" she questioned. "Are you arresting me?"

"You are a suspect," he answered.

"Do you actually believe that I had something to do with this case?" she asked. "I would never do anything to hurt Morgan."

"I would like to believe that," Craig replied. "I have some incriminating evidence against you though. I can read you your rights and ask you again about having your lawyer present. I want to make it clear though that you are not under arrest. I am just asking you a few questions. I am trying to get to the bottom of this."

Elizabeth sat silent as she stared across the table at Craig. "I can't believe that you think I have something to do with this," Elizabeth responded. "Morgan is my best friend. She is like a sister to me and I would never do anything to hurt her. I don't know what kind of evidence you have that proves otherwise."

"I have your journal," Craig said, as he opened it to the first entry about him and Morgan. "Are you jealous of Morgan?"

Elizabeth grabbed the journal and set it in front of her. "Just to let you know," she explained. "I will answer your questions because I didn't do anything wrong and I have nothing to hide. I don't need my lawyer. I am jealous of Morgan. I have liked you from the moment I met you. It was hard for me when I found out that you two were dating. I came to the realization though that I should be happy for both of you. You were never mine to begin with so she didn't steal you away from me."

Elizabeth read the entries in the journal that Craig directed her to. "I remember writing this," she continued. "I was upset the night that Morgan interrupted us at the club. But then I saw you two dancing and I knew that something was going on."

"So this isn't a case of 'if I can't have him, no one can?'" Craig asked.

"No," she answered. "As I told you, I am happy for both of you. There is no need for me to be hateful about it. That would only result in me losing my best friend. It's not worth it."

"I also have these pictures that were brought to my attention," he replied, showing them to her.

"I have never seen these before," she told him. "Where did you get these?"

"These look like surveillance pictures," Craig said. "Did you hire someone to follow us around?"

"I didn't hire anyone to do anything," she replied. "I told you that I have never seen these before."

"I also have a copy of your bank records," he stated. "According to this, the money you received from your settlement is gone. That was enough money to pay people to do your dirty work."

"What do you mean it is gone?" she asked, as Craig handed her the paper. "I didn't spend it and I sure as hell wouldn't have used it to pay anyone off. That money was supposed to be for my future."

"Did anyone else have access to your account?" Craig questioned.

"No," Elizabeth answered, getting frustrated. "I don't understand what is happening here. I didn't pay anyone to hurt Morgan or take pictures of the two of you."

"How well do you know Daniel Milano?" Craig asked.

"I have known him since high school," Elizabeth told him. "Is he involved in all of this?"

"Daniel has come into a lot of money lately," Craig replied. "He has had a lot of bad luck in business too. I think you have been bailing him out. What happened to all the money you had?"

"I don't know," she responded, in tears. "I didn't spend it!"

"Well someone did," Craig said. "You told me that you were the only one with access to it."

"I am," Elizabeth told him. "I don't know where it is."

"Let me tell you what I think," Craig stated, getting frustrated. "I think that you were jealous of Morgan and wanted her out of the way. I think you paid someone to take pictures of us and follow us around so you would know where we were and what we were doing 24/7. I think you employed Daniel Milano, among others, to terrorize Morgan and spent your settlement to pay them."

"NO!" Elizabeth screamed. "I would never do that!"

"That's enough, Detective," Richard Brinkman ordered, as he entered the room with his lawyer.

"Daddy," Elizabeth cried. "I would never do any of the things Craig is accusing me of. You have to believe me."

"I do," he replied. "You shouldn't be talking to him without your lawyer."

"I don't need a lawyer," she stated. "I didn't do anything wrong."

"Detective, you need to leave," Richard told Craig. "I want to talk to my daughter."

Craig knew he was going to have to arrest Elizabeth in order to keep her there. Craig approached her and began to read her rights to her. "What are you doing?" Richard asked.

After Craig was finished telling Elizabeth her rights, he answered, "I am placing your daughter under arrest."

"I think you are too involved in this case," Richard replied. "You need to remove yourself from it."

"I'll find another detective to handle this," Craig said, as he left the room.

Craig tracked down Detective Jacob Logan and filled him in on the case. He returned to his office in a state of shock. He didn't mean to be so rough on Elizabeth but he had to know the truth. He honestly believed Elizabeth had nothing to do with the case but the evidence told a different story. There were so many unconnected pieces of the puzzle. He knew the way to complete it was to find Daniel and hopefully, he could somehow clear Elizabeth.

Craig grabbed his coat and decided to leave. There wasn't much more he could do since he was ordered to remove himself from the case. That was probably for the best because he didn't want to risk the case being dropped due to a technicality. It had been a long night and he didn't want his hard work to be dismissed. Anyway, he had a beautiful woman to go home to and he couldn't wait to see her.

Chapter 16

Morgan awoke to a dream come true. Lying beside her was Craig and he had his arms wrapped around her. For the first time in a long time, she felt safe. She didn't want to leave her safe haven but she knew she would have to in a few minutes. She promised John a morning jog and she wasn't going to disappoint him.

Morgan carefully moved Craig's arm from around her, trying not to wake him. She knew it was late when he had gotten home and he needed his rest. She began to move across the bed. "Where are you going?" Craig asked sleepily, as he pulled her back to him.

"I promised John that I would go jogging with him this morning," she answered. "I have to get up."

"I don't want you to go," he replied. "I like having you next to me."

Morgan rolled over onto her side so she could face Craig. "You came home late last night," she stated.

"Yeah," he agreed. "I made an arrest in your case."

"You did?" Morgan asked. "So you found Daniel?"

"No, we haven't found him yet," Craig answered. "I arrested Elizabeth."

"Elizabeth?" Morgan questioned. "I don't understand. Why would you arrest her? She wouldn't be involved in anything like this."

"I don't think she's involved either," he told her. "But I have evidence that proves otherwise."

Craig told Morgan about the package he received. "Do you have any idea who sent it to you?" Morgan asked.

"I have no idea," he answered. "The evidence is pretty damaging though."

"I just can't believe Elizabeth would want to hurt me," she replied. "She's been my friend since we were little girls. We're like sisters. Why would she do this?"

"I think she is jealous of you," Craig responded.

Craig told Morgan what Elizabeth had said during the interrogation. "She's always been supportive of us," Morgan told him, in disbelief. "She always seemed so happy for us. Was that all an act?"

"It could have been so we wouldn't suspect her," he stated.

Morgan wasn't sure what to think. She didn't want any of this to be true. How could her friend of so many years be involved in all these crimes? How could Elizabeth have become so desperate for a man that she was willing to harm Morgan to get him? The question that bothered Morgan the most though was how far would she have gone if she hadn't been caught? Would she have killed Morgan to get her hands on Craig?

"Everything is going to be fine," Craig told her, as he examined the look on her face.

Morgan smiled at him. "I hope so," she said.

Craig pulled her closer to him. "I am so glad that you were here last night when I got home," he told her. "I could get used to this."

Craig ran his hand along Morgan's cheek. "You are so beautiful," he whispered.

Morgan smiled again. "You should kiss me," she instructed.

It was Craig's turn to smile. He wasn't going to argue with her. He did exactly what he was told. "I missed you kissing me," she said.

"There is more where that came from," Craig replied, getting closer for another kiss.

"As much as I would love to stay in bed with you," Morgan stated. "I promised John we would go for a morning jog. I don't want to disappoint him."

"Ok," he responded. "I'm going to let you get dressed while I go talk to John. I want to fill him in about Elizabeth's arrest. I think I am going back to bed after that."

Craig left the room and found John in the kitchen. "I heard you come in late last night," John said. "I'm surprised you're up."

"Morgan's getting ready to go jogging with you," Craig replied. "I thought I would update you on Morgan's case."

Craig explained the events of the night before to John. "I didn't see that coming," he stated. "It didn't even occur to me to suspect Elizabeth."

"I think she fooled us all," Craig told him.

"Hey John!" Morgan said, as she entered the room. "Are you ready to go?"

"Yeah," he answered. "I'll go get my shoes on and meet you outside."

After John left the room, Craig instructed Morgan to be careful. "Wake me up when you get back ok?" he asked.

"I will," she confirmed.

Craig gave her a passionate kiss. "I love you!" he told her.

"I love you too!" she said.

"How are you doing?" John asked, as they started their jog.

"I'm ok," Morgan answered.

"I was just checking," he replied. "I wanted to make sure that you were ok after hearing about Elizabeth."

"I'm shocked," she responded. "I can't believe she would do this especially over a man. There were times in school that we had a crush on the same guy but we never fought over anyone. She always was supportive and seemed happy for me when I was dating Daniel and then Edward. I just don't understand."

"Hopefully soon, we can get some answers," John said. "It would be nice if we could find Daniel. I don't think he is innocent in all this."

"I don't either," Morgan told him. "The more I think about it the more I think this is all a well constructed plan. Someone is running the show."

"We'll figure it out," John stated. "Until then, know that Craig and I will do whatever is necessary to protect you."

"I hope you don't think that Craig and I are throwing our relationship in your face," Morgan said.

"I don't think that," he replied. "I hope you are not going to apologize again for what happened between us. If it will make you feel any better, I always thought it would be you and Craig. I just thought I would take the chance while I had it."

"I'm just glad you are fine with it," she responded.

"I am happy for you two," John said. "I hope you know that."

Morgan stopped jogging. "What's wrong?" John questioned.

"Nothing," she answered, as she stared at the entrance to the cemetery. "I just didn't realize where we were at until now. This is where Edward is buried. I haven't been here in awhile. Do you mind if we stop for a few minutes?"

"That should be fine," John told her. "Just don't wander off without me, ok?"

Morgan agreed and the two walked into the cemetery and quickly found Edward's grave. "I'll give you some privacy," he stated. "I'll be right over here in case you need something. We probably should be headed back shortly so just a couple minutes, ok?"

Morgan nodded and turned her attention to the tombstone. "Hello Edward," she said. "I'm sorry I haven't been here in awhile. Things have been a little complicated but I'm sure you already know that. I guess I wanted to stop by to tell you that I found someone, someone that I love. Not that I have forgotten about you or stopped loving you."

Morgan began to cry. "I'm sorry. I know you hate it when I cry," she continued. "I guess I just want your permission to move on. I know that sounds silly but I was with you for a long time. I think you would like Craig. He is so good to me and he loves me."

Morgan wiped her tears and smiled. "You know I will always love you and you will have a special place in my heart. I feel like I need to move on. This is where I need to be. Somehow I think you would understand that."

"That was beautiful, Morgan," Daniel said, as he approached her, applauding. "Now do you have a heartfelt speech prepared for me?"

Morgan began to panic and turned her attention to the direction John was last standing. "He's not there, Morgan," Daniel informed her. "Do you really think I would approach you without taking care of him first? I'm surprised that Craig isn't with you but then again whose to say I didn't take care of him too. You'd be surprised how easy it is to get to someone who is sound asleep."

Morgan wanted to cry but she willed herself to stay strong. "You didn't do anything to Craig," she said.

"What makes you so sure of that?" Daniel questioned. "I got to Officer Martin without any problems."

Morgan's mind was spinning. She wasn't sure what to think. "Why are you doing this?" she asked.

"I have my reasons," he answered, grabbing her arm. "You are coming with me."

****

Craig awoke with a jolt. He had a bad feeling something was wrong. He stared at the clock and began to wonder why Morgan and John weren't back from their jog. Craig heard a noise coming from the living room. He grabbed his gun and quietly entered the room. "John!" Craig shouted. "You scared the hell out of me!"

John stood there trying to speak but was having a hard time catching his breath. "Where's Morgan?" Craig asked. "Where is she?"

"I'm so sorry, Craig," John replied. "She's gone. They took her."

"Who took her?" Craig questioned, angrily.

"We were jogging and ended up out at the cemetery where Edward is buried," John explained. "She asked if we could stop for a few minutes. I thought it would be ok. I was no more than a few feet away from her the whole time. I saw Daniel coming toward her but before I could say anything or get to her, someone jumped me. I am so sorry. You trusted me to watch her and they took her."

Craig's mind was racing. "How did you get away?" he asked. "Why are you not with her?"

"I did everything I could to get to her," John answered. "I hope you know that. They planned it this way because they wanted me to deliver a message to you. They told me to tell you that they have her and you need to come find her. You need to go question Elizabeth again and find out where Morgan is."

Craig felt numb. He couldn't think straight. "I need to change clothes," he said. "Then I'll head to the station."

Craig entered the bedroom and stared at the bed. Just hours ago, Morgan was lying there with him. They were back together. He wasn't going to let someone take her away from him again. He knew what he had to do.

They arrived at the station and Craig immediately found Detective Jacob Logan. "Morgan has been kidnapped," Craig told him. "I need to talk to Elizabeth Brinkman. She has information that will lead me to Morgan."

"You can fill me in as we walk," Jacob said. "I will let you go into the room with me but I'm asking the questions."

Craig reluctantly agreed. He would do whatever he had to do to find Morgan but he wasn't sure he would be able to keep his mouth shut.

Craig and Jacob entered the interrogation room, where Elizabeth and her lawyer were waiting. "I don't know what else you could possibly have to ask my client," David Michaels stated. "She doesn't know anything."

"We have a new development in the case," Jacob explained. "We have reason to believe that Miss Brinkman has information about it that she hasn't told us yet."

"What is this new development?" David asked. "Why am I just hearing about it?"

"Morgan is missing," Jacob answered. "She was taken this morning by Daniel Milano and at least one other man. We have reason to believe that Elizabeth knows where she is."

Elizabeth and David looked at each other. "I don't know where she is," she said.

"I don't have time for any of your games," Craig stated. "I don't think you understand what kind of danger Morgan is in. If you ever cared about her, you will help me find her."

Jacob glared at Craig. "I do care about her," Elizabeth replied. "If I knew where she was, I would tell you."

"I am getting so tired of this," Craig told her, raising his voice. "I am so sick of this innocent act. We have all this evidence against you. You know what is going on and I want you to tell me."

"I don't know anything!" Elizabeth yelled. "Anyone could have had access to my things. I wrote things in my journal. It was suggested I do that as a form of therapy to get me through the accident. I have never seen those surveillance pictures before nor do I have any idea who took them. As for my bank account, no one has access to it but me. I told Morgan the other day that I was planning on using that money to get a place of my own. I was going to use it so I could start taking care of myself. I don't know where the money is."

Elizabeth began to cry. The pressure was getting to her. She wished someone would believe her. She just wanted to go home. "I didn't mean to upset you," Craig said, as he sat down across the table from her. "I just don't think you understand how serious this is."

"I do understand," Elizabeth replied. "But I don't know where she is."

Craig sat there in thought. Something about this wasn't right. There was a piece of the puzzle still missing. "You said that anyone could have had access to your things?" he questioned. "Are you sure that you are the only one who has access to your account?"

"The only person's name on the account is mine," she answered. "The only other person that could possibly have access to it is my father."

"Where is your father?" Craig asked.

"He's not involved in this," Elizabeth told him.

"Humor me," Craig replied. "If your father is behind all of this, where would he have taken Morgan?"

"My family owns several acres of land around our house," she stated. "He might have taken her there."

"Thank you!" Craig said.

"I hope you find her," she told him.

Craig exited the room with Jacob on his heels. "I know what you're going to say," Craig said. "I'm sorry I took over

244

in there after you asked me not to. I have to find Morgan and I'm afraid we are running out of time."

"I understand," Jacob replied. "Let's just get out there and see if we can find her."

****

"Why are you doing this?" Morgan asked. "Is it all because I wouldn't go out with you?"

"I did it for the money," Daniel answered. "Don't be offended, my dear. We all have a price."

"What happened, Daniel?" she questioned. "Did your business go belly up? Did someone come along and offer to bail you out?"

"Shut up!" he replied, wrapping a hand around her neck. "I don't want to hear another word from you."

Morgan surveyed the area. She knew exactly where she was. She and Elizabeth used to play in this clearing when they were young girls. Off to the left, she saw the woods where she would climb trees and play hide and seek. To the other direction, she located the old tree with the remnants of the tree house Elizabeth's father had built. She knew Daniel would have never found this place on his own. Elizabeth must have told him about it. "The cops are on their way," the man Morgan recognized as the other assailant when she was first attacked told Daniel.

"Good," Daniel said. "It seems Elizabeth did her job. Once Masterson gets here, the fireworks can begin."

Daniel turned his attention back to Morgan. "Ok, Sweetheart," he stated. "This is what I want you to do. You better do exactly what I tell you or I will kill Masterson. Don't think I won't. He means nothing to me but I know he means a lot to you. Although seeing you go through that kind of pain would pleasure me greatly, that's not the plan right now. Anyway, I digress. As soon as I let go of your arm, I want you to run into the woods. Do you understand?"

Morgan nodded, a little confused. "You do what you are told and you might just make it out of this alive," Daniel continued by saying. "Get ready, Dear. Here they come."

Daniel let go of Morgan's arm and she took off running towards the woods. She wasn't sure what was going on or why

245

Daniel would let her go. He must not have been informed that she knew these woods like the back of her hand.

Morgan stopped running and took a look around. She wasn't sure what she was supposed to do next. Was she supposed to continue running or find a place to hide? She decided that she should do one or the other because she didn't want to be a target. She didn't want to be captured again either.

Morgan was startled by a noise off in the distance. She decided to hurry to one of her surefire hiding places that she had found as a child. She hoped she would be safe there.

****

Craig and John arrived at the Brinkman estate with a handful of officers. Craig directed a few of them to check the house and the outlying buildings for any clues to where Morgan might be. "What do you want me to do?" John asked, still feeling guilty about Morgan's kidnapping during their morning run.

"Stay here and see if they find anything," Craig answered. "If they don't, send a party into the woods and start looking for her. Assume that the kidnappers are armed so have everyone buddy up and watch each other's backs. I'm going to go look for her."

"You're not going out there by yourself," John ordered.

"I know she is out there," Craig replied. "We are wasting time."

"Be careful," John told him. "We will join you as soon as they are finished searching the buildings."

Craig made a mad dash towards the woods. He had a bad feeling that this whole thing was a trap so he decided to proceed cautiously. All he wanted to do was find Morgan and make sure she was safe.

Craig drew his gun and wandered slowly through the woods paying attention to every sound. He prayed that he would find Morgan so they could get out of there. Somehow he knew that it wasn't going to be easy. He knew that she spent a lot of time in these woods as a kid and if somehow she had gotten away from Daniel, she would be difficult to find. She knew every hiding place and exit. He just prayed for a little luck and hoped that the connection he felt to her would help him locate her.

The trees seemed to engulf Craig as he wandered aimlessly through the woods. He felt like he was walking around in circles. He investigated every nook and cranny he could find but it was like looking for a needle in a haystack. He was startled by something he saw out of the corner of his eye. He aimed his gun and was ready to fire at the first sign of danger. "Craig, it's me," Morgan whispered, as she stepped out from behind the foliage.

Craig let out a sigh of relief as he lowered his gun. "If we stay here, we are sitting ducks," he told her, as he grabbed her hand. "We have to MOVE!"

The couple maneuvered their way through the woods. Morgan directed Craig to a secluded hideaway. They needed a place to talk so they could get a plan in action. "Can we get back to the house from here?" he asked.

"We would have to backtrack," she answered.

"We don't want to go back that way," Craig replied. "What is in this direction?"

"There is a clearing over there," Morgan explained, pointing to the northeast. "There is a pond with an access road next to it. The road leads to the main road."

Craig wasn't sure what to do. He didn't want to risk going to the clearing for fear that they might be ambushed. Without the trees as cover, they would be easy targets. They could take a chance and circle back around but he wasn't sure where the perpetrators were.

The snap of a twig alerted Craig and Morgan that someone was nearby. Neither one of them could tell who it was but they knew they had to move quickly before they were discovered.

Craig decided that they were going to try to circle around and make their way back to the house. He was hoping with some luck they would find one of his officers along the way. He knew they would have to be careful because one wrong move could be their undoing. It was a chance they would have to take if they had any hope of getting through this alive. He was thinking of the worst case scenario because he wasn't sure what Daniel was capable of. He still didn't have all the answers to fill in the holes of his investigation but he would get them in time. His only concern right now was to protect Morgan and to get them to somewhere safe.

Craig grabbed Morgan's hand and began to lead her through the woods. Morgan wasn't sure what Craig's plan was but she trusted him enough to put her life in his hands. She knew he would take care of her and she prayed they would get out of this safely.

"Where do you two think you are going?" Daniel asked, as he stepped out from his hiding spot.

Craig pulled Morgan closer to him, unsure of Daniel's next move. "Victor," Daniel said to the man standing behind the couple. "Take Masterson's gun."

The man did as he was told and along with Daniel directed the couple towards the pond and access road. "Why are you doing this?" Morgan asked Daniel.

"I already told you that," he answered. "Don't make me repeat myself."

"Who are you working for?" she questioned.

"I'm not working for anyone," Daniel told her.

"Who gave you the money to bail out your sinking business?" she asked.

Daniel swung around and pointed his gun in Morgan's face. "SHUT UP!" he yelled.

Craig pulled Morgan behind him. "Put the gun down!" he ordered. "No one needs to get hurt."

Daniel lowered his gun and motioned for Craig and Morgan to walk in front of him. "I can't believe how stupid you are," Daniel stated. "It was so easy for everything I planned to fall into place."

Daniel paused, expecting Morgan or Craig to say something. When they didn't, he continued. "Morgan, you provided us with a great opportunity this morning," he explained. "You bringing Officer Martin with you was an added bonus. I knew at that moment that I could use him as bait to lure Masterson out to find you. Even Elizabeth did her part. All this time, she has been proclaiming her innocence. But as soon as you asked her where Morgan might be, she had an answer almost immediately. Doesn't that strike you as funny? I can't believe how easy this was."

The foursome arrived at the pond and access road. "I still don't understand why you are doing this," Morgan stated.

"You rejected me," Daniel told her. "I came back to town to get back together with you. That night we went to your Christmas party together and you led me on to believe we had a chance. Then you informed me that you were in love with Masterson. To tell you the truth though, it didn't really hurt as much as I thought. It made me angry and now I want revenge."

"Daniel, I'm sorry if I hurt you," Morgan replied. "I never meant to do that. We dated in high school though. After all that time, how could you expect me to just pick up where we left off? Too much time has passed. I have moved on."

"Maybe you have," Daniel stated. "Anyway, it has been a real pleasure watching you suffer these last few months. Now that I think about it you have had a real rough time lately. Sorry about Edward. That must have been heartbreaking."

Morgan knew that Daniel was being sarcastic. "You bastard!" she said, angrily. "You better not have had anything to do with that."

"I can honestly say that I didn't have anything to do with Edward's death," Daniel replied. "That would have been a great way to get my revenge on a spoiled brat like you. One day, you will learn what it is like to have to work for something. You can't have everything handed to you."

Morgan stood there trying to figure out where all of this was coming from. It sounded to her as if Daniel had a lot of pent up anger towards her that had been escalating for longer than just a few months. Why was he so angry with her? It had to be more than just her rejection of him.

"I don't understand why you are SO angry at me," she responded. "Everyone thinks that I have life so easy. What the hell did I do to any of you? Daniel, why do you hate me?"

"This is beyond hate," he answered. "I am going to have so much fun watching you suffer, watching you go through so much pain."

Daniel raised his gun and pointed it at Craig and Morgan. Without hesitation, he pulled the trigger.

Chapter 17

Morgan regained consciousness in the corner of a cold concrete room. Her swollen and burning eyes were making it difficult for her to focus. She got to her feet and braced herself against the frigid wall. Despite feeling weak, she slid herself slowly across the surface. She had to figure out where she was which proved challenging. All she had to depend on was her sense of touch and a small amount of light peeking through a tiny window, which was too high for her to reach.

Morgan stumbled several times as she slowly found her way around what she calculated to be a twelve foot by twelve foot room. It wasn't furnished with much. From what she could tell, it only had a cot, a toilet, and a sink. It felt like a prison cell. The building seemed familiar to her but she wasn't sure why. She felt like she had been here before. The faint scent of cedar and oak brought all kinds of childhood memories back to her. She was in Richard Brinkman's old wood shop.

"Come on, Morgan!" an eight-year-old Elizabeth said, as she ran past Morgan. "Daddy told me that he has a surprise for us."

"I wonder what it is," Morgan replied.

The girls raced to the wood shop. They had been there a number of times before but the projects Richard was working on were never for them until now. The two knew the rules to being there before they even arrived. The first rule was to push the button outside the door before you came into the building. The button was a signal to the person inside that someone was coming into the shop. The girls also knew that they were not allowed to touch anything. Richard believed in safety first and if the girls were going to be there, they were going to abide by his rules.

That was one of the happiest days of Morgan's life. She and Elizabeth learned that Richard was working on a tree house for the girls to use as their secret hideout. The two were so excited that they would have a place that was theirs and only theirs.

The wood shop was different now. All the equipment was gone and it was cold and dark. It was nothing like Morgan remembered it. She knew that someone had taken a lot of time to set the room up that way for her. She had to find a way out.

The overhead light flipped on and blinded Morgan. She couldn't see anything but she did hear the door at the other end of the room open. Terror filled Morgan as she tried to find a place to hide. If she could have blended into the wall, she would have. She felt the new presence approach her and Morgan tried to scream but nothing came out. "Morgan, it's Abby," she told her. "I am here to help you. I brought you some water and food. I also brought you some towels so you can clean up."

Morgan reluctantly took a drink of the water hoping it would soothe her throat. "Why are you helping me?" Morgan asked, her voice cracking.

"Because this has gone too far," Abby answered. "This is not the way things were supposed to go."

"Are you going to help me get out of here?" Morgan questioned.

"I can't do that," Abby replied. "It's not safe. Morgan, I only have a few minutes. I need for you to drink this water and eat this sandwich I brought you. I have a few extra bottles for you and I will bring you more later, along with a blanket. Right now, you need to let me help you get cleaned up. I have a sweatshirt here for you to change into."

Morgan agreed and let Abby escort her to the sink. Morgan was horrified by the image she saw in the mirror. Blood covered the right side of her face and the front of her clothes. Flashes of that afternoon crowded her mind. She knew she was about to break down but willed herself not to in front of Abby. Before Morgan could say anything, Abby began to apologize.

"I'm so sorry about all of this," she said. "I want you to know that I was only paid to follow you around and harass you. Maybe one day you will let me explain it to you and you can forgive me."

"What happened to Craig?" Morgan asked, bracing herself.

"I think I got you cleaned up," Abby replied, ignoring Morgan's question. "Hurry up and change."

Morgan did as Abby asked. "Can you leave the light on?" Morgan questioned.

"I don't know if I can do that," she answered. "I can probably leave it on long enough for you to eat your sandwich but I can't guarantee how long it will stay on. Since the switch is outside, I can't control it. I'm sorry."

"Thank you," Morgan said.

"I'll be back later to check on your water supply," she told Morgan. "Do you need anything else? Would you like anything special to eat?"

Morgan started to cry. "You have to pull yourself together," Abby stated. "Daniel is going to be here before too long and you have to remain strong. Can you do that?"

Morgan nodded. "I'll be back later," Abby said, trying to reassure her.

As soon as Abby exited the room, Morgan dropped to the floor and cried. Memories of earlier in the day flooded her mind. Daniel shot Craig. Morgan tried desperately to help him but Victor grabbed her and pulled her away from Craig's side. She remembered being dragged away kicking and screaming. Then everything went black.

Morgan starting crying harder when she realized she wasn't sure what had happened to Craig. She had asked Abby but she didn't answer her inquiry. She hoped and prayed that he wasn't dead. That was the only conclusion that she could come to though. Daniel didn't care about Craig so why would he offer Craig any type of help? Unless by some chance someone had found Craig and got him the proper medical treatment, there was little hope that he was still alive. She couldn't give up on that little bit of hope. It was the only thing that was going to get her through this ordeal.

Morgan decided to eat her sandwich. She really didn't feel like eating but she had to in order to regain her strength. She knew she had to remain healthy if she was going to get out of there. She wasn't sure how helpful Abby was going to be in her escape or to even what extent she could trust her. Morgan knew she would have only herself to rely on.

Morgan must have drifted off to sleep without realizing it. She was awakened by the sound of the door opening. She prayed it was Abby but she was quickly disappointed by the appearance of Daniel. "How are you doing, Princess?" he asked, as he approached her. "Are you happy to see me?"

Morgan rose to her feet. "Go to hell!" she told him.

"You first," he replied.

"What do you want?" she asked.

"I came to check on you," he answered.

"You don't care about me," she stated.

"You're right," he responded. "I don't care."

"Then just leave me alone," Morgan told him.

"What fun would that be?" Daniel said.

"Where's Craig?" Morgan questioned.

"Don't you remember, Sweetheart," Daniel answered. "I shot him. He's dead."

Morgan willed herself not to cry. "You bastard!" she yelled, as she slapped him across the face.

In one quick motion, Daniel shoved Morgan against the wall and wrapped a hand around her throat. "Now you listen here, bitch," he whispered, leaning into her. "You did this. This is all your fault. You're the reason my mother asks me every time she sees me why we aren't together. You're the one who has constantly distracted me to the point that my business suffered and I was labeled a failure. I've been planning this for a long time and when the opportunity presented itself, I couldn't say no. Now you are finally getting what you deserve."

Daniel squeezed Morgan's throat and then let go. Morgan grasped for air. "Don't mess with me," he told her. "Next time, it will be worse."

Morgan shook in fear as she watched Daniel's departure. She knew that Daniel's plan was to kill her. She knew it wouldn't be long before he succeeded. She had to figure out a way to escape. She had to try to convince Abby to help her. As much as she hated to admit it, she had to trust Abby because she was her only hope.

****

Craig opened his eyes but didn't recognize his surrounding. His memory was foggy and he couldn't remember what had happened to him. He started to sit up but experienced an intense pain in his chest which caused him to groan loudly. "You need to lie still before you rip your sutures," Abby told him, as she hurried to his side.

"Where am I?" he asked. "What happened?"

"You're in a safe place," she answered. "You were shot. Don't you remember?"

Craig seemed confused. "I was shot?" he questioned.

"Yes," Abby replied. "Daniel shot you."

"Where's Morgan?" he asked, trying to sit up again. "I have to find her."

"No," Abby corrected him. "You need to rest. You had quite a bit of damage from the bullet but luckily, it didn't hit your heart."

Craig closed his eyes trying to remember exactly what happened. He remembered standing beside Morgan, listening to her and Daniel argue. He saw Daniel raise his pistol but before he could react, he felt the bullet explode into his chest. As he hit the ground, he could hear Morgan screaming as Victor took her away. He must have lost consciousness because that was all he could remember.

"Does Daniel have Morgan?" Craig asked.

"Craig, you need to rest," Abby reminded him. "You're not going to be any good to anyone if you don't allow yourself to heal. I'm going to go talk to the doctor. I'll be right back."

Craig scanned the room, trying to figure out where he was. He noticed an IV unit to the right of him and a needle stuck in his arm. There was also a monitor that posted his vital signs. He was pretty sure that he wasn't in a hospital though. The room looked too homey like a guest bedroom. He concluded that he was in someone's house.

"Can you tell me how I got here?" Craig asked Abby, as she walked back into the room.

"It's a long story," Abby explained, as she sat down in a chair next to the bed. "I was watching from the woods when you got shot."

"Wait a minute," Craig interrupted, angrily. "You saw Daniel shoot me and did nothing to stop him from taking Morgan. Why wasn't he arrested right then and there?"

"We didn't have the authority," she answered. "We aren't cops. We couldn't have arrested him. We just anticipated something bad was going to happen and were ready in case someone got hurt. After Daniel left with Morgan, we rescued you and brought you here for medical treatment."

"Who are you working for?" Craig questioned.

"I can't tell you that," she answered. "This whole situation got out of hand before we realized it. No one is going to incriminate themselves in all this. What is going on now was not part of the original plan."

"What was the original plan?" Craig asked.

"We were trying to keep you and Morgan apart," she replied.

"Why would you do that?" Craig questioned, becoming upset.

"I told you that it is a long story," Abby repeated. "I can't tell you anything else. Even if I could, I don't think you are physically ready to handle it."

"Do you know where Morgan is?" he asked. "Is she safe?"

"She is safe for now," Abby answered.

"What the hell does that mean?" he questioned, angrily.

Abby's attention was directed to Craig's monitor. It began to beep as his blood pressure shot up. "You need to remain calm," she warned him.

"Why haven't you called the police and told them where Morgan and I are?" Craig yelled. "Have you told them that we are ok? This whole ordeal would be over with if you would tell them what you know."

Craig was having a hard time catching his breath. He knew he needed to try to relax but not knowing where Morgan was and what condition she was in was upsetting him. He wanted to find her and he couldn't understand why Abby was so unwilling to help.

"Craig, you have to calm down," Abby ordered. "Getting upset is not good for you."

Craig's monitor beeped louder and with more urgency as his blood pressure rose. "Get the doctor," Abby told the man guarding the door. "I think he is going into cardiac arrest."

****

Morgan sat motionless in the corner of the room. She felt withdrawn. She couldn't comprehend what was happening. Daniel was not the man she remembered. The hostility that he felt had consumed him all these years and transformed him into a monster. She couldn't understand why he hated her so much. Did he really blame her for all the problems he was experiencing?

Morgan slowly stood up and decided to stretch her legs. She had to convince herself that the Daniel she used to know no longer existed. She knew the man she loved all those years ago had been replaced by someone she didn't recognize. She saw no remnant of him anywhere. This new Daniel was violent and enjoyed taking pleasure in her pain. In his mind, she had brought him to this new place. Was it really her fault? Did she invent this madman?

Morgan thought back to the comment Daniel made about Edward. The police informed her that his shooting was an open and shut case. The man had been Edward's client and he invested his life-savings into a deal that suddenly went south. He lost his house and his wife so the man took drastic measures to make sure that Edward paid. There was no indication anyone else was involved. She really didn't think Daniel was connected to the case. The comment he made was just said out of spite. This convinced her that Daniel was just trying to antagonize her and he had succeeded.

Was that what he was doing when he told her that Craig was dead? She wasn't sure whether to believe him or to just dismiss it as another attempt to hurt her. Tears welled up in Morgan's eyes. What if Daniel was telling the truth? She didn't know if she could handle another man she loved being taken from her. She had finally gotten the strength to move on after Edward's death and now she would have to do it again. She felt her heart breaking as she replayed the scene of Craig's shooting over and over in her mind. Was there any way he could have survived or was that just wishful thinking on her part?

A feeling of fear washed over Morgan as she heard the door open. She was frightened that Daniel had returned to finish what he had started earlier. The light flipped on and Morgan let out a sigh of relief when she realized it wasn't Daniel. She didn't recognize the man who had entered the room and his presence alone made her feel more uneasy. "Morgan," the man called as he approached her. "My name is Andy. I am here to check on you."

"Where's Abby?" she asked.

"Abby had other things to tend to," he answered. "She asked me to bring you some supplies. I'll set your blanket on the cot."

Andy put the folded blanket down and then handed the food and bottles of water to Morgan. "Thanks," she said.

Andy offered her a warm smile. "Are you ok?" he questioned. "What happened to your neck? Did Daniel do that to you?"

"Daniel attacked me the last time he was in here," she explained. "He wrapped his hand around my neck and squeezed."

"That's not going to happen again," he informed her.

"How can you guarantee that?" she asked.

"I'll do the best I can," he answered.

"Can you help me get out of here?" she questioned, trying hard to steady her voice.

"I am doing what I can to make that happen," Andy replied. "I need you to hang in there just a little longer. Can you do that?"

Morgan nodded. "I'm scared," she answered, trembling. "Daniel comes in here and he is so violent towards me. I am afraid he is going to kill me. Why are you and Abby being so nice to me?"

"This has become much bigger than it should have," Andy replied. "Abby and I are trying to make it right. All I can tell you is that it started out as a plan to keep you and Craig apart. When we thought we succeeded, the plan was dissolved and we were paid handsomely for our services. The only thing we were asked to do was to not incriminate each other if for some reason we were interrogated about any of this. Apparently, Daniel decided to continue with his own agenda. He's the one who set the fire at your brother and sister-in-law's house. Please don't tell him you know that."

"I won't," she said.

"I need to go," Andy told her. "Someone will be back later to check on you. Please know that we are doing what we can to protect you."

Morgan grabbed the blanket and wrapped it around her shoulders. It wasn't warmth she was looking for though. It made her feel secure. She wished she could hide in it for awhile.

She sat down on the cot and thought about what Andy had said. She couldn't believe that someone had devised a plan to keep her away from Craig. The only person she could think of that would have motive to do that was Elizabeth. She had admitted to Craig that she was jealous of Morgan. She couldn't believe that Elizabeth would sink to this level though. If Morgan knew she was going to be in this situation, she would have just told Elizabeth to take Craig. As much as it would have broken her heart, she would have let him go.

Morgan felt betrayed. She felt like a fool. Elizabeth was so convincing with her caring and supportive attitude. How could Morgan had fallen for that? She dealt with clients all the time who twisted the truth to make themselves look better and she always saw right through them. Why did she let Elizabeth manipulate her like that?

Morgan opened the plastic bag that Andy had brought her food in. Inside she found another sandwich, a small bag of chips, and a candy bar. It didn't seem like much but she was grateful that they were trying to take care of her. Andy had given her a little bit of hope but she still wasn't sure how he was going to protect her from Daniel. Morgan just prayed for this nightmare to end.

****

Craig opened his eyes and found an old friend staring back at him. "Hey!" he said. "What are you doing here?"

Andy McNamara let out a sigh of relief. "You had us scared there for awhile, Buddy," he replied. "How are you feeling?"

"Groggy," Craig answered. "Is it over?"

"Is what over?" Andy questioned.

"This whole mess," Craig stated. "Where's Morgan?"

"Daniel has her," Andy told him.

"What are you doing here?" Craig asked again.

"The FBI is investigating Daniel for real estate fraud," Andy answered. "Your inquiry about him to the police in Florida brought us here."

"He has my girlfriend," Craig responded. "Do you know where he is?"

"Yes," Andy replied. "I've been working undercover."

"Have you seen Morgan?" Craig questioned. "Is she ok?"

"I talked to her earlier," Andy told him. "She is scared. I tried to reassure her that I was there to protect her. She doesn't know who I am though."

"When are you going to get her out of there?" Craig asked.

"As soon as we can," Andy answered.

"I don't understand," Craig said. "Can't the local police go in and arrest Daniel? We have him on kidnapping and attempted murder, among other things."

"It's not that easy," Andy explained. "If we go in there now, there will be a lot of people in danger. Daniel doesn't care what happens to him or anyone else. He has nothing to lose."

"Has he hurt her?" Craig questioned.

Andy didn't want to answer that question. "He attacked her earlier today," he answered, reluctantly.

Craig's eyes welled up with tears. "She needs me," he replied. "I can't do anything to help her. You need to get her out of there today."

Andy could tell Craig was getting upset. "Craig, you need to calm down," he instructed. "We don't want you to flat line again. You're not going to do Morgan any good if you are dead."

Craig took a deep breath and began to calm down. "Can you give her a message for me?" he asked.

"I can't do that," Andy responded. "Both Morgan and Daniel think you are dead. We need for them to continue thinking that."

"Promise me that you will take care of her," Craig stated.

"I'm doing the best I can," Andy replied. "I better go. I don't need Daniel getting suspicious."

After Andy left, Craig began to think about Morgan and the hell she must be going through. He wished he was strong enough to get out of this bed but right now, there was nothing he could do for her. He had to rely on someone else to do that and just the thought of that frustrated him. He wanted to be the one to save her but Andy was right. Craig had to rest his body and heal because he wasn't going to be able to help her if he was dead. "Hang on, Baby," Craig whispered. "I'll be there as soon as I can."

****

"Do you need anything else before I leave?" Abby asked Morgan, as she handed her more supplies.

"I would like to leave," Morgan replied.

Abby smiled. "Soon," she said. "Andy told me about what happened this afternoon with Daniel. I don't know what I can do to stop him."

"He's extremely angry with me," Morgan stated. "I think he gets some twisted pleasure from hurting me. I just want to survive this."

"Andy and I are doing all we can to protect you," Abby responded.

"How did you get involved in all this?" Morgan asked.

"We needed someone with access to you during the day," Abby answered. "I was supposed to get close to you and be your friend. But the day you told me off in the elevator, we decided to try a different approach. I was supposed to make you feel guilty for Craig's marriage ending. We thought maybe the guilt would make you change your mind about being with him. Sorry if I was hard on you."

"Don't be," Morgan replied. "On some level, I probably deserved it. I wasn't very nice to you."

"I am trying to make up for it now," Abby said. "I helped make this mess. I figured I should help clean it up."

"I appreciate everything you have done," Morgan stated.

"I wish there was something I could bring you to do," Abby responded. "I don't want to press my luck though. I had to convince Daniel to allow me to bring you food and water. If it was up to him, he would have let you starve. You must get bored in here."

"I'm ok," Morgan told her. "I probably would go nuts if it weren't for you. At least, I have a little bit of company."

"Try not to worry," Abby replied. "I'll be back in the morning. Andy will be keeping an eye on things tonight."

Morgan ate a banana she found in her bag of goodies and then settled in to try to get some sleep. She didn't know how much rest she would get. Daniel was out there somewhere and she knew that he was capable of just about anything. She didn't know if Andy would be able to stop him if he decided to attack during the night. Morgan said a little prayer that somehow she would make it through the midnight hours unscathed.

Morgan closed her eyes and visions of Craig filled her thoughts. She didn't know what she was going to do now that he was gone. She knew somehow she would pick up the pieces and eventually move on. She didn't want to move on though. She wanted Craig to be here with her. Why was this happening again?

Tears fell from Morgan's cheeks onto the mattress on the cot. She didn't want to show weakness especially now. She had to pull it together and remain strong. She knew she couldn't let her guard down for one second. If Daniel saw how vulnerable she was, he would use it against her and she didn't want to give him the satisfaction. She had to muster up as much courage as she could and fight him with everything she had.

Morgan tossed and turned trying to find a comfortable spot on the cot. Eventually, she fell asleep but it proved to be a restless night. Nightmares of Craig's death and Daniel's relentless harassing consumed Morgan's mind. One of her nightmares became reality when she was awakened by a noise in her cell and the feel of someone covering her mouth with his hand.

Chapter 18

Craig was out of bed and sitting in a chair on the other side of the room. Several days had passed and he was finally starting to feel stronger. Since Craig was able to eat and drink without the assistance of the IV, the doctor decided to disconnect it. He still had the heart monitor as his constant companion but he was hopeful that wouldn't be for much longer. "How are you doing?" Andy asked as he entered the room.

"Better," Craig answered. "You haven't been here in a few days."

"Things have begun to escalate," Andy replied. "We'll be taking Daniel into custody sometime today."

"It's about damn time," Craig said. "How is Morgan?"

"She's not doing so well," Andy answered.

"What the hell happened?" Craig questioned. "You were supposed to be watching her."

"Daniel went into her room the other night," Andy explained. "By the time I got there, he was laying on top of her. As far as we could tell, he didn't hurt her or do anything else to her physically. I don't know what he said to her but whatever it was left her visibly shaken. She hasn't said a word to anyone since it happened. She has been eating very little. I think she is doing that just to keep her strength up. She has been drinking water though which is comforting. Other than that, she is withdrawn. It's almost like she's lost hope."

"You need to get her out of there now!" Craig ordered. "You should have done *that* days ago."

"You, more than anyone, know the chain of command," Andy replied, defending himself. "I can't do anything until I get the ok to proceed."

Craig knew it wouldn't do any good to argue with him. He did know how things worked. "When do you move in?" he asked.

"I am going to go meet my team now," Andy answered. "If things go smoothly, this should be over within the next couple of hours."

****

Morgan sat in the corner and stared into space. She felt disconnected and numb. She wasn't in the mood to talk. She didn't want to associate with anyone especially Andy and Abby, who had promised to protect her but that promise fell short. Several nights ago, Daniel had attacked her again. This time it wasn't physical, but emotional and verbal. She would never forget what he said to her.

Morgan remembered the strange noise she had heard and then the hand covering her mouth. She knew it was Daniel. She could tell from the scent of his cheap cologne. "You shouldn't let your guard down," he said. "You never know when I will visit you."

Morgan began to shake as she felt his breath on her cheek. Daniel removed his hand and climbed on top of her. She was so grateful for the blanket that separated them. "Don't make a sound," he ordered. "I will snap your neck."

Daniel positioned himself on top of her and pinned her down. "Don't worry," he whispered in her ear. "I'm not going to have sex with you. That would just disgust me."

Morgan tried to find solace in his statement but the fear she felt was more consuming than she ever imagined it could be. "Get off me!" she ordered.

"Not until I am finished talking to you," he replied. "I have some information to share with you."

"I don't want to hear anything you have to say," she stated.

"You'll want to hear this," he responded. "I wish I could see the look on your face because it will be priceless. Your husband, Edward, cheated on you with Craig's ex-wife, Valerie."

Morgan's head began to spin. "You're lying!" she said, trying not to sound upset and angry with no success.

"I think it is just amazing how I keep coming up with all this information," Daniel boasted. "I am getting so much pleasure out of this."

Morgan heard footsteps as someone entered the building. Someone grabbed Daniel by the collar of his shirt and pulled him off her. "I hate you!" Morgan screamed.

"The feeling's mutual," he replied, smiling.

"What the hell are you doing?" Andy asked Daniel as he pulled him away from Morgan.

"I thought I told you to take a walk," Daniel stated.

"I'm not going to let you terrorize her anymore," Andy told him.

"I am in charge of this operation," Daniel said, getting in Andy's face. "You will not tell me what to do."

"I just think she has been through enough, Sir," Andy responded, hoping he didn't just blow his cover.

"I will decide when she has had enough," Daniel replied, as he pushed his way past him and out the door.

Morgan wasn't sure how to feel or even what to think. She was in a state of confusion. Daniel knew how to push her buttons but she wasn't sure if he was just making things up as he went along or if he spoke the truth. She was having problems processing all the information she was receiving. Edward never would have cheated on her. Somehow Daniel had found out that Valerie cheated and he decided to link it to Edward just to hurt Morgan even more. She just couldn't make herself believe that Edward was capable of doing something like that.

It was difficult for her to accept a lot of things lately. She had given up any hope that Craig was alive. She knew that he would have moved heaven and earth to find her but there had been no sign of him. Her heart ached at the thought of a life without him. It angered her that whoever set out to keep Craig and her apart had succeeded. She hoped they were happy.

Morgan pulled herself up from her corner, hoping her wobbly legs would hold her. She leaned against the wall and closed her eyes. It had been a few days since she had slept and she was beyond exhausted. Every time she closed her eyes, she saw Daniel and her imagination ran wild. She was afraid of what he might do next. She had to stay alert and fight him with everything she had.

Morgan knew she was falling into a depressive state. She had given up any hope of being rescued. She couldn't depend on Abby or Andy to help her escape. For some reason, they were both slow to react. Were they afraid of Daniel or was money the driving force behind their involvement? The only thing Morgan was sure about was that if she wanted to get out of there, she would have to do it on her own.

She grabbed a bottle of water and an apple that Abby brought her that morning. She knew she had to keep her strength and energy replenished. No matter how paranoid she was feeling about Daniel, she had to clear her mind and regain her mental faculties. Feeling sorry for herself was no longer an option. She had to concoct her getaway plan. She had to depend on herself because it was obvious no one else was going to help her. It was time to fight back. She wasn't going to let Daniel win the next round.

Morgan grew impatient as she waited for the opportunity to put her escape plan into action. She finally heard the door open and she was prepared to attack whoever it was. She was pleased when she saw Daniel. It was time for her to turn the tables on him and she would take great pleasure in torturing him. "You're coming with me!" he ordered, as he grabbed her arm.

"No, I'm not," she protested.

"Woman, don't test me!" he yelled, angrily. "I'm not in the mood for it!"

Daniel pulled her towards him. "You are not taking me anywhere!" Morgan shouted.

"You have gotten some of your spunk back," he replied. "Are you ready to fight back?"

"I'm not going to let you push me around anymore," she responded.

"What are you going to do about it?" he asked, moving closer to her. "Punch me? Slap me across the face? Take your best shot."

Morgan was terrified. She knew if she attacked him, he would retaliate. She would be lucky to make it out of that room alive. "I'm not going anywhere with you," she told him.

"Yes, you are," he threatened, as he pointed his gun at her. "You will do exactly what I tell you to do. You see I have the upper hand here and I need a hostage. Looks like you're it."

"Is that the same gun you killed Craig with?" she questioned.

"As a matter of fact, it is," he answered.

"If you expect me to go with you, you need to answer a few questions," Morgan instructed.

"I don't need to do anything," Daniel replied.

"Do you want me to go willingly or would you like me to put up a fight?" she asked.

"I don't care either way," he answered. "You're going with me whether you like it or not."

"Just answer my questions," she stated. "And I'll go without a fight."

Daniel let out a frustrated sigh. "It's time to go," he told her, raising his voice. "Then I will answer your damn questions."

Morgan noticed the desperation in Daniel's voice. She knew someone was closing in on him and this might be her chance to escape. She remembered the night she knocked Reginald Montgomery to the ground. She wondered if she could do the same to Daniel.

Morgan walked towards the door, knowing the whole time Daniel had his gun pointed at her back. This situation was different from the one she encountered with Montgomery. In that instance, she had the gun and was in control of what was happening. This time the tables were turned and she had to survive.

As she approached the door, she heard voices. She wasn't sure who was outside the building. If it was Daniel's men, she was not going to allow them to surround her. If she was going to die, she was going to go down fighting.

As Morgan turned back towards Daniel, she slammed the door shut. She noticed that Daniel was distracted by the voices outside and he was wondering how he was going to escape.

Morgan knew this was her chance to grab the gun. There was only one thing she could think of to do.

Morgan gained momentum as she quickly closed in on Daniel. She knew she only had one shot so she kicked him with every bit of energy she had. Daniel dropped to the floor wincing in pain. She gathered up the gun that had fallen from his hand. "I'm not going to be your victim anymore," she proclaimed, as she pointed the gun at him.

"You don't know what you're doing," he said, as he knelt on the floor.

"I know exactly what I'm doing," she stated. "I am not going to let you terrorize me anymore. You put me through hell!"

"You deserved it!" he yelled. "You made my life hell! I am so tired of being labeled a failure. I've explained this to you before and I won't do it again."

"Tell me who you are working for!" she demanded.

"I'm not working for anyone," Daniel replied. "My agenda was to get revenge on you and I succeeded. Craig's dead."

Morgan was too angry to let his statement affect her. "You were working for someone," she stated. "I want to know who. Was it Elizabeth?"

Daniel smirked and Morgan smacked him in the face with the gun. "What are you going to do, Morgan?" Daniel asked, spreading his arms out. "I don't have anything left to lose. I'm going to jail or I'm going to die. So shoot me! Then you won't have to keep looking over your shoulder."

"Don't tempt me!" she said, angrily.

"You don't have the guts!" he replied.

Morgan switched off the safety on the gun. "You wanna bet?" she asked, in a voice that scared her. "Tell me why I shouldn't? I thought you were my friend. But this whole time you have been plotting against me. You lied to me about Edward's affair. You schemed to keep Craig and me apart. You killed Craig. You terrorized me for months. You tell me why I shouldn't kill you?"

Morgan heard someone outside the door. She quickly moved to Daniel's side and put the gun against his temple. "Don't even think about moving!" she threatened.

The door slowly opened. "Morgan, put the gun down!" Andy ordered.

"No!" she replied. "I will not let you hold me hostage anymore. If I let him go, that is what will happen."

"I'm with the FBI," he stated. "You are free to go. I'm here to take Daniel into custody."

"You're lying," she said. "Show me your shield!"

Andy flashed his badge. "Morgan, let him go," he said, "then this whole thing will be over with."

"Can you promise me that he's not going to be released due to some technicality?" Morgan questioned. "Can you promise me that he's not going to get some sort of deal?"

"With as many charges as there are against him," Andy answered. "He is going to be spending the rest of his life in prison."

Morgan stepped away from Daniel but kept the gun pointed in his direction. Daniel and Morgan locked eyes. "You're not worth it!" she said, furiously. "I hope you burn in hell!"

Morgan turned and walked towards Andy. "He's all yours," she told him.

Morgan exited the building and took a deep breath. It was good to get some fresh air. She watched as a couple of agents brought Daniel out of the building and put him in the backseat of an unmarked car. "Are you ok?" Andy asked, as he approached her.

"No," she answered.

"I have something that might make you feel better," he replied. "Come with me."

Andy escorted Morgan around the corner of the building. She stopped dead in her tracks when she saw Craig standing there. She caught her breath and her heart skipped a beat. "I'll leave you two alone," Andy said.

"Is that really you?" Morgan asked, as tears ran down her cheek. "I thought you were dead. Why didn't anyone tell me you were alive?"

"They couldn't" he answered.

"Do you know how much pain I felt thinking you were dead?" she questioned. "Where were you? How come you didn't come find me?"

"Daniel shot me in the chest," Craig explained. "I wanted to find you but I physically wasn't able to. You know I would have done whatever I had to do to find you."

"Did they tell you what he did to me?" Morgan cried. "Daniel put me through hell."

"I know, Baby," he said, with tears in his eyes.

Morgan hurried over to Craig and he wrapped his right arm around her. They both wept. "I'm so sorry," Craig whispered. "I wish I could have done more for you."

"I hate to interrupt," Abby said. "We need for you both to go to the hospital and get checked out. There is an ambulance waiting for you and Dr. Walters is going with you."

Andy approached the group. "I'm going to head to the station and question Daniel," he informed them. "I'll let you know what I find out. Abby, you need to come with me."

After the couple loaded into the ambulance, the doctor started taking Morgan's vitals. "What happened to you?" Morgan asked Craig. "Where were you?"

"After I was shot," he answered, "Abby took me to Dr. Walters. He removed the bullet from my chest. I did give them a scare though. When they told me that Daniel had you, I got so upset and I went into cardiac arrest. Things are fine now. There is no damage to my heart and I am getting stronger."

"I'm sorry I got you involved in all of this," she replied.

Craig grabbed her hand. "We're in this together," he stated.

"You both seem to be doing well," the doctor interrupted. "We are still going to the hospital though, just as a precaution."

"I think that is a good idea," Craig told Morgan. "I want someone to examine you and make sure everything is ok."

They arrived at the hospital and a nurse escorted the couple to an examining room. "The doctor will be with you shortly," she said.

"I'm glad we have a few minutes alone," Craig said, as he pulled Morgan close to him. "I'm sorry I wasn't there for you."

"I'm just glad you're ok," she replied, wrapping her arms around his neck, being careful not to bump his left shoulder. "I thought you were dead."

Craig kissed her on the forehead. "It will take more than a bullet to keep me away from you," he whispered. "I love you!"

Morgan tried to hold back the tears without success. "I love you too!" she told him.

Craig wiped a tear from her cheek as he pulled her closer. He passionately kissed her. "I should have done that earlier," he said. "God knows I wanted to."

"I think we were both in a state of shock," she replied. "We have been through a lot the last few days."

"I don't ever want to be apart from you again," he responded.

They began to kiss again, each one longer than the last. "I'm going to ask you to keep that to a minimum," the doctor said, jokingly as he entered the room. "Actually, it is nice to see you both feeling better."

The doctor instructed Morgan to take a seat on the table. As he examined her neck, he asked her several questions about the abuse she endured. He wanted every detail she could recollect pertaining to her ordeal with Daniel. Craig's heart broke as he listened to Morgan's experience. He wished he could have been there to rescue her. "Everything seems to be fine," the doctor said. "I heard that you didn't eat or drink much over the last few days. Is that true?"

"I didn't eat much," she answered. "I did drink plenty of water though."

"I don't think you are dehydrated," he replied. "To be on the safe side though, make sure you drink plenty of fluids and get something to eat. You are free to go."

The doctor turned his attention to Craig. "I want to check your wound and change your bandages before you leave," he instructed. "Morgan, I want to show you how to change his bandages so he doesn't have to come to my office everyday. I'll grab the supplies we need if you'll help him remove his shirt."

Craig flashed his sexy smile at Morgan as she began to unbutton his shirt. She giggled like a schoolgirl. "Ms. Garrett," the doctor said. "Do I need to go get a nurse to do that?"

"No," she replied, blushing.

Morgan finished her assignment and carefully slid Craig's shirt off. "Does it hurt?" she asked, as she looked at the bandage on his chest.

"It's sore," he answered.

"It will be for awhile," the doctor told him, as he removed the gauze. "You're lucky the bullet didn't hit anything major. An inch or two to the right and you wouldn't be here. Everything looks like it is healing nicely. Make an appointment with my office for late next week and we'll remove the sutures. You both can go home but I have several conditions. Craig, get plenty of rest and don't overexert yourself. Try not to use that arm. If the wound starts to look worse or you experience any unusual pain, get to my office or to the emergency room. If you have any concerns or questions, call. Understand?"

Craig nodded. "Morgan, make sure you check the wound throughout the day and replace the bandage like I showed you," the doctor continued explaining. "You need to also get plenty of rest, push the fluids, and eat. Not too much food at one time. Work your way up to a full meal. If you have any problems, you also need to call. Before you go, I want to ask you about your mental state. You have been through an ordeal. Do you need me to prescribe something to help you relax and sleep?"

"I think that would be ok," she answered.

He wrote her prescription and handed it to her. "I'm also going to give you this card. If you need to talk to someone, you can call her. She is a great counselor and will help you through this."

The couple thanked the doctor as they exited the room. John was waiting for them in the corridor. "Thank God you two are ok," John said, smiling ear to ear.

John shook Craig's hand and patted him on the back. "So fill me in. What happened?" Craig asked, as John gave Morgan a hug.

"FBI came in and took over the case," John explained. "Apparently, they have been investigating a case of real estate fraud that Daniel is involved in. That was their main concern.

273

They shut us out of the case. They had agents keeping an eye on you both but the whole thing was a setup to capture Daniel."

"I know," Craig replied, angrily. "I kept telling Andy to get Morgan out of there but the higher ups had a different agenda."

"I need to take you to the station so we can get your statements," John told them. "They want every bit of evidence they can get to put Daniel in jail."

Morgan was frustrated and angry with the whole situation. All she wanted to do was go home, take a shower, and get some sleep. She didn't feel she needed to jump through hoops for the FBI since they were so slow in protecting her. "Excuse me for a minute," Morgan said, as she looked in the direction of the restroom. "I'll be back. I just want to freshen up a bit before we leave."

Morgan hurried to the bathroom to splash some water on her face. As she stared at her reflection, tears filled her eyes. So many different emotions washed over her. She just wanted to crawl in a corner and hide. She examined the faint bruise on her neck and flashes of the horrible things Daniel had done to her flooded her mind. She broke down just like she knew she would. That's the main reason she excused herself and rushed to the restroom. She couldn't let Craig see her like that again.

She was so frustrated. She couldn't let go of the anger she was feeling towards the FBI and the way they treated her case. She felt expendable like a pawn in a game they were playing. It made her so mad that her life, or even Craig's life, meant nothing to them. She wondered what would happen if she refused to help them. She would either not get the justice she deserved or she would be imprisoned. Either way, they would get what they wanted despite her protest.

She was worried that Daniel would get off easy with the FBI. They would nail him for the whole real estate scam and that would be it. He would rot in jail but not because of what he did to her or Craig. This made her question her career as a lawyer. She didn't see the need to continue down that road if the system was going to fail her.

Morgan leaned on the sink and closed her eyes, trying to hold back the tears. *I'm not done with you yet.* Her eyes snapped open and she caught her breath. She knew Daniel wasn't in the room with her but he would always be a part of her now. She had allowed that to happen and she wasn't sure how to rid herself of him.

There was a knock at the door. "Morgan, are you ok?" Craig asked through the door.

When Morgan didn't answer, Craig opened the door and peeked inside the room. "Morgan?"

Morgan didn't want to look at him. She was ashamed of herself and didn't want Craig to think any different of her. She wasn't sure what to do with all these emotions and she didn't want to burden Craig anymore than she already had. "Are you ok?" Craig asked, as he put his hand on her back.

Morgan almost jumped out of her skin. She began to shake uncontrollably as she cried harder. Craig pulled her close to him. "Talk to me," he pleaded. "Tell me what's going on."

"I can't do this anymore," she cried.

"You can't do what?" he asked, feeling helpless.

"I can't handle all these emotions I am feeling," she answered.

"Talk to me," Craig repeated. "Please let me help."

Morgan backed away from Craig. She looked up at him and could see the concern in his eyes. "I am angry," she told him. "I hate the way the FBI handled this case. They had their own agenda with no concern for me. Daniel hurt me. He threatened me. They did nothing to save me until it was convenient for them. I'm not trying to feel sorry for myself but I got handed a lot of empty promises. Now they expect me to give them a statement to help their case and the rest be damned. As long as they get him on this fraud charge, they aren't going to care if he goes to trial for kidnapping, attempted murder, and arson."

"We will do everything we can to see that he is tried for ALL his crimes," Craig replied, trying to reassure her.

"You know what the worse thing is though," she explained. "As he sits in prison, he will have the satisfaction of knowing that he got to me. He will always be in my head. My trust is shaken. I trusted Daniel and look what he did to me. I trusted Abby and Andy to take care of me and Daniel still got to me. Hell, I can't even trust my best friend because I don't know what her involvement in all of this is. This whole experience has made me paranoid. I can't close my eyes without seeing Daniel and reliving the attacks. I should have killed him."

"You don't mean that," Craig stated.

"Yes, I do," she told him with conviction. "I should have killed him. I had the opportunity. I had that gun pressed against his head and I was so tempted to pull the trigger. If he were dead, I would be free and maybe have peace of mind. I will never forgive him for the things he did and said to me. He told me that you were dead. I am so very happy that you're not but I still have these feelings of grief. Maybe that has to do with Edward. I am still not certain Daniel wasn't involved in Edward's death. He planted doubt in my mind about Edward. He told me that Edward cheated on me with your ex-wife. Am I supposed to believe that? Is it true or was that just another one of his mind games?"

Craig was devastated. "I don't know," he said. "All I know is that Valerie had an affair. I have no idea who it was with. I can guarantee you that I am going to find out."

"I don't think it would make any difference," Morgan replied. "I think somewhere in the back of my mind I will always have doubts about Edward's fidelity."

"What can I do for you?" Craig questioned.

"You can tell me I don't have to go to the station and make a statement," she answered. "All I want to do is go home and take a long hot bath. Then I want to crawl in bed next to you. I just want to feel safe again."

"I will do the best I can to make you feel safe," he replied. "I feel like I disappointed you before in that area. I wasn't there for you when you needed me. I am so sorry for that."

Morgan wiped her eyes. "There is no need for you to be sorry," she responded. "I got you involved in this. I was the one he was after, not you. If I could take one moment back, I would have taken that bullet for you."

"And you probably would have been killed," Craig stated, not wanting to think about it.

"I just realized something," Morgan informed him. "There is still someone out there who initiated this whole thing. Is someone else going to be coming after us or is this really over?"

"Well, as much as I hate to suggest this," Craig replied. "We need to go to the station and make our statements. We need to find out what is going on. All the evidence we have points to Elizabeth. Daniel is in custody and hopefully, Abby is cooperating. One way or another, we are going to get the answers we need."

"Let me splash some water on my face and I'll be right out," she said.

As the three entered the station, Andy approached them. "I am glad you're here," he said. "Morgan, if you'll come with me, I'll get your statement. Craig, you can go with Officer Martin."

"No," Craig protested. "I'm not leaving her. You can take our statements together or not at all."

"Ok," Andy said. "Follow me."

They entered an interrogation room and Morgan took a seat at the table. "Let's get started," Andy instructed.

"Before I tell you anything, I have a few things to say to you," Morgan replied.

Andy stared at Morgan, dreading what she was about to say. "I don't have time for this," he told her.

"You will either make time or I'm leaving," Morgan threatened.

Andy sighed and sat back in his chair. "Ok," he said. "I'm listening."

"I would like to thank you for allowing me to be a pawn in your investigation," Morgan explained, sarcastically. "You promised to take care of me and you didn't. Every night I was living in fear that Daniel was going to kill me. My skin crawls every time I think about how he touched me. Now I have to live with every memory because of you. Why did you make me endure all that knowing what I was going through? Was I that expendable to you?"

"I was just following orders," Andy replied.

"Since when did a cop's job become more important than a human life?" Morgan questioned.

"I'm sorry for what you went through," he stated. "I did everything I could to protect you."

"Don't patronize me!" she responded. "I will give you your damn statement and then I want to see Elizabeth. You owe me that much."

Andy went to the door and asked an officer to bring Elizabeth up to interrogation. Still angry, Morgan decided to comply and give her statement to Andy. She made sure he heard every horrifying detail from the time she was kidnapped to her release. "Are you happy now?" she asked, glaring at Andy.

"Thank you, Morgan!" he replied.

"I want to see Elizabeth now," she said.

"In a few minutes," he told her. "I want to get Craig's statement first then I will take you to her. I would like to listen to your conversation from the adjoining room."

"No!" she protested. "I will not let you use me to spy on my friend."

"Then you can't see her," Andy replied.

"Fine," she responded. "But I'm going to tell her that you are listening so she doesn't incriminate herself."

"Craig, are you ready to make your statement?" Andy asked, as he glared at Morgan.

After Andy took Craig's statement, he escorted the couple to the room where Elizabeth was being held. "I want to do this by myself," she told Craig. "You can watch from the other room but I need to go in here by myself."

Craig gave Morgan a kiss. "Ok," he agreed.

Morgan entered the room and found Elizabeth sitting at the table. "Hello Morgan!" she exclaimed, surprised to see her. "They told me that I had a visitor but I never imagined it would be you. Is everything ok?"

Morgan sat down at the table. "I need to tell you something," she said. "Before we start talking, you need to know that the cops are watching you from the other room. Don't say anything that might be incriminating."

"I've told them everything I know," she replied. "I don't know what else they want from me."

"I want you to know that I am not in here to gather any information for them," Morgan told her. "I just need to understand some things."

"Ok," Elizabeth said.

"Are you involved in any of this?" Morgan asked.

"No," she answered. "I would never hurt you like that. I don't know who sent that evidence to the police and I don't know where my money went."

"I believe you," Morgan stated. "I have to ask though. Are you jealous of me?"

"Yes," Elizabeth answered. "I always felt like I fell short when it came to you. When I first met Craig, I fell head over heels. Maybe it was because he saved me. But then I found out he fell for you and once again, I felt like I was on the outside looking in. I realized though that I wanted you to be happy. I love you. You're my sister. Maybe not by blood but you know what I mean. We have always been supportive of each other so why should this be any different? I would never hurt you intentionally and you know that."

The two women smiled and wiped their eyes. Morgan was relieved that she could let go of the negative emotions she was feeling towards Elizabeth. She was sure Elizabeth was innocent and she would do all she could to prove that.

A commotion outside the room drew the women's attention to the door. The door opened and Richard Brinkman entered the room. "There you are!" he said to Elizabeth. "They told me that you were here and I wanted to make sure they weren't harassing you again."

"Dad, I'm fine," Elizabeth replied. "We are just talking."

"What are you doing here?" Richard asked Morgan. "Are you trying to get information to use against my daughter? I know the cops are on the other side of that glass."

It occurred to Morgan that Richard had been drinking. "I am just talking to her as a friend," she explained. "I'm trying to help her."

Richard turned and slammed the door to the room shut. That is when Morgan saw him remove a gun from his coat pocket. "Dad, what are you doing with that?" Elizabeth questioned, in a panic.

"I have to explain things to you," he answered. "I have to make you understand."

"Put the gun down and we can talk," Morgan instructed, trying to take control of the situation.

"I can't do that," he said. "If I do, the cops will arrest me and I have to tell you something."

"Ok," Morgan replied. "I'm listening."

"Elizabeth had nothing to do with any of this," he explained. "This is all my fault."

"What did you do, Dad?" Elizabeth asked.

"I did it for you," he answered. "I couldn't watch you be unhappy anymore. I had to do something."

"So you decided to keep Morgan and Craig apart?" she questioned.

"I did it for you," he answered. "I was so tired of her getting everything and you getting nothing. When I realized it wasn't working, I put a stop to it. I'm sorry that Daniel hurt you, Morgan. That was not part of the plan."

"You planned the attacks on me and John?" Morgan asked.

"Yeah," he told her. "You weren't supposed to be with Craig. Elizabeth was. Why couldn't you have just left him alone?"

The women looked at each other, confused. "Are you the one who set me up?" Elizabeth questioned. "Did you send the police the evidence they have against me?"

"I didn't have a choice," he responded. "Daniel was going to expose me. I couldn't let him do that. I would go to jail and you would be all alone."

"I'm going to be alone anyway," she stated. "You are going to jail for what you have done. Did you take my money? Did you use it to pay these people to hurt Morgan?"

"No," he told her. "Your money is safe. Talk to my lawyer and he will let you know where it is. I couldn't let Daniel get his hands on it so I moved it."

Elizabeth turned her chair towards her father as the door to the room slowly opened. "Mr. Brinkman," Andy called. "We need you to put the gun down."

"Not until I know my daughter is exonerated," he said.

"She will be," Andy replied. "Just put the gun down before someone gets hurt."

Morgan gasped when she witnessed Richard raise the gun to his head. "You don't understand," he said to Elizabeth. "You don't need me anymore. There's no reason for me to be here anymore."

Elizabeth began to cry. "Daddy!" she whispered. "I will always need you. Please don't do this."

Richard stared at Elizabeth as he lowered his gun and dropped it on the floor. The older man dropped to his knees in front of her. He laid his head on her lap and sobbed.

Andy and John hurried into the room and took Richard into custody. Craig watched from the doorway as Morgan went over to Elizabeth to comfort her. "I'm so sorry, Morgan," she cried.

"This is not your fault," Morgan replied, as she wrapped her arms around Elizabeth.

Elizabeth saw Craig standing in the doorway and invited him into the room. "I have something to tell both of you," she said. "I am so happy for the both of you. I pray that God gives you the strength to get through this whole ordeal. I wish you nothing but the best. Now get out of here! Go get some rest and recover."

"Are you going to be ok?" Morgan asked.

"I'll be fine," Elizabeth answered. "Someone will make sure I get home."

"Call me if you need anything," Morgan replied.

"I'll call you even if I don't need anything," Elizabeth stated, smiling.

Craig and Morgan walked hand in hand to the front door of the precinct. As they approached it, they saw Valerie and Stephanie waiting for them. "Daddy!" Stephanie yelled, as she ran to him.

Craig gathered her up with his right arm and held her tight. It was so good to see her. "Mommy said that you hurt your arm," she said. "Are you ok?"

"Yes, I am now," he replied smiling at her. "Would you like to go with Morgan for a few minutes? I want to talk to your mom alone."

After Stephanie and Morgan left, Valerie asked, "Is it ok that I brought her here? She was worried about you because she hadn't heard from you. I wanted to reassure her that you were ok. I didn't tell her that you had been shot. I just told her that you hurt your arm."

"That's fine," Craig replied. "I am going to ask you though if you or our parents can keep her for a few more days. This whole ordeal has been exhausting and I would like to get my strength back before I start to take care of her again."

"Yeah sure," she responded. "I think everyone will understand that. So is it over?"

"All except for one thing," he answered. "I have a question to ask you and I need the truth. Don't forget. I can tell when you're lying."

"Ok," she stated, confused.

"Who did you have an affair with?" he asked.

"Why is that important now?" she questioned.

"I'll make this easy for you," Craig replied. "Did you have an affair with Edward Garrett?"

"No," she answered. "I didn't even know him."

Craig stared at Valerie. He knew she was telling the truth. "What is this all about?" Valerie asked.

"Let's not talk about it anymore," Craig stated. "I appreciate you being honest with me. Now let's go get our daughter."

****

The couple arrived at Morgan's townhouse. It had been a long day and it felt so good to be home. Morgan decided to take a shower while Craig figured out dinner. He was answering the door to collect the pizza when Morgan appeared on the stairs. "I hope pizza is ok," he said, as he closed the door.

As they ate, Craig told her that he had asked Valerie about the affair. "I'm relieved that it wasn't with Edward," she said. "I'm sorry it had to happen but I'm glad it wasn't with my husband."

"I'm sorry it happened too," Craig replied. "But if it hadn't happened, I wouldn't be here."

After the couple finished their meal, Craig decided to take a shower. "Do you need any help?" Morgan asked, with a sexy smile.

Craig wanted so badly to say yes. "I think I'll be ok," he answered. "Can you help me with my bandage when I'm done?"

After Craig was finished, Morgan applied the new bandage to Craig's wound. After she set the supplies down on the nightstand, Craig grabbed her hand and pulled her to him. "I want to ask you something," he said, as he got down on one knee. "I know that we have been through so much the last few days and this probably isn't the right time to do this but I can't wait anymore. Will you marry me?"

Morgan's eyes filled up with joyful tears. "Before you answer," he continued by saying. "I don't have a ring to give you but I can give you my heart. It's already yours anyway."

Morgan smiled at him. "Yes," she whispered. "I will marry you."

Craig stood up and pulled her close. "I promise I will love you for the rest of my life," he told her.

"And I promise I will love you for the rest of mine," she repeated.

The couple sealed their promises with a kiss.

Chapter 19

"What should we name her?" Morgan asked.

"I don't know," Craig answered, staring at the cute little face. "Maybe we should ask Stephanie."

"I think we should name her Belle," she replied, as the golden retriever barked. "I think she likes it."

Morgan and Craig smiled at each other. They were so glad to have the newest addition to their family. Stephanie was so happy to finally have the puppy she always wanted.

"Daddy!" she said. "Can we take Belle outside and play?"

"Sure," Craig answered, as he grabbed some of Belle's toys. "Are you coming with us?"

"I'll be there in a few minutes," Morgan responded.

Morgan stood at the backdoor and watched Craig play with Stephanie and Belle. She couldn't believe how far her life had come in the past year. She was so happy that the nightmares of what happened had finally stopped. She continued to see Dr. Walters and followed his recommendation to see a counselor. She felt that she was in a much better place thanks to them. She was also relieved that Daniel was being held in a prison several states away. He couldn't hurt her anymore and that brought her peace.

Surprisingly, she had also developed a friendship with Abby over the past several months. She had finally come to terms with the fact that Abby was trying to help her and that it was only causing her pain to continue to be angry. With Morgan's help, Abby received a few years of probation for her involvement in the case.

Things didn't turn out so well for Richard Brinkman. He was ordered to undergo psychiatric treatment for his mental breakdown. He would then be evaluated on whether he could stand trial.

As soon as Morgan felt she was getting her life back to normal, she made the agonizing decision to leave the law firm. With her faith in the justice system still on shaky ground, she decided to take her career in a difference direction. With everything she had been through with Daniel, she wanted to provide her expertise to other victims of violence. Jaime and Elizabeth helped Morgan create a non-profit organization to bring more awareness to violence against women. Little by little, Morgan was asked to make public appearances to share her story. Because of this, she was hired as a legal consultant for one of the agencies. Morgan finally felt like she was making a difference.

Morgan had decided not to dwell on any of the bad things that had happened. She had a bright future ahead of her. She and Craig were married several months ago in a private ceremony. All of their family and close friends were in attendance. The ceremony was held in the backyard of Elizabeth's newly purchased home. With Jack as her escort, Morgan appeared in her strapless ivory satin gown holding a bouquet of assorted lilies. She remembered immediately catching Craig's attention and the smile that emerged on both their faces. It was such a perfect moment and a beautiful way to start their new life.

As she rubbed her tummy, Morgan knew that there was more excitement to come. After being told that she couldn't have a baby, she was now eight months pregnant with a baby boy. The couple decided to name the child Benjamin Thomas, after Morgan's late father.

Morgan glanced at her watch. She had a couple of hours before Jamie and Elizabeth were coming over for Elizabeth's bridal shower. During her months of physical therapy, Elizabeth had taken a liking to her therapist and apparently, the feeling was mutual. Elizabeth was also making progress with her therapy. She was walking with a cane now and she couldn't wait until she didn't need to rely on it anymore. Things were really looking up for her friend and Morgan couldn't be happier.

With a smile on her face, Morgan opened the door and joined her family. It was such a beautiful day and she wasn't going to let it go to waste.

www.ingramcontent.com/pod-product-compliance
Lightning Source LLC
Chambersburg PA
CBHW021340250626
47155CB00002B/718